Pr:

Filled with relevant issues that are handled with delicate poignancy, *Kept* is a refreshing change to the normal Christian fare. I urge every woman to read this book. Too often, I found myself on its pages as one character or another, and more than once I became so immersed in the characters, I forgot they weren't real people. I related to them, I. cried for them. I laughed with them, and most of all, I hoped for them. One of the most surprising and best books I've read this year.

> — MaryLu Tyndall, best-selling author of Legacy of the King's Pirates series

Gutsy and fast-paced, *Kept* sweeps the reader in and doesn't let go until the final, riveting page. With keen insight into human nature and the tangled relationships of our times, author and pastor's wife Sally Bradley explores romance against the backdrop of God's infinite, redeeming grace.

> — Laura Frantz, author of *Love's Reckoning*

Sally Bradley's *Kept* is one of the top ten books I've ever read. The story captivated me from the first page and held me until the last. It's one of the few novels I've ever read where I totally believed the character's surrender to Christ. It's honest and real. Miska's fragility and strength were so true to life, I experienced each high and low with her. The story was not predictable, and Bradley made me totally suspend disbelief. I fell in love with these characters. Novel Rocket and I give it our highest recommendation.

> — Ane Mulligan, president of novelrocket.com, author of *Chapel Springs Revival*

Vibrant characters, compelling questions, modern-day issues… *Kept* is a contemporary Christian classic along the lines of *Redeeming Love*.

Impossible to put down, this story pulls us into the heart of Chicago and shows us how God's hand can work, even when we repeatedly make the wrong choices. Sally Bradley's voice is gripping and clear, and her debut is a shining beacon of how very relevant Christian fiction can be.

— Heather Day Gilbert, author of *God's Daughter* (Amazon Norse bestseller) and *Miranda Warning*

At the intersection of immorality and redemption, Sally Bradley's *Kept* will redefine contemporary Christian romance. Rife with engaging characters, powerful storytelling, and authentic emotion, this romance will challenge how we view the fallen and reaffirm the swoon-worthiest men are those whose deepest passion is for Christ.

— Nancy Kimball, award-winning author of *Chasing the Lion*

KEPT

Sally Bradley

To Steve
For promises kept

I Corinthians 6:11—"And such were some of you…"

CHAPTER ONE

Mark was leaving—again.

Miska Tomlinson let the gauzy curtain fall across her living room window, obscuring the view of Chicago's lakefront eighteen stories below. If she'd known a year ago that their relationship would stall like this, she might have thought twice about accepting his offer of a drink. That would have saved her this roller coaster of pleasure and pain.

The pain was worth it, though, wasn't it? The two of them hiding out in her condo three or four days at a time. No one hassling them, no one knowing…

She fingered a curl. Why was he packing his bag a good two hours before he had to be at the ballpark?

"Miska. Baby." Mark's voice drifted from the bedroom into the living room. "Have you seen my wallet?"

"Didn't you put it on the nightstand?"

Something thumped in her room. "Oh, yeah. Found it."

Right. She smiled at his words. *He'd* found it. Next he'd be searching for his phone, his keys, his shoes. Maybe even his toothbrush.

He wandered into view, stopped at the end of her bed where his duffel sat, and tucked his shaving kit and toothbrush inside.

All pleasure from the last three days vanished.

She returned to the window. She couldn't obsess. He probably had a good reason for leaving early. If she just waited…

Miska scanned the view that had convinced her to risk her inheritance and live house poor. Grant Park, Chicago's version of Central Park, spread below her, treetops finally decked out in vibrant spring green. The faded-jean blue of the sky contrasted with Lake Michigan's cerulean waters, and a handful of white boats dotted Monroe Harbor.

But the jewel of the park was Buckingham Fountain. The massive fountain of granite and pink marble held court in the park's center. Any second now the ten-o'clock water show would begin, the first of the year. The center jet would soar a hundred fifty feet into the air, and dozens of other jets would try to catch it.

Someday, maybe, she'd take Mark down there and share it with him, his hand in hers as the music played and the water danced. Someday, when he belonged to her.

Mark's bag zipped shut. His footsteps crossed to the kitchen island behind her, bag thumping to the floor, then turned her way. "What're you looking at?"

"Buckingham Fountain. Isn't it beautiful?"

He wrapped his arms around her and pressed himself to her back. "Mmm. Very."

The fountain's center jet leaped high into the air. Smiling, she relaxed against him while the rest of the jets sprayed high then low, splashing to a song she couldn't hear.

He said nothing while the fountain played, just held her.

When the hundred-plus jets fell back to their usual height, she turned in his arms and slid her palms across his defined chest. Her gaze trailed over his full mouth and square jaw, both so tempting. But she couldn't bring herself to meet his eyes. "Your bag's packed?"

"Yep." He cleared his throat, then ran a hand through his thick blond hair until it stood on end. "It's too beautiful to stay inside. We should go out for breakfast—or brunch. For something."

Out? In public? She held still. "You want to go somewhere? Together?"

"If you're not comfortable with it, we don't have to."

"No, I'd love that." Of course she was comfortable with it. Her smile morphed into a grin. He matched it, and she stood on tiptoe and kissed his cheek, just a peck so he didn't get any new ideas. "Where should we go?"

"There's a great diner a few blocks from here. Best hash browns and French toast anywhere."

"Sounds perfect, except I'll have to run twice today."

He followed her to the kitchen island where her Kate Spade bag—the last purse Mom had bought—lay beside his keys, phone, and baseball cap. He picked up the worn hat. "Wish I could run with you."

He could, if he really wanted to. "Next time you're in town."

A thud sounded in the hallway outside her condo. Then another, followed by deep muffled voices. She ignored it as she slipped her purse strap onto her shoulder.

But Mark, filling his pockets, glanced toward her front door. "What's going on out there?"

"The condo next door sold. Someone's moving in."

He tugged the hat's curved brim low. Bag over his shoulder, he followed her to the front door where he held up a hand and listened.

Silence.

Miska opened the door and stepped into the empty hallway. Mark followed and locked the deadbolt with his key. "Ready?" he asked with that aw-shucks grin that had won her over.

So ready. This changed everything. She grabbed his hand and tugged him forward, flashing him a flirtatious look. "Let's go."

His fingers tightened around hers, pulling her to a stop just steps from her door. That longing smile hinted around his mouth.

What would he do? They were in public, after all, even if the hallway was empty.

Mark didn't do public.

He stepped up against her and slipped an arm around her waist. His head lowered, and she closed her eyes with him, already warm from a barely begun kiss in a silent hallway where anyone could walk out—

A doorknob clicked.

Miska opened her eyes.

A tall, dark-haired man burst through the doorway beside Mark and plowed into him.

Mark's weight fell against her, and she backpedaled into the wall, the back of her head smacking it, while Mark crashed beside her.

Tall-Dark-and-Klutzy stared at them, his mouth hanging open. "Oh, man, I'm sorry." He offered his hand to Miska where she half-sat, half-leaned against the wall. "Are you okay?"

She grabbed his hand, all knuckles and long fingers, and let him pull her up. He was incredibly tall—well over six feet, maybe closer to seven. She scanned his lean face and the scruff he hadn't shaved that morning, pausing on his nice brown eyes. "I'm fine."

"I didn't realize anybody was out here." He looked at Mark. "You all right?"

Mark tugged the hat over his forehead. "We're good."

The guy towered over Mark's six-three height.

Mark reached down for the duffel bag, and the man's lips parted. His eyebrows rose.

Great. He'd recognized Mark.

Behind Tall-Dark-and-Klutzy, a second man—not as tall but similar enough in looks that they had to be related—stepped out of the condo and laughed. He smacked Klutzy's back. "Dude, why couldn't you run over Mark Scheider yesterday? Before he shut out the Cubs?" He shot Mark a grin. "Sorry about my brother. You'd think he'd have grown into those feet by now." He shrugged as if it were a lost cause. "I'm Garrett Foster. This is my brother, Dillan. Could we get an autograph?"

Klutzy closed his eyes, his head lolling back a bit.

"Why not." Mark held out a hand for paper and pen, the gesture friendly but irritation clear in his voice. "Then we have to go."

As Garrett searched his pockets, he looked at Miska as if seeing her for the first time. "Oh. Right. Didn't mean to hold you up. Or knock you down." He grinned and elbowed his brother.

Miska mashed her lips together.

"Dude, I don't have any paper. And none in the condo. We're moving in. Guess it'll have to be next time. You have a place here, I take it?"

Klutzy glanced her way as if he knew all about them.

But how could he? "Mark's just visiting. Actually, we've got to run. We're meeting someone."

Garrett nodded. "Of course. It was nice meeting you, Mark and…"

Mark grabbed her elbow, sending the men a clipped nod. "Let's go."

"No name?" Garrett turned to his silent brother as they passed. "Did I hear that right?"

Mark mumbled beneath his breath.

They walked down the hallway and turned the corner into the floor's lobby where the elevator doors waited. Mark pressed the call button and stepped back, his face and neck flushed. He adjusted the hat again and glued his gaze to the floor.

"You okay?" she asked. "Did that guy hurt you?"

He let a huge rush of air escape, shoulders slumping. "I'm fine."

Really? The way he kept staring at the floor? She slipped an arm around his waist just as the Foster brothers walked around the corner.

Mark pushed her arm down.

Garrett flashed her a smile she wasn't even beginning to buy. "Off to bring up more boxes. Dillan says you're our neighbor." He stuck out his hand. "I didn't catch your name."

"Miska Tomlinson." She shook his hand, feeling Mark seethe beside her. Easy for him to be rude. He didn't have to live next door to these guys. "Nice to meet you both."

A ding announced the arrival of an elevator.

As the doors opened, Mark held her back. "I think I left my phone at your place." He glanced at the brothers as he pulled her toward the hallway. "Have a nice day."

"Same to you, man," Garrett called to their backs. "See you later."

Miska followed Mark down the hall. What was he doing? Just regrouping? Or…

At her door, he fumbled with his keys. She gave him a moment before pulling out her keys and unlocking the door. Their first time in public, and they hadn't even made it to the street.

Mark shoved his way inside.

She followed and eased the heavy door closed, leaning against it while he emptied his pockets, phone included, onto the island. He dropped his bag by the barstools and walked past her dining room table and white leather couch until the wall of windows stopped him. He stood there, hands on hips, staring toward the lake.

So. No breakfast date. No taking that first step in front of the world. Her jaw clenched. If only they hadn't run into those men.

In the kitchen she opened the refrigerator and grabbed eggs and milk. She could still make pancakes, still finish their days together on a good note. But next time he was in town, she'd make really bad French toast and they'd—

His phone buzzed.

Out of habit, Miska glanced at it. *Darcie* flashed across the screen.

The name numbed her brain, freezing her where she stood.

Again the phone buzzed.

Miska couldn't move, couldn't take her eyes off it, even though Mark's footsteps approached. He snagged the phone and walked away before answering. "Hey, babe." He entered her bedroom.

Hey, babe.

The door banged shut.

Silence swarmed her.

Somehow she managed to swallow. The motion freed her body but not her mind. She set the milk down and opened the egg carton. Scrambled eggs sounded good. Or maybe sunny-side up. She cracked an egg against the counter, then threw the whole thing into the sink.

Mark could get his own breakfast.

She eyed her door. What were they talking about?

Wiping her hands on a dishtowel, she tiptoed toward the bedroom. She really shouldn't listen. But she was already there, waiting for her pounding heart to quiet, ears straining.

"Aw, babe. I'm sorry."

Amazing how he sounded sorry and loving, as if whatever Darcie was going through was his pain too. But she knew what he thought of Darcie. He'd told her.

He sighed. "I know, I know. We'll keep trying, okay?"

Keep trying?

"Darcie, hon, it's not your fault. It's just one of those things…"

Oh. Her throat tightened. So he was lying to her *and* Darcie.

"Look, I don't blame you."

She needed breakfast. Eggs. Pancakes. She marched back to the island. Hash browns and bacon. Maybe she'd hunt down that diner herself. See what kind of company hung out there. She passed his duffel bag and kicked it.

Kicked it again.

She rested her elbows on the island and buried her face in her hands. Maybe she should call Darcie and tell her how her husband had hit on her last spring. How he'd pretended to be single long enough for her to lose her heart to him. If only she knew how Darcie would react—and whether or not Mark would return.

He had to return. No, he had to leave Darcie. She couldn't live like this forever. He had to make a choice. It was long past time for that.

Her door clacked open, and Mark's footsteps sounded.

Miska pulled herself up, wiped her cheeks just in case. She faced him, fighting the tension in her jaw. "How's Darcie?"

He studied his phone. "She's fine."

"Not pregnant again, huh?"

He met her eyes.

"But you'll keep trying, right? That's good."

"Miska—"

She smacked the granite. "It's been a year, Mark. A year of you waffling on whether you're going to commit to me or not. To your wife or not. You need to decide."

He pulled the cap off and eyed it, mouth tight. "Is this an ultimatum?"

"No." Of course he loved her. He would choose her over Darcie once he thought it through. "Nothing's keeping you with Darcie except your wedding band. If she were your girlfriend, you'd have been done with her as soon as you found out she'd cheated."

He said nothing, just watched her.

He would choose her, wouldn't he? He and Darcie—he'd said they were done. "Mark, we can't even go outside these four walls without you freaking out over being seen together. How do you expect—"

"Maybe you need to choose. Either take me like this or don't take me at all."

She shook her head, her voice locked in her throat. He couldn't mean it. "You said—" She pressed her fingers against her mouth. "When I found out about Darcie, you said the marriage was dead already. That you'd give it a few months."

But twelve months wasn't a few. What an idiot she was to let it drag on this long.

She turned her back to him. Did he really expect her to keep waiting? For what? To see if his wife got pregnant? What kind of disgusting relationship was this?

Mark's hands settled on her shoulders.

Miska flinched, but he said nothing, did nothing. She swallowed, the weight of his hands increasing. What kind of a woman was she? She hugged herself, her hands sliding up to her shoulders and knocking his fingers away. He turned her, and she folded into herself, nose tucked into the crook of her elbow.

"Miska. Baby."

A tear slipped free and vanished down her arm. She squeezed her eyes shut. This wasn't what she'd planned to be—or do. This was *not* who she was.

Mark tugged her arms free and pulled her close.

She pressed her face against the soft cotton T-shirt and took him in— his faint cologne, his broad chest, the feel of his arms tight around her. Was she strong enough to risk losing him? Could she survive without him?

His cheek rested on top of her head, and he toyed with the ends of her curls. "Miska, you're the best thing that's ever happened to me."

"Then stay."

"I need more time. I promise. Just a few more months."

She pulled back enough to see his eyes. "When?"

"A few—"

"*When*, Mark?"

"Will you trust me?"

"Haven't I?" Even after he'd lied? "Give me an end date. July? August? When?"

He searched her face, eyes softening. His mouth worked, and finally he spoke. "The end of August. By then…" He shook his head.

Four months of waiting and wondering. So many days home with Darcie. So few here with her. But she'd take it. "I'll wait through August. And not a day more."

Mark nodded, releasing her.

She took a step back, arms wrapped around her middle. He adjusted his hat and tucked his phone, wallet, and keys into his pockets.

So he was still leaving early.

He picked up his duffel bag and settled the strap onto his shoulder. He pushed the bag behind his back, then stood beside the island and fingered the counter's edge.

When he looked up, his smile was heartbreakingly tender. "You know if I could do things over…"

He'd have married her. That's what he'd said when she'd confronted him about the wife he'd failed to mention. His words had melted her. She'd known he'd choose her soon.

But he hadn't.

If she could go back to that day, she'd throw him out of her condo before her heart was too far gone to think straight, before he kept her a prisoner in this messed-up relationship.

But it was too late. She was vested in Mark, in the beauty he brought her each time his team came to Chicago. There had never been anyone like him before, and there could never be anyone like him again.

As she walked him to the door and whispered good-bye, she vowed to do everything in her power to make Mark choose her. Everything.

Darcie'd had her chance.

Now it was Miska's turn.

Dillan Foster pressed the lobby button as the elevator doors closed on his view of the baseball player and woman retracing their steps.

Behind him, Garrett's head thumped against the elevator's paneled interior. His brother chuckled. "Wow, that was fun."

Dillan shot him a look. "If by fun, you mean awkward."

"Come on, dude. It's not every day you find your neighbor's messing around with a pro athlete. He wasn't happy about being seen here, was he?"

"Can you blame him?"

"I don't know—she's pretty hot. I wouldn't complain."

Typical Garrett. "You remember you're engaged, right?"

"Uh, yeah. But the eyes still work, you know?"

Yes, he knew. And Garrett was right. The woman was hot. Stunning. Long black curls, silky skin, the perfect shape— Dillan glanced at his brother.

Garrett grinned back. "Good to see your eyes still work. I wonder sometimes."

"He's married—and not to her."

"How do you know?"

"Remember last spring when he threw that perfect game? Remember his wife was there afterward and you said she looked just like Tracy?"

"Oh, right." Garrett straightened. "She was something. That guy knows how to pick 'em."

The doors dinged open.

Dillan grunted and walked out.

The last pile of boxes sat at the end of six bronzed Art Deco elevators. Tracy, Garrett's fiancée, leaned against the wall, safeguarding boxes while she messed with her phone.

Garrett spread his arms. "Tracy, my love."

She smiled and looked up.

Garrett wrapped her in his arms.

At least Garrett had picked his fiancée right. A guy couldn't do much better—unless a quieter version was out there.

Dillan ran a hand over his hair. For the next five months he'd get an up-close view of their relationship. Garrett's suggestion that Dillan move in with him until the wedding, rent-free, had seemed perfect at the time. He could handle anything for five months, right? And by the time he moved out and Tracy moved in, he'd have enough to buy a fixer-upper of his own. How bad could it be? He picked up his boxes of books and called an elevator. Today he had a really sick feeling he'd find out.

"One last trip up, some unpacking, and we can eat." Garrett filled Tracy's arms and then his own with boxes. "Or maybe we can knock over the celebrity couple again. What do you think, Dill?"

"What couple?" Tracy flashed him a grin. "Do we have famous neighbors?"

An elevator opened. Dillan stepped inside and elbowed number eighteen. "Just a ballplayer having a fling with our neighbor."

"Oh." Tracy's face fell. "Poor girl. I can't imagine how she must feel."

Poor girl—right. "Her name's Miska." He focused on the elevator's buttons. Why had he volunteered that?

"Miska? That's different. But pretty. What's she like?"

Different. Pretty. He replayed their meeting. The woman's soft hand in his, her big dark eyes with all that makeup women wore. Her hair falling around her shoulders, toned arms bare beside the snug, white shirt—

"Dillan?"

He could see how Scheider could get lost in a woman like her, a woman so opposite the blonde beauty at home. But he couldn't remember anything past how she looked. Had she been angry they'd been caught? Ashamed?

Did she even care?

As the elevator slowed, he banished the mental picture. "Didn't have time to tell."

"Well, I can't wait to meet her. Maybe you guys are next door to her for a reason. Wouldn't that be something?"

Garrett followed her off the elevator, shaking his head.

For once Dillan agreed with him. She was just a neighbor—a neighbor he'd never see again five months from now and probably wouldn't see much in between. What reason could there be for living next door to her? Because clearly she was a temptress, a woman who made men lose their minds and souls. Mark Scheider had to know all about that.

Inside the condo, Garrett and Tracy carried their boxes to the living room while Dillan entered the smallest bedroom by the front door, the room that would be his office until the church addition was finished. Next time he moved his not-so-small library, he'd get a dolly. He lowered the boxes and let them go inches above the ground.

They caught his big toe.

The instant he closed his eyes against the pain, the exotic beauty of the woman next door filled his vision. He jerked his foot from beneath the boxes and grabbed his toes with one hand while he leaned against the wall with the other. Great. Too late. She was already in his mind.

God, help.

Garrett would laugh at him, roll his eyes, make some snide remark. But Dillan had seen where his brother's life had taken him. He remembered perfectly the shock and anger they'd all felt, remembered Mom's tears and Dad's stony grief. Saw firsthand the pitiful looks people at church sent his parents' backs—and probably his—before Garrett returned from the East Coast in shame. He had no idea how deeply his choices had affected them. But Dillan did. He'd lived through the nightmare of wondering if Garrett would be arrested or not.

Of course to hear Garrett tell it, he was a different man.

Nope. Not after that elevator conversation. Not with the way he talked lately, full of innuendos and double meanings. With each one, Dillan found himself stiffening, then catching the glance his parents shot each other. They had to feel like he did, that the old Garrett, the one he said he'd left back in New England, had followed him home and lingered just outside their vision, waiting for the right moment to mess with them again.

Dillan lowered his foot and wiggled his toes. Then again, why would someone like Tracy fall for him if he hadn't changed? That had to mean something.

From the other end of the condo, Garrett's muffled voice floated into the room. Tracy laughed. Dillan dug into the top box, pulling out commentaries and youth curriculum. He stacked them on his desk, ignoring the sudden quiet.

That woman's figure flashed before him.

He popped open the bottom of the empty box and flattened it. The ripped packing tape clung to his hand, and he yanked it loose and flung the box at his doorway. It banged against the thick, white molding and flopped to the ground.

"Dude. Don't be damaging my walls."

Dillan closed his eyes. He loved his brother. Really, he did. In a distant, hope-things-work-out-for-you-knucklehead kind of way. Right now, though, all he wanted was to escape to Grant Park and explore the lakefront and brand-spanking-new greenery. Anything to get away from Garrett.

Garrett, who had it all.

CHAPTER TWO

Miska woke Friday to the sun painting her ceiling and walls in golden tones. She lay in bed as the gold faded to cream, wishing the week were over and she was already rid of the depression that hit every time Mark left. She had a new novel to edit for Melissa, her old boss in New York, but she knew better than to start it today.

Not when she felt so empty. So lost. Not when she felt such insane relief that Mom wasn't around to know about her relationship with Mark—and then hated herself for the very thought.

What she wouldn't give to hear Mom chew her out right now.

A run should cheer her up. She forced herself out of bed and pulled on black yoga pants and a teal shirt and hoodie. She tugged her curls into a messy bun, then brushed her teeth. Like Mom always said, a girl never knew when she'd run into her perfect man. With the way things ended with Mark, she wasn't taking any chances.

Outside, an icy breeze prickled her skin. She crossed quiet streets and found her stride beneath the freshly leafed trees she'd admired from her condo. The trees opened up, and the majesty of Buckingham Fountain spread before her. The center jet sat low and quiet, water tumbling over the edge of each basin and spraying from the mouths of greened copper seahorses. After six months of a dried-up fountain, she couldn't get enough of the water. It breathed life into her, washing her emotions clean.

Maybe she'd be back to her old self in just one day. Wouldn't that be something?

A gust off the lake pressed her pants against her thighs. The last of the tulips waved. In the park, everything made sense. The compromises she'd made—she understood them all when she stood by the fountain or ran beside the lake. Out here, in the baby green of spring, life could be—would be—perfect.

Fatigue setting in, she started for home.

A freakishly tall man jogged toward her, his dark hair slightly messy as if he'd just gotten up. She studied the toasted skyline behind him, then glanced his way.

He was almost beside her, going the opposite direction, but his gaze was on her. As he passed, she realized who he was.

The guy who'd flattened Mark.

She twisted to look over her shoulder, only to see that he'd done the same. He opened his mouth to speak—then wiped out on the sidewalk.

She jerked to a stop, hand flying to her mouth.

The man rolled into sitting position and dabbed at his knees before checking his palms. He looked up, mouth twisted into a frustrated smile, cheeks pink. "You gonna help me up?"

"Me?" She laughed, relieved that he was all right. "After yesterday, isn't this karma?"

He chuckled and climbed to his feet. "I don't know about karma."

One knee was skinned and red. Blood trickled down the other.

She cringed as she walked closer. "Are you okay?"

"I'll be fine. Watch it." He pointed to the ground, and Miska halted. "That crack there took me down."

"You sure it was the crack?"

He shrugged. "Either that or you, right? I saw you coming but wasn't sure if it *was* you."

"Do I look that different without makeup?"

"Actually, no." He looked at the trees beyond her.

She cocked her head.

His gaze dropped to hers. "It's Miska, right?"

"Yes. Sorry. I don't remember your name."

"Dillan."

Right.

He jerked his chin toward their building. "Looks like you're heading back."

"I am. You run every day?"

"Four, five days a week. But living here…" He looked around. "I should take advantage of this while I can."

"You sound like you won't be here long."

"A few months. I'm staying with my brother and saving up for a house."

A house. She wrinkled her nose. "Let me guess. Suburbs?"

His smile crinkled the skin around his eyes. "You say it like the suburbs are evil."

That had been her experience, although the city held the same problems, if not worse. "I'm a city girl. I decided years ago that I'd live downtown."

"And here you are."

"Here I am." She returned his smile. How nicely it softened his face. What did he think of her, especially after yesterday with Mark? He'd been so quiet then. Was he friendly today because she might be a way to get to a famous athlete?

"Well, I gotta run." He pointed his thumb over his shoulder. "I'm taking a few laps around the fountain and calling it a morning. See you."

So he loved the fountain too. Suddenly she found herself hoping she'd been awake enough when she'd brushed her teeth. "Enjoy your run. Don't trip." She flashed him a smirk as she turned toward home.

"I told you," he called after her. "It was that crack."

She held up her hand in acknowledgment. Liar.

Inside her condo she refilled her water bottle and guzzled it as she paced through her living room and kitchen, cooling down. She checked her phone. Nothing from Mark—just a text from her half-sister Adrienne, asking if she was up.

She replied, then showered and dressed. She spread her Devacurl cream through her curls, scrunched them, and opened her makeup bag.

A thick envelope rested there.

Two gift cards lay inside, one for Jewel-Osco, her usual grocery store, and another for Peapod, the grocery delivery service. She checked the amounts Mark had scrawled on them. Three thousand dollars at Jewel. Two thousand at Peapod.

She bit her lip. All that money—that had to be enough for the rest of the year. No, probably longer than that. A lot longer.

A slip of paper in the envelope caught her eye. Mark had written a note in his broad, messy scrawl.

Hope this makes things easier for you. Save the Peapod for when you're on a deadline. Or getting ready for me.

The note ended with his name and a winking smiley face.

She fingered the gift cards. Months and months without having to pay for food—she was that much closer to financial freedom because of his thoughtfulness.

Her phone rang in the kitchen.

Miska hurried to it.

The area code said Chicago—Adrienne was probably calling from her office. Miska answered. "Hey, girl."

"Oh. Umm…" A man cleared his throat. "I was trying to reach Miska Tomlinson."

Not Adrienne. And still not Mark. "Who is this?"

"I'm… I really need to speak to Miska."

"I screen her calls, so if you'd like to speak with her, you'll need to tell me who you are."

"I see." The man sighed, ultimate weariness in the sound. "Tell her it's her father."

Her knees buckled. Miska grabbed a bar stool and pulled herself onto it. "Excuse me?"

"My name's Jack Tomlinson. I—I haven't spoken to her in years. But if you'd tell her—"

"You're Jack Tomlinson."

"Yes. It's very important I speak to her."

Her dad was looking for her. She squeezed the center of her shirt. Was this for real? "How do I know it's you?"

"How do you know?"

"Tell me something about her." She held her breath. The last time she'd seen him, she'd just turned two. She had no memory of him. None. Did he really have memories of her?

"I—" He cleared his throat again. "She has curly, black hair."

"Something else. Her brother..."

"Brothers. Wade and Zane are fourteen months older. They're blond."

Was that all he could say about them? Birth order? Appearance? "Wouldn't a father know stuff about his own kids?"

Silence hung on the other end.

"Come on, Jack. What kind of a man doesn't know anything about his kids?"

"A man with a whole lot of regrets."

Oh, please. She rubbed her fingers across her eyebrows. "What was my—" she gritted her teeth "—Miska's mother's name?"

"Claire Friel."

"Why did you leave her?"

His voice quavered. "Because I was a young, stupid fool."

Just like Mom had said. She moved the phone away and drew in a shuddering breath.

"Miska?" she heard faintly.

She raised the phone to her ear. "What does my name mean?"

"Mariska means 'of the sea.'"

It *was* him. She closed her eyes. "Or bitter."

"To me it meant the first. The *bitter* would be up to you."

"Easy for you to say, the man who didn't stick around. Who left his kids to fend for themselves, left them to watch their mother fill his place over and over."

"Miska—"

"Don't tell me I shouldn't be bitter."

He sighed.

"Why are you calling me?"

"Because I'm hoping you'll give your foolish father another chance."

"To do what?"

"To get to know his daughter."

His words rattled around the room. Her dad wanted to know her?

"Miska, I'm fifty-five. I've had three decades to think about the women I left. And too late I'm realizing what an awful—" His voice caught. "I've wasted a lot of time. I've hurt a lot of people. And I don't know how much time I have left—"

Her stomach seized. "Are you dying?"

"No." He chuckled. "Sorry. Not yet. But I'm pretty sure middle age is past. I've got joints that tell me when storms are coming."

"It's been twenty-eight years."

"I know."

"Twenty-eight years! How can you walk away—" She clenched her fist. She'd never had a dad, didn't remember the loss of him. So where was all this anguish coming from?

"I'm sorry, Miska."

She stared at the floor.

"I can never make up for what I did. But I'd like to get to know who you are now. If it's not too late, I'd like to spend time with my daughter."

It had been a lonely four years since Mom died. She'd felt like an orphan, even though Jack had been alive somewhere. Now here he was. Asking to see her.

Did she want to see him?

Of course she did. She nodded. Yes, yes, yes.

"Miska?"

She laughed, realizing he couldn't see her nod. "I'd like that."

His relief gushed out. "Thank you."

She fought back the urge to thank him. "Just promise you won't disappear for another twenty-some years."

"As much as I can, I promise."

Afternoon light deepened the hollows of her half-sister's cheeks. Adrienne eased her drink onto Miska's kitchen island and stared at her. "He what?"

"I know. It sounds crazy, but he wants to get together. He wants to be a dad. Finally."

Adrienne's brown eyes darkened. "Who cares what he wants? Like coming back after all these years makes it okay."

This wasn't the reaction she'd expected. "Of course it doesn't. You can't make up for twenty-eight years of neglect—"

"Thirty-one years!" Adrienne jumped up from Miska's barstool and marched to the window where marshmallow clouds hovered over the lake. Her chest heaved as if she'd sprinted there. "Do you know what my only memory of him is? The only rotten thing?"

"Hey, he left us both—"

"It's my mom chasing him through the house, hanging onto him, screaming for him to stay, trying to pull his suitcase out of his hand. Then he turned and shoved her. She fell and broke her wrist—had surgery and pins—and he never, never showed up again."

Miska eased onto a stool. Maybe not having memories was a good thing. "I'm sorry."

"Don't be sorry. He's scum." Adrienne swore and looked around the room.

What was she looking for? Jack? Something to throw? "Calm down. He's not here."

"He's lucky he's not here. I can't believe he had the nerve to call you." Her gaze zeroed in on Miska. "What'd you tell him?"

Oh no. How had she ever thought her sister would be okay with this? "I told him I'd like to meet him."

Adrienne stalked her way. "Are you insane? Do you know why he called?"

"I'd like to think it's because I'm his daughter—"

"You have money, Miska. He wants money."

Her inheritance was in her condo. Wade's and Zane's inheritance—
there probably wasn't much of that left. "No, he doesn't. He didn't say a
word—"

"Not yet."

"If you could have heard him—"

"Miska, wake up!"

She jerked at Adrienne's volume.

"He's never cared about any of us. Never! So why now? Why all of a
sudden?"

"People change."

"Not without reason. He'll ask for money, then he'll vanish again. You
won't hear from him until—"

"Stop it!" Miska's feet hit the floor, her hands in fists. "Stop trying to
ruin this!"

"I'm trying to protect you. He's a lousy, despicable man who couldn't
keep his pants on—"

"And now he wants to make up for it. What's wrong with that? Just
because he hasn't called you yet—"

"He did call me! I told him when his first wife got over her pill
addictions, we could talk."

Miska swallowed.

"I told him if he ever came near me, I'd beat him within an inch of his
life, then castrate him while he was down. Do the women of the world a
favor."

There was the Adrienne she knew and loved anyway. "I didn't realize
you felt that strongly."

"Well, I do. He doesn't deserve another chance. Not with a single one
of us."

What if she wanted to give him one?

"My mom used to watch you and Wade and Zane and your mom.
We'd take the long way everywhere, right past your house just in case his
car was there."

"Adrienne, he left when I was two."

"I'm not saying it made sense. But she was always watching for him, always hoping. And when she didn't see him, she'd pop pills." She scowled at the stool between them. "It's a sorry way to grow up."

"You think I don't know that? You think my mom didn't have her own issues? I get that what he did is despicable. I do. But if you could have heard him on the phone—"

"I did hear him. He's a joke of a human being now just like he's always been. I'm not giving him a minute of my time. Don't you either."

"Maybe I want to spend time with him."

Adrienne glared down her nose. "Then I don't want to spend time with you."

What?

Long, brown hair whipping against her neck, her sister marched to the couch, stilettos attacking the floor, and snatched her lime green messenger bag.

"Adrienne, wait."

Adrienne stared at the bag, her look morphing into one of pure revulsion. "What?"

"You can't be serious."

"I am. I hate him, and I won't spend time with anyone who patronizes him."

"But we've been friends a long time—"

"More than that—family. Yet you seem ready to throw us away for a man who threw *you* away when you were in diapers. Why is that?"

"He's our father, Adrienne."

Her jaw ticked. "No, he's a paternal ancestor who put as much into my life as my ten-times great-grandfather. I owe him nothing. Neither do you."

"You're being extreme."

"You think so?" Adrienne took a step closer, a good two inches taller in her heels. "You can look back over your mom's life and not hold him responsible?" She shook her head. "What would Claire say if she knew?"

Miska held still beneath Adrienne's hardened gaze. "She'd at least talk to him. Face to face."

"Fine. Talk to him. Tell him what a pathetic man he is, then leave him. It'd serve him right." She hefted the bag's strap onto her shoulder. "But don't give him a second more. Or we're through."

CHAPTER THREE

The squeak of the condo door broke Dillan's concentration. He stuck a finger in his commentary, sat up on the couch, and looked down the hallway to the entrance.

Garrett closed the door and yanked off his yellow, paisley tie.

"Hey, Gare."

"Dillanator. Whatcha reading?"

"Something for youth group."

"Still working?" Garrett headed to the master bedroom off the side of the living room. "Dude, it's after six."

Dillan glanced at the microwave clock as his brother closed his door. Huh. So it was.

It had been a long, slow day, full of unpacking and reading and note taking. He set the book aside and turned on the TV. On SportsCenter, three former athletes dissected the NBA playoffs, then showed highlights from the afternoon's Cubs game.

Garrett's voice came from the kitchen. "How long till football starts?"

"Too long." Dillan stretched across the couch, feet hanging over the ratty armrest, hands tucked behind his head. "Is this where I ask how your day went?"

"If you like living beneath a bridge."

Dillan chuckled.

"So what'd you make me for dinner?"

"Dinner?"

"You're here all day."

"Uh, working."

"You've got no commute. Dude, that's got to be worth a meal."

Dillan pointed down the hallway. "I commute. Bedroom two to bedroom three. Then I double my commute going to the kitchen for lunch."

"Don't hurt yourself." Garrett's eyes landed on Dillan's knees. "Too late. What happened?"

"Nothing." He fingered a scab. "Went running."

Garrett snickered as he opened the dishwasher.

"Aren't you Mr. Clean, working in the kitchen."

"Someone's got to clean your mess." Garrett turned the faucet on. Water splashed, and he wiped his chin on the shoulder of the Chicago Bears jersey he'd changed into. "Would it kill you to put stuff in the dishwasher?"

"Since when do you care how the place looks? Or are you trying to keep Tracy in the dark until after the wedding?"

"I happen to like a clean house."

He remembered Garrett's room in high school, the last time they'd lived under the same roof. Dillan shot him a look.

"People change, Dill."

"I'll believe it when I see it."

The words were barely out of his mouth before he regretted them.

Garrett focused on the skillet and spatula in the sink, jaw tight. He scrubbed the pan and stashed it in the dishwasher.

Nice one, Dillan. He hadn't meant anything by it, but there was too much history for him to blame his brother for taking it the wrong way.

Garrett wiped off the stovetop.

Dillan stood. Glanced back at the TV, then out the windows at the glittering lake. What could he say—

"You eaten?" Garrett asked.

"No. You got something in mind?"

"Tracy said dinner's on her tonight. In honor of us being moved in."

"She's cooking?"

"Buying. Chinese."

"Nice."

"Yep. She should be here soon." Garrett closed the dishwasher and dried his hands. His eyes focused somewhere south of Dillan's waist. "What happened to your hands?"

Dillan fisted them. "I told you. Nothing."

Garrett laughed, and all was right between them again. "Dude. You wiped out good. Wish I'd seen that."

"Just replay any other wipeout, and you're there."

Garrett chuckled, then cocked his head toward the front door.

A faint female voice sounded.

"Yes. Food."

So it began, third-wheel time with his brother and soon-to-be sister-in-law. He stuck his hands in his pockets.

Garrett flung the door open and looked the wrong way, toward Miska's door beside theirs. He straightened, smiled, and stepped into the hallway.

Umm... Who was out there? Miska?

A new, deeper female voice reached him before the door fell shut. Great. He followed Garrett out of the condo.

Miska and another woman stood beside her door, Miska listening while the other woman, eyes hard and jaw tense, smiled at Garrett.

He was deep into some story already, hands in the air, chin up, mouth curved in a grin that—

Garrett was flirting?

Dillan looked back at the new woman. She'd locked eyes onto him. "Who's this?" she asked.

Garrett back-handed his arm. "My big brother, Dillan. Literally."

He held his hand out, not wanting to but not knowing what else to do. "Hi."

She took it, shook hard. "I'm Adrienne."

"Miska's older sister," Garrett added as if they went way back.

Adrienne sent him that tight smile. She was on edge over something. Miska too. He could see it in the way she stood, her eyes empty of the life they'd had that morning. The awkward moment he and Garrett had just experienced was nothing compared to whatever had happened between these two.

"They're clearly related, aren't they?" Garrett asked as if they weren't standing right there.

"Weird how that works." Miska's beauty was all soft and natural while Adrienne's paler looks had a jagged edge to them. While they resembled each other, there was a definite difference. "You must each look like a different parent."

Miska spoke. "We have the same—"

"Different moms." Adrienne tossed her head.

Garrett wrapped his arms across his chest. "Did you grow up together?"

"Same town." Miska glanced at Dillan. "How are your hands and knees?"

Garrett shifted, his upper body leaning back and his head tilting as if to say *oh, really?*

"Fine." He opened his palms, dropped his hands to his side. He didn't need to see the damage again. "I'll be good in a day or two."

Garrett winked at Adrienne. "Until the next wipeout."

She laughed.

He asked her what she did, and while she told him about the publisher she acquired for, Dillan leaned against the doorjamb. There had to be some way to get Garrett back inside before he flirted himself out of a fiancée.

Miska shifted too. "You were home today, weren't you?"

"I'm working here until I move out. What about you?"

Her warm brown eyes met his. "I work from home."

"What do you do?"

"I freelance for a few publishers."

"Freelance?"

"Edit. Adult fiction."

"Same one as your sister?"

"Her house is one of them."

Miska looked back at Garrett who was telling Adrienne about the law firm he worked at while running his thumb up and down the edge of his bicep.

Hopefully that wasn't intentional.

Miska shifted again, yanking Dillan's gaze back to her. She was so beautiful, so female. *So immoral*, he reminded himself.

"What's chasing you away in a few months?" she asked.

"Garrett's wedding. I'm living here until then."

"Some brotherly bonding?"

"Something like that."

She nodded. Looked back at Garrett and Adrienne who were even deeper in conversation.

Oh, the dreaded awkward silence. Dillan cleared his throat. "So how do you keep from talking to the walls?"

"Getting lonely in there?"

He hadn't meant it that way. "I'm used to working around people. In there all I hear are sirens and horns."

"You'll get used to it, but you have to find ways to get out. You know, go to a club, find something going on in town, get outside and walk through the crowds."

Go clubbing? No, thanks. He wasn't looking for anyone remotely like her.

Adrienne and Garrett interrupted them with a laugh. Adrienne leaned in to Garrett, her fingers slipping across his wrist.

Dillan frowned. *Come on, man.*

Out of sight in the floor's lobby, an elevator dinged.

Garrett turned toward the sound, the move taking him out of Adrienne's reach. "Maybe that's dinner."

Dillan hoped.

Tracy rounded the corner, two bulging, brown paper bags in her arms, oversized, pink purse dangling from her elbow.

Garrett's face brightened as he walked to her. "Hey, my little fortune cookie."

Dillan held back the urge to shake his head. Seriously?

Garrett bent down to kiss her, and Dillan looked away, right at Adrienne—who watched with some sort of odd interest—and then at Miska. She studied Tracy, mouth tight, shoulders stiff.

What was this— Oh, right. Maybe he and Garrett weren't the only ones who'd noticed Tracy's resemblance to Mark Scheider's wife.

Tracy smiled up at Garrett, talking softly. He shrugged as he took the bags of food, then led her back to where he'd been standing so closely to Adrienne. "This is my fiancée, Tracy." He nodded at Miska. "And our neighbor, Miska."

"So nice to meet you." Tracy held out a hand, and Miska took it. "Just a few more months, and we'll officially be neighbors."

Miska flashed her a smile, the tension gone.

"And this is Adrienne, babe. They're sisters."

Tracy turned to Adrienne, and the smile on Miska's face faded. She ran a finger along her temple, then glanced at Dillan.

He forced his attention back on Tracy. Stink. Caught looking. Hopefully she didn't think he'd been checking her out.

'Cause he hadn't been.

"You should join us for dinner," Tracy was saying.

Dillan blinked and straightened.

Fake friendliness registered on Adrienne's face. "We couldn't."

"I bought a ton. Really. There's plenty for everyone. The more the merrier, right?"

Did Tracy, Garrett, anyone but him see the condescension behind that woman's smile?

Adrienne sent her sister the slightest eye roll. "Miska and I already have plans for the—"

"Actually, I don't." Miska crossed her arms and smiled at Tracy. "I've got some work to catch up on. Dinner sounds great. What can I bring?"

Tracy grinned. "Just yourself. I've got it all here."

"Okay then." Miska gave Tracy a forceful nod. "Thanks."

Adrienne almost glared at her sister.

"Well." Miska patted her shoulder. "I don't want to keep you. Have fun without me."

"Always do." The fake smile crossed the woman's face again. "Very nice meeting you all."

Yeah, right. Dillan opened the door, escaped inside.

Except it wasn't an escape, not with Miska joining them.

With a sigh he opened a kitchen cabinet and grabbed four plates. At least he wouldn't be a third wheel.

For being Darcie Scheider's twin, Tracy whatever-her-name was all right.

Even better, as dinner went on, Tracy looked less and less like Darcie and more like her own person. Tracy's hair was long with big, loose curls, a lot like Darcie's had been until she chopped it last month.

For whatever reason, this girl was just nice.

Miska passed the Triple Delight to Dillan, who dished seconds onto his fried rice. No wonder the guy ran every day. He and Garrett could both pack it away. But when one was six foot thirteen, one probably needed a lot of food.

Dillan glanced at her and did a double take. "Need anything?"

Not a thing. "A fortune cookie, maybe?"

He handed her one from the pile beside him.

"You have to read it out loud," Garrett said.

Tracy nodded. "So we can laugh." Her fortune had said she should avoid taking that long trip which led to her bugging Garrett about where they were going for their honeymoon.

After removing the wrapper, Miska cracked the cookie and pulled out the slip of paper. The words made her blink.

"Read it," Tracy said.

"'You will soon inherit great fortune.'"

Garrett and Tracy chuckled. Dillan raised an eyebrow and returned to his food.

"What do you think, Miska? Any lump sums of money in your future?" Tracy asked.

If they only knew. "Let's hope."

Garrett picked up his own cookie and tossed another to Dillan who caught it against his chest. "Bet I know what yours says, Dill. Something about ducking. Or taking a nice trip."

Garrett didn't let up, did he? "How tall are you?" she asked.

Dillan tore open the wrapper. "Six nine."

Six nine? No wonder Mark looked small beside him.

Dillan read the strip of paper. "Get ready, Gare. Softball coming. 'Love is in your future.'"

Tracy aahed, and Garrett snickered, nudging Dillan with his elbow. "Mom and Dad do get back from Florida tomorrow."

Dillan smirked and tossed the paper onto Garrett's plate. "Looks like I got yours."

So Dillan was single? She pushed the thought away. "Your parents are snowbirds?"

Garrett nodded. "Dillan house-sits for them while they're gone."

"Miska, what about you?"

She forced her gaze to Tracy. "Me?"

"Do you have family in Chicago? Other than Adrienne?"

"Some. We don't see each other much."

"Is Adrienne your only sister?" Garrett asked.

Dillan stilled.

Why had that question grabbed him? Miska forced herself not to look at him. He'd all but ignored Adrienne. He couldn't be interested in her. "I have two brothers and six half-brothers and sisters. Adrienne's the only one I see."

"Now that's my concern with my brothers." Tracy looked at Garrett. "I know guys are different this way, but I can't imagine only seeing my brothers a couple times a year, you know? Is it their decision not to get together or yours?"

Garrett shifted. "Tracy."

"I'm sorry. That was too personal, wasn't it? I just get going sometimes—"

"It's okay." When was the last time she'd talked to her brothers, much less seen them? "We aren't close. Some stuff..." She waved it away. "My father only stayed with a woman long enough to have a kid or two. I don't really know any of my half-siblings except for Adrienne and her brother, Alec. And Alec never liked me. So it's just been Adrienne and me, I guess."

They stared at her. Which meant they had perfect families.

So why not bare it all? Shock 'em good? "Actually I just heard from my dad this morning. First time since I was two."

"Since you were two?" Tracy grabbed her hand. "That's not right."

"I know." She looked Tracy in the eye. This one couldn't hide her thoughts if she tried. "Is it wrong that I want to get to know him?"

Tracy shook her head emphatically. "Of course not."

"That's what I think. Adrienne hates him, though."

"And you're caught in the middle."

Story of her life.

"Miska, you'll always regret it if you don't get to know him. I would. Sure, it's been a long time. I get why your sister would be angry. But if he's coming back now, he deserves another chance." She faced the guys. "Right?"

Miska looked at Dillan.

He'd leaned back in his chair, arms crossed, gaze locked onto his plate.

Great, she'd shared too much. "I shouldn't have bored you guys with this."

"No." Tracy grabbed her hand again. "You have to talk to him. If Adrienne's trying to keep you from him, she's wrong, although I'm sure she means well. He's *your* dad. You should meet him."

Dillan nodded his support. Garrett did the same.

"Okay then." She released a small laugh. Tracy was right. Adrienne was being unreasonable. "We made dinner plans for next week. Guess I won't break them."

Tracy grinned at her. "Definitely not. Go have fun."

As the conversation moved to other things, Miska found herself loosening up with these new neighbors. How different Garrett and Dillan were from her brothers. They'd have been all over the new girl at their table. Of course Garrett was engaged, but that had never stopped Wade or Zane.

Even quiet, serious Dillan lightened up, reminding her of the guy who'd joked after wiping out that morning. Something about him appealed. What was it?

He was so tall, tall enough that it compensated for the serious lines that cut across his forehead, for the tight way he held his mouth. For the way he only spoke when spoken to and focused more on his food than on the company. If he were to cut loose and laugh, relax more and smile, he could be a good-looking man. She'd seen it that morning. And if he ever let a woman run her fingers through that dark hair, mess it up a bit—

Dillan glanced at her.

Could he read thoughts?

He scraped the last of his rice onto his fork.

She'd caught him watching her in the hallway after Tracy arrived. Maybe his fortune cookie had it right. Maybe…

While Garrett joked about something that had happened at work, she shifted in her chair, arching her back as if she were stiff, making sure the V-neck of her shirt dipped just low enough.

Dillan glanced her way, eyes landing right where she wanted.

But he jerked his gaze away as if he'd been stung. He scooted his chair back and leaned his elbows on his knees, gave her the back of his head, and focused on Garrett.

What on earth was that? What, was he gay?

Garrett's eyes flickered from her back to Tracy, who had no idea what had just happened, her attention glued to her fiancé. What *had* just happened? What guy turned down a peek?

Dillan stood and grabbed his plate, silverware, and empty rice boxes. He reached for her plate, then paused, his gaze never leaving the table. "You finished?"

"Oh. I am." She handed him the plate. "Thank you. I'll pack up the leftovers."

Tracy shook her head. "You don't need to do that."

Miska waved off Tracy's words and put lids over the orange chicken and chicken with broccoli. She followed Dillan around the island.

He glanced at her from where he rinsed silverware in the sink. "You can put those in the fridge."

"Sure." She opened the stainless steel door. A pristine white interior greeted her, along with a gallon of milk, a twelve-pack of Dr Pepper, apples, bread, mayonnaise, lunch meat, and processed cheese. "Wow. I think this doubles your refrigerator contents."

Dillan smiled at the silverware. "Tracy, you're doing this every night, right?"

"Sorry, Dillan. Got to find your own girl."

His own girl? So he wasn't gay?

She closed the fridge.

Tracy set two more containers of leftovers on the island. Miska grabbed them and turned, bumping into Dillan who'd somehow ended up behind her.

He stepped back, hands raised. "Sorry."

"My fault." She stacked the food in the fridge and closed it again. Now what?

Garrett and Tracy talked in low tones, Garrett wearing that flirty grin that seemed to go everywhere he did. Dillan leaned against the counter and stuffed his hands in his pockets. His body language said uncomfortable.

He was right; she'd stayed too long.

She slipped past him and rounded the island where Garrett and Tracy could see her. They both looked up. "I need to head out. Thanks so much for dinner."

"You're going?" Tracy asked.

"I am. Have some things to do yet. But thanks for inviting me. I enjoyed it."

Tracy stood and wrapped her arms around Miska. "Me too. We'll have to do it again sometime."

Relax. Tracy was one of those women who thought everyone wanted a hug. Normally she would, but not from someone she'd just met. Tracy released her, and Miska stretched her mouth into a smile. "Sounds great." She said good-bye to Garrett and Dillan and walked down the hallway toward the front door.

Dillan followed.

She opened the door, glancing into the closest bedroom as she did. A cheap desk and computer chair, a simple bookcase filled with what looked like textbooks and reference books.

He reached above her and held the condo door open.

She smiled up at him. "So that's where the magic happens, hmm?"

"The magic." He tugged his earlobe. "Yeah, we'll go with that."

She laughed, and he smiled with her. "You have a good night, Miska."

So he wanted her to go. A decent-looking, single man who had no interest in her. "'Bye."

"'Bye."

She slipped through the doorway, and the door closed behind her. No lingering. No flirting. Nothing.

Engaged Garrett was more flirtatious than Dillan.

She pulled her keys out of her pocket and unlocked her door. The evening had somehow left her feeling flat. What time was it? Eight? What did she have to look forward to? The gym? Writing a new post for her blog? Mark's game that was recording?

She checked her phone for the twentieth time that day. Still nothing from Mark. Of course he couldn't have called since she'd last checked, not with his team playing.

Her couch beckoned, and Miska obeyed, her hand finding the remote, the on button, and Mark's recorded game that had started an hour ago. She curled up in the couch's cool leather embrace and scrolled through the footage, checking every view of the dugout for Mark since he wasn't pitching.

There he was, leaning against the padded dugout railing, an inning later back-pounding a guy who'd homered, and, when the game ended an hour and a half later, lining up with the rest of the team near the third-base line to high-five each other.

She grabbed her phone and texted him. *Miss you, love. Can't wait until you get back.*

Message sent, the screen faded to nothing.

Nothing.

She should have gone out with Adrienne.

CHAPTER FOUR

I f she'd passed him on the street, Miska would have known Jack Tomlinson was her father.

While the waitress sliced deep-dish, spinach pizza, Miska studied his face, a male version of herself. Curly, black hair, his streaked with silver. Golden skin tone. Brown eyes the same wide shape and color as hers. His lips, his jaw, an aged version of her own. The main difference were the lines edging his eyes—lines Wade and Zane were beginning to sport—either laugh lines or worry lines.

Adrienne would hope they were worry lines. Sleepless, scared-for-his-life worry lines.

The waitress left, and with her fork Miska cut off the tip of the pizza. The first bite of rich tomato, gobs of mozzarella, and buttery cornmeal crust was savory heaven.

Jack chuckled. "Told you it's good."

"It's amazing. I can't believe I've lived here all these years and never tried it." She weighed her words, then threw caution away. "Mom always preferred Giordano's."

"She knew I liked Lou Malnati's." He set down his fork. "You want to talk about it?"

His tone was gentle, warm, as if he were asking her to share some terrible burden.

Was it being unfaithful to Mom to want to know his side of the story? He was her father, after all, the man who influenced her appearance and height. Wade and Zane had inherited Mom's blonde hair and average stature. Having a relative she actually looked like felt better than expected.

It had to be okay to listen to him.

She shoved her hands into her lap. "Okay. What happened?"

He looked at traffic crawling past on State Street. "I married my first wife too young."

"Jody, Adrienne's mom."

"You know them?"

"Adrienne and I are friends."

He smiled as if it made him happy. "How'd that happen?"

"We were in the same high school for a year. For some reason she watched out for me." They weren't here to talk about her and Adrienne, though. Not yet. "You married Jody too young."

"We were twenty-one. Adrienne was born five months later, her brother a year later."

Her brother. Shouldn't he have said his son?

"Jody and I didn't have much in common. She should never have married me, really. And I shouldn't have asked her. But she was pregnant, and everyone said we should get married, so we convinced ourselves that what we felt was love." He looked down at his pizza. "I met your mom at the office. She was getting her master's at night and working for the company during the day. Don't know how we found time to have an affair, but we did."

"Why'd you do it?"

"You've seen pictures of your mom at that age. She was beautiful."

"She was beautiful when you left her. In fact, she was beautiful up until the cancer. So why did you leave?"

He studied her. "Miska, when you're young and… and stupid, you think love is a feeling that never fades. When it does, you think you're settling for less than you deserve. So you look elsewhere."

"So you fell out of love with Jody and my mom and all the rest."

"I was just in love with the idea of love—with romance, you know? That high you get when love is fresh and exciting? I wanted that."

She thought of Mark, even though their situation was different. They'd been together a year, and he hadn't given any signs of getting bored. Then again, he hadn't left his wife either. "How did you know you needed to leave Jody for my mom?"

He chuckled. "Claire was pregnant with twins, and Jody guessed I was having an affair. Someone had to go. Jody wanted to maim me; Claire didn't." He shrugged. "At the time it made sense."

"So what happened? You and Mom were together four years. Longer than you were with Jody."

"Not quite four years. Six months before I left, I was seeing someone else."

Seeing someone else. Could he really use that term when he'd been raising three kids with his wife? It wasn't high school.

"I left her for a woman I met at a bar. Cute little thing. Married her a week after the divorce. Had a baby with her and then another affair. My history in a nutshell."

He held her gaze, sorrow and regret lining his eyes.

"How many women were there?"

"Wives?"

"Wives. Girlfriends."

"I married another woman after Lana, then decided marrying was foolish. Getting a divorce so I could move on was too much."

"Not to mention the child support."

The street suddenly fascinated him.

"You never paid child support?"

"Nine kids? Five different women? I never made that kind of money."

"Don't you think fathering them demands you take care of them? If you knew how Adrienne and Alec grew up—"

"Did you suffer for anything?"

"No, but we were the exception."

"Then don't fight their battles. I sent money for Adrienne and Alec until I realized Jody was spending it on her drug of choice. I helped Lana awhile, and then it became too much. Plus I wasn't making money for a time."

How had he survived?

He shifted the half-eaten piece of pizza around with his fork, a frown creating wrinkles between his dark eyebrows.

She picked up her water and sipped it.

"Eventually they all made it, Miska. They all made more than I did. And Lana took my book advance, so we were even."

She choked on her water, a few drops sputtering from her mouth. His *what*? He handed her a napkin, and she dabbed her chin. "You wrote a book?"

"On poetry during the Civil War. The university I taught at published it. Then Lana sued me for child support. Long story short, I lost my job and the advance, and left the country."

"You wrote a book."

He nodded as if she were slow. "Yes."

Her chest tightened. "I write too. Well, I edit, but I love words. I write when I have free time. Mom was such a numbers girl that I wondered where I got it."

"You and Adrienne." His eyes flashed with fatherly pride. "My girls. My wordsmiths."

My girls. Adrienne had no idea what she was missing.

Mom and Wade and Zane—they'd been bored with the written word, always wanting to *do* something rather than read something. Now it made sense. This man, this mostly stranger, had made her who she was, even without being around.

Adrienne was wrong. He'd given them much, and Miska was grateful for the chance to bond with him, even if there had been almost three decades of neglect. What mattered was today, this chance to know the father who'd suddenly gifted her a sense of belonging. "Jack, why have you come back?"

He grabbed her hand, squeezing like she mattered most. "Because I know how much I missed. And I'm tired of it. I don't want to miss any more."

Jack took a cab to work while Miska walked the few blocks home. Her phone rang outside her building.

It was Mark.

She answered as she pushed the building's revolving door. "Hey, how are you?"

"Busy, baby. I've missed you. Thought about you every day since I left."

"Me too." She hated going so long without talking to him. If only they could snuggle through the phone. "You looked so good last night."

"Thanks. I haven't thrown a complete game since—"

She laughed. "No, I meant you." She lowered her voice. "You looked wonderful. It made me hurt to watch you."

"Did it?" His voice lowered too. "Wish I could drop by for an afternoon."

"Milwaukee's only two hours away. When's your next off day?"

"Thursday."

The word was full of promise. He'd visited her during the off season but never on an off day. She waved at the doorman behind the desk and opened the glass door to the elevator bank. "Should I work extra hard tomorrow so I can take Thursday off?"

He groaned. "I think so. You'll definitely have company."

"What time?"

"I'll surprise you. Be ready."

She would be.

CHAPTER FIVE

Miska's alarm woke her Wednesday morning. She went through her routine—washed her face, brushed her teeth, dressed in black running pants and a soft gray and white striped hoodie, and pulled her hair up. She took the stairs to the lobby and headed into an overcast, cold May morning, following her usual route around Buckingham Fountain and the lakefront.

On her way back, she stopped beside the fountain to catch her breath and guzzle her water. The fountain's basins mirrored the metal gray of the sky. Miska looked toward the lake and instead found Dillan Foster several yards to her right, watching her.

Well, good morning. She waved her fingertips as she finished her water bottle.

He strolled to her, his head turned toward the lake as if he suddenly couldn't tear himself away. What a confusing man. Here he was, watching her, when almost a week ago he'd given every sign of being uninterested.

"Hey, there," she called as he neared. "What a lovely March morning, huh?"

He chuckled, hands stuffed into the pockets of his navy blue running pants. "May, March. What's the difference?"

Already the warmth from her run faded, and she fought to keep her teeth from chattering. "You're a hardcore runner, coming out in this cold. Or did you move here from Alaska?"

"There's a place I'd like to visit. Like in August, when it's ninety-five here."

"Right now ninety-five sounds wonderful."

He smiled, scanning the watery horizon.

What was he thinking?

He wiped his forehead with the collar of his sweatshirt.

"I don't know how I ever lived away from the lake."

He looked at her. "Where'd you move from?"

"New York."

"You like it?"

"To visit. Not to live."

"What brought you back?"

"The publishing house laid a bunch of us off when the economy tanked. I came back here, bought this place, and started my own editing business."

"So something good came from the bad."

Interesting, now that she thought about it. "That might be a first."

"You're just young. Give it time. You'll see more."

"Young?" That was relative. "I'm thirty."

He eyed her. "No, you're not."

"Want to see my license?"

"I thought you were twenty-five or six." He chuckled as if it were funny.

"What?"

"Nothing."

She sent him a come-on look, and he laughed. "Tell me," she said.

"It's not that funny." He peeked at her, humor tugging at his lips. "You're older than me."

"Oh, sure. Rub it in."

He snickered.

Miska stuffed her smile away. "It isn't easy turning thirty. The body starts to slow down, you can't go without sleep like you used to—"

"Wait, wait, wait." He searched the space around them. "Where'd I put that violin?"

She smacked his arm, and he fake-stumbled sideways, his grin erupting. She knew hers matched his. "Just so you know, you could pass for thirty."

His smile vanished. "Hey now. Play nice."

"If you're not thirty, how old are you?"

"I'm twenty-eight for... three more weeks."

"So you're almost my age."

"Almost. But not." He raised his eyebrows, a smirk on his lips.

She rolled her eyes, walking away to throw the bottle in the trash.

When she turned back, he still watched her. "What kind of books do you edit?"

"Fiction. Romance."

He nodded and looked back at the lake.

"My favorite was a historical during the Chicago Fire. Really interesting stuff."

With one foot, he nudged the decorative fence surrounding the fountain. "Chicago history is full of good coming from bad."

"Like?"

"Like Grant Park here. Rubble from the Chicago fire? Under our feet."

"Really?"

"Yep. Lots of debris and rubble were thrown out here which made the land eat into the lake and the park grow larger. People got sick of its ugliness and the squatters and turned it into the showpiece it is."

"Huh."

"So without the fire and trash and rubble, Grant Park isn't nearly this big, and we don't have our view. Good from bad."

"Interesting. Is that why you like Grant Park?"

"That and the fact that the Cubs used to play here."

"No, they didn't."

He crossed his arms. "Oh. Okay."

"I've never heard that. Where'd they play?"

"Randolph and Michigan Avenue. Northwest corner of Millennium Park."

She studied the skyscrapers providing a silver backstop for Millennium Park. "When was this?"

"Before the fire. They lost everything, then rebuilt the ballpark a few years later. Didn't stay long, though."

Mark would love this bit of trivia. "I'll have to check your Cubs info myself, just to make sure you aren't dreaming it up."

He shrugged as if what she thought didn't matter.

"Well, I'm freezing. I'm heading back." She turned to go.

Dillan stayed where he was.

"You coming?"

He jerked his head toward her as if he hadn't heard. Then he nodded and fell into step beside her, and they began jogging.

She matched his pace, pleased that it pushed her a little. "I don't know what you do for a living."

"I'm a pastor."

A pastor? She shot him a glance, trying to picture him in clergy robes or that collar Catholics wore. Strange. He seemed so normal, except he never showed interest in her. This sure explained it—he wasn't allowed to marry. "How long you been doing that?"

"Five years. I'm the assistant."

"What's the assistant do?"

"Everything. Run the youth group, behind-the-scenes stuff, teach a Sunday School class—lots of variety."

"Sounds intriguing."

He looked her way, his smile a bit smug, as if he knew she were faking interest. Guess his job made him good at catching little white lies.

"What's Garrett do again? And Tracy?" she asked.

"Garrett's a lawyer. Tracy's a nurse for a pediatrician in the suburbs."

"So that's why she isn't living with you guys."

"Well…" He quieted as they turned west toward their building, cars whizzing by. "They're waiting until they get married."

What? Seriously? She shot him a look, but he focused ahead as if what he'd said was normal. They were waiting to what? Live together? Or have sex? "What about you?"

"Me?"

"Can a pastor marry, or are you single the rest of your life?"

"We can marry. The Bible doesn't say anything about pastors not marrying."

"So why haven't you?"

"Haven't met her yet. You?"

"Me?"

"Yes, you. You *are* thirty."

"I'm seeing someone."

"Ah."

"What's that mean?"

His forehead crinkled. "That I was listening?"

"Wasn't an I'm-listening kind of sound."

"What kind of sound was it?"

Miska studied his profile. "It sounded judgmental."

"Did it?"

"It did."

"Huh. Strange."

She waited for him to say more, but he kept silent. A car honked as it flew by. Ahead of them, traffic flooded Michigan Avenue. "You're judging me for dating a married man."

"Who?" They stopped at the edge of the sidewalk, the don't-walk hand flashing. He planted his hands on his waist and gulped in air. "That guy you were with when we moved in?"

"Yes. Mark Scheider. *That* guy."

"He's married, huh?"

"His marriage was over before we met."

"Mmm-hmm."

There he went again. "Stop it."

The walk sign flashed.

He took off across the intersection, and Miska raced to catch up. "It's the twenty-first century, Dillan. We're not in Victorian America."

"Aren't you perceptive."

They dodged a car trying to turn and jogged onto the sidewalk. She grabbed his arm and pulled him to a stop. "You don't have any right to judge me."

"You're right. I'm not the one you answer to, but you keep hearing judgment when I haven't said anything. So maybe what you're hearing isn't coming from me."

She tossed her head and studied him. He was right; she'd overreacted. It was probably her own past that haunted her.

But Mark and Darcie didn't have children, no little boys or girls growing up in a dysfunctional family. It'd be best for her to break them up before Darcie went and got pregnant. "You're right. Sorry."

Dillan held up his hands. "Like I said, you don't answer to me."

They trudged to the revolving doors where he motioned for her to go first.

First?

Miska straightened, her fatigue gone. What if she got pregnant first?

That would change everything.

Dillan ran with Miska Thursday morning.

But not on purpose.

He left earlier than usual, but she was stretching in front of the elevator when he reached their floor's lobby, one hand holding her foot up behind her, her other hand bracing herself against the wall.

She nodded over her shoulder. "Hey, there."

He grunted, hoping she took it as an insult.

She didn't, instead flashing a beautiful smile.

The elevator doors opened, and they rode down to another cool morning which she loved and told him so.

Something had her in a good mood.

All he could think about was the way he'd copped out the day before, trying to get her to think about her conscience and God, hoping she'd figure it out on her own.

Didn't seem like she had.

He endured the forty-minute jog and said good-bye outside his door. Inside the condo, he slid down the hallway wall and let his head thump it. Why did he have to run into her?

"What's with you?" Garrett stood beside him, dressed in another one of his expensive suits.

Nice tie, though. "Went running."

"Figured that. You look frustrated."

"Little bit."

"Don't forget the couch is being delivered."

"Right. Sometime between eight and six."

"Or nine. They just called. Don't spill anything on it or cut yourself and bleed all over it. Tracy would shoot me. Or you. Probably you." Garrett flashed him a grin, stepped over him, and left.

With time to kill, Dillan lazed through his routine. He showered and dressed, had his devotions, watched the lake awhile, then obeyed his growling stomach and headed to the kitchen. Great chef he wasn't, but he could make an omelet with the best of them. With his earlier start, he needed a full stomach to make it to lunch.

He grabbed eggs and milk, tomatoes, green onions, and cheddar cheese from the refrigerator. His stomach tightened and growled, jabbing him from deep inside.

He should have eaten first.

He mixed eggs and milk, then set them aside to chop vegetables.

What next? He pulled a skillet from the cabinet. Oh, salt and pepper.

He set the skillet beside the cutting board, but his aim was off. The skillet's handle banged the knife, and the knife flipped over the edge of the counter, somersaulting toward his feet.

Dillan jumped out of the knife's way. His toes hit the floor but slid from beneath him. The floor came up fast, and he flung his hands down. His chest smashed on top of his arms. Something snapped, and pain rocketed up his right arm while his forehead smacked the bottom corner of a cabinet.

A warm, sticky liquid filled his eye. Oh no.

He rolled onto his back and wiped his left hand across his right eyebrow. Blood slid down the side of his head, into his hairline, into his ear.

This was bad. He forced himself up, wincing at the slightest movement of his arm.

Blood poured down his face, a thick, wet curtain over his eye. His pulse throbbed in his wrist.

On his feet, he teetered and leaned against the counter. He had to stop the bleeding. He rooted through the few kitchen towels Garrett had, streaks of blood following his hand. "Sorry, Gare. I owe you towels."

Not that these were in good shape anyway.

With his left hand, he held a beige towel over his right eyebrow, his right arm tucked against his chest. It felt like a bad game of Twister. How was he going to get to the hospital? He couldn't drive.

Dizziness washed over him, and he sagged against the counter. He'd have to call 911—over a cut and sore wrist. Man, this was messed up. He'd never hear the end of it.

Where was his phone?

He used his one clear eye to scan the kitchen and living room. The phone wasn't in sight, and he couldn't make himself think. This wasn't good—

Miska.

While he growled at the idea of asking *her* for help, relief sagged his shoulders. He couldn't drive, he couldn't find his phone, but Miska was home. She would have to do.

CHAPTER SIX

The drive home from the hospital was less tense with rush hour over and Dillan no longer bleeding. Miska peeked at him, crammed into the front seat of her Volvo, his fingers tapping his jeans.

The ER hadn't been busy. By the time she'd parked and made her way inside, they were stitching him up. When they finally let her see him, X-rays had already shown a broken bone by his wrist. She waited while they splinted his arm. What were neighbors for? Besides, Mark was probably still sleeping. She'd be home before he knew she'd been gone.

Dillan sighed.

Miska glanced at him. "So what story are you going to tell Garrett? That you were making breakfast or shaving with a chainsaw?"

"I might go with the chainsaw." He shifted and gritted his teeth. "You look like you're going out."

She glanced at her dark skinny jeans and gauzy, scoop-necked shirt with cutaway shoulders. "I've got plans later on."

"Hope I didn't ruin them."

"You didn't."

"Good." His fingers resumed their tapping. "Have you heard from Garrett?"

Dillan had asked her to let Garrett know he'd miss a couch delivery. "No."

He shrugged, hissed in a breath, and resumed staring out the window.

She parked in their building's garage. Silently they rode the elevator to the building's main level where she called an elevator for their floor.

He adjusted the sling around his black splint, wincing again.

"How will this affect your work?"

"It'll make typing difficult."

"You type a lot?"

An elevator opened, and he motioned her ahead of him. "When I'm working on stuff for church."

"Stuff?"

"Youth group lessons, Sunday School lessons. Stuff."

She held up a finger. "Ah, stuff."

He rested against the wall and watched her.

She held his gaze.

"Thanks again, Miska. You didn't need to wait at the hospital, but I appreciate it."

"No problem."

"Somehow I'll—"

"Make it up to me. I know—you keep saying that. We weren't there that long, and it made no sense to leave when they were close to releasing you."

"So how do I make it up?"

"Dillan."

"Humor me."

"Fine. Next time I hurt myself, you take me to the ER. Deal?"

"Deal." He stuck out his left hand, and she shook it. His fingers were long and slender, his palm smooth, his hand so different from Mark's.

He let her go as the elevator opened to the seventh floor. A fifty-something man, straight from the gym, entered and sent Dillan and his blood-stained shirt a double take.

Dillan nodded at him. "Know how to get blood out of a shirt?"

The man frowned. "Pretty sure you wash it in cold water. Better Google it, though."

"I will. Thanks."

The man nodded.

Dillan smiled at her over the guy's head. Miska bit her lip into submission.

The elevator stopped at ten, and the man left.

Dillan shifted. "So what are you up to?"

"Just—stuff."

"What kind of—oh. Hah. Funny. Editing stuff?"

"Friend stuff. I took today off."

"And I messed it up."

"Will you stop? You didn't mess up anything. My plans aren't until later."

"Good. There's nothing worse than messing up someone else's stuff."

"So true." She gestured to his arm. "Much better to mess up your own stuff."

"Except it hurts."

"Poor baby."

He raised his chin. "I'm tough, though. I can handle it."

She laughed. "No painkillers for you."

"Not while people are looking, anyway."

Her smile faded. How was Dillan single? He was that wholesome, surprisingly attractive guy next door who would do anything for his lady. He was someone a girl could grow up with and suddenly view as a man she could—

Could what?

At the least, he seemed to be a man she could trust.

Which was saying something. After the debacle of her fifteenth birthday slumber party, she'd never trusted her brothers again. And her brothers' friends—guys you wouldn't leave any girl alone with, no matter how much you disliked her. Then there was Dad, all of Mom's boyfriends. Men in general—untrustworthy.

So what made Dillan seem trustworthy?

He was single, and not once had he come on to her.

Then again, she'd caught him watching her a time or two. Maybe instead he was the worst kind of pervert, lulling you into false safety with the real man hidden from the light of day.

The elevator opened. Dillan held out a hand. "After you."

He couldn't be a pervert.

In their hallway, he adjusted his sling. "Next stop, bloodbath."

"It can't be that bad."

"You have seen my shirt, right?"

"Tell Garrett your arm hurts. He'll have to clean it."

"Except he'd get Tracy to do it."

Dillan's door opened. Garrett stepped out—tie flung over his shoulder, dress shirt rolled past his elbows, wadded paper towels in his hand.

Dillan glanced at Miska. "I stand corrected."

"Next time you don't want to deal with a delivery, just say so," Garrett said. "I walked in and thought I was on a slasher set."

"That bad?" she asked.

Garrett gestured to the door. "There's a bloody handprint back here. Do you have any blood left?"

"It was touch and go. I saw a bright light, heard someone calling my name—"

"But you had too much left to do, right?"

"The Memorial Day cookout *is* coming up."

"Lucky for you. Hey, Miska, did you see he bled all over your door?"

"He what?" She feigned shock. "I can't imagine how that happened with blood spurting out of his eyebrow."

"Spurting?"

Dillan sighed. "She exaggerates."

"He had a towel over his eye when I opened the door. He lowered it to show me, and the blood went—"

Her door opened. Mark poked his head out. "Miska, I've been—" His gaze traveled from her to Dillan and Garrett.

He was already here? "When did you get in?"

"Hey, it's you!" Garrett pointed at Mark. "Dillan, it's him. It's déjà vu all over again." He whacked Mark's shoulder with the back of his hand. "See how I did that? That's a baseball quote. Yogi Berra. Nice, huh?"

Mark sent him a look as he stepped into the hallway and spoke to Miska. "Ten minutes ago."

"We really need to stop meeting like this. In case you forgot, I'm Garrett. My brother, Dillan. This should make you thankful he only collided with you. Obviously it can be—and is—worse."

Mark eyed Dillan. "What happened to you?"

"Paper cut." Garrett set a hand on Dillan's shoulder. "Bad one. He almost didn't—"

"Will you shut up?" Dillan shook his head, his face an emotionless mask. "Broken arm and stitches. Miska was kind enough to drive me to the ER which is why there's blood on her door."

Mark pointed out the drops. "I saw that. I was starting to wonder if you were okay."

"You were worried?" She laced her fingers through his. "That's so sweet."

Mark raised his eyebrows at the guys.

Fine. Like they didn't know what was going on. "Garrett, I hope your couch makes it in one piece—"

"It's here. Come try it out sometime."

Flirt. He'd said that for Mark. "Dillan, no more running with paper. If you need anything, I'm next door."

His gaze bore into her doorknob. Did he think she was making fun of him?

"He's a big boy." Mark tugged her toward her door. "He can take care of himself."

"And if he can't," Garrett said, "I'm here. You and Mark go have fun."

Mark smirked and pulled her closer.

Yes, Mark was here. Mark was the one who mattered.

Not Dillan. Not the boy next door. Not those dark, trustworthy eyes. She let Mark lead her inside and wrapped her arms around him as the door fell shut.

When Miska walked into the living room after fixing her hair, Mark was bent over her laptop. Her heart jolted. "What are you doing?"

He jerked upright and spun, shielding her desk from view. "Miska."

"Yes, it's me. Surprise." She stalked toward him. "What are you doing to my computer?"

"Just checking the radar. Heard it might storm—"

She reached around him and opened the computer.

A wad of cash lay across the keyboard.

Her shoulders slumped. "I thought you were messing with it."

"Why would I do that?" He held her close. "I just wanted to leave you a gift. It's getting hard to find new hiding places."

She accepted his kiss. "Why do you have to hide them?"

"You want me to hand it to you? As I walk out the door?"

Good point. But some part of her wanted to push him. "Why not?"

"I don't think you want that. Wouldn't it make you feel…"

She ran her tongue over her teeth, crossed her arms. "Feel what?"

He plopped onto the couch and tugged her onto his lap. "I just want to take care of you. I don't want it to come across any other way."

"So take care of me."

He grinned and snuggled her close.

"We've already done all of that. There's more to taking care of me than sex."

"I know. I want to take care of you. I want to give you everything."

Did he? She studied his blue, blue eyes. "What's keeping you?"

"We agreed to wait until August."

"I said that was the longest I'd wait. But if you know you want to take care of me—and you know I want to take care of you—"

He kissed her again, pressing her tightly against him.

Miska shoved him back. "Mark!"

He swore. "What is the matter with you?"

With her? "I'm sorry. What was I thinking, trying to have a conversation? Will you answer my question instead of trying to start things again?"

"We agreed on August, Miska. Don't push me."

"*Push* you?"

"After what I witnessed with those two idiots, you think I'm ready to make that call?"

"Wait, you—what? What are you talking about?"

"You flirting with Beavis and Butthead. Makes me wonder how close you've been with them since I've been gone."

Miska slapped him.

He dumped her onto the couch and shot to his feet.

She jumped up, her hand stinging. "Get out."

"With pleasure," he spat.

He glared at the island and stalked there, grabbed his keys and phone, and shoved them into his pockets. He stormed back to the laptop and grabbed the pile of cash. Shook it in her face. "Here."

She crossed her arms.

He swore again and threw the money at her feet.

He marched away, his words stinging worse than her hand. Her gaze landed on his wallet beside her laptop. She looked up—he was at her door, his hand on the knob. "You left your wallet."

Mark stilled. Tilted his head back. Frustration screamed through his clenched fists.

She waited. He wouldn't leave without his wallet.

Slowly he turned and made his way back.

She picked up the wallet before he could. "All I did, Mark, was be a good neighbor. I'd think you'd want a woman like that, a woman who cares about others."

He yanked the wallet from her hand. "All I want is a woman who's faithful to me. Forget everyone else."

He left, slamming the door.

Miska stayed where she was, hoping he'd come back to apologize, but after a minute passed, she figured he was really gone.

She collected the money scattered across her floor. Each bill was a fifty, and she counted them, finally ending at two thousand dollars. He'd never left this much. Not for one day.

And she'd ruined it.

Her mind ran through all the ways the money could sustain her. Health insurance. A mortgage payment. Utilities. Advertising if work ran low. Gas. Taxes. Yeah, taxes.

She rested her head against a couch cushion. *Don't ever call them,* she could hear her mom saying. *If they walk out, let them. If you beg them to come back and they do, you'll never feel secure.*

Sitting on her bed back then, thinking her seventeen-year-old life had ended, she had listened and nodded. Mom knew everything.

Today she wondered.

One marriage that lasted four years. Then one man after another. She could still see their faces, even though none of them stayed.

Even when they'd been the ones to come back.

No one stayed.

No one.

Her shaking became hard jerks that jolted her, and tears dripped from her chin before she realized she was sobbing.

It had been so long since she'd cried over a man. Gotten angry, gotten drunk, gotten even—yes. But tears…

Because Mark wasn't coming back.

CHAPTER SEVEN

"I can't believe Scheider showed up again." Garrett chuckled from the kitchen where he scrubbed newly found dried blood off a lower cabinet. "I love messing with that guy."

On the new couch, Dillan adjusted the pillows beneath his arm. He didn't want to think about Scheider. Or Miska. He focused on the TV. "Celtics are down by five."

Garrett grunted and kept scrubbing. "Dude, I seriously wonder how close you were to bleeding out."

Tracy smiled from the oversized chair where she worked on the wedding's guest list. "People don't bleed out from cuts above the eye."

"I don't know, my little Florence Nightingale. Miska said it was spurting. Must be why he had her take him to the hospital instead of calling 911."

Tracy sent Dillan a puzzled look. "Why didn't you call 911?"

"Because I couldn't find my phone. Couldn't think straight. Started feeling... fuzzy."

"Like you were going to pass out?"

He narrowed his eyes. "Don't repeat that."

She smiled and returned to her list.

Garrett turned on the faucet. "So what do you think about Miska and Mark? Think we'll all be friends someday?"

Dillan held back a snort. "No."

"Me neither. I don't think Miska likes me."

"Miska?" Dillan turned. "You mean—"

Garrett grinned at him. "What gets me is that you still felt faint after you saw what she was wearing."

"I did not feel faint."

Tracy set down the pad. "What was she wearing?"

Garrett had to bring that up. But the truth was that Dillan hadn't even noticed until they left the ER. Then the sheer shirt over the low, white camisole, the shoulders of the shirt cut away with the billowy fabric covering her forearms, the skin-tight jeans that hugged... everything—Dillan fiddled with the Velcro on his sling.

"Sheesh, guys. Bring it up then don't tell me, why don't you?"

He focused on the basketball game as if he hadn't heard.

"She was—" Garrett bumped a cabinet. "Just a... I don't know. She looked like she bought her wardrobe from Victoria's Secret. I shouldn't have mentioned it."

No kidding.

"How was the baseball player?" Tracy asked.

"Fine." Garrett plopped onto the other end of the couch and stretched his legs. "A little friendlier than last time."

"Which isn't saying much." Dillan snickered. "That dumb Yogi Berra quote. I have to say, Tracy, it was fun watching Garrett press Scheider's buttons."

Tracy laughed while Garrett ducked his head in false modesty. "What can I say? I'm quick on my feet."

"I'd like to be quick on my feet and avoid her," Dillan said. "I've run into her too much."

"Dude. You'd be dead without her."

Tracy laughed again. "It can't be that bad, Dillan. What, is she trying to seduce you all the time?"

He shook his head. "Like you wouldn't believe."

"Yes, well, she's lost. What do you expect?"

"I expect to run along the lakefront and enjoy some peace and quiet. You should have heard the way she jumped all over me when it came out that you two weren't living together."

"That came up?" Tracy pursed her lips. "Interesting. What'd she say?"

"She confessed that Mark was married and said I shouldn't judge her."

"Dude." Garrett made a face. "What'd you say that brought that on?"

"I said, 'Oh,' or something like that."

Tracy picked up her bag and searched through it. "She feels guilty."

"She should."

She pulled out a DVD case and stared at it. "I can't stop thinking about her, wondering if maybe God put us here for her."

Nope. Not him. What if warm weather came, and she dressed for that? "I don't see it."

"See what? You don't think she could be saved?"

"God can save anyone he wants to. I just don't see her being interested in God."

"So you think she's too much for God."

"No—"

"That's what you're saying."

Dillan glanced at Garrett who held up his hands. "I'm not here."

Tracy made a face. "I'm serious, Dillan. I don't think avoiding her is the way to go. Be smart, yes, but don't avoid her. She needs what we have."

So he'd smartly avoid her? That would work.

"Garrett." Tracy tapped the DVD case. "You've been around her type. How does someone like her think?"

Dillan stilled, waiting for a reaction. Been around her type... yeah, that was one way of putting it.

But Garrett only shrugged. "Sometimes they don't have much of a personal life. They've got men and maybe some close friends, but those friends are like them—always on the prowl. She'd have some downtime to think, but my guess is that she'd try to avoid it." Garrett glanced at Dillan. "I did."

Who was this Garrett look-a-like? Dillan couldn't remember a more honest, open moment from his brother since... well, since they were twelve and eleven and huddled in the basement while tornado sirens went off and trees doubled over.

Maybe Garrett *had* changed.

And maybe Tracy had something to do with it. She was obviously good for him, accepting him despite his past. Brotherly love for her surged through Dillan.

"I wonder how many girlfriends she has." Tracy focused on Garrett. "If it's all about men, all about the next fling, maybe she's kind of lonely when she has those down times. Maybe..." She tapped the DVD again. "Is there some *Rambo* or *Predator* movie on?"

Garrett's mouth fell open, and he spread his arms. "I knew it! I converted her! Come here, baby."

Dillan laughed.

Tracy rolled her eyes. "Please. No. I've got a girls' movie. Someone at work gave it to me. I can use you guys as an excuse to see if she wants to hang out. You know, you're watching *Rambo* and basketball, and I'm about to pull my hair out."

Garrett worked the remote. "*Rocky* started fifteen minutes ago."

"That's perfect. I hate that movie."

Garrett sent Dillan a confused look.

"She hates it, Gare. So it's perfect."

Tracy slung the bag's strap onto her shoulder. "Exactly. You guys enjoy your guy night. I'm going to try to go next door."

Interesting plan Tracy had. Hopefully she came out unscathed. "Knock an SOS on the wall if you get into trouble."

She flicked his earlobe as she passed.

Dillan grabbed it. "Ow."

"I thought we'd use the whippoorwill call."

He exaggerated rubbing his ear. "Is she that loud?"

Garrett raised an eyebrow. "Scary thought. Go get 'er, tiger."

"I will. Pray for me, guys."

Right. *God, keep Tracy safe. Make Miska be nice to the poor girl.*

The door shut behind them. Garrett leaned forward, eyes on the game. "You want to watch *Rocky*?"

"Not especially. What else is on?"

Garrett flipped through the listings. "*Pride and Prejudice. Les Mis*—"

"*Rocky* sounds awesome."

CHAPTER EIGHT

Miska peeked at Tracy sitting in the dark beside her, gaze glued to the TV screen where *Downton Abbey*'s Matthew Crawley surveyed his future estate. Tracy's arrival with a plea of escape from what the guys were watching had been a surprise. But she'd had no reason to say no. Adrienne had never shown up to drink their sorrows away, and the last thing Miska wanted was to sit alone and relive her argument with Mark.

If she and Adrienne weren't going to get drunk together, watching *Downton Abbey* was a good second choice.

And Tracy was all right, after all.

Someone pounded at her door.

Tracy jumped. "Wow, that scared me."

Miska paused the show. "I'll see who that is. You want popcorn?"

"Sounds great."

She padded down the hall in her bare feet. "There's a box in the cabinet above the microwave."

Miska released the deadbolt and opened the door.

Adrienne teetered in the hallway. "Misky." She grabbed the doorframe. "What's up?"

"Not you for much longer. What'd you drink?" Miska pulled the door wide open to give Adrienne room to maneuver.

"Just shots, I think." Adrienne trailed one hand along the hallway. "Why's your place so dark?"

"We're watching TV."

"We?" She lowered her voice. "Is Mark still here?"

Tracy popped her head into view. "Hi, Adrienne. Good to see you again."

Adrienne stared at Tracy. "You're—aren't you Garrett's little fiancée?"

Miska tensed. A wasted Adrienne was unpredictable. "Tracy brought *Downton Abbey* over. Have a seat. We're making popcorn."

A kernel popped as if to verify her words. Adrienne seated herself at the island. "So how was your love fest with Mark?"

Tracy peered into the microwave.

"Fine." If she pretended he left five minutes earlier than he had. "What happened to tonight? I thought you were coming over."

"Oh, that." Adrienne waved a hand. It fell and smacked the granite. "Got stuck dealing with an author issue, then got talking with someone new in the office, and we went out for drinks. Didn't mean to blow you off. You ended up with company anyway." She flashed Tracy a useless fake smile.

Tracy asked Adrienne about her work. Miska took over popcorn duty as they talked.

"So what are Garrett and his brother up to?" Adrienne asked.

"They're watching *Rocky*, I think."

"Ah, *Rocky*." Adrienne laid her hand over her heart. "My fave."

Smiling, Miska pulled the popcorn from the microwave. "Yo, Adrienne, want popcorn?"

"No, I'm gonna head out. Need to sleep off those shots. You girls enjoy your show."

Miska handed Tracy the popcorn and followed her sister down the hallway. "You need a cab?"

"I'll get one. See you."

Miska watched her walk away. What was going on in Adrienne's life that she hadn't waited to drink with her? She closed the door and returned to the kitchen. One girl had to be as good as another. "You want something to drink?"

"I'll take pop if you've got it."

She'd been thinking Bailey's. Or Bacardi. "A&W okay?"

"Perfect."

"Glass or can?"

"Can's fine."

The woman was too easy to please. Miska grabbed cans from the fridge. She handed Tracy one and curled up on her end of the couch. A dry night. Oh, well. She popped the top and drained a good third of the can.

"You and Adrienne seem close."

Cold seeped into her fingers. "We are. She looked out for me in high school. Then I did an internship at her publisher, and we've been good friends since."

"You don't seem much alike, though."

"Our families were different. Her mom's spent most of her life high on something. So Adrienne went without a lot. A hard life, you know?"

Tracy nodded.

"My mom, on the other hand, worked hard, made a lot, gave us everything she could. She was an amazing woman. She was our glue." She swirled the root beer. Vodka was calling her now.

"You said *was*. She's passed?"

"Four years ago. She was twenty-six when I was born, and I was twenty-six when she died. I've always wondered if she had any idea when I was born that she'd just hit middle age."

"Probably not."

"Makes me wonder, you know? Like maybe middle age was back in high school and the end's just around the corner. Or maybe I'm twenty years away from middle age."

"Those are some heavy thoughts."

Thoughts she no longer wanted to think about. "What about your family?"

Tracy studied the popcorn bowl. "My family's closer to yours, except my parents are together. My older brothers are the best. They've always spoiled me. You know how brothers are."

All too well.

"We're even closer now." Tracy gave a nervous laugh. "My family became Christians while I was in college. I was the first. I had this friend in high school who invited me to youth group—"

Dillan flashed in her mind. "Youth group—what is that? Dillan's mentioned it."

"Oh." A startled look crossed Tracy's face. "It's a weekly church meeting for teenagers. We'd play games, eat junk food, study the Bible. It was life changing."

"So that's what he does every week? Plays games, eats junk food, studies the Bible? That broken arm will ruin any games."

Tracy laughed. "I doubt it'll make a difference. Dillan's not much of an athlete."

"Really? But he's a runner—" Who wiped out while running. "I see your point."

"You should see him with the kids, though. He's so good. I hope he's still youth pastor when our kids are old enough." She sighed as if the idea made her infinitely happy. "Anyway, I started going to youth group with my friend and learned how God loved me and made a way to pay for my sins so I could go to heaven."

Ah, there was the God stuff. It obviously worked for Tracy, which was great. "Can I ask a question?"

"Ask away. I'm an open book."

"Dillan let it slip that you're not living with Garrett until you're married."

"It's no secret. Sure, we're waiting until our wedding night for sex."

Their wedding night? "Why?"

"Because God says to wait until we're married. His plan is for one woman and one man to be married until death separates them. Doing it any other way brings pain. That's all it is. I want to have a great marriage with Garrett, and part of that means doing it God's way. Waiting."

"But you guys are engaged. You're getting married—when?"

"Late September when it's nice and cool."

"And you're still waiting? To have sex?" The words squeaked out, but Miska didn't care. Garrett and Tracy were already committed to each other. They loved each other. Why wait? "How do you know if you're even compatible? I mean, what if you get married and find out—" She grimaced and shook her head.

Tracy laughed. "I'm not worried. I adore Garrett. He's funny, he's handsome, he takes care of me. It's hard to wait, as it is. I'm not worried about—" She waved a hand in the air. "Yeah. Not happening."

"So Garrett's waited too? You've both waited all this time?"

Tracy's smile vanished.

Oh no. "I'm sorry. I shouldn't have asked."

"No, it's okay. Garrett and I—we both have our pasts. Mine's just a lot longer ago than his. He hasn't waited. *I* haven't waited. I can't tell you how much I wish I had."

"Would you really want to come to him as a clueless virgin when he wasn't?"

Her nod was solemn. "I would love that."

It didn't make sense, and yet it did. The concepts struggled in her mind, one part of her justifying her needs, the other reminding her of guys who'd manipulated her.

Jared, the first. The junior who'd pressured her to prove she loved him—when she was fourteen. Then Gordon. Thad. Guys who'd gotten her drunk enough to not think straight.

She'd been careful after that, waiting until she knew she loved them. But she ran through five more names, men—boys—who'd said they loved her, then got bored.

"How do you know it'll last? It always seems like it will, but you were just on the mountaintop, you know? Mountaintops fall into valleys."

"That's where doing it God's way comes in. Feelings never last. Life takes over. Marriage has to be based on commitment, on decision, on vows to neglect all others and remain true to that one person. No matter what happens."

"What about when that person isn't faithful to you? What happens when you find out things you didn't know about them?"

"Divorce can't be an option."

Oh, really? "If divorce weren't an option, I wouldn't be here. People should be allowed to do what makes them happy. If a marriage isn't working, it's wrong to make someone stay in it. Mark's wife hasn't been faithful to him. Why should he pay for that?"

Tracy said nothing.

"I think it's cool that God works for you, but I see too many holes. There's too much—too much—" What was the word? Her breath came faster. Everything Tracy said felt so wrong. "There's too much bondage. Why should people remain faithful to someone who's not faithful to them?"

"But wouldn't it make a great story? Imagine being the unfaithful person and finding that the person you hurt, the person you rejected, still loved you. Still remained true to you."

"They're an idiot. That's an awful story."

"But imagine being loved like that, Miska. Isn't that the kind of love we long for in a man? A love that remains, no matter what?"

Chapter Nine

A love that remains.

The phrase flitted through Miska's head all night, woke her gently with the sun. It was different. Unique. Something of substance.

What if the one man a woman longed for *was* in her past? And what if all that time he'd waited as she went from one man to another?

Wow, that could make an amazing story.

Love That Remains. She wrote it on a piece of paper, added some notes, and slipped it into her idea file.

The phrase bounced along in her head as she ran through Grant Park and down the lakefront running path. Boats bobbed on the harbor's choppy waters. The wind whipped through hair she'd forgotten to put up, flinging curly wisps into her face, but she smiled anyway at each person she passed. Today was a beautiful day, a wonderfully cold, gray, overcast day.

Her book idea had come.

Beside Buckingham Fountain, her phone chimed.

A text.

She read it as she jogged. *Sorry about yesterday. Forgive me?*

It was a beautiful, gorgeous, perfect day.

What a rotten, rotten, rotten day.

Dillan tossed the can opener onto the counter and glared at the can of tuna that rolled to a stop in the hallway. Twice it had slipped from between his upper arm and his chest and made him chase it. He should be glad he hadn't gotten it open or his splint would smell like tuna.

He flopped onto the couch. His wrist ached, and his stomach growled. He had to eat something so he could take pain meds, but there was nothing in the place that didn't require two hands to make.

The only two hands available were next door. Miska.

His stomach growled again, his insides prodding him. All right, already. He'd ask her.

He took the can and opener next door and knocked.

When she opened the door, her natural beauty hit him. Her glossy, black hair—straight today—draped over her shoulders. Her makeup was minimal, much lighter than yesterday, and she wore looser jeans and a flowy, silky white shirt. She smiled, her teeth brilliant against her skin and lips. "Hi, Dillan. What's up?"

"Hey, Miska." Had a woman ever appealed like she did? Yesterday was nothing compared to her innocent look today. She even smelled good— He sniffed. No, that was whatever she was cooking. Smelled… Mexicany.

"Oh, you brought me tuna. You shouldn't have. Really."

He held out the can and opener, forcing a chuckle over his stomach's gurgle. "This is for me. But I can get you a can."

"I hate tuna. It stinks."

"Tastes good."

"How can that be? Taste is linked to our nose. If it smells bad, it shouldn't taste good."

Did she hear his stomach? "Something to think about."

She waved him in. "I bet you love the smell of coffee and hate the taste."

"Guilty."

"You've got major taste bud issues." At the stove she picked up a wooden spatula and stirred something in a pan. "I'd get that checked out."

"Costs money. I'll live with my stinky tuna."

"Hope you enjoy living alone then." She softened the words with a smile. "What do you need?"

"I'm embarrassed to admit it, but I need to hire a new can opener and wondered if you'd be interested in the position."

She looked at the can, an eyebrow raised in painful contemplation. "That's your lunch?"

"Didn't we have this conversation? I like tuna."

She took the can and opener and set them aside. "And I already told you it smells bad. We won't be opening this in my house."

His stomach was about to eat him, he knew it. "Fine. Open it in my place."

"Do you know that the smell of tuna can linger on someone's hands, even after they wash them? I can't take that risk."

She wasn't so pretty anymore. "Will you just open it already so I can leave and we can pretend this never happened?"

"Wow. You're grumpy when you're hungry."

"I'm also grumpy when my arm hurts because my stomach's empty which means I can't take my pain killer."

"So irritable." She turned back to the stove.

He lifted his good hand from the counter, palm up. What was this?

"Here." She picked up the skillet, filled with some reddish, brownish, meatish stuff. "Follow me."

Follow her? He watched her walk around the island to the table behind him where a single plate and glass sat with a few other bowls. One held chopped green onions, another some leafy stuff. Parsley maybe? Another held lime quarters. Next to that sat a small container of Greek yogurt and a plate of taco shells.

Miska set the skillet on a hot pad. She headed back to the kitchen but pointed at the chair in front of the plate. "Sit."

She was feeding him? "Miska—"

"A can of tuna is a pathetic lunch."

"I have an apple. Pretty sure I can wash that myself."

"Don't argue with me."

"And mayonnaise and bread. It was going to be a sandwich."

She returned with another plate and glass. "Do you see how much chicken is in that pan? There's enough to feed both of us for a couple days."

He peered at the skillet. "That's chicken?"

"It's chipotle chicken, one of my favorite meals. Humor me and let me feed you something decent."

He eyed her.

She eyed him back. "I'm not opening that awful tuna. Eat here or starve."

"So you're saying this tastes better than tuna?"

She arched her eyebrows as she set four tacos on his plate. "I did not just hear that."

"Kidding. It's nice of you to feed me, but I feel bad. You don't need to."

"I know, but I enjoy cooking. And sharing what you cook is... nice."

"Well. Thank you." Man, the words were hard to say. She seated herself, and he sat across from her. "What kind of tacos are these?"

"Only the best tacos ever. I cook the chicken in a chipotle sauce, then shred it. You put green onions and cilantro on it with some Greek yogurt and squeeze lime over it. Delish."

Sounded good. And the smell of the chicken wafting up at him... He propped his shells against his lime quarter and followed her lead, dishing chicken into the shells and adding the toppings. He paused and closed his eyes. *God, help me figure out what to do here. Kind of in over my head.*

"Are you praying?"

He opened his eyes and winked at her, a finger over his mouth. "Don't interrupt." Stink. *Help me not flirt with her, either.*

"I didn't mean to interrupt. Go ahead."

He lowered his head again. *God, this isn't good. She's too pretty. I get distracted—*

"Aren't you supposed to pray out loud?"

He kept his head down but sent her an evil glare.

She bit her lip, a smile escaping.

"God, thank you for the food you've given us. Bless Miska for sharing with me. In Jesus's name, amen." He cleared his throat, eyes on his plate. "Why'd you cook so much? Did you know I was coming?" He took a bite of his taco, the paper-thin shell almost melting in his mouth. The flavors of smoky chipotle and cilantro, green onion and sour-cream-like yogurt blended with the lime juice. He groaned before he could catch himself. "Oh, man, is this good."

"Isn't it?"

"Yeah. Wow, Miska. No need to answer my question. I could eat this every day."

"I know. The meat is the most work so I make a lot and freeze it. Then I can have it whenever I want. I'll send some home with you."

He shook his head, his mouth full.

"Are you arguing again?"

He swallowed. "That's taking days of chicken tacos from you. What kind of guy does that?"

"A starving guy who's fortunate to fall into my good graces. Eat. There's plenty."

First taco gone, he squeezed the lime over the second. The tart scent tingled in his nose. He hadn't eaten this good since Thanksgiving, just before Mom and Dad went south for the winter. "This tastes like something I'd get at a nice Mexican restaurant."

Her smile warmed him. "Thanks."

He finished the taco and started on the third. "Where'd you learn to cook?"

"My mom. She loved cooking. We usually tried a new recipe each weekend."

"What was your favorite?"

"We came up with a great beef stew recipe, one that's creamy and not so strong on the beef flavor."

Sounded wonderful.

"There was this massive lasagna we made when my brothers had their team over after a game. Forgot all about that one. Haven't made it in years."

She studied the tabletop, probably trying to remember the recipe. Someone lucky was going to eat that one of these days.

Hopefully not Mark.

Not that it mattered if she made it for Mark. Why did he even care? He drank his water, watching her force an escaping cilantro leaf back into the taco. Her hair slipped over her shoulder as she took a bite.

A beautiful woman who took neighbors to the ER, then cooked for them. Could he really blame Mark? "How'd you meet Mark?"

She jerked her face up from the taco, smearing a little yogurt on the edge of her mouth. She dabbed at it with her napkin. "Mark," she said, a whole lot of wistfulness in her voice.

What did that mean?

"I met him at a club two Aprils ago. I was there with my girlfriends, and he was with a few teammates. We hit it off." She toyed with her taco. "He was really good to me, you know? Sent me flowers, bought me stuff. He treated me like…"

Like?

"I had no idea he was married until he threw that perfect game. One of my girlfriends called me before the game was over, told me to watch it. I was so thrilled for him. Then after his team gets done dogpiling him, they show him kissing this woman."

He shouldn't have asked. Where was his brain?

"Her name's Darcie. She's a local news anchor in Milwaukee. Monday through Friday. I found it ironic that his perfect game was on a Saturday when she wasn't at work. Imagine if it had happened a day earlier." She smiled, some contrary emotion twisting it. "I still might not know."

A guy couldn't keep a secret like that. Not for long. "You wouldn't want to not know."

"True, but I wish I'd known right away. I wish one of the guys had let it slip. I wish he'd been wearing his ring. Something."

"You sound like you want out. He isn't—isn't forcing you, is he?"

She cocked her head and smiled at him. "You're sweet, Dillan. Someday a girl's going to get very lucky with you."

His skin warmed. "Yeah, well, not today." Yikes. That was even worse. Time to shut up.

"Let me turn the question on you. Why aren't *you* with someone?"

God? Got an answer for that? He shrugged. "Just not the right time yet."

She leaned back in her chair.

He took another taco bite.

"So you can ask a personal question which I answer, but I don't get the same from you."

He rearranged the crumbs on his plate as he chewed and swallowed.

"You've got a little yogurt on your mouth."

"Yep. Did that on purpose."

She chuckled.

He wiped his mouth and blew out a sigh.

"So?"

"I'd like to find the right someone. It'd be nice to know whether she's right around the corner or three years out or ten."

"So you're... what? Looking for the right girl? Not looking? It's a big city, you know. Are you coming out of a relationship?"

"Nope."

She nodded. Looked at him. Nodded again. "Wow, it's like pulling teeth with you."

"You were expecting Tracy?"

"Tracy would be deep into the story by now. I like her. She's real."

"Yeah, she is."

"So you agree. Good. At first I didn't think someone could be that open, you know? She shared a lot last night."

"Did she?"

"Yeah. She was so determined to be a friend. Now I'm glad."

He fiddled with his glass. "Cool."

"But you can't sidetrack me. I want your story. Spill it."

There wasn't much to spill. So many of his college and seminary buddies were married and on kid three. Here he was, dateless for the first four months of the year. What was up with that? What was wrong with him?

"I'll make it easy on you. I'll pack up leftovers so you can have this tomorrow. Then you won't have to look at me while you talk."

But he wanted to look at her. He watched her carry the skillet and bowl of green onions to the kitchen. She opened a drawer and pulled out a box of Ziploc bags.

"Miska, don't. I already feel bad enough eating this."

"Shut up and tell me your story."

"Maybe I don't want to."

"Why? What have you got to hide?" She filled a bag with chicken. "I'm getting really curious. If you don't tell me, I'll ask Tracy."

"Don't do that. Don't ask Tracy."

"Ha." Her eyes sparkled. "Now I'm crazy curious. What's your story, Foster?"

"It's rather boring."

"I doubt that. Not with you being so reluctant." She set the spoon aside and faced him, arms crossed. "So. Who was your first girlfriend?"

He pushed his chair away from the table. "I gotta go."

"No!" She ran around the island and held her hands up in front of him. "Come on, Dillan. I was honest with you. Why won't you be honest with me?"

He swallowed as he looked down at her. Her dark brown eyes searched his, her long lashes flicking. What a beautiful woman. In every way. Every single—

He felt himself tip toward her just a little and jerked upright. His leg banged the chair behind him, and he let out an embarrassed laugh.

"What I wonder," she said, "is why a guy like you isn't with Tracy."

"Have you noticed that Tracy talks a lot? Don't get me wrong. I like her. But I couldn't live with her."

"So?"

"You are ridiculously persistent."

She smiled and tilted her head.

"That wasn't a compliment."

"I'm very patient, Dillan."

More like stubborn. "I haven't dated much. Okay? Had a group of friends in high school that hung out together, guys and girls. Dated some in college but nothing serious. Met a girl during seminary—"

"Seminary?"

Yeah, thanks for that reminder, God. "Grad school for pastors. Met a girl then. We dated a year, broke up. Then got my first job as an assistant pastor. The head pastor didn't want me dating single women in the church, so I didn't. Took the job here at the church I grew up in. Haven't dated much since."

"Why?"

He shrugged. "No one's interested me, and I want to be careful about dating someone I go to church with. I don't want to cause problems in case it doesn't work out."

"I don't get it. Rarely does it work out. So just do it."

"Thanks for the tip, Nike. I'll keep that in mind."

She rolled her eyes. "So that's it?"

"Yep." He rubbed his neck. "Like I said, not much to tell."

"No, I mean you hemmed and hawed over that. I don't get it."

Of course, she didn't, Miss Picks-Up-Married-Guys-At-Clubs. At least she hadn't laughed at him. Or over-shared about Mark.

She handed him the paper bag. "Here you go. Lunch for tomorrow. Enjoy."

He took it from her, careful not to brush her fingers. "Thanks. You're a great cook."

"We'll have to do it again."

No. Way. "Sure." He forced a smile. "Well, back to work."

"Me too." She followed him to her front door. "Now you can take your pain killer."

Right, his arm. He'd completely forgotten.

CHAPTER TEN

Miska's windows were black with night when she and Adrienne returned to her condo Friday night. Miska stretched across her couch, head pounding, and willed the pain to leave.

Adrienne's purse clattered to the floor. "Since when do you get headaches from a couple drinks? You're getting soft, Misky."

She squeezed her eyes shut. "I think the guy beside us messed with my drink."

"I told you that place is no good."

"Sorry, but I'm not into your crowd."

Silence settled, and the band of agony relaxed. She'd thought a night out would be just what she needed. Evidently not. "Aid, you don't need to stay."

"I'll wait awhile."

Miska focused on relaxing, peaceful things. Like lunch with Dillan, his long body across from her, brown eyes studying hers, cheeks darkening with embarrassment. He was so sweet, so kind—

But he wasn't into her.

So much for relaxing thoughts. "What are you doing this weekend?" she asked.

"Tomorrow I'll be recovering from tonight, and Sunday Alec and I are going to Mom's for lunch so we can lie about what a wonderful mother she was."

Mother's Day. She'd forgotten.

"Well." Adrienne stood. "I'm gonna go."

Miska struggled to sit up.

"I'll see myself out. Get some rest, Sleeping Beauty." Adrienne closed the door behind her, and silence returned.

Peaceful thoughts, peaceful thoughts. What was Dillan doing?

After lunch, she'd found the lasagna recipe. Maybe she'd make it Monday and invite him over. Mentally she sorted through her clothes. She'd need something really sexy without being obviously sexy.

She closed her eyes and drifted off. When a knock sounded, she eased up, her head okay with the movement. What time was it?

The microwave said 9:58. Almost time for Buckingham Fountain's light show.

The knock came again. She eased off the couch, then plodded down the hallway to the door, and looked through the peephole.

Tracy?

Miska opened the door. "Come in. Quick."

Tracy's mouth was already open, as if she'd been about to speak. "What's going on?"

"Buckingham Fountain." Miska hurried to the window, Tracy beside her. "Watch."

The fountain's layers were faintly lit. Spotlights gilded the motionless seahorses.

"Just wait," she whispered.

The center jet shot up, and the entire fountain flashed to colored life. The layered basins turned red, then orange, pink, and purple. Fountains on the edges shot toward the center jet, as if supporting the main spout.

One color faded into another, fountains rising and falling until the light and water calmed. Again, spotlights highlighted the four seahorses.

Miska leaned against the wall. "That never gets old."

"Garrett proposed to me out there, in the dark with the lights and music going. You might have been watching."

"I might have. What are you doing in so early on a Friday? You work tomorrow?"

"Nope. How about you? Big plans for the weekend?"

What had she decided? Cooking? Planning an outfit for Monday? "I'm about as exciting as that fountain will be for the rest of the night."

"What are you doing Sunday?"

"Nothing. Sundays are the worst, you know? The end of the weekend drags, but you can't race through it because then it's work for five days straight."

"You could come to church with us."

How fortunate that it was dark. She pressed her lips together to keep any derogatory sound from escaping.

Except it would give her something to do on Mother's Day, something very un-mommish. Plus Dillan would be there. In his environment. That might be interesting. "What time?"

"What time?" Tracy sounded startled. "Church starts at 10:30. It's forty minutes away. You want me to pick you up? Maybe 9:40?"

"Sure. Why not?"

"Well, okay."

For once Tracy had nothing more to say.

And now Miska had two outfits to plan, something churchy for Sunday and something sexy for Monday. The second one she had no problem with. But the first one—she was going to have to Google church attire.

Dillan cleaned up well.

Beside Tracy and Garrett in the last row, Miska had a plain view of the back of his head, despite him sitting on the opposite side of the auditorium, a few rows from the front.

While a silver-haired man welcomed everyone, a brunette behind Dillan sat forward and whispered to him. He leaned back, his chin craned toward his shoulder as he listened. The guy beside him turned too. A smile cracked Dillan's features, and he twisted to say something, grinning as he spoke.

His gaze landed on Miska.

Her breath caught.

A very long second passed before he lifted his chin in greeting.

She nodded back and looked away. What did he think of her being here?

The man on the stage called Dillan who stood, smoothed his tie as he walked up to an extra-wide table beneath the podium, and bent down for something.

The other man spoke. "As our custom is, we want to honor all our moms today."

Tracy coughed like a fly had kamikazed down her throat.

"In a bit, the ushers will have a rose and chocolate for each mom, but—" he raised a finger and gave an impish grin "—a select few will get yours first."

Tracy coughed again. And again.

Garrett sent her a concerned look.

"Dillan and I got together Friday and added some categories. What'd we call them, Dillan?"

He set small gold boxes on the table. "Unique categories, I think?"

Still hacking, Tracy slipped past Garrett and disappeared into the foyer while the man chuckled. "We'll go with unique. Let's get started. Tallest mom."

The crowd laughed. Even Garrett snickered.

"Guess who came up with that one. Shari? Where's Shari?"

A dark-haired woman stood and made her way to the front, shaking her head.

Miska glanced at Garrett. "My mom," he whispered as the audience clapped. "Six one."

Dillan's mom. She took the rose and box and returned his hug. He kissed her cheek. She shook her head at him again, but a smile covered her face, so similar to the one Dillan wore.

"Now we go the other direction. Shortest mom."

Shari Foster walked back to her seat. The man she sat next to had mostly dark hair and was a handful of inches taller, just sitting. He wrapped an arm around her shoulders, and Miska caught her profile as she said something.

"Who's the oldest mom?"

Dillan and the man on stage—probably another pastor—scanned the audience. In front of Miska four hands went up, pointing to someone beside them.

"Emma Holbrook, it's great to see you. Ron told me that Emma turns ninety-one today."

Everyone applauded again, and Miska joined in. A man in the same row as Emma walked to the front to get the rose and candy. Dillan gave him a handful of roses.

Her heart melted a little.

On it went. The youngest mom. The mom with the most kids. The mom who'd been mothering the longest. Emma Holbrook again. The mom with the most boys. The mom with the most girls.

Miska's nose tingled more with each round of applause.

There was an award for the mom who'd come the shortest distance—two doors down—and an award for the mom who'd come the farthest—from Alaska for a granddaughter's birthday.

The tingle spread to her eyes. She blinked rapidly and pinched her nose. If only her mom could come back from wherever she was. Would she have won that award?

"I'm going to take the blame for this one," the pastor said, "just in case. The loudest mom. Heidi Rivers, come on up."

A woman a few years older than Miska slowly stood.

"Anyone who's been at Heidi's boys' games knows how much she cheers them on. We wonder how the kids ever hear the coach."

Heidi looked overcome, and as she walked up to strong applause, three boys in the pew she'd left stood and clapped. Three boys ranging from fourteen to maybe ten.

Dillan said something as he gave her the rose and chocolate. Heidi nodded and wiped an eye.

The pastor also said something to her as the applause wore on, and she managed a teary smile before heading back to her seat, her boys still standing, still clapping.

The story was clear. A single mom—abandoned by some waste of a man—working alone to provide for her kids. How awesome that those boys realized what she was doing.

How she wished she and Wade and Zane had done the same.

How she wished Mom were here so she could make up for it.

The tingle in her nose spread beneath her eyes. Tears dribbled down her cheeks. From the corner of her eye she caught Garrett do a double take.

She had to get out of there.

She grabbed her purse and stepped past the long legs he slanted out of her way. How lucky that they'd sat in the back.

The foyer was empty. She sagged against a wall, and the tears won. Her shoulders shook. Four long years without her mom, and some days it felt like it had just happened. She turned her back to the doors as emotion poured out of her.

Mom.

She was so alone.

She sucked in air between silent sobs. It had been months since she'd missed her mom this badly. Why had she ever come with Tracy?

A large hand settled on her shoulder. Startled, she turned and, through her tears, saw the tall, tall man beside her. *Dillan.* He'd left the auditorium for her?

She buried her face in his chest and let the tears run. His long arms tentatively held her, and she let herself cry.

Wait. *Two* arms?

She struggled for some sort of control, the man's cologne penetrating her runny nose.

His arms released, and she stepped back, embarrassed to have flung herself at—

Garrett stood before her, awkward concern etched across his face. "You okay?"

She shook her head, panic flashing through her. How could she have mistaken Garrett for Dillan? She couldn't look at him. "I'm sorry." She wiped her face, feeling the makeup smear beneath her eyes. "I need to leave."

"Miska?" Tracy's voice sounded from a side entrance. She hurried to Miska and flung her arms around her, fingers tangling in her hair. "Oh my goodness, honey. What's wrong?"

Tears pushed for release.

"I think it was too much," Garrett whispered. His voice quieted further. "The mom stuff."

"Honey, I'm so sorry. I didn't even think about it being Mother's Day." Tracy pulled back and peered into her face. "You want me to take you home?"

Home was where Mom was. But Miska nodded. Anywhere but here.

CHAPTER ELEVEN

The smell of tomato and garlic permeated the restaurant. While the waitress filled Dad's plate a second time, Miska noted all the families celebrating at Lou Malnati's.

"Another piece, Miska?" Dad asked.

"No, thank you."

The waitress left.

"Don't get me wrong, Dad." Saying that still felt strange. "I love Lou's pizza, but if I were a mom, I wouldn't celebrate Mother's Day here."

He chuckled. "Where would you go?"

"Somewhere quiet and dark. Someplace where you'd need a babysitter."

"Which is how you end up with another baby for the sitter. Have a man in mind?"

She shrugged.

"If you're single, it can't have been for long."

"What's that mean?"

"It means you're a Tomlinson. A Petrosian, really."

"A what?"

"Peh-trow-zhee-en. It's the Armenian in you. Petrosian women are never lonely long."

"I'm Armenian?"

He sent her a puzzled look. "What did you think you were?"

"Mom was Dutch, Irish, English, and German. So Dutch, Irish, English, and German."

"Not me. I'm Armenian and Hungarian."

She sank back in her chair. Did she even know where Armenia was? "Wait. Explain how we ended up with an English surname."

"My grandfather was first-generation Hungarian American. His name was Tamas."

"Tuh what?"

"Tuh-mosh. He hated it—it marked him as an immigrant. So he changed it. Tamas became Tomlinson."

"But Tomlinson is a real name. I did a report on it in middle school."

He smiled over his forkful of pizza. "He had a crush on a girl whose last name was Tomlinson. Guess he never got over her."

"And the Petrosian?"

"Armenian. You look just like my mother—and my aunts." He set his fork down and studied her. "How are you doing? I should have remembered earlier that you were the only one without a mother today."

She'd spent all her tears. "Zane and Wade are in the same boat."

"They're men. It's different. And they're caught up in their own... issues."

That was putting it nicely. "Have you talked to them?"

"Some." He sighed. "Zane's cordial. We've met for drinks a time or two. He's the one who gave me your number. But Wade—I don't think he knows how to talk to me. Are they angry with me?"

She shrugged. "They never talked about you."

He studied the room behind her. "They were bad, weren't they?"

"They were." There was no sense softening the truth. "It's the main reason we don't see each other much. Through high school they were always using me to get to some girl, and girls befriended me to have a sleepover at my house. If you know what I mean."

He stared at his plate, mouth twisting.

"Why does that bother you? How is it any different than what you did?"

He looked up, eyes lit with surprise. Didn't he see himself for what he was? What he'd been?

"They're not good men, Miska."

She shrugged. "They're my brothers, your sons."

"It pains me because at some level their behavior is my fault. Mine and your mother's."

"Mom's fault?"

"Miska." He flashed a fatherly smile. "I don't mean to make your mother look bad. She was a single mom doing the best she could."

"You *have* no idea."

He blinked at her.

"How would things be different if you'd done it right?"

"Miska, please."

"Humor me. What if you'd stuck it out with someone?"

"For starters, you and the boys wouldn't exist. It would be Jody, Adrienne, Alec, and me." He chuckled. "And probably a few others."

"So we were a mistake."

"No. Never." He crossed his arms. "Children are the good that come out of bad situations. You, your brothers, your half-sisters and brothers—all gifts."

Some gift if he'd chosen to neglect them. "What would you say if I were in a similar situation?"

"What do you mean?"

"If I were dating a married man. Would you say that was a mistake—"

"Yes."

"You don't think anything good could come from it?"

"No."

"What if his marriage was already dying? What if we really connected and were happy together? Couldn't that be the right thing?"

"Never. If you're seeing a married man, end it."

"I think you're wrong."

"I'm not. I was the married man. None of those relationships had a chance because I didn't respect—"

"Mark respects me. I know he does."

Dad studied her. "Except everything's rushed. Secretive. You have to meet on the sly, and there are certain people and places he wants you to avoid. So *he* doesn't get caught. And it's always sex. Just sex. You talk some, but most of those rushed moments together are just sex."

"No." She lifted her chin. "We talk a lot. Skype, phone, texts. When he comes to town, there's lots of talking too. He makes me happy. I make him—"

"He's no good, Miska. You send a married man packing."

"Or maybe you hang on to love when you find it. Maybe his first marriage was wrong and *we're* the ones meant to be."

He grabbed her fisted hand. "Then you have that conversation. You find out if you're right. And if he's not serious about you, then you kiss him good-bye. Right? Okay?"

Against her will, she nodded. The one thing her parents agreed on—and she'd done the opposite.

Stomachs satisfied, they walked to her building, a strong lake breeze whipping her hair. Cars honked and sped past while pedestrians crossed into and out of Grant Park.

Inside her building, they waited for an elevator.

Dad's fingers trailed across a paneled door. "Did you know," he said, "that this building used to house *Encyclopedia Britannica's* offices? I dreamed about working here."

She flashed him a smile.

An elevator dinged, the doors opened, and a familiar, older couple stepped out, talking over their shoulders to people behind them. Garrett and Tracy followed.

"Miska!" Tracy engulfed her in a hug, her faint floral scent following. "How are you?"

Miska flashed her a smile to let her know the morning was no longer an issue. "Just fine. How are you all?"

Dillan walked out of the elevator, behind him the brunette who'd spoken in his ear that morning.

Up close she looked several years younger. What was she doing here?

"We showed Garrett's parents the condo. Oh, Shari, Dave—" Tracy touched the older woman's arm. "This is Miska, Garrett and Dillan's neighbor. Miska drove Dillan to the ER."

Shari's mouth formed an *oh*, and her eyebrows rose. "Thank you so much. We couldn't believe the pictures Garrett sent. So much blood."

Miska could feel Dillan's embarrassment. "It's not a big deal. I was happy to help."

The brunette spoke. "We're pretty sure he would have bled to death if you hadn't been there."

Garrett elbowed Dillan. "Told you."

Dillan sent Miska an uncomfortable smile.

Shari pointed toward the brunette. "You haven't met our daughter. She just got home from college."

The brunette held her hand out. "I'm Jordan. As in Michael."

Miska smiled as she shook her hand. A sister. "Of course. Who else?"

Dave Foster broke in. "I wanted to name the boys Butkus and Ditka, but Shari said no."

"Thank you, God," Garrett muttered to the ceiling.

"So what are you up to?" Dillan asked, his eyes flicking toward her dad.

Miska introduced her dad who shook hands with everyone. Small talk continued for a few minutes. The Fosters were off to the Art Institute before heading home. Miska wished them a good time before saying good-bye and calling another elevator.

Once inside, the doors shut, Dad spoke. "Seems like you've got good neighbors there."

"So far."

"That tall one—you know him very well?"

"A little. Why?"

He shrugged. "He was watching you."

A tingle zigged across her shoulders. "So?"

"So I think he's interested."

"Not Dillan. He doesn't date much."

"Then I would take him seriously. A guy like that focusing on you—"

"Dad."

"Trust me, Miska. I know men. He's interested."

Could that be? Quiet, serious, Mr. No-Emotion Dillan Foster? She watched the floor buttons light up and tried to ignore the thrill that wafted through her.

Chapter Twelve

Dad's words stayed with Miska. Was Dillan interested? If so, what should she do about it?

Because in eleven days, Mark would be back in Chicago.

Other than his apology text, which she'd replied to, she'd heard nothing from him. Then again, he'd had a big series at home against the Cardinals and was starting a long road trip on the West Coast.

So what, if anything, should she do about Dillan?

She couldn't lie to herself—the man intrigued her. And like Mom said, one never knew...

The memory decided for her. She'd make lasagna and invite him over. See where things went.

On Monday, Miska woke to a downpour and lightning. She dressed, brushed her teeth, and pulled her hair up before heading to the seventh-floor gym.

Garrett was just leaving, his shirt sweat-soaked, hair threatening to drip on her. "Miska," he said, his voice full of sunshiny cheer. "How have we not crossed paths here?"

"Blame the weather. I prefer running outdoors."

"You and Dillan both." He shook his head as he left.

Miska chose a treadmill beside a window and warmed up before setting an incline. As she ran, she watched the wind whip rain through the small space between the buildings, watched lights turn on behind lowered shades—

"Snooping?" Dillan asked beside her.

Her feet faltered, and she grabbed the rails.

Chuckling, he turned on the treadmill beside her. "Didn't mean to scare you."

"You're not brave enough to run in a thunderstorm?"

"If I can't dodge the raindrops, I probably can't dodge the lightning."

She smiled, pleased that he'd chosen the treadmill beside her. "How's the arm?"

He started at a walk, fiddling with the speed. "Better, but I won't be keeping up with you."

"Wimp."

He pointed out the window. "What *is* that?"

She looked.

The incline on her machine grew.

She turned back to see him messing with the controls. "Hey!" She swatted his hand away.

"Wimp."

She laughed as she fixed her incline.

"I saw you leave yesterday. Everything okay?"

The warm feelings faded. "I'm fine. It was—I didn't expect all the Mother's Day stuff."

He nodded.

"Some days are great and I can think about her with no problem, and then other days, like yesterday, can be a nightmare."

He nodded again.

Either he was a terrible conversationalist or a great listener. "Mom was this short, blonde thing. Full of energy, always happy. She decided the morning my dad left that she wasn't going to let single parenthood keep her from living a full life—and it didn't."

"What'd she do for a living?"

"She was a finance whiz. Some friends started a computer business and she got in early, sold at the peak. She was a magician with money. We never wanted for anything—which is so different than Adrienne's life. Obviously we don't talk about our moms."

He nodded, adding a sympathetic smile.

"What about your parents?"

"My dad's retired. He worked for the state and still consults for them. Mom stayed home with us kids. Now they spend half the year in Florida. Jordan spends her winter break there."

"Can't say that I blame her."

"I need my seasons. When we go down for Christmas and I'm packing my shorts and swimsuit, it just feels… off."

"Something's very wrong with you."

He pointed to his new cast. "My arm. Broke it."

She flicked his shoulder, relishing his smug smile.

Miska spent another forty minutes beside Dillan. For the first time, conversation came easily. They talked about high school and college, family pets and vacations, how good the Bears would be in the fall, and whether or not the Bulls and Blackhawks would make it to the next playoff round.

It was a great start to what would certainly be a great day.

In her condo, clean and dressed, Miska returned to her editing. She was deep into the book when her phone rang on the end table.

She glanced at it. Mark.

It rang again, and she debated what to do. He'd apologized and she'd accepted, but other than his short text, there'd been no communication.

Despite everything she'd told Dad, he wasn't safe yet.

She picked up the phone and answered, letting distraction color her voice. "Hello?"

"Hey, it's Mark. How are you?"

"Oh, hi, Mark." She saved the document and set the laptop beside her on the couch. "How are you?"

He cleared his throat, then cleared it again. "Just woke up. Think I'm catching a cold."

Poor baby. "Sorry to hear that."

"Did I call at a bad time? You got a few minutes?"

"I'm in the middle of an edit. What do you need?" There. Polite but not too cold.

"I've been thinking. I didn't like how things ended the other day."

"Me, either. I don't like being accused of something I didn't do."

"I'm sorry. It's just—after what Darcie did, I don't trust too easily."

You mean after what you've done. "I'm not Darcie."

"I know."

Silence fell. Miska let it continue. He'd called. He had things to say. She wasn't going to make it easy.

"I just wanted to tell you in person that I'm really sorry."

His words broke her resolve, and she grinned. "So when are you coming over?"

"What?"

"You said 'in person.' We're not together."

"Oh." He gave a sheepish laugh, and something rustled in the background. "Told you I just woke up."

"You're still in bed?"

"It's only seven thirty here." He talked about how his arm felt, about the massive bruise on his thigh from the comebacker that nailed him last week. He talked about plans he and some teammates had to go deep-sea fishing in Seattle and about the fish they'd caught there last year.

Before long, she couldn't keep the smile off her face or the laughter from her voice. Dad was so wrong about Mark. This wasn't about sex. Even if Mark wanted to, he couldn't see her for almost two weeks. No, this had everything to do with who they were. This was a real relationship.

"I miss you, Miska."

His longing swirled in her chest. But how many times had he said it? Last November. Christmas Eve. Late January. So many other days during the season. "We don't need to be apart, Mark. You've had all these years with Darcie. You know what life's like with her, but you don't know what life's like with me."

He chuckled in her ear. "I think I do."

"Maybe that's just a taste. Do you realize I can take my work wherever I want? Where would you live in the off season if you could choose?"

"Maybe I like Milwaukee."

"You're Texas born and bred. You hate cold."

He sighed deeply, as if he were stretching.

"Where would you spend your winter?"

"Honestly? Somewhere warm and tropical. Hawaii. The Caribbean. With you." His words were a seductive caress. "What do you think? The Bahamas? Jamaica?"

"Or maybe the Maldives. Bora Bora. Fiji. Imagine two or three months there."

He groaned.

"You do your work, I do mine, we go to the beach, come back in for the night—"

"You're making reservations, right?"

"Only if you're not with Darcie after August."

She had him. She'd painted paradise, and it only included her. If he wanted the life he said he did, if he were a real man, he'd jump on it.

No waiting for August.

But silence answered. "Are you there?"

"I'm thinking."

"What is there to think about? You love me; I love you. I give you freedom to spend your precious offseason however you want. I'm freedom, Mark. Me, not Darcie—"

"I told you not to push it, and I meant it."

"Don't you try to string me along. Don't you test me."

"Go get your—"

"Don't come back to me on September first 'cause I won't be there—"

"Go look up *nag* in your dictionary. See whose picture—"

She laughed at the juvenile cutdown. "Are you serious? You went there? That's supposed to put me in my place?"

"You're nagging me, Miska."

"You're on thin ice with me. Thought of that? I live in a big city. Lots of good-looking men everywhere I go. Lots of rich, good-looking men. Single too. I'm not going to play this game much longer, and I'm giving you plenty of warning."

Silence.

She couldn't even hear him breathing. Was he listening? "We've been playing this long-distance romance for too long, and I'm about done. You either make me an honest woman, or you make your bed with Darcie. You go past August, and you won't see me anymore. That's a promise."

The call ended.

Miska screeched at the phone. Of all the idiotic, stupid men out there, and she had to run into this one. Of all the brainless, bonehead jocks in the world— She banged the phone down on the end table. She picked up the laptop and set it down hard on the coffee table. If only Mark were here. She'd bang his head against her desk.

Ooo, he made her mad.

She clenched her hair behind her neck. She was never going to get anything done now. She might as well do some yoga or cook or—

The lasagna!

Suddenly she was glad Mark had called. It put things into such perspective. She and Mark were far from a done deal. It would be wise to keep her options open.

And Dillan was option number one. Dillan, who just might like lasagna.

CHAPTER THIRTEEN

While the lasagna baked, Miska got herself ready—fresh makeup with bold eye shadow, eye liner, and lipstick, and a sleeveless, plum-colored shirt with a decent amount of cleavage. She played with her hair, finally leaving it down, and touched up the polish on her toes and fingers.

By then the lasagna was done—the basil, oregano, tomato sauce, and sausage smelling as wonderful as she remembered. Amazing that Dillan wasn't knocking on her door already.

Dillan and his silly tuna. She smiled at his cuteness. What the guy needed was a woman to feed him. Among other things.

She sprayed herself with perfume, took one last look in the mirror, and left. Outside his door, she took a deep breath.

Faint laughter sounded deep inside the condo.

What if he had company?

There was no going back. Everything was ready. He had to be there. He had to come over.

She knocked on the door and waited. She wasn't in a rush. Really. She'd just cooked a little too much. Was he hungry?

She raised her hand to knock again, but the lock turned on the other side.

The door opened just enough for Garrett to poke his head around it. His hair was messy, as if he'd just gotten up.

"Did I wake you?"

"No. I just—" He waved a hand behind him, eyes fighting to stay above her neck. "I'm home sick today. Not feeling good. Just resting. Watching a little TV."

He was rambling. Good. She'd dressed well.

"Can I help you with something?" he asked.

"I was looking for Dillan. Is he here?"

"It's his day off. He's with Jordan."

A brother who hung out with his little sister. How perfect was he? "That's so sweet. What are they up to?"

"I don't know—exploring the city, I think. Or was it the beaches? Or swimming over to Michigan? Can't remember."

She rewarded his lame joke with a smile.

He grinned, gaze finally staying north of her shoulders. "What'd you need him for?"

"Oh. Nothing." No, there had to be something. "He said something in the gym this morning, and I wanted to ask him about it. I can do it later." She flashed him a smile, hoping it looked nonchalant. Disappointment seeped through her. "I'll let you get back to your nap. Feel better."

"Yeah, thanks." He closed the door.

Miska returned to her condo. She sank onto a bar stool and flopped across the island top, arms spread. First Mark, now Dillan. Her forearms glided over the cool granite. What next?

Back to work.

She could almost hear Mom's voice. How many times had she said that, the Monday morning after a man had moved out? Back to that thing she loved that could never throw her aside. Look how far she'd come, freelancing for two New York publishers and a Chicago one. Look where she lived, how she lived. Yes, man-money helped—a lot—but still...

Day off. What kind of nonsense was that? Who took off Monday?

She ate a large square of lasagna, then wrapped up the steaming leftovers. There was a second, smaller lasagna in the refrigerator. Maybe she'd try again tomorrow.

She finished off the meal with a salad. Now it was back to work.

But as the afternoon wore on, all she could think about was the threat she'd made to Mark and how Dillan hadn't been around to make it legit. Maybe she needed to go out. Make sure those rich, single, good-looking men were out there.

The longing built until she could think of little else. She ate a light dinner and called Adrienne who was still at work. "Aid, I need to get out. You up for hitting a club?"

"I can't." A drawer closed on Adrienne's end. "Something happened, and I'm going to be here late."

"But I'm dying. Your stuff can wait."

Adrienne laughed. "No, it can't. I probably won't leave the office until seven. By the time I get home, it'll be eight. You know how early I get up. Got to save the partying for the weekend."

"But my weekend stunk, remember? I need another one."

"Go solo. I've seen you in action; it won't take long."

Going alone wasn't something she normally did. "If I turn up dead tomorrow, I'm holding you accountable."

"Just don't do anything stupid. Don't go to his place; don't take him to yours."

"You're no help."

"I know. Sorry. Have fun."

Fine. She'd go alone.

Miska searched her closet, finally settling on a sleeveless black sheath dress. If Garrett thought this afternoon's outfit was something, he'd love this one. She pulled it on and smoothed the low-cut square neckline. She pulled on her favorite, sparkly-black stilettos and twisted in front of the mirror. A little more makeup, something fun with her hair—tonight would be good.

An hour later she sipped her drink as she surveyed men in the poorly-lit club. Two blonds over there, one smiling and starting toward her. No blonds. She looked away, hoping he'd catch the snub. A well-built Hispanic man, another blond—

There. A tall, dark-haired man with his profile to her, deep in conversation with the blond and the Hispanic. She studied him. Maybe Garrett's height. Maybe Mark's. Hair a rich chocolate brown, face clean-shaven, his build—what she could see through the blue dress shirt and dark suit pants—lean and athletic.

He must have come from work. What did he do, dressed like that? Something that made money, for sure.

She let her gaze roam over him, though he wouldn't be the one to notice.

The blond nudged his friend, then nodded in her direction.

She pretended not to see that, but when the man faced her and showed the strong lines of his jaw, she held his gaze, letting her interest show.

He said something to his friends, pushed back from his table, and approached her. He came closer, taking her in with his eyes, his mouth working to control itself. He was taller than she'd thought, which made her even happier.

"May I sit here?" he asked as he sat on the stool beside her.

"I was saving it for you."

He caught the bartender's attention and ordered a drink. "I'm Eric. And you are lovely."

She ducked her head as if his words were sweet. "I'm Mariska. Thanks for coming over."

He raised his eyebrows, but she didn't care. They both knew where this was going.

She asked him about his work and where he lived, not paying attention to his answers as she finished one drink and moved to another. When he said something funny, she touched his knee and leaned toward him as she laughed. His eyes lingered where she wanted, and her body warmed when his fingers covered hers.

A few drinks later, he led her to the dance floor and pressed her close while the music played. His hands roamed, and she let him go where he wanted, not caring, not stopping.

But when he whispered, "Mariska," and she looked up, the lights emphasized the green of his eyes. She blinked. He should have deep brown eyes that matched his hair. And he wasn't quite tall enough. Another three inches maybe.

"Mariska," he whispered again, "where can I take you?"

It wasn't him she wanted. He was close, but he wasn't right. And no matter how far she went tonight, no matter how many times she satisfied herself, it wouldn't be enough. The buzz cleared long enough for her to see his desire to get her alone and do whatever he wanted.

She couldn't think past Dillan messing with her incline in the gym and playing dumb when she'd said there was something wrong with him. About Garrett's arms wrapped awkwardly around her while she cried. Had she really expected to find men like them here?

"No." The word came out in a whisper. She pushed Eric back. "No, I can't."

"What?" His laugh flowed with incredulous disgust.

"I need to go." She turned, searching for the exit.

"This way." He grabbed her hand and tugged her after him.

"No—"

His grip tightened.

"No!"

Around them people turned to look, gazes darting from her to him to her again.

He stepped up against her, his whisper fierce. "Don't play with me. You made it clear what you wanted."

The room shifted. She closed her eyes.

Eric wrapped an arm around her and marched her outside where the street seemed to dip. He pulled her closer as he waved for a taxi.

"No," she whispered again.

He tugged her to him and kissed her, his mouth digging into hers.

She pushed against his chest, but his arms locked around her, keeping her flush against him.

Did it really matter who it was? In the end it wouldn't last. She could pretend he was someone else.

Except he didn't smell right. His cologne was closer to Garrett's—

She couldn't kiss Garrett. She would never do that to Tracy. So whose arms was she in? Not Garrett. Not Mark. This man was taller.

Dillan.

She wrapped her arms around his neck and molded her body to his.

He chuckled and loosened his death grip.

"Dillan," she breathed.

He tensed. "Sorry. You're stuck with me."

No, she wanted Dillan or—no, just Dillan. What would it be like to have him hold her? Have him look at her without that emotional shield across his face?

"Cab's here."

She opened her eyes. They were on the sidewalk, people watching them. Heat flooded her cheeks. What was she doing?

Eric opened the cab's door and gestured for her to enter.

"No—"

He grabbed her arm and pushed her partway in.

She spilled across the backseat.

He shoved her deeper inside, then half-sat on her. He yanked the door shut.

"Where to?"

Eric rattled off a Gold Coast address.

"No!" She lunged upright. "I don't want to go with him."

The cab driver twisted in his seat, his tattoo-covered arm draped across the back of the front seat. "You forcing the woman?"

"Of course not. Just take us—"

"Take me to a police station. Please! I changed my mind."

"That's it. Out." The man jerked a finger toward the sidewalk. "Or I do what she says. Police or nothing, bud."

Eric swore.

"A cop just passed us. I can catch him fast."

Eric flung more insults as he shoved the door open, but she didn't care. He was out.

The door slammed.

"You okay? Need the cops? Hospital?"

"No. Thank you."

Eric stood on the sidewalk, hands on hips, glaring.

She swallowed the awful taste rising in her throat. "I need to go home." She gave him her address and sat silently while the cab drove down brightly lit streets. The motion made her queasy, and she closed her eyes, letting

Eric's face blend with Dillan's. Eric might have resembled him, but he'd been nothing like him.

All she wanted was one good man. Just one.

Pete, the evening doorman, held open the glass doors to the elevators.

She tripped through them but managed to stay upright. Why couldn't Dillan have been at that club? Where'd he been today?

An elevator opened. She stepped inside and pressed eighteen. Well, she'd had enough. She needed to see him.

The eighteenth floor lobby was deserted. She trailed a hand down the hallway as she walked home, tipping when the wall dipped inward for a door.

Dillan wouldn't reject her. She nodded emphatically as she knocked on his door. What should she say? Or should she just kiss him?

The door opened, and Garrett looked her up and down, eyebrows raised. "Uh, Miska?"

"You again." She crossed her arms and leaned against the doorjamb, head spinning.

"Yeah, I live here." His forehead crinkled. "You okay?"

"No, I need to see Dillan."

"He's still not in."

She slipped past him.

"Hey—"

He reached for her, but she scurried down the hall.

The living room was empty, the TV playing a Cubs and Mets' game. The kitchen was as spotless as her own. There was nothing anywhere that said Dillan was nearby.

She turned to Garrett, her shoulders slumping. "Where is he?"

"Out."

The closed door to the master bedroom caught her attention. "Is he in there?"

"I told you. He's not home."

She pursed her lips and cocked her head, looking at Garrett from beneath her eyelashes. "Why don't we see what happens in there?"

"Oh-kay." Garrett took her by the shoulders and spun her toward the exit. "I don't think you want him seeing you like this."

"You don't like my dress?" Her stomach kept swirling. "Slow down. I don't feel right."

He propelled her even faster toward the door. "I bet you don't."

"Garrett—"

"I've already cleaned blood. Don't need to be cleaning barf." He reached around her to open his door, grunting when she got in the way. "I'm sure your lovely toilets will keep you company tonight."

She let him push her into the hallway and smiled up at him.

He held out his hand. "Keys?"

"Don't have any. Guess I'll have to spend the night with you."

He took her beaded clutch and opened it. Held up her keys. Jangled them. "Magic."

She leaned against the wall as he tried one key before switching to another. He pushed the door open and spread a hand before her. "Ta-da."

Wasn't he sweet? She took her purse back and grabbed his hand, but he slipped out of her grasp. "Aren't you coming in?" she asked as she stepped inside.

His smile was tight-lipped, his laugh forced. "Night, Miska." He pulled the door shut between them.

She stared at the door. He'd said no?

The bathroom called, and she raced for it, making it with just enough time to lift the seat of her lovely toilet before her stomach heaved.

CHAPTER FOURTEEN

Morning sun invaded Miska's bedroom with blistering shame, taunting her awful headache. She tugged down the blackout shade and fell back in bed, her insides sick, her conscience sicker.

She'd thrown herself at Garrett.

It had been so long since she'd gone after a man, since she'd been single and in need of fun. She curled in a ball beneath the silvery blue comforter. She'd been desperate, foolish.

And now she was paying for it—although paying less than at other times. Eric didn't know where to find her. He was forever gone, and he'd taken nothing of her with him.

But Garrett... She rubbed her fingertips against her forehead. What would Tracy say?

She dozed through the morning, trying to forget that she'd just thrown away a budding friendship with the soon-to-be girl next door—the one who wouldn't sleep with her fiancé until she'd married him, the same man who'd turned her down even when no one had been there to know.

Some girls had all the luck.

By eleven, her headache began to fade. By noon, her stomach felt normal enough to keep food down.

She shuffled to the kitchen and slumped over the counter. The thought of all the men she'd run through in less than twenty-four hours sickened her. Mom would be appalled. Wade and Zane—impressed.

How disturbing that she was like her brothers.

Garrett was clearly a mistake. She was drunk. Wasn't in her right mind because Garrett was someone she'd never go after.

Even though you did.

Eric was just a substitute for Dillan. A sorry substitute. That left Mark and Dillan. Not so bad. And if Mark would make up his mind, she wouldn't be interested in Dillan. Which meant it was all Mark's fault.

"Now I feel better," she whispered.

She poured the last of the milk and popped whole grain bread into the toaster, then searched for her phone. It lay on the floor beside the toilet. She checked her messages. One text from Adrienne asking how last night had gone.

Nothing from Mark.

In the kitchen the toaster dinged. Food and a shower, a little makeup and Advil—that would make her feel better. Then she could put yesterday behind her.

The afternoon sped by as she edited. Her stomach rumbled around five, and she made a salad, scarfing it down while she worked. This book had everything going right for the heroine. The stranger she'd hit on—he'd turned out to be good in every way.

Too bad real life hadn't cooperated.

She took another break to clean up the kitchen, then returned to edits.

A knock sounded at her door.

Miska looked out her window. What time was it? Six thirty? Seven?

At her door, she looked through the peephole. Tracy stood outside.

Miska stepped back, stomach churning. Of course. She swept her hair over her shoulder and drew in a slow breath. Tracy had every right to bawl her out, every right to call her whatever name she wanted. Miska would let her, then apologize and hope nothing worse happened—that in the months to come they could be good neighbors even if they weren't friends. She forced a plastic smile and opened the door.

Tracy looked up from the DVD case in her hand. "Miska! How are you?"

"I'm—fine." She swallowed the tangle in her throat. "I'm fine. You?"

"Good. Ready for the NBA playoffs to be over. 'Course then it'll be baseball." Tracy heaved a sigh. "Men and sports, although I don't think I'd understand a man who didn't like sports. Oh, well. I thought I'd see if you were busy or if you wanted more of the Crawleys."

The picture on the front of the DVD registered. Tracy wanted to watch more *Downton Abbey*? After she'd hit on Garrett?

"You can say no, Miska. I won't be offended."

"Oh! No, I was just… thinking. I'm actually—" Miska gestured behind her. Maybe Garrett hadn't told her yet. Could that be? She laughed in relief. "I was working. My brain's a little fried. Come on in."

"Don't stop on my account."

"I'm not." Really, they were both too polite sometimes. The thought made her laugh again. "I didn't realize how stiff I was until I got up. I've been at my desk awhile."

Tracy followed her into the kitchen. "What are you working on?"

"A romance. Very unrealistic. Girl chases sexy man for a night of fun and discovers he's the man of her dreams. So not real."

Tracy nodded. "No joke."

Miska opened the fridge. "Root beer?"

"Can I bug you for water? My dress was a little snug."

"Sure. No popcorn tonight?"

"If you want some, go ahead. But none for me." Tracy leaned against the counter, one lip pooching out. "Just veggies and fish in my future."

"You look fine to me."

"Please come to my next fitting. The lady got on me like I was living off fudge."

"Tell her it's that time of the month."

"It is, actually. Maybe that's the problem. I better be careful, though, just in case. Tell me what you had for dinner. I'll live vicariously."

Miska remembered Garrett's hands on her shoulders, propelling her down his hallway. "Just a salad with a hard-boiled egg."

"Seriously? Do you eat like that every day?"

Miska handed Tracy her glass. "I missed my run this morning. I haven't missed in… months."

"You run every single day?"

Every day she was home alone.

"What made you miss?"

Tracy really didn't know. Why hadn't Garrett told her? "I was stupid last night and woke up with a hangover."

"Oh, honey."

The word endeared Tracy to her, and after a moment she realized how much Tracy sounded like her mother. *Oh, sweetness.* Mom's voice rang fresh in her ear, clearer than it had been in months.

Tracy's face swam.

"Miska." Tracy clutched her hand. "What's wrong?"

She shook her head. "I'm okay." Tracy *would* find out. Why not tell her herself? Control the damage? "I need to tell you something."

Tracy eased onto a stool. "Okay."

"I—" She clamped her lips together. If only she could do it over. The last thing she wanted was to ruin this delicate friendship. "I went out last night."

Tracy nodded.

Miska jumped on her understanding. What people did when they were drunk, that didn't count, right? "There was this guy. We had a lot to drink, and he tried to get me to go home with him."

Tracy's voice was tender. "Did you?"

"No. The cab driver kicked him out and brought me home. But I was really drunk, Tracy. I wasn't thinking straight, and I just wanted someone to talk to." She swallowed. "I knocked on Garrett's door."

Tracy stiffened.

Miska grabbed her hand. "Nothing happened. I promise. Garrett was more than the perfect gentleman." Far more than she'd deserved. "But I was feeling sorry for myself and so drunk that I kind of... I kind of hit on him." She grimaced at the words. "I just couldn't stand having that between us. And obviously you didn't know."

Tracy's mouth tipped into a sad smile. "No, I didn't."

"It was my fault. I was drunk, I was lonely, and Garrett was just there. But he totally turned me down and unlocked my door for me and left. He never stepped inside. I want you to know that. He's—you've got a real gem on your hands, and I'm completely jealous."

Tracy studied her.

"I couldn't keep that between us. You're my friend, and I'm really sorry."

"I'm your friend, huh?"

"I hope you are. If you want to leave, I get it."

"No, Miska. I forgive you. It's not okay, but I forgive you." She sighed.

Miska held her breath, not feeling safe yet.

"He turned you down? Just like that?"

"He did. He said something about having had enough of barf and blood and me spending the night in my bathroom."

"Did you?"

"Oh, yeah."

Tracy rested her chin on her hand and traced patterns in the granite.

What was she thinking? "Are we okay?"

"I think so." She glanced around the kitchen. "Thanks for telling me."

Miska fiddled with her glass. Tracy might not completely trust her, but at least she hadn't thrown her away. For the moment, she'd be thankful for that.

"Why is it..." Tracy moistened her lips. "Why go looking for a man when you're with Mark? Do you have some sort of understanding?"

"The only understanding I have is that I don't know where we stand. He tells me he's leaving his wife, but then..." She fiddled with a dish towel. "I'm tired of being jerked around. I want him to make up his mind."

"Why would you trust a man who'd have an affair?"

"Because she had the affair first. He's tried to put it behind them, but that's a hard thing to get over."

"So his having an affair doesn't mean anything. It's not like he's getting revenge."

"If it were revenge, don't you think I'd pick up on that? After a year?"

"A year, huh? I hate to say it, Miska, but I wouldn't trust any man willing to have an affair with me, no matter what his wife did."

"No offense, Tracy, but I think it's pretty crazy to wait for your wedding night for sex."

Tracy laughed. "That's fair. You know why we're waiting?"

"Why?"

"Because I want to be able to trust him. I want him to know that I'm faithful to him and I want to know that he's faithful to me. No doubts, no wondering. I want our marriage to last, and if we jumped the gun, I'd never trust him. What kind of a relationship is that?"

There was truth in her words. If she and Mark married, it wouldn't be all roses, but real life wasn't like that anyway. Only the romance genre pretended otherwise. Besides, it wasn't like Tracy or Garrett hadn't been with other people.

"Wait. Neither of you are virgins. So how does that figure into waiting and trusting each other?"

"All of that was before we met. We were different people then."

"Tell me."

"It's not that interesting."

"Then I won't put it in a book."

Tracy laughed. "You write too?"

She could never tell Tracy about her blog. "When I've got a few brain cells left after editing."

"Well, I'm not too worried about ending up in a story." She blew out a sigh and spread her palms across the counter. "Okay. My junior year in high school I dated this guy. Ethan."

"*Ethan*. I dislike him already."

"Good girl. He was a senior, had this surfer-dude look in the middle of the 'burbs. We sat next to each other in two classes because our names were in alphabetical order."

Miska straightened. "I don't know your last name."

"Coleman. And he was Cone. So he was always right behind me. He was gorgeous—"

"If you're into surfer dudes." She pretended to stick a finger down her throat.

"I know. Who likes that?" Tracy grinned and shuddered. "Anyway, at the time my sixteen-year-old brain thought he was gorgeous and funny. We dated a couple months before he tried to take things farther. When I didn't want to, he pressured me. Told me if I loved him—"

"You'd prove it. Because love is action, not talk. I think Ethan had cousins at my school."

"Probably. So I gave in. Didn't want to at first, but I got used to it and began to really like it, and then it was over. He moved on. I was devastated."

"Then what?"

"A friend invited me to her youth group, and everything changed. I read what God said in the Bible and vowed to wait until my wedding. Since then, I have."

"All that time? Going without?"

"Nine long years. But it ends in three months and four days. I can't wait."

"What about Garrett?"

Tracy paled. "Oh, no no no."

"Come on."

"Miska—"

"Please. Tell me."

Tracy eyed her. "Why?"

"Because guys don't wait, Tracy. They don't. If he's only been waiting since he met you, I'm not buying it. And if he is waiting, I want to know why. Because it doesn't make sense."

"Why couldn't it make sense?"

"Because he's living differently than every other man I've met. They don't wait for marriage, Tracy. If you don't put out, they go elsewhere."

"I disagree."

"Prove me wrong. Tell me Garrett's story."

Tracy fiddled with her cup. "Fine. The condensed version."

It would do.

"Garrett picked bad friends in high school, guys that got their hands on magazines and passed them around."

Miska frowned. What guy didn't like those magazines?

"He hid it from his parents, but he was with a couple girls in high school. Once he went to college, he got tired of hiding it and went pretty wild. It caused a lot of problems between him and his parents. Then he went to law school and lived with guys who partied all the time. You know."

She did. "How long ago was this?"

"Maybe a year before I met him. Maybe nine months. He moved back just as I moved here and started my job. He was very quiet when we met, very introspective."

"What happened?"

"I can't get into it. It's not something he wants to talk about, not something his family likes to remember. But he went through something about a year before we met that made him stop and look at his life, made him get right with God. That's part of the reason he came back to Chicago. He wanted to fix things with his family and have some accountability."

"So he'd gotten out of that right before you met." Miska swished the words around in her mouth, then spit them out. "Not that long, really."

"Long enough."

Maybe. "I can't picture him introspective."

"Yeah, he's loosened up. Jordan and Dillan say the quiet Garrett was a little unnerving. But considering what God was doing in his life, it makes sense."

"What does that mean? 'What God was doing in his life'?"

"It means that God was bringing things to his mind, working on him to get rid of sin. It's what God does to all of us Christians every day. He's molding us, making us more like him—if we let him."

Sounded boring. Miska held the words back. She wouldn't hurt Tracy by saying them.

But the light in Tracy's eyes faded.

Rats, it must have shown. Miska ran a hand over the granite, wiping away imaginary crumbs.

Garrett, the partier. She could see it.

But his brother... "And then there's Dillan."

"I know. Talk about brothers being opposite—in every way. Sometimes I wonder who God will send him, you know? Who my sister-in-law will be." Tracy rested her chin in her palm. "Dillan deserves the best."

Which wasn't her. She knew it. Dillan—the man who didn't date much while his brother partied through school—deserved a woman she couldn't even begin to imagine. Someone sweet and honest, someone kind and gentle, someone who probably didn't exist.

Just like the men in the novels she edited. Crazy sexy—and dedicated to one woman.

Poor Tracy. Poor Dillan. Like the rest of the world, they were in for disappointment.

The conversation turned to other things before Miska popped the disc into the DVD player. As Mary Crawley ruined her sister's romance, Tracy's words about Dillan and Garrett returned. *Brothers being opposite—in every way.*

Curled up in her corner of the couch, Miska stilled. Surely Tracy didn't mean that Dillan— She couldn't mean—

There was only one way to find out.

Tomorrow. Lasagna. Lunch.

Chapter Fifteen

This time Miska went for simple. The condo was clean, but she left the stack of paperwork on her desk. Already wearing her favorite jeans, she changed the scooped-neck shirt for a black camisole and form-fitting, lightweight, gray sweatshirt zipped halfway up her chest.

She brushed her teeth, dabbed a little perfume on her wrists, then went for the pièce de résistance. She carried the small lasagna to the hallway and waved its herb and tomato scent by Dillan's door.

He and his tuna had no chance today.

Lasagna safely on her table, she hurried back to Dillan's door and knocked before the scent vanished. He opened the door quickly, like he'd been about to leave.

"Hey. How's the arm today?" she asked.

He looked at the blue cast as if he needed to ask it. "Better. Doesn't hurt much anymore."

"That's great." Yes, he was very different than Garrett who would have said a lot more, teased her, and given her something to go on. "Remember that lasagna recipe I mentioned? I found it and made some for lunch. You hungry?"

His eyebrows went up. "Lasagna?"

"I can't eat it all, and I thought of you and that sad can of tuna. You got a few minutes?"

He nodded as if he didn't need to think twice. "Definitely. I love lasagna. Thanks, Miska."

"No problem."

Inside her condo, the aroma wrapped around them. He inhaled, long and deep. "Man, I was sure I was making this up a minute ago. I could smell it next door."

"Really?" Ah, she loved playing dumb. "Have a seat at the table. I'll grab dressings."

Instead he followed her to the fridge. "Anything I can help with?"

She looked up at him, aware of his warmth. "Umm, drinks maybe." She nodded at a cabinet. "Glasses are up there."

He turned his back to her as he opened the cabinet, muscles in his shoulders bunching beneath the thin fabric of his T-shirt. She searched the fridge for salad dressings before he caught her staring.

"What do you want to drink?"

It felt so good to have him here. Almost like he belonged. "Water's fine. You want A&W?"

"I'll do water."

She set the salad dressings on the table while he filled glasses. By the time he joined her, she'd cut the lasagna into pieces and slid a piece onto his plate.

He eased onto the chair across from her, her usual seat with the view out the windows. "This looks great."

"Thanks." She gave herself the smallest piece. "Do you want to pray again?"

"Sure." He lowered his head and closed his eyes, and she did the same. "Heavenly Father, thank you for the food you've given us and for the income you've provided Miska. Please bless her for sharing with me, and bless this food to our body. In Jesus's name, amen."

She mumbled an amen, feeling very fake. But when in Rome and all that. She slid her napkin onto her lap. "May I ask why you pray before you eat?"

"Keeps the calories from sticking to you." He dished a large helping of salad onto his plate before looking at her and breaking into a grin.

She took the salad bowl from him. "You're hilarious."

"So I hear." He drenched his salad with honey mustard dressing, negating any value the lettuce had. Well, he was in his twenties. Clearly his metabolism was still going.

"Do you think it's wrong not to pray over food? Because I never have. Today's the second time I've ever had my food prayed for."

This time his expression was more serious as if he were a bit shocked. But then he shrugged and took knife and fork to the lasagna. "It's not wrong. My family always prayed at meals. It's just a way of thanking God for what he's done for you."

She dribbled balsamic dressing over her lettuce. "What's he done for you?"

"He's done everything. He's given me hope, a future; he's given me health. He's given me a great family, work that I love. Peace. Security."

His words rolled around in her mind. She could see crediting a higher power with family, because no one could pick that. "I don't understand health. You run. You're the one taking care of your body." She waved a hand at his salad. "Except for that."

He swallowed a bite and grinned at the dressing-drenched lettuce. "Honey mustard is my weakness."

"Do you drink it?"

"Only for breakfast." His smile faded. "Miska, I can do everything I want to take care of myself, but if God doesn't give me health, I won't have any."

"That's not true. You put the work in and you get the results."

"Then someone's in an accident. Or they get some rare disease. Their muscles deteriorate or—" He pointed at her. "Look at Lou Gehrig. A professional athlete. Active. Healthy. Goes from being one of the best athletes to dead in a few years."

"So God killed him."

His brown eyes roamed her face.

"Don't think I'd want to believe in a god like that."

"You have to go back to the beginning, Miska."

"The beginning of what?"

"Of man. Have you read any of the Bible?"

"Some. In college."

"If you go to the beginning, you read how God made the first man and woman."

"Adam and Eve. I've heard that story."

"Only it's not a story. It's truth."

His words hovered between them. Miska waited for the punch line, waited for him to smirk and tell her he was kidding, but the serious look on his face stayed there. Remained. Watched her digest the realization that he was a complete lunatic.

How horribly sad. How wrong that such a wonderful guy would believe such—such stupidity. "Dillan, don't say that."

"Why?"

"Because we know how the world began."

"How?"

"The gasses caused an explosion that brought about the very basic forms of life, and millions of years later, here we are. Everyone knows that."

"Everyone who rejects God, everyone who wants to bury their head in the sand."

"Hey now—"

He crossed his arms. "What evidence is there?"

"Science has proven it."

"No, it hasn't."

"Okay, *you* prove it."

"In so many ways science has proven that evolution couldn't have happened, that the earth is nowhere near millions of years old. Mt. Saint Helens—the volcano in Washington that exploded back in the eighties? All the stuff scientists said took millions of years to occur—the rock layers, the trees in the rock layers—all of that happened in one catastrophic event. They know what the area was like before the eruption, they went back in as soon as they could, and it had completely changed. Completely. All these new rock layers that weren't there before the explosion—they happened over days and weeks, Miska. Days and weeks. And there have been more eruptions and new rock layers since."

Her mouth fell open. Had he ever said so much at one time?

"And then there are scientific calculations like the rotation of the earth, the magnetic field, the size of the sun if the earth had been around that long. Nothing—nothing!—could have survived the speed of the rotation or the heat of the sun or the force of gravity. And when's the last time an explosion created something complex?"

Holy cow. "Dillan—"

"Does a fertilizer plant explode and create the best fertilizer known to man?"

She raised her eyebrows, pretending boredom.

"Of course not. That's absurd. So why do we believe an explosion brought about the most intricate form of anything anywhere?"

"I'm not a scientist, Dillan, but those guys are way smarter than you or me. I trust that what they tell me is the truth."

He pointed at her. "Exactly. You have to trust. You have to have faith in what they say. Because whether you believe God made the world or that the world evolved, both beliefs go back to the same thing."

"Which is?"

"That no one was there in the beginning. No one. Either way, it's a religion that you have to put your faith in."

A religion?

"When you go back to the beginning, the Bible says that God made the world. He made man and woman and put them in charge of the earth. God told them there was one thing they couldn't do. Everything else was theirs to enjoy. But they chose to disobey God, and they brought sin into the world."

Sin? Wow, this guy talked like he'd come out of the fifties.

"And sin brought death and destruction. We see it every day. So that's the answer to your question. Man caused his own death, his own destruction. Not God."

"Let's pretend what you've said is true. Then isn't God to blame for leaving the world as it is? Look at what happens every day in this town—all the murder, abuse, crime. What kind of god lets that continue?"

He nodded. "Man ruins everything in the beginning of the Bible, but what follows is the story of God's love for us, of his decision to come down and give us a way out of our mess."

"Really."

"God makes this incredible promise, that someday he'll send a perfect sacrifice—Jesus—to pay for what we've done. Everyone who believes will be forgiven. They'll have eternal life in heaven when life here is over."

What had she ever seen in him? He was a nut job. "When does the spaceship come?"

His shoulders drew up, straight and stiff. "You've never heard this, have you?"

"Never."

"Then it makes sense that it would sound crazy, but it's the truth. It's what our country was founded on, the beliefs of the Bible. That there are rights and wrongs, absolutes."

"Dillan, it's outdated."

"Really? So we push the Bible aside, say it doesn't apply, and our society gets worse and worse. You said so yourself."

"But that's not..." That's just how life was—hard, difficult. People weren't fair, couldn't be trusted. Everyone had to look out for themselves or be taken advantage of. There *was* no other way.

But to imagine that there could be something better—

"Miska. Tell me."

She jerked her gaze to his. What had he seen?

"I won't judge you."

Was that what he thought? That she was going to confess some great sin? "It's just what you said. Life is hard. Unfair."

She toyed with her lasagna, pulling cheese to the side, pushing sausage and beef in another direction. Tomato sauce clung to everything. "I'll probably regret this later, but you and Tracy and Garrett—" She swallowed the words, then let them out. "Tracy told me last night about her past and Garrett's past."

He frowned at his plate. "Oh."

"She didn't go into detail about Garrett. I guess he did some things your family didn't like."

He set his good hand on his hip, elbow out, and stared at his plate.

"Tracy and Garrett, they're… waiting."

He gave a slow nod.

"But…" How did she ask this without it coming across wrong? "Why are they waiting? If neither one is a virgin?"

"It goes back to the Bible."

"Which says?"

"That sex is to be saved for marriage. For that person you marry."

"Why?"

The planes of his face tightened.

"You don't seem to want to talk about this."

"It's not that. It just seems kind of obvious."

Really?

"If you're faithful to one person for your whole life, there's a lot less pain and risk. If you wait until marriage, there's no fear of being left for another—"

"That's not true. That happens all the time."

"Sure, but in what circumstances? Someone strayed from the relationship. Or they never married so it didn't seem wrong to throw that person away."

"People in marriages divorce all the time."

"They do, but how often would it be if people did things the way the Bible says? If they followed God's plan, if they waited until they were married—"

"Have you waited?"

There. It was out, the question she'd been longing to ask since last night. Miska waited for the answer, hoping to hear yes, hoping to hear no. Hoping…

He looked from her to the plate in front of him, to the lasagna with only a couple bites taken.

He hadn't waited? Really? After everything he'd said? After this whole insane conversation? She stabbed a piece of lettuce. Then another.

"Why do you want to know?" he finally asked.

He sounded beaten. Of course. Because he'd been caught. Fake. Hypocrite. She jammed the fork into her mouth, stabbing her tongue. Liar.

He looked up. "Why, Miska?"

She chewed her food. Glared at him. Swallowed. "Because men don't wait. Ever. All the boys I knew in high school, my brothers, my father, men my mom dated. Men *I've* dated. They don't wait. Garrett didn't—"

"Some do."

"Name one."

He heaved a sigh and looked her in the eye. "I have."

She stilled in her chair.

He held her gaze, his honesty undeniably clear.

He'd waited? For marriage? Which meant— "You're a virgin?"

He gave a simple nod.

"Why?" She couldn't keep quiet. "Dillan, that makes no sense. Why would you do that to yourself?"

"It's the other way around. Why would I want to go against what God says is right? Against the guidelines he's put down to protect me?"

"*Protect* you?"

"Yes, protection. God doesn't tell us to wait to yank us around. It's for our own good."

She could feel her heart breaking. "You're almost twenty-nine. And you've never..."

He nodded again. "I've never."

"How can you wait? How can you deny yourself every day?"

He straightened and looked around the room.

"You're even embarrassed about—"

"No, I'm not."

His harshness froze her.

His eyes were dark, his jaw and mouth tight.

"I'm sorry. I'm not making fun. I just... I don't get it. It's not natural. It's just not."

"So you wouldn't want a man who was a virgin."

"No." She folded her arms across her stomach. A man like that would be so clueless, so inexperienced.

"You'd rather have a man who brought risks, who'd proven he didn't stick around. A man who valued sex more than the woman who gave it to him, who used her and kept her around as long as she made him happy. Forget about what she wants."

She looked up to find him studying her. For several long seconds, their gazes held.

He sighed and ran a hand through his hair. "To me, it's the other way around. Imagine a man coming to you and saying, 'Hey, I've waited for you. All these years I've kept myself for you. Kept myself pure for your sake, for us. And now here it is. I give it to you, Miska. And no one else.' You're telling me you wouldn't want that?"

I give it to you, Miska.

A tear slid down her cheek before she could stop it. The image of a man like Dillan—no, Dillan himself—offering such a gift was heartbreakingly wrenching. Because it would never happen. Not to her.

She covered her face, struggling to keep herself together. She pictured Mark. Kendall. Jared. Gordon. So many others. None of them had come to her like that.

She hadn't gone to a single one like that.

Dillan cleared his throat. His silverware clanked against his plate. His chair scraped.

She drew in a shuddering breath and wiped her face. When she looked up, he stood over her trash can, scraping the remains of his meal into the trash.

She hurried to her feet, frantic to think of a way to get him to stay. "Do you want to take some home? I can pack up—"

"I'm fine."

"You hardly ate."

"Yeah, well…" He set the plate in her sink, then stood there and looked at it. "I should go."

She disgusted him. She knew it. If she were the only woman left, he would never bring his virginity to her.

Well, it would be his loss. She knew how to give a man a good time. Knew well. Anyway, he couldn't be right. He was the only virgin she knew. The only one.

One person couldn't be right.

She followed him to the door. If he were a virgin, it was his own stupid fault. All this pious nonsense about waiting. No, she wasn't buying it. He was deformed somehow. Or he'd been turned down or made fun of in some way. He probably wasn't even a virgin. Maybe he was gay—and ashamed of it. Saying he was waiting for the right woman, all that Bible nonsense—that was his way of hiding it.

What kind of man said no to sex? Not a masculine man, for sure.

Dillan opened her door and looked at her. He stopped, his forehead lined. "What?"

"I didn't say anything."

"You've got this look on your face."

"A guilty look? The look of someone who's seen the error of her ways?"

His eyes narrowed. "No, the look of someone who's ticked."

"I wouldn't know what you're talking about."

"Right. Thanks for lunch and the interesting conversation." He tipped his head in good-bye. "See you."

Not if she could help it.

She slammed the door behind him.

In the kitchen she glared at the table and dishes. What a joke lunch had been.

She snorted. What a joke Dillan had turned out to be.

Her closed laptop called from her desk. She eyed it. Wouldn't this be an interesting blog post, sharing his whacked-out view. It would be different than her usual posts.

She settled onto her chair and woke the computer. Dillan could tell his version of things all he wanted, but so could she.

And far more people listened to her than to him.

CHAPTER SIXTEEN

"Misky, this tastes amazing." Adrienne took another bite of salmon and spoke around her full mouth. "Makes me want to learn to cook."

Seated at the island beside Adrienne, Miska dug into her own fish. "Someday you'll have to or you'll turn into a blimp."

"Until then, I'll mooch off you."

Which hadn't happened in a long time. "Where've you been? You seeing someone?"

A smile twisted Adrienne's mouth.

"I knew it. How long?"

"Just this week."

"No way."

"Really. Other than that, I've had tons of work."

"You should bring your work here. I miss that."

"I know. That seems so long ago."

It *was* long ago, back when Adrienne had been her roommate—until their different lifestyles became too much. Even that had only resulted in Adrienne moving out, not in seeing each other less.

Something stood between them now.

Adrienne looked up, and Miska returned to her plate, filling her fork with asparagus. "What are you thinking?" Adrienne asked.

"I just hate how busy life's gotten."

"What's going on? You're only seeing Mark right now, unless Kendall's coming—"

"He's not," Miska snapped. There was a name she didn't want to think about until she had to.

"Fine. Whatever. But Mark's hardly around. Plus we haven't gone out much—which reminds me. How was Monday night?"

"Fantastic."

"Oh. So you found another—"

"That was sarcasm."

"Then what's got you all busy?"

"I went to Dillan and Garrett's church on Sunday."

"You're kidding."

"Nope."

"Have you ever been to church?"

"First time."

"So you had this thirty-year streak going and you ruined it?"

"Yep."

"How was it?"

"Awful. I left early."

"Good for you. Why on earth did you go?"

She wrapped an arm around herself. "I don't want to talk about it."

Adrienne shrugged and took another bite.

The earthy smell of fish, asparagus, and the olive oil they'd been cooked in wafted around Miska. The pleasure was lost, though. She dropped her fork to her plate and sighed.

"Okay, what's wrong?"

"I just don't feel right. Ever get that way? Where everything feels off?"

"Sure."

"What do you do?"

"Whatever will help. Did something happen?"

"No." Maybe. "I had this weird conversation with Dillan yesterday."

Adrienne glanced at her as she picked up her wine goblet. "Oh, yeah?"

"Get this. He says he's a virgin."

Adrienne coughed on the sip she'd taken. She set her glass down and wiped her chin. "Man, that burns."

"Sorry. Can you believe that?"

Adrienne coughed again.

"He tried to convince me to wait for marriage."

"Like it's not too late for you."

She shrugged the words away, even though they rankled. "There's no way he's telling the truth, is there?"

"There are groups where it's common for people to wait until they get married."

"I can't even wrap my mind around it."

"Yeah, it's weird." Adrienne pushed her asparagus around. "Garrett and Dillan grew up that way?"

"I guess."

"Interesting."

"What do you know about people like that? Should I be worried since they're next door?"

"They're harmless." Her smile grew. "And usually a bit of fun."

"You've got a story. Tell me."

Adrienne shrugged. "I grew up next to a family like that. They had teenage boys."

"You corrupted them, didn't you?"

"No, although I tried. The oldest kept trying to convert me, telling me there were consequences and stuff like that."

"To some extent, that's true."

"Duh, of course. There are consequences to everything we do, some good, some bad. Anyway, those little cultures actually teach their young to wait until they're married. From what I remember, a lot of them follow that. But not all."

"So Dillan's telling the truth?"

"You didn't believe him?"

"Aid, I've never known a man in his twenties who was a virgin. I just—I don't get it."

"He's saving himself." She rolled her eyes. "Like he's all that."

On the edge of the island, Adrienne's phone chirped. She reached for it and read the text, a smile covering her lips.

"Who is it?"

"No one. Gimme a minute."

While Adrienne texted, Miska carried plates to the kitchen and rinsed and stacked them in the dishwasher. When the kitchen was clean, she looked up at Adrienne who wore a wide grin while she read her phone's screen. Miska moved to look over her shoulder. "So who is it?"

Adrienne hid the text. "Gotta run. Got a date all of a sudden." She tucked the phone into her new lime-green purse and checked her reflection in the mirror above the desk.

"You're bailing on me, girl. I deserve to know."

Adrienne shot her a smirk. "Later. Maybe."

"Well, be careful." Miska followed her down the hall. "Don't do anything I wouldn't do."

Laughing, Adrienne opened the door. "I'm meeting a guy. Feel better?"

"No. Some men aren't safe."

Adrienne flashed her a grin. "True, but I'm not safe either. And I love watching them discover that."

Early Friday morning, Dillan crossed into Grant Park, searching for Miska. He'd seen her ahead of him yesterday, his first morning running outside after his broken arm, but he'd run another direction before she could see him. He'd do the same today, if necessary.

She was nowhere in sight.

This mid-May morning was warmer than anything yet this spring. It hinted that summer was days away, and he relished the feel of running in shorts and a T-shirt, even if he was a bit cool. His arm seemed okay lately, and other than doing everything with four fingers and one thumb, he felt almost normal.

He jogged past Buckingham Fountain, crossed Lake Shore Drive, and jogged down the stairs to the running path. He paused at the edge to watch waves dance at his feet. The breeze picked up, sending icy cool all down him. He breathed it in. Today would be a scorcher in the suburbs, but not here on the winter-chilled lake.

"Are you following me?"

He flinched at Miska's voice.

She stood beside him, dressed in black shorts and a soft pink tank top, hands on her hips. The pink drew out matching color in her cheeks and neck. And arms. And legs.

"Of course you're not following me. You tried to avoid me yesterday. But now you're stuck." She tilted up her nose in an exaggerated manner.

"I haven't been avoiding you."

"He lies? Shame, shame, Reverend Dillan."

Behind his smile, he clenched his teeth. "While I'd love to talk, I have to be ready for work in an hour. Thought I'd run along the lake." He pointed at Shedd Aquarium where it protruded into the lake. "Looks like you're done, though, so—"

"I've got time."

Awesome.

She fell into step beside him. He sped up, but she matched him. "I've been thinking about the other day."

Of course she had. Nothing heated things up like revealing his virginity to a woman having an affair.

"I wanted to continue our conversation—"

"I don't."

She sent him a sudden glance. Good. Maybe she'd catch on.

They passed a jogger going the other direction, then another. A couple bikers. More joggers. Waves slapped the harbor wall. Shedd Aquarium bobbed closer.

Finally she spoke. "Sorry for the other day. If you want to wait for the right girl, who am I to question that?"

Dead right.

"You hear me?"

How could she still run *and* talk? "Yeah."

"Can I ask you about Mark?"

"Scheider?"

"I need a guy's perspective. Tracy said something about not being able to trust him if we ended up together."

Good job, Trace.

"What do you think? You and Mark—" She panted, and Dillan tried not to be happy about it. "Apples and oranges, I know. But I think I trust you."

What was it with this woman and frank discussion? He stopped and bent over, planting his good arm low on his thigh.

Miska slowed beside him and walked in a tight circle, hands on hips, sucking in shallower breaths than he did.

He craned his neck to look up at her. "You want to talk while we walk back?"

"Sure."

Good. He'd give her what she wanted so she'd leave him alone. Panting less, he drew himself up.

Behind her, the row of trees shielded them from traffic. Skyscraper tops poked higher. The red CNA Center behind Metropolitan Tower, Sears Tower—or whatever it was called now—standing tall and dark. It was a different world from where he'd grown up, from subdivision after subdivision, strip mall after strip mall.

And here he stood with a woman who wanted an honest opinion about the man she was having an affair with.

He'd give it to her.

She surveyed the same view he did. "It doesn't get old, does it?"

He couldn't help it. He let himself take her in. "Nope."

"So." She started back the way they'd come. "About Mark."

He cleared his throat.

"I know you live differently than he does, but…"

He followed the pink flush in her cheeks and neck and arms and the skin exposed by the scoop neck of her tank top.

She turned toward him.

He looked away.

"I don't know if you can put yourself in Mark's shoes or not."

He massaged his throat. Yeah, a little.

"I don't know what Garrett did. If he was just partying—"

"It was more than that."

"Oh." She peeked at him. "Would most people think it was bad?"

"They would. You would."

"Oh," she said again, surprise in her voice. "What happened?"

He'd already said too much. "That's Garrett's story. Ask your question."
So he could get this conversation over with.

"Tracy said I wouldn't be able to trust Mark—if he left his wife for me.
I know to a certain extent that's true. There'd always be some doubt. But is
it always true that a relationship that begins like ours couldn't last?"

"You mean a relationship that begins with an affair?" How dumb *was*
she?

Shame tainted her voice. "Yes."

He pressed his lips together.

"I think Mark really loves me. His marriage was a mistake. But even my
dad, the master of affairs, says an affair will never last, and I can't get that
out of my head. Since then, Mark and I can't talk without arguing. For a
year everything was good. And now—now I wonder."

He nodded. The beginning of the end, most likely.

"What do you think?" She held his arm, made him face her. "Do you
think Mark and I have a chance?"

Her touch flamed through him, and Dillan raised his hand to his scalp,
removing himself from her fingers. "All I know is that any guy willing to
have an affair with you doesn't care about you. It's all about him, about sex.
It's just sex. But women want a relationship. So he goes along with it until
the sex isn't worth the relationship."

"How do you know?"

Come on. "I'm sure you've seen it, the way a guy looks at a woman
who's made it clear how far she'll go. He doesn't care about her; he wants
one thing."

She looked away. Her jaw tensed. Her eyes shone, and she lowered her
head.

Oh, great—she was gonna cry on him. He studied the nearest boat
bobbing in the harbor.

"So," she finally said. She brought her fingertips to her lips and played
with them. "You think Mark is just here for the sex."

Duh. "Most likely."

"Then what do I do?"

"About Mark? Send him packing."

"No, I mean how do I find out what he's here for? Me or the sex."

He rolled his eyes, not caring if she caught him. "Tell him no sex."

"Until?"

He shrugged. "Marriage?"

She caught her breath. "He won't wait that long."

"Right. Because he's here for the sex." *Listen, woman.*

"But don't men have needs? A guy who's used to having sex—he's not going to turn that off. It's not realistic."

"Then come up with some arbitrary date. Either way, the second you say no, he loses interest. He doesn't love you. He doesn't respect you. There is no real relationship."

She lifted her chin and stared at him.

He stared right back. She'd asked for it, so there it was. What she did with the truth was up to her.

And if she didn't like it, maybe she'd leave him alone.

He turned toward home. "I'm heading back."

She nodded and walked beside him.

Dillan kept silent, waiting for her to go off.

A minute passed before she looked up. "Thank you."

He shrugged her words away.

"I think you were really honest with me when most men wouldn't be. So thank you."

Absolutely. No problem. After all, he only had her best interests at heart. He scratched his neck, his sarcasm bringing discomfort. *God, why can't I avoid her?*

"Do you have plans for lunch?" she asked.

"I do." Good old tuna sandwich, apple, and chips. He'd have to send Tracy a thank-you for opening up a bunch of cans over the weekend. Now every time Garrett opened the fridge, he got to listen to him complain about the odor.

"If you ever need a can of tuna opened, let me know."

Funny lady. "You'd do that?"

"You were honest with me. It wasn't easy to hear, but I'm grateful."

Her words stopped him. "Miska—"

"Don't, Dillan." She pressed her hand to her mouth. "I need to go." She hurried up the steps that led to the street.

Dillan stood at the lake's edge and watched her disappear. If only he could do it over—with true compassion, the way a real pastor would.

Because it sure looked like Tracy was right. Something was going on inside her. And all he'd done was shove her away.

CHAPTER SEVENTEEN

As usual, Dillan disappeared over the weekend. For a single guy who said he didn't get out much, he seemed to have an active social life.

His words, though, hung around and haunted Miska. It was uncanny how he'd described Eric, the guy from the club, who'd known how far she was willing to go and wanted her for his own desires. But hadn't she gone to the club for the same thing? For a man to use?

She ground the guilt away. There was no point thinking about the past. She had a decision to make—what to do when Mark arrived Thursday evening.

Did he love her? Or just love her in bed? All the time they'd spent together, the nights and mornings they'd shared—what if it were all for nothing?

Dillan's suggestion was risky. What if Mark became angry? What if he left her?

Complicating everything was her body, ready to ovulate exactly when Mark would be here. She could get pregnant by him and bind them together. How could she take Dillan's advice and miss that chance?

The options plagued her, equally important. She had to know how much Mark loved her, but if she wanted to get pregnant by him, this next visit was it. The one window she had.

Then she'd always wonder if she'd trapped him. Like Mom had trapped Dad, like Jody had trapped Dad. She'd never rest easy.

And Dillan would never, ever look at her again.

Miska, he isn't looking at you now.

The beginning of the week passed between work and exercise. By Tuesday evening, she'd almost finished her current project and called it a night with a jog down eighteen flights of stairs to pick up a delivery the doorman said had come.

The package was from Kendall Sullivan, the NBA player she'd met last winter.

Why was he sending her a package now?

She sorted the rest of her mail while she rode the elevator up. But her hands shook. What did Kendall want? His season was over. She hadn't expected to hear from him until October at the earliest.

In the common hallway, Garrett and Tracy stood outside his door, a frown on Tracy's face.

"Miska," Garrett called. "Whatcha got there?"

"Just mail." She hoped.

Tracy held up a DVD. "Guess what? Season two!"

"That's my favorite season." She glanced at Garrett. He hadn't acted liked she'd ever been a drunken fool, and for that she was grateful. Even Tracy had moved past it. "When do we watch it?"

"Tonight?" Tracy sent a poochy lip at Garrett who rolled his eyes. "He has to head back to work *again*. I may need to get a job there if I want to see him."

He pecked her on the cheek. "Can't be helped. Once the case is over, I won't have to work so much."

"He lies. It'll be another case then."

"That'll teach you to marry a lawyer," Miska said.

"True love can't be helped, though. Farewell, dear barrister. Until we meet again." Tracy held out her hand, queen-style, for him to kiss.

Garrett raised his eyebrows at her hand. "This Abbey stuff is going to your head."

"It's *Downton Abbey*, and they don't kiss hands. Do they, Miska?"

"I don't remember. Maybe?"

He shook his head. "You two debate that while I earn us some moolah." He pulled Tracy close and gave her a quick kiss. "I'll give you a call if I'll be back before nine."

"So see you tomorrow? At church if you're not working?"

Already down the hall, he held up his hand in an I-heard-you wave.

When he was out of sight, Tracy sighed. "I'm sorry, but Matthew Crawley is a poor replacement for that man."

Miska unlocked her door and pushed it open. "Matthew's got some great eyes."

"I did notice that. Who's the package from?"

"Oh. A friend." She'd almost forgotten it. "Why don't you start the DVD while I make popcorn."

"I'm on it."

Miska set the package and mail on the counter beside the fridge where Tracy was unlikely to see it. With kitchen shears, she cut through the large manila packaging. The contents were wrapped in several plastic bags, and as she unwrapped them, she realized what they were.

Cash.

Why was Kendall sending her more money?

She finished unwrapping the contents. Four stacks of rubber-banded twenties with a letter tucked into one. She glanced over her shoulder.

Tracy fiddled with the DVD player.

Miska opened the letter.

Surprise, Miska! Since my favorite hockey team's playing your Blackhawks for the Stanley Cup, I thought I'd swing by for a few days, take in a game. You like hockey? I've got tickets for game one, May 28. I'll get in May 27. Here's the extra money, per our arrangement. See ya' then, hot stuff.

Her stomach turned. She swallowed and fingered the money.

What had their arrangement been? An extra four thousand for visits outside his NBA schedule? She'd already received his May payment and put it right on the mortgage. That had been easy to take, but him coming here again, staying in her bed, wanting her...

He doesn't care about her; he wants one thing.

She pressed a hand against her forehead. She'd been flattered when Kendall paid her attention at that club six months ago. Mark had been vacationing with Darcie, and Miska was sure she'd never hear from him again. Kendall was charming enough, and she'd already felt the pinch of not having Mark's gifts. She'd assumed one guy was as good as another.

How wrong she'd been.

His last trip to Chicago had been in March. She'd breathed easier once he'd left. Six months of his payments with none of his presence. She'd never imagined he'd want to see her during his off-season.

"What's this?" Tracy asked.

Miska flipped a crumpled bag on top of the money and turned.

Tracy was looking at the open laptop, head cocked to the side. Miska's blog dashboard was up, the post box blank but the title there.

"Oh, that." Miska hoped her laugh sounded realistic. "It's a friend's. It's nothing." She kept her walk toward the desk normal. What had Tracy seen? How much had she guessed? "Let me shut it down, and I'll get that popcorn."

"Sure." Tracy walked to the kitchen.

Miska glanced over her shoulder, making sure the money was covered.

"I wish Garrett didn't have to work so much." Tracy took two glasses from a cabinet. "Makes me wonder how we'll ever see each other once we're married."

Miska logged out of the dashboard. "You'll be living together. That'll make it easier."

"I'll have a commute, though. I'd love to stop working so I can be available whenever he's home, but we decided not to do that until the kids come."

"You planning on waiting long?"

"No, maybe a year. There's no guarantee it'll happen right away, you know?"

Miska mulled that over. True.

"You got plans for Memorial Day?"

Mark's last game against the Cubs was Memorial Day afternoon, and Kendall got in sometime the next day. "Morning plans. Why?"

"Our singles group from church is grilling out at Garrett's parents' place that night. You should come. We're just going to eat, goof off, be lazy. What do you think?"

Dillan's home, a bunch of Christian singles. All virgins? Tracy and Garrett weren't, so unlikely. Still… it could be interesting. "Sounds like fun."

"Cool. It starts at five. We can ride together, if you want. Garrett's taking Dillan to the Cubs game for his birthday, so they'll get there later."

She sorted through Mark's schedule. Wasn't he due to pitch that day? "Sounds good."

Miska closed the laptop and turned as Tracy's elbow bumped the bag. It slipped to the floor, revealing the stacks of cash.

Miska froze.

Tracy stared at the money, then at Miska.

The stare woke her. "That was my package. It's from a client—they like to pay in cash."

"You make this much from editing? Holy cow. You are not cheap."

She was far cheaper than Tracy knew. She hurried to the kitchen. "Let me put it away. Then I'll make popcorn."

"I'll get the popcorn. You take care of your money."

Miska grabbed the cash and stashed it in a desk drawer, out of sight but not forgotten.

As the popcorn popped, Tracy talked about discovering the flower order was wrong and the cake tasting she and Garrett had on Saturday. Even when Tracy stopped talking to watch Matthew Crawley fight in the trenches of World War I, Miska couldn't forget the money—and what she'd have to do to earn it.

Was money truly worth it?

No. Never.

She'd send Kendall a message after he left, telling him she was releasing him from their agreement. She'd even save some money to send with it. Then she could throw away the red sheets and duvet he liked and move on.

Mark would be enough for her.

He had to be.

Melissa Leach, Miska's former boss, stretched the cheese hanging off her pizza until it broke and dangled from her finger. "I can't believe all the times I've been to Chicago and never eaten here. Makes me almost consider moving." She winked at Miska as she piled the cheese on top of the slice. "But then I couldn't get my thin crust."

"I never liked that stuff." Miska glanced out the window at pedestrians strolling by, taking in the same view she'd first had with her dad.

"What an unbiased Chicagoan you are."

Miska smiled and cut another bite of pizza with her knife and fork. She popped it into her mouth while Melissa picked up her slice. Such a New Yorker. "Can't fold this stuff in half, you know."

"Shouldn't have to eat it with a fork. Seems un-American if you ask me." Melissa took another bite and set the pizza down. She chewed and swallowed as she wiped her fingers on her napkin, then sighed.

Here it came. When Melissa called last night and asked if they could get together while she was in town, Miska had sensed something was up. The sigh, the fading smile—it all reminded her of when she'd been pink-slipped. "Melissa, just tell me."

She stilled. "That obvious?"

Miska nodded.

"Okay then. They're closing the Relentless line."

Oh no. Her shoulders slumped. She closed her eyes. So much of her work. "When?"

"We're contracted through the end of the year. I've got maybe three months of work for you."

Three months? She thought through the recent titles she'd edited. Five of the last twelve had been for the Relentless Hearts line. "I can't remember the last time a romance line closed."

"The newer lines have gotten some big names, plus we lost a lot of shelf space last year. Our e-sales just aren't strong enough. We're moving the authors that are selling well into one of the stronger lines."

"But e-books are huge in romance. Are you sure it's that bad?"

"Miska, the decision's been made. We've been talking about it for the past two quarters. We've gone over the Q1 numbers, and they're not good. Not good." Melissa fiddled with her plate. "It won't go public for a while. None of our authors know. But we have to be a good percentage of your income."

Miska rested her elbows on the table and held her head in her hands. What was she going to do?

"When I get back, I'm meeting with Randy Husner, and I'll let him know what good work you do. I've got friends at other houses. I'll let them know you're available."

"Thanks." But they already had their holes filled. She'd just go on a list of names, if she were lucky, and have to wait for an opening.

"Feel free to use me as a reference."

"Sure. Thanks, Melissa." Going back to an office job didn't thrill her like it had right out of college. All the meetings and hours of work—her experience still didn't qualify her for a senior editor position. The only jobs she fit wouldn't pay nearly enough, and no employer would grant her time off each time Mark came to town.

What was she going to do?

"Miska, it'll be all right."

She couldn't look up and nodded instead.

"Get a mani-pedi, a massage. Have a night out with the girls. You'll feel better."

As if spending more money would solve her impending financial troubles. "Thanks for letting me know."

"I knew I wouldn't sleep well until I told you. Just keep it between us."

"Sure." She'd have to ask Adrienne about openings at her house. She faked a smile. She was getting too good at those. "I'm sure it'll work out. It's just a little overwhelming right now."

"Of course." Melissa picked up her pizza again. "But you've got that inheritance to fall back on. You'll land on your feet."

Miska cut another piece off her pizza. She was living in that inheritance. There was nothing to fall back on.

Nothing but men.

CHAPTER EIGHTEEN

The news ruined her afternoon. Miska set editing aside and contacted publishers she hadn't worked with lately as well as friends who'd moved up the editorial ladder. She texted Adrienne about jobs at her house.

Adrienne said she'd check.

By dinner, Miska felt sick with anxiety. To distract herself, she watched the recording of Mark's afternoon game. It had ended after four. He was probably just now flying out of Dallas. Give him two hours for the flight, another hour and a half to get to her. She checked the clock. He should be at her door around nine thirty.

She'd be ready by nine.

When the knock came at seven thirty, she panicked. The condo was clean, but she had yet to shower and touch up her makeup. She looked through the peephole.

Just Tracy.

She sagged in relief and opened the door.

"Garrett's working again," Tracy announced. "If he isn't careful, I *will* end up in love with Matthew Crawley."

"Then he'd be sorry, wouldn't he?"

"He would." Tracy walked in. "You get the popcorn, I start the DVD?"

"I can't tonight."

"Oh." Tracy froze. "Oh my goodness, I just walked on in, didn't I? I am so sorry, Miska."

"Don't worry about it."

"I. Am. Mortified." Tracy pulled Miska's hand to her cheek. "Feel how hot that is? I have almost never been so embarrassed."

"Stop it." Miska laughed. "I'll watch Matthew Crawley with you. It'll just be awhile."

"Great. So what's going on?"

"Mark's in town."

"Oh." Tracy pressed her lips together and glanced toward the living room. "Oh. I see. He's, umm, he's coming to see you?"

"They're here to play the Cubs."

"Right. Oh, right. The Cubs are playing Milwaukee this weekend..." Her words trailed off, and Miska guessed she was realizing that the game Dillan and Garrett were going to would be against Mark. "Maybe after he leaves?"

Except Kendall was coming in, right on Mark's heels. "I've got some things going on next week too. I might not be free until the weekend."

"With the way Garrett's schedule is filling up, I'll probably be sitting home alone all weekend. Watching dear Matthew." Tracy glanced at the DVD case, then peered up at her. "You be careful, okay?"

The warning chilled her. "I'll be fine."

"Okay. Well—okay. I'll be praying for you."

Praying? "For what?"

"That you'll see the truth. That you'll be free." Tracy paused. "If you feel something in your spirit, listen. Okay?"

The warning made her throat grow thick. "I will."

"All right, then. You have a good night."

"You too." She watched Tracy head down the hall. "Tell Matthew hi for me."

Tracy waved and smiled.

Miska closed her door. Something in her spirit?

She thought through the night to come—the lingerie she'd picked out, the music ready to go on her iPod, the perfume, the lights she'd turn on for just the right ambience. Tonight was the night she'd get pregnant—or tomorrow or Saturday or Sunday or Monday morning.

It was the decision she'd come to after a week of thinking, after the news Melissa had delivered, after the money and impending arrival of Kendall. The answer to everything was a baby with Mark. Mark's baby meant no more Kendall. Mark's baby meant no worries about finding work. Mark's baby meant *Mark*.

What would Tracy think? Would she say go for it? Get pregnant? Or take Dillan's advice?

He doesn't care about her; he wants one thing.

Not Mark. He loved her—even though they hadn't talked much since their last argument. He'd asked her to wait so they could talk in person and see each other's face. How she wanted to see his face.

Being apart wasn't good for them. No wonder their relationship struggled, especially since she'd put an end date to the relationship. She needed to back off, let him enjoy his time with her. His decision would be easy then.

She showered and curled her hair the way he liked it. She slipped into a cream teddy and perfected her makeup, then dabbed on perfume.

But in her bedroom, standing in front of her closet, she couldn't put on the cream lace dress she'd picked out. After debating, she slipped into a favorite pair of jeans and pulled on a lightweight, fitted, peach shirt.

There. Comfortable. Relaxed. Just Miska as she was. Take it or leave it.

Around nine fifteen his key sounded in the lock. The lamp on her desk gave her enough light to reach the door as it opened.

Mark slipped inside, duffel bag over his shoulder. "Miska," he whispered. He set his bag aside and pulled her into his arms, into a hug that warmed her in ways she'd forgotten.

When he finally released her, he set his hands on her neck and jaw. "I've missed you," he whispered and leaned down to kiss her. His lips were gentle on her mouth, waiting for her response.

She wrapped her arms around his waist, her back arching as he held her tight. He felt so good, so right. What was missing was here. She knew it.

Finally he drew back and grinned, eying her up and down. "Baby, you look so good. It's like coming home."

He kissed her again. Kissed her again and again. His hands tangled in her hair, then slid down her back.

"Mark." She pulled back and covered his hands on her waist. "I don't... I don't want us to sleep together while you're here."

The fog in his eyes vanished, and he searched her face. "What's wrong?"

"Nothing. We're fine. It's just…" She toyed with the edge of his sleeve. "I get so caught up in you when you're here. I think we should take some time to really look at us. As a couple."

He shifted, and she raced to convince him. "I won't say a thing about you making a decision. That's not what this is about. We just need time to focus on us without getting lost in all the great sex we have."

He chuckled, pressing his nose into her hair. "Bringing that up doesn't help."

"I know. I'm sorry." Would he understand at all? "It's just this once, Mark. For us, for you. So we'll make the right decision."

He studied her, his blue eyes scouring her for something more. "You sure we're okay?"

"Yes."

"I know I haven't been the easiest guy—"

She pressed her hand to his mouth. "I'm past that. This weekend is for us. So we'll know what it's like if we decide to be together."

His palm settled on her cheek, and his thumb traced a gentle path above her eyebrow down to her earlobe. "You're sure this is what you want?"

Eyes closed, she nodded.

"Can I still kiss you?"

She looked up. His mouth curved in a tender smile. "Please," she whispered.

He lowered his mouth to hers and gave her a slow, excruciating kiss. "Okay, Miska. I'll wait until you're ready."

He loved her.

The knowledge burst in her while fear she hadn't acknowledged vanished. He truly loved her.

Dad had been wrong. Dillan too. Mark loved her, loved her for her.

She kissed him as he pressed her against the wall, glad she'd waited. There might not be a baby this time, but there would be one in the future.

Which meant, ironically, that Dillan and Tracy were right after all. Waiting did matter. Because all she knew as she kissed him over and over was that she'd never been so happy.

CHAPTER NINETEEN

Dillan's parents lived in a typical suburban neighborhood, the home an updated two-story with white siding and black shutters, an asphalt drive out front with a scuffed backboard over the garage. The driveway was full, and cars blanketed both sides of the road.

Tracy parked on the street three doors down.

"You don't get reserved parking?" Miska asked.

"Got to fight for it like everyone else. Looks like a lot of people beat us here."

They'd watched the first inning of the Cubs and Hogs' game, but after Mark gave up five runs, Tracy convinced her their time would be better spent with the Crawleys. They got caught up in the story and didn't leave the Loop until five.

The front door was open, and Tracy walked inside. "Mom, Dad? It's Tracy."

"In the kitchen," a woman called.

Miska followed Tracy past the carpeted staircase into a wide, open kitchen and great room.

Shari Foster stood at the sink, washing a colander of grapes. People filled the great room. Several sprawled across the checkered couch and floor while two surfed via a Wii.

"Hi, honey." Shari dried her hands, then hugged Tracy. "I was beginning to think you'd met up with the boys after the game."

"No, we got busy with something. Mom, you remember Miska."

Shari held her hand out, and Miska took it. "I do. It's good to have you, Miska. Make yourself at home."

Miska followed Tracy outside onto a wide, two-level deck where more people spread out. By the doors six people played an intense game of Rook at an umbrella-covered table. On the lower level, Jordan Foster sat with a blond football-player type who looked like an all-American from the fifties, complete with a high-and-tight haircut.

Jordan glanced up as they neared. "Tracy! Miska, right?" Jordan gave Tracy a hug, then pulled Miska into a quick one. She smelled like silk. "Miska, this is Matt. He just got home."

"From?" Miska asked.

"Marines." He sent her a friendly grin. "Done with that. Time to start school."

"Miska rescued Dillan when he about killed himself."

"Ah." Matt nodded knowingly as he pulled another chair toward them and motioned for Miska to take his. He perched on the deck railing.

"How long were you in the military?"

"Four years. Mostly in Hawaii."

Tracy shook her head. "We prayed you'd survive that torment."

Miska laughed with Jordan, and Matt smirked. "Yeah, well, it wasn't all a beach party."

When Dave Foster opened the patio door and called that food was ready, Miska joined everyone inside and filled her plate. Tracy and Jordan introduced her to people, the names swirling through her head. She'd be lucky if she remembered anyone besides Matt.

They took their food to the deck and talked while they ate. Two men joined them, but neither singled her out. They asked Matt about his last year as a Marine, about why he was getting out.

"Hey, Dillan," someone called behind her. She heard the sound of hands clasping, a smack on a back, guys doing their guy thing.

She focused on the conversation around her rather than glance over her shoulder for Dillan, but a fold-out chair scraped beside her, and she couldn't not look. Dillan, all six feet nine inches of him, towered beside her as he nudged a chair next to her, his plate in his good hand. His face and forearm were darker than normal, the bridge of his nose a touch red from an afternoon at Wrigley.

All around her people called out greetings. Matt jumped up to shake his hand, and Miska hid a smile at the obviousness of a guy trying to impress the brother of a girl he liked. Sweet, though. Wade and Zane wouldn't have cared.

"How are you?" she asked when Dillan finally sat beside her, plate in hand.

"Good. You?" He glanced at her, then picked up his burger and took a bite.

"Fine. How was your weekend?"

He chewed fast, swallowed. "Busy. But good. Nice to have a day off, isn't it?"

"It is."

He stuck his fork into a piece of watermelon and popped it into his mouth.

Around them people quieted.

Miska looked up.

Matt, the other men—their eyes locked onto Dillan as if he were doing something fascinating.

He eased back in his seat as he finished chewing. "I didn't know you were coming."

"Tracy invited me. This where you grew up?"

He nodded, eyes still on his plate, his fork stabbing another piece of watermelon.

She watched him a second longer, and when she turned back, she caught the men's gazes going from Dillan to her and back again.

What were they seeing that she wasn't?

Behind her, the chatter picked up. Garrett's voice rose over others as he told someone about how bad the Hogs' pitcher looked.

Miska focused on her food. Garrett would think his presence at Wrigley had something to do with Mark's performance, but Mark hadn't even told his pitching coach yet about the pain in his shoulder. Let Garrett have his moment.

Matt stood as Garrett pulled up a chair beside Tracy. "Hey, Garrett."

"Mattie, good to see ya'." Garrett grabbed the hand Matt offered and pulled him into a male hug, finishing with the slap on the back. "So you're a regular civilian, huh?"

"Yep. Glad to be back in the flat, boring Midwest. How was the Cubs game?"

Cam, one of the other men, perked up. "You were at the Cubs game?"

Garrett picked up his plate and sat. "Second row. Right behind home plate."

"Nice."

Dillan shifted, his foot bumping Miska's. "Sorry."

"Shall we talk about the game?"

A smile tugged at the corner of his mouth. "Cubs won so…"

"How much did Garrett heckle Mark?"

"Not much."

"Then he's taking credit for the win."

"You know Garrett. But Mark didn't look good. I wonder if he's hurt."

"Hmm." She sipped from her can of lemonade.

Dillan scooted lower in his seat, his voice beside her ear. "Is he?"

She peeked at him.

This time he didn't look away. A smile spread over his face. "He's hurt? What's wrong?"

"I didn't say he was—"

"Don't take up poker."

She hissed out a frustrated breath. "You can't breathe a word. No one knows."

"Wow. I feel like an insider." He grinned, rubbing his chin. "You know, this might help me get into my place sooner. What's it worth to you?"

"If you say *anything* to *anyone*—"

"So a lot. Let me think. You know, my car needs an oil change."

"Dillan—"

"Yeah, you probably don't know how to change oil. You could do my grocery shopping."

"Stop it."

"I know—you have to open a can of tuna every day until I get my cast off."

"That's just wrong."

He snickered.

She smacked his arm. "It's not funny. I can't believe you read that on my face. Don't you dare say anything to Garrett."

He filled his fork with potato salad. "You know I'm messing with you."

He focused on his food, and Miska returned to the conversation. Again, Matt and Cam watched them, looking away as she caught them. Seriously, what was going on?

The deck and yard filled up as the crowd in the house filed outside with their food.

When he finished eating, Dillan joined the guys on the lawn. Someone tossed him a football, and he caught it against his chest with one arm. Not bad for a wounded klutz.

While the girls talked, Miska's gaze drifted to Dillan. The other men joked with him, treating him like a good friend, like a guy worthy of respect. So much better than the constant ribbing Garrett gave him.

"Hey, ladies," Garrett hollered from the lawn. "You up for Frisbee soccer?"

"Bring it!" Jordan called.

Tracy scowled at Miska. "I stink at sports."

"So hold down the sidelines." Jordan hauled Miska to her feet. "Me, I need to show up Matt before he gets a head like Garrett. You playing, Miska?"

Dillan stood out in the crowd heading toward the empty green space behind the Fosters' house. "Absolutely." She kicked off her sandals and stashed them under her chair.

Jordan tugged her forward. "Miska's on my team."

The teams divided with Garrett joining Jordan, Miska, and six others. Dillan stood across from her at the soccer field's center line and quirked an eyebrow.

"What?" she asked.

"Shoeless Miska Tomlinson?"

"Worked for Joe Jackson, didn't it?"

He shrugged.

Miska's team started with the Frisbee. Jordan and Garrett made a great tandem with Jordan flinging the Frisbee true and straight to Garrett who jumped higher than everyone else, snagged it, and sent it into the soccer goal. In a matter of minutes, they were ahead, two to zero.

After the other team got the Frisbee past her and into her team's goal, Miska gave up on defense and switched to offense, running down the opposite side of the field from Garrett. He caught sight of her before anyone else did and sent the Frisbee flying. She snagged it by a fingertip and threw it toward Jordan, but it arced away and landed in the grass.

Beside her, Dillan ran backwards as they headed toward the other end. "Nice try, newbie."

"Newbie? Do you know how tempting it is to trip you?"

"You wouldn't—" His foot flew out from beneath him. He caught himself before his head could slam into the ground.

Miska gasped. "I swear, Dillan, I didn't trip you."

"I know." He grinned at the Frisbee that landed a few feet ahead of them. His teammate grabbed it and sent it the opposite way. "I was distracting you."

"Oh, of course."

They jogged farther down the field. Dillan's team kept the Frisbee near her goal, and she and Dillan stopped to catch their breath. Behind the trees on the far side of the park, the sky began to turn pink and lavender. She squinted at the occasional ray of light that jumped between swaying leaves and tried to blind her.

Somewhere someone was grilling. "Smell that?"

Dillan sniffed the air.

"What is that? Ribs? Steak?"

He pointed behind them. "It's coming from over there."

She looked but couldn't find the source. When she turned back, Dillan was yards ahead of her, sprinting for the Frisbee heading their way.

"Dillan!" She chased him.

The Frisbee stayed up, and Dillan leaped high into the air, nabbing the edge and pulling it into his palm. He landed hard on his feet, almost falling to his knees as she skidded to a stop. He flung his arm out for balance.

Two of his teammates stood alone by her team's goal. Once he stood—

Miska leaped onto his back.

He laughed beneath her. "Uh, foul."

She wrapped her arms around his neck, her legs around his waist. "Drop the Frisbee and no one gets hurt."

People began to laugh and cheer. Someone wolf-whistled.

"Miska." Dillan coughed. Laughed. "Get off." He twisted, his left arm coming back to his chest to fling the Frisbee.

Miska lunged over his shoulder for it.

He laughed again, straightening. "Are you serious?"

She slipped. With a yelp, she tightened her hold around his neck, one hand grabbing a fistful of shirt.

He stumbled back a step.

Safely on his back again, she made another grab for the Frisbee.

"Please." Amusement tinged his voice. He held the Frisbee out, way beyond her reach.

"No fair. Your arms are like six feet long."

"And you climbing on my back is fair." He brought the Frisbee in close, let her reach for it, and held it out again. Pulled it close, let her reach for it, held it out again. And again.

Across the field laughter grew. Jordan flopped onto the grass, an arm across her stomach, while Garrett watched with his hands on his hips. "Let me have it, Dillan. You're making a scene."

"So?"

"So I can live with this. Can you?"

"Watch me," he said and started to run.

She jerked backwards. Her mouth flew open, and she grabbed his shoulders. "Dillan!"

His long legs ate up the distance. Miska hung on, each fist clenching the front of his shirt, each step jouncing her up and down. She pressed her cheek against the side of his head, his hair cushioning her jaw. They passed everyone until only one man stood between them and the goal.

Dillan leaned over the shorter guy's head and tossed the Frisbee in.

His team erupted.

Miska slid off his back and landed in a heap on the ground. Dillan high-fived Cam, then turned to her, a grin across his face. He offered her a hand up.

She swatted it away. "You cheated."

"Oh, I'm sorry. What was I thinking?"

On her feet, she flipped her hair over her shoulder. "You weren't, I'm sure. There's not enough oxygen up there. How are you even alive?"

Laughing, Cam shook his head and jogged downfield.

Dillan pointed toward his ear, his chest heaving beneath his crumpled Cubs T-shirt. "You've got grass in your hair."

She ran her fingers over her curls. "Did I get it?"

"No, it's still—" He brought his hand closer. "You're right below it."

She shook her head, moved her hand up. "Here?"

"Let me."

Her hair gave beneath his fingers, a curl separating his skin from hers. And then his fingers were in front of her, a blade of grass—brown and jagged at one end—in his hand. He tossed it to the ground. "There."

"Any more?"

"Don't think so." He checked both sides of her head. "You're good." He took a step toward the center of the field, and Miska fell in beside him, seeing the Frisbee take off at the other end.

Cam said something to a guy who glanced over his shoulder at her and Dillan.

"Why does everyone keep looking at us?"

"What do you mean?"

"While we were eating and just now. Every time I look up, guys are watching us."

He shrugged. "Got me." He eased into a jog and began to leave her behind.

"What are you doing?"

"Playing defense." He smirked over his shoulder. "I'll explain it to you some time."

Wasn't he funny. She matched his pace, staying behind him, out of sight. Across the field Garrett noticed her, and she fell back, letting Dillan put distance between them.

Garrett zipped the Frisbee to her.

When Dillan turned, his mouth fell open. She caught the Frisbee, and he came at her, arms stretched out, huge frame blocking her angles. She aimed the Frisbee above his head, waited until he jumped, then threw the Frisbee between his feet.

But his giant foot knocked it to the ground. He scooped it up and sent it the other way.

She growled out her disgust.

Jordan jogged to her and slipped an arm around her shoulder. "Good try, but it's pretty much impossible to get it past Godzilla over here."

Dillan snorted. "Godzilla?"

Jordan peered at the back of Miska's head. "You've got grass in your hair."

Grass? "Dillan, you said my hair was fine."

He watched Jordan pull a few pieces from the back of her hair. "I didn't check the back."

Really?

He winked at Miska, then jogged down the field.

"Did he just wink at me?"

Jordan stared at Miska, then Dillan. "Did he?"

Yes. He had. "It's no big deal."

"Umm…" Jordan swallowed and sent another questioning look Dillan's way. "You're good. No more grass."

Jordan jogged across the field, saying something to Garrett as she passed. Garrett glanced toward Dillan who stood a good ten yards ahead of Miska, his hand shading his eyes while he followed the action at the other end of the field.

So it was a big deal. Evidently he didn't wink at women very much.

But he'd winked at her.

Chapter Twenty

Tracy's tire was as flat as a tire could be.

Beneath the streetlamp, Garrett fingered the nail responsible. "Dad should have something to plug this. Miska, you okay if Dillan takes you home?"

It was nice of him to ask, but that was more than okay. "Sure."

"How will you get home?" Tracy asked him.

"I'll spend the night at Mom and Dad's. Take the train in tomorrow."

The street was almost bare of cars, and the Fosters' driveway was empty except for Dillan, his friend Cam, and another guy who talked while dribbling a basketball.

Dillan looked up. "Thought you ladies were leaving."

"Tracy's got a flat. You mind letting Miska ride home with you?"

Dillan deadpanned a look of irritation. "As long as she doesn't jump on my back again."

Miska smirked.

He smirked back.

"Can't promise that, Dill." Garrett grinned at her. "Too bad about Mark stinking up Wrigley, huh?"

Tracy smacked his ribs. "Garrett."

Miska checked an invisible watch on her wrist. "I can't believe you made it this late into the evening before your first comment."

Garrett laughed. "I'm so mature. It shocks me too. Pass along my condolences, will you?"

"Right."

He laughed again, heading for the garage.

After telling Tracy good-bye, Miska fell into step beside Dillan. "Where's your car?"

"Right here." He held up a key fob, and a gray Chevy Trailblazer beeped, the lights coming on.

She opened her door and slid inside.

He started the engine and waited while she buckled her seatbelt, then met her eyes. "So. How do I get to your place?"

"Very funny."

He chuckled and shifted into drive.

She settled into her seat and watched dark homes slide past. They made small talk until he turned south onto a highway. "I don't think Tracy took this route."

He checked traffic to his left. "Tracy lives farther south. She probably took I-90."

"I wouldn't know. I didn't pay attention."

"What if something happened to your ride? How would you get home?"

"You mean like right now?"

"Ah." A smile tweaked his lips. "She's quick."

"You get around Chicago much?"

"More than I'd like. We've had church members in Chicago hospitals so I know my way around."

"Ever do a funeral?'

"Twice."

"That had to be awful."

"They're not the reason I became a pastor."

"Did you know the people who passed?"

"My grandfather and a man from our church."

"Oh." He seemed so calm about it. She watched streetlights flash across his face. "You did your grandpa's funeral?"

"It wasn't easy. But he was a Christian, so I knew where he was."

"You mean heaven."

He nodded.

Silence settled between them. It felt comforting, natural, and for a moment she pretended that she and Dillan were a couple, that they were heading back to their place.

But that was crazy. He was a pastor, of all things. He made a living off telling people that they couldn't sleep together.

"So what made you—" she began as he started to say something. "Sorry. Go ahead."

"You go."

"What made you become a pastor?"

"My pastor got me thinking about it. When I was in high school, he talked to some of us about going into the ministry."

"Going into—" The phrasing sounded foreign. "You mean being a pastor."

"Yeah. Sorry."

"I'll catch up on the lingo. Continue."

He smiled at the road. "He helped us teach a Sunday School class, small stuff like that, kind of ease our way into things. As time went on and I prayed about it, I realized being a pastor was what I should do."

The guy prayed about everything. "Did you *want* to be a pastor?"

"Definitely." He shot her a look. "I love what I do. I spend hours each day studying the Bible, what God says, how it applies to us. Then I get to share it with people and watch it change their lives. It's pretty cool, frankly."

"Really?"

He looked her way again, eyebrows up. Laughter escaped him. "Yeah, Miska, really. I love my job. You couldn't pay me to do anything else."

"Huh."

"You don't think much of pastors."

"It's not that." Had she ever known a pastor before? "I guess I thought—" No, she couldn't tell him what she'd always believed about men in a church. That they weren't men, weren't masculine, were out of touch.

"What made you want to work with books?" he asked.

"I like to read. Getting paid to read is a pretty good gig."

"Exactly. I get paid to study the Bible. A pretty good gig."

Hmm. Okay.

Her phone chimed. Miska pulled it out of her purse and read the text. "Looks like Garrett fixed the tire."

"That's good."

"How come Tracy ended up with Garrett and not you?"

"That's a weird question."

"Let me guess. He met her first."

"He probably did."

She waited for more, but he said nothing. "You're taking the easy way out. Why'd she go for him?"

"You sound like you don't like Garrett."

She shrugged. "You just seem more like Tracy's type."

"Seriously?" He sent her a pained expression. "Why?"

"Now you sound like you don't like Tracy."

"Tracy's fine. She's just not my type."

"And your type is…"

"Nope." He shook his head. "Not going there."

"Come on, Dillan."

"Why would you think Tracy's my type?"

"I don't know. Opposites attract, I guess. She's talkative, you're not. Garrett's just as talkative as Tracy. I wonder how those two will get a word in edgewise."

"They'll be fine."

Probably. "How about you tell me your type, and I tell you mine."

"I would assume I know your type."

"Meaning what?"

His eyebrows rose like it was obvious. "Mark?"

"What do you know about him?"

"Plays baseball—"

"Yes, definitely. Has to play baseball."

"He's tall—"

"Absolutely. Has to be a giant."

"He's blond."

"You do realize you're only describing him."

"What? Isn't that your type?"

"That's not who he *is*, Dillan. That's the surface. It's what he's like that matters."

Dillan snorted. "You want me to tell you what he's like? I can do that. He's rude, unfaithful, arrogant—"

"Hey now—"

"Selfish, self-centered. That's your type?"

"He is not self-centered. I did what you suggested, and it worked."

Dillan's eyebrows scrunched together. "What I suggested?"

"Yes. Told him no sex to see if he split."

"You—oh."

He took in the news, the tiniest bit of irritation flying over his face.

"Don't you want to know how it went?"

"I don't want to talk about Mark."

"You brought him up."

"Then let's change the topic."

"Okay. What should we talk about?"

His jaw tightened. "You know what bugs me about him?"

"Mark? I thought we weren't talking about him."

"Changed my mind. You know what gets me?" He shook his head. "The arrogant way he views everything and everyone. If he were married to my sister and treated her like… I'd be all over the jerk."

She drew back. Jerk?

"Relationships aren't sacred to him. When I marry, I'm not throwing it away for nothing. I'd do everything I could to make it work. To make it great."

"That's easy to say now."

"Yep. And it's easy for Mark to say what you want to hear too."

"So you don't like my boyfriend."

He pursed his lips. "I don't know. Can you call a married man your boyfriend?"

She rolled her eyes.

"Hey, you said you liked it when I was honest. You see him, what, every time his team comes to Chicago?"

"No," she snapped. "More than that."

"Not much more, I bet. How often do you see him when baseball's over?"

His question surprised her. She opened her mouth. Closed it.

"I think he's taking advantage of a beautiful woman who shouldn't be taking crumbs—" He clamped his mouth shut. His jaw twitched, and he clenched the steering wheel.

A beautiful woman. There was no way he meant to say that. But to know how he viewed her… *A beautiful woman. Taking crumbs.* Was she taking crumbs? When she could do better?

He glared at the road like it had yelled at him.

"Dillan."

He grunted.

"What you said—"

"Yeah, I shouldn't have—"

"No, thank you." She pressed her hands into her lap. Why couldn't Dillan, who'd have no trouble going out in public for breakfast, be right for her? "Don't let it make things awkward."

The hum of tires throbbed between them.

"Hey. Say something."

He stared out the windshield a few seconds longer. "So. How 'bout them Bears?"

She laughed. "Really? That's what you came up with?"

"You said say something. You weren't specific."

"The Bears aren't even practicing yet. Are they?"

"Mini-camp is a week and a half away."

"What about the Blackhawks? They're in the Stanley Cup Finals."

"Not much of a hockey fan."

"Not enough to jump on the bandwagon?"

He glanced in his side mirror. "Nope."

"Just so happens I get to go to the first game Wednesday."

"Mmm."

"A friend has tickets."

He grunted again.

Miska looked at him. He was staring at his rearview mirror.

She swiveled in her seat in time to see blue and red lights flash behind them.

Dillan groaned. "Great."

"How fast were you going?"

"Too fast." He slowed and pulled onto the shoulder. His jaw clenched.

He had to be frustrated. Or embarrassed. "It's no big deal, Dillan. Everyone gets pulled over."

"Yeah, well." His fingers tapped a rhythm against the steering wheel. "This will be my second ticket."

"Ever?"

He sighed and looked at his rearview mirror again. "This year."

"This year?" The laugh burst out of her. "It's not even June."

His scowl softened. "It's almost June."

"I'd hate to see your insurance bill. Need anything from your glove box?"

"Oh yeah. You'd think I'd have that down."

She opened the compartment. A receipt for his last oil change sat on top of his insurance card and registration. She handed him the papers.

"Thanks."

The cop closed his door and walked up the side of the SUV. Maybe she could flirt with him and get Dillan out of trouble.

The man stopped just behind Dillan's door. "You know how fast you were going?"

"No, sir."

"Sixty-seven in a fifty-five. You have anything to drink tonight?"

"No."

It was Memorial Day. Of course there'd be cops all over. She ducked her head until she could see the man's face.

He caught her movement and shifted to look at her.

"Officer, it's my fault." She flashed him a smile. "He was answering some questions for me, and I guess I distracted him."

The cop ignored her. "I need your license, proof of insurance, and registration."

Dillan handed him the papers.

"Where you headed?"

"The Loop."

"Coming from?"

"Uh, church activity."

The cop looked up from the license. "Church stuff?"

"Yeah. I'm a pastor."

He was so getting a ticket. She leaned forward again. "Yes, he's my pastor, and he was answering some questions for me."

Dillan narrowed his eyes at her.

"Sit tight. I'll be back."

The cop walked back to his vehicle. He'd barely looked at her—and Dillan had told him his job. "You're so getting a ticket."

"It's just money." He stuck a finger inside his cast and scratched. "And I'm loaded."

"You are?"

"I was. Not after this."

"Are you embarrassed?"

"Completely."

"Don't be. Ask me when I got my last ticket."

"When was your last ticket?"

She shrugged. "Never."

"Oh, nice one." She laughed while he shook his head. "Here I thought you were trying to make me feel better."

"No, just trying to make you laugh."

His smile said he was mildly amused. "I'm laughing on the inside."

"You should let it out. It's good for you."

He studied her, his mouth curving a little more.

She watched him back, watched his amusement fade into awareness. His eyes, so dark in the night, slid across her face, down her cheek and mouth, and back up to her eyes. She swallowed. This moment, right here, was where some other guy might lean across the inches separating them and kiss her. But not Dillan, even though he kept hold of her gaze.

What was he thinking? And why did she think about kissing him after the past few days with Mark?

The thump of a car door ended the moment. The cop returned and handed Dillan his information. "Make sure you obey the signs. Slow down, and have a safe night."

"Thank you." Dillan sorted through the cards and paper. "Huh." He handed her his insurance card and registration. "Would you put that back?"

"Sure. He didn't give you a ticket?"

He slid his license into his wallet. "Nope."

"Seriously?"

He set his wallet in the cup-holder between them. "Seriously."

She picked it up and flipped the soft leather open. "Does this mean you're still loaded?"

"Guess so. Good to be me, huh?"

"Or me. I'm the one with your wallet."

"Good point." He shifted into drive and eased onto the highway.

Miska pulled his license out. His serious face stared back at her. Six nine, two hundred fifteen pounds. "You are not two-fifteen."

"You planning on impersonating me?"

"Right. People think I'm over two hundred pounds all the time."

"At least you're aware of it."

She flicked his cast.

He chuckled and let it fade into a sigh. "So."

She slid his license back and closed the wallet. "So what?"

"Why'd you tell him I'm your pastor?"

"Because you are."

His glance questioned her.

"You're the only pastor I know. And we were having a serious discussion."

"Were we? I can't remember."

She settled back in her seat and watched the glittering skyline approach. "You were telling me how beautiful I am."

He didn't say a word.

"You change your mind?"

"You trying to get me pulled over again?"

"No, just helping you remember."

He chewed on his lip.

So the moment was really over. She adjusted her seatbelt.

"Miska, what do you… How do you see yourself?"

"What do you mean?"

He pressed his lips together, slowing through the curved interchange ramp. "You are beautiful." He glanced her way. "Don't you see that?"

She caught her breath.

"You're kind. Caring. Don't—don't throw it away on Mark."

He looked back at the road, but Miska couldn't take her eyes off him. He was the beautiful one. All six foot, nine inches, two hundred and more like forty pounds of him. He was a gorgeous man, in and out.

And she wished she'd met him before Mark.

Oh, how she wished she'd met him first.

CHAPTER TWENTY-ONE

Working was pointless. Absolutely pointless.

Dillan pushed his chair back and stretched his good arm high over his head. Maybe he needed a break. He checked the clock. Four-thirty. There had to be something good on ESPN. That might get his mind off Miska.

He swallowed, remembering everything about the night before. The way she'd looked running down the field, dark hair bouncing around her shoulders. Her teeth bright against her skin, her cheeks flushed. The feel of her on his back, her scent when he turned his head. Oh, man. He dragged his hand down his face. The way she looked at him after he'd been pulled over, like she was waiting for a kiss.

She wasn't. But it had been tempting.

Which was scary.

He tapped his fingers against the laptop, staring at his notes. He pictured Miska between Jordan and Tracy, the three of them laughing about something, looking so different yet seeming as if they belonged together.

He clenched his jaw. He couldn't go there. She wasn't a Christian.

The intercom buzzed.

He jumped on the interruption, hurried into the hall, and pressed the speak button. "Yes?"

"This is Scott downstairs. I've got a package for Dillan Foster."

"Be right down."

He grabbed his keys and left. Had to be the commentaries he'd ordered. Maybe that would help him focus.

An elevator came quickly, and he rode uninterrupted to the main lobby.

Scott stood behind the front desk, on the phone. Across from him a well-dressed African-American man waited.

The man flashed him a smile, and Dillan nodded back. The guy looked familiar. Tall, just a couple inches shorter than he was. Well dressed in a bright orange sweater with light blue shirttails and collar sticking out. Dark jeans and boat shoes. His hair in short dreads and a diamond in each ear. Some fat silver watch on his wrist.

Where had he seen him before? Was he new to the building?

No, he hadn't seen him here.

Scott hung up the phone. "You can go up, Mr. Sullivan."

Dillan blinked. Kendall Sullivan? Shooting guard for the Detroit Turbines? Now he could picture the man in the hated jersey, playing for the Bulls' rival.

"Thanks." Sullivan tapped a knuckle against the raised desktop and walked past Dillan, a wheeled suitcase in hand.

What was he doing here? Dillan faced Scott. "You got a package for me?"

"I do." From beneath the desk Scott pulled out a box. "Here you go, Dillan."

"Thanks." So he was just Dillan while Mr. NBA was Mr. Sullivan. Good to know.

Sullivan was still waiting for an elevator when Dillan entered the glassed-in lobby. The man smiled again. "Whatcha got there?"

"Just books." Dillan took a deep breath. Whatever the guy said, he was not going to act like Garrett. "Are you Kendall Sullivan?"

His smile grew. "That's me." He stuck out his hand, and Dillan took it. "And you are?"

"Dillan. Foster. Nice to meet you."

"You too. It's always a pleasure to meet someone in Chicago who isn't a Bulls fan."

"Actually…"

The elevator dinged, and Kendall laughed a deep, rolling laugh as the doors opened. "Do I want to get in an elevator with you?"

Dillan grinned. "We'll keep the rivalry on the court."

"My man." Kendall slapped him on the back as they entered. "Chicago's too cool of a city to pretend I hate it."

He pressed the eighteen. "Lots better than Detroit."

"You don't hear me disagreeing." Kendall reached for the floor buttons, then stopped. "You live on eighteen?"

"Yep. You headed there?"

"Oh, yeah. Love the views." He laughed that deep, throaty laugh again, but this time the sound grated.

Dillan held the smile on his face. He wasn't going to... He couldn't finish the thought. There was no way. No way. "What are you doing in town?"

"Just having some fun in my off season. My hockey team's playing for the Stanley Cup. Got to support my boys, you know?"

Dillan's stomach turned. This couldn't be.

"You like hockey?"

He tried to smile at the guy, but it fell flat. "Not much."

"I used to play. Fun sport."

He stared at his toes. "What made you choose basketball?"

"My coaches thought I could make it. I gave up hockey in middle school, but I still love it."

Dillan nodded. The elevator slowed, and he jammed his lips together. What on earth was Miska doing?

"You play basketball?" Kendall asked. "You're tall enough."

"No." He followed Kendall out of the elevator, and the man turned down his hallway. Dillan muffled a groan. *God, no.* He couldn't be seeing Miska. She couldn't be... sleeping with another athlete. He slowed his steps, finally stopping to retie his shoe.

Kendall glanced back at him. "Have a good day, man."

"You, uh, you too." The words were foul in his mouth. Kneeling on the floor, still tying his shoe, he watched Kendall walk past his door and stop at Miska's.

He knocked.

The door opened immediately, as if she'd been waiting. She stepped into view, and Dillan froze. Long curls danced across bare shoulders, a gauzy, pink top barely covering what had to be covered. She wore tiny, white shorts, and between the top of the shorts and the bottom of her shirt, a band of tanned skin showed.

Kendall's face lit up. "Hey, sweet thing." He held her face in his hands and lowered his mouth to hers.

Dillan wanted to look away. So much. But he couldn't tear his eyes from the awfulness of what he was seeing—Miska's hands on Sullivan's waist, Sullivan's fingers traveling down her shoulder, her arm.

He'd never seen her like this, flaunting everything, kissing a man she'd never mentioned, letting his hands run across her body. What had happened to Mark?

Forget Mark. What had happened to last night?

He couldn't watch. She was nothing but a skank. A whore. He stood, the contents of his box thumping inside, and started for his door, toward the couple displaying their immorality to anyone who happened to look.

She pulled back from Sullivan and peeked at Dillan.

He searched his keys. So she was embarrassed. Good. She should be.

Her voice was almost a whisper. "You coming in?"

Sullivan grabbed his suitcase. "Absolutely."

Dillan jammed his key into the lock, unable to keep from glancing her way. Miska had already disappeared, but Kendall sent him a wink.

Dillan set his jaw. He tossed the box beside his desk, then wandered into the living room. The windows beckoned him, and he took in their view, trying to empty his mind of what he'd just discovered. Of what he was pretty sure was going on next door.

The woman knew how to cast a spell on him, just like she had with Scheider and Sullivan. He rubbed his throat. It was amazing, really, how she could seem so innocent and sweet, all soft and safe around him. And the next day be opening her home to some other guy.

Some guy with boatloads of money.

His words from the night before came back to him, his warning not to waste herself on Mark. She had to have been laughing at him. She wasn't wasting herself on Mark. She was wasting herself on him and Sullivan and who knew who else.

She was disgusting.

And she and Mark and Sullivan—they could have each other. His fist fell against the window. He'd learned his lesson this time. She was a beautiful woman on the outside only. Inside she was all filth and perversion and—

He sighed. He was a fool. A stupid, stupid fool. From now on he'd keep his distance.

He didn't want any part of her.

When the front door squeaked open and Tracy and Garrett entered, laughing about something, Dillan still leaned against the window. He pushed off the glass and turned toward the recliner, hoping he looked busy.

"Dillmeister." Garrett set his briefcase on the counter. "What's up, bro?"

"Not much." He plopped onto the couch and flipped the TV on to SportsCenter.

"You eaten yet?"

"Nope."

"Everything go okay with Miska last night?" Tracy asked.

Oh, yeah. "Yep. How's your tire?"

"Between Garrett and your dad, it's as good as new." She sank onto the far end of the couch, water bottle in hand. "More sports. Do you watch anything besides sports?"

Dillan grabbed the remote and turned the TV off. Tossed the remote onto the coffee table.

Silence filled the room.

"Dill?" Garrett asked. "You okay?"

"Yeah." He cleared his throat. "Just—kinda bored."

Tracy watched him, eyebrows furrowed.

He stood, waved a hand at the TV. "You guys watch what you want. I've got stuff to do."

"Like?"

"Work. A run." Actually a run sounded good.

He slipped past Garrett and grabbed an empty water bottle. While he filled it, he heard Tracy whispering. He rolled his eyes. He just needed to leave.

No, he *needed* to calm down. Miska shouldn't be able to ruin a perfectly good day. How dumb was that?

Tracy picked up her bag. "I think I'll say hi to Miska, see what she's got going on."

"She's busy." Dillan snapped the cap onto the bottle. "She's... entertaining."

"Entertaining?"

"Oh, yeah. She and Kendall Sullivan seem very close."

Garrett cocked his head. "Kendall Sullivan?"

"That's what I said."

"Detroit's Kendall Sullivan?"

"Nice guy. Very friendly."

"Who's Kendall Sullivan?" Tracy asked.

"Basketball player for the Turbines."

"Another—another athlete?"

He could see it all coming together for her. "She's a classy lady, isn't she?"

"Are you sure that it's..." She held out a hand.

"Saw it myself, Trace." He glanced at Garrett who looked shocked— which was saying something. "She actually wears clothes for Mark. Kendall, not so much."

"So what..." Tracy sank back to the couch. "She's dating two athletes? Do you think—I mean, why? Do you think she's..."

He decided to say the words Tracy couldn't find. "Do I think she's prostituting herself? Absolutely."

"Dillan."

"What?"

"Don't be so hard on her."

"Come on, Tracy. I know you want to see her get saved and all that, but get real. This woman is so far gone."

"You don't know that. You don't know what's going on inside her."

"And you do? What's she said? That she's agonizing about which guy to sleep with? I'm beginning to wonder how much Mark's paying her."

"Dillan!"

He jerked his chin at Garrett. "Am I right?"

"Probably." Garrett sighed. "Tracy, a woman with two rich guys? You know what's going on."

"Yes, but you don't have to be so cynical about it."

"We aren't." Garrett's voice stayed calm. "A woman doing what she's doing? She's into it for money."

"But what about Mark? She talks about him all the time. This other guy doesn't fit."

"Yet he's right next door. Go figure." Why did he care? Why? "I'm going for a run."

In his room he pulled off his Bears jersey and tossed it in the hamper. He stared at his open closet, at the mix of T-shirts, button-downs, dress shirts, and suits. Why had he ever met Miska? He blinked, unable to move. *God, why?* He'd had every intention of forgetting her, of leaving her to her life and moving on with his. Like he'd told Tracy, she was too far gone. He'd known it from the moment he'd met her.

But he hadn't been able to avoid her.

Okay, that wasn't completely true. He'd run into her a few times, and he'd enjoyed her company and her looks enough that he'd allowed himself to run into her again, to pretend a friendship existed where none did.

At least she'd never propositioned him. Would he have been strong enough to resist that?

Well, he was now.

Against his will, he saw Miska standing in her doorway again, saw the scant clothing, saw Kendall's hands on her.

He gritted his teeth. It was his own stupid fault he was feeling this way. But he let the image play in his mind, branding into his brain who she was. What she was.

He wouldn't forget.

CHAPTER TWENTY-TWO

Miska pushed a kalamata olive around her plate while her father took another bite from his panini.

"Mmm," he mumbled around the bread. "Good."

She glanced across the crowded café. Tables were filled with people on lunch break and suburbanites enjoying a day downtown. In the corner a couple with two-year-old girls in ponytails scarfed their food while the baby boy banged his high chair.

What a life.

"Don't you like your salad?"

She looked at Dad. He'd polished off another three bites while her mind wandered.

"Told you the sandwiches are great. A little bread wouldn't hurt you."

"I'm not that hungry." She stabbed a forkful of lettuce and olives. She'd eaten too well while Kendall was in town—a different brand of average deep-dish pizza, a steak place, a sushi restaurant, and two breakfasts at a great diner. Not to mention the food at the hockey game.

She was thirty now. She wasn't burning calories the way she used to. She couldn't afford to put on a few pounds.

Which was ridiculous. She set her fork across the plate, not caring that it clattered. How crazy that a few pounds could make a difference between staying in her home and having to sell. How wrong.

She'd done everything she could to make sure Kendall had a good time, despite how sick it made her. Once, while he was on the phone, she'd thrown up in her bathroom and knew she couldn't do it anymore. When he'd said he'd be back in two weeks for game seven, she'd wanted to dash for the bathroom again. But he'd handed her his June payment, another ten thousand in cash, and said he'd bring the extra four grand if he came back.

Fourteen thousand more. Another chunk out of her mortgage. Another several months closer to the home being all hers. She could do it a little longer.

"You okay, Miska?" Fatherly concern creased Dad's forehead.

She smiled at him. "I'm thinking."

"About?"

"Just… work stuff."

"What's going on?"

"I'm losing an editing client in a few months."

"Ah. Have any new leads?"

"I've got feelers out. Too early to know, though."

"Something will show up."

"Right." Spoken like someone who wasn't affected by her forthcoming money woes. Maybe that fourteen thousand should go in the bank, just in case.

The thought made her instantly nauseous. Something would come along before things got bad. Hadn't they before?

Of course those things had been Mark and Kendall.

She shivered. She couldn't handle another man.

"They keep this place so cold. Here." Dad handed her his jacket. "This will help."

Arguing wasn't worth the effort. She draped the jacket across her shoulders. "Thanks."

"It's the least I can do."

The least he could do. Yes, there was so much more he could have done. Her sinuses tingled. Great. Nothing like crying in public. She pressed her fingertips against her nose.

"What is it?"

Her fingers fought back the pain. "I just wish you'd been there."

"Been where?"

"Everywhere I was. Everywhere Wade and Zane and Mom were. We were never a family." She stared at the couple in the corner, at the man playing got-your-nose with one of his girls. What would her life be like if her parents had stayed together? Then again, switch the gender on all the kids, and she could be looking at her own family months before it came apart.

Dad cleared his throat. "I've told you how sorry I am."

She dragged her gaze to his. Saying it once made it better? "You could say that every day for the rest of my life, and it wouldn't fix a thing. *Dad*."

"You'll feel better if you forgive me."

"How do you know?"

He shrugged. "Forgiveness makes a difference."

"Who did you have to forgive?"

He stared at his half-empty glass.

Exactly. What did he know about how she felt?

Her gaze wandered again to the happy family. The mom scolded a twin while she wiped the baby's hands. The man laughed and shoveled another forkful of pasta into his mouth.

What was wrong with her that she couldn't catch a man like that woman had?

Movement between her and the family distracted her. Her eyes adjusted.

A man in a dark blue suit smiled at her.

She blinked back. He thought she was looking at him? He raised his eyebrows, and she turned toward the other side of the restaurant, watching a handful of people leave through the glass doors. *Get the hint, buddy?*

"Miska." Dad wiped his mouth. "You don't know what my family was like."

"That would be because you've never told me."

"It wasn't *Leave It to Beaver*. Not even close."

"Who wants *Leave It to Beaver* anymore? Or do guys really wish their wives wore dresses and pearls while they made dinner?"

He studied her.

She sniffed, the pungent scent of olives and vinegar penetrating her nose. "I'm sorry. It's not been a good week."

"So I see." He went back to his sandwich, lips pursed, eyebrows raised.

Miska rolled her eyes. "I'm thirty. You don't need to treat me like I'm a smart-mouthed thirteen-year-old."

"Then don't act like one."

She shot to her feet. Her thighs banged the table, and the jacket fell. "I've got better things to do than listen to this." She grabbed her purse. "Thanks for lunch. Talk to you later."

"Miska—"

She held up a hand as she walked away, longing to break into a run. She ran her palm down the snug white sheath she wore and sucked in a breath. Looked like he wanted to make up for everything after all, including treating her like a child.

He had no right.

Outside, she stopped on the busy sidewalk, not caring that people had to veer around her. She breathed deeply the mix of lake-fresh air, car fumes, cooking oil, and tires. Ahead of her a horn honked, then blared. This she could manage. This she understood.

Her dad, she did not.

She turned for home, glancing in the restaurant's windows.

Her dad wrote furiously in a notebook.

She halted. He was writing? He hadn't bothered coming after her? But what should she expect? He'd chased skirts, never his children.

Someone stopped beside her. "Miss? You dropped this."

She forced herself to look away from her dad.

The man in the blue suit stood beside her. "Are you all right?"

"Yes."

He held out a white business card.

"What's this?"

He grinned at her, a dimple forming in one cheek. "You dropped this."

She had? She took the card. *Allen Carmichael, attorney—*

She threw the card to the ground. "I did not drop that," she snapped and marched down the street.

"Come on." He laughed, right behind her. "Don't be like that."

She whirled on him. "And what should I be like? Huh, Allen? You don't even know my name."

"Your dad said it was Mariska."

"My dad."

"He said you needed a good, stable man in your life. I saw the way you were looking at that family. I could give you that."

She jerked her finger at him, her whole body shaking. "My *dad* doesn't have the first clue about what I need. And you're definitely not it. So no thank you."

She spun on her heel and stormed away from a father who gave her name to strangers, from a man who wanted her just for fun, toward the home that was her haven—until she'd invited Kendall inside.

Until she'd invited Mark.

She dashed tears from her eyes. A horn blared in her ear, and someone jerked her back. She blinked at the cab that had been turning the corner, a foot or two from where she'd almost stepped off the curb. The front end of the cab still lurched.

"Watch where you're going," someone warned.

"Sorry."

The cab continued, the walk sign flashed, and she darted across the street. Another block and she'd be home. Safe in her apartment. Safe alone.

How she wished the man of her dreams waited there for her. *How was lunch?* he'd ask. *How's your dad?*

She'd tell him how he'd treated her, and he'd take her in his strong arms—well, one strong and one in a cast—and hold her close. And it would be all right.

Everything would be all right.

Except that it could never be all right. She'd seen the revulsion on Dillan's face. He knew now what she really was, how cheap and easy she was.

A man like him would never look at her.

She'd made a terrible, horrible mistake when she'd let Mark into her life. But how could she have known that the most perfect man she'd ever meet was thirteen months away from moving in next door?

What she wouldn't give to do those months over.

Safe inside her condo, she changed out of the dress and threw it in her hamper. She should burn it. Blue-suit man had appreciated it too much.

Blue-suit man…

She dressed, then called her father, ignoring his hello. "What are you doing, giving my name out to men?"

"Calm down, Miska. You make it home okay?"

"You mean did I get assaulted by Allen? No, I fought him off. Yes, I'm home."

He chuckled.

"It's not funny. I can't believe you told some stranger my name. You're supposed to look at every man interested in me like you're going to kill him."

"I thought you said you were thirty."

He had no *clue* how to be a dad. "When it comes to men, could you pretend I'm thirteen? Don't give out my name."

"I know Allen, some. We've had lunch together. He isn't a stranger."

"He is to me."

"You need a good guy, Miska."

"I'll find him myself, thank you."

"You mean Mark?"

"No." *No?* She sucked in a breath. "Could you do me a favor and just play Dad? Chase the guys away? Love me no matter what?"

"I'm doing my best, Miska."

She rubbed her forehead. Today his best was lacking. "I need to go."

"You know it's awfully hard to be a good dad when you didn't have one yourself."

So there it was. It wasn't his fault, just like it wasn't Wade's fault or Zane's fault that they couldn't make a marriage last. "You know, Dad, I'm sorry you had a rotten family life. I am, because I know what that's like."

"Don't throw that back at me."

"I'm not. Honestly. But don't you think someone needs to stand up and say enough? That it's time to quit passing on the mistakes of our parents? Don't you get tired of that?"

He didn't say anything.

"I have a nephew I never see because he lives with his mom who hates Zane's guts. And Zane thinks his son will be fine without him because he was fine without his dad. And I wonder what that little boy will grow up to be, what he'll do to a woman twenty years from now. And all I wish is that some man out there would step in and be his dad and show him how to be the right kind of man."

"Like I wasn't, you mean."

"It's the truth, isn't it?" She groaned. "I'm sorry. I don't mean to rub your past in your face. I'm just thinking out loud. Wishing I could make things better."

"Some things can't be fixed."

"But we can't give up on the future either." What did her future hold? True love? A hot, faithful man who'd love her no matter what? Could Mark be that for her?

What about Dillan?

She pushed that idea away. Dillan *would* be faithful to his wife, just like he'd said. She tightened her grip on the phone. "I really have to go."

"Miska—"

"No, Dad. I'll talk to you later." She hung up. Already she hated some woman she didn't know, some woman who'd end up with a crazy-tall, decent-looking guy who'd love her in ways Miska couldn't imagine.

If only Dillan had never seen Kendall. If only she'd never met Mark. If only...

She set the phone aside. "Enough," she whispered.

Nothing changed. Kendall's red silk duvet was still on her bed, the phone cord he'd forgotten still on her counter. He was still coming back. Mark was still coming back.

And Dillan—Dillan would never look at her again.

Chapter Twenty-Three

Miska was retouching her resume when the knock sounded. She glanced at the clock. Ten twenty-five at night. Who on earth?

Tracy stood outside, grinning. "Come with me. Hurry."

"Where?"

"There's no time. Come on."

Miska followed her.

Tracy opened the door to Dillan and Garrett's place.

Whoa. "Tracy—"

"Hurry up. Before he gets here."

Inside hushed chatter and laughter sounded from the living room. Around the kitchen corner, two heads popped into view, peering down the dark hallway.

Miska sniffed. "I smell chocolate."

"Surprise party for Dillan—and he's in the building."

The living room and kitchen opened up to over two dozen people crouching behind the island and furniture, tucked away in the kitchen or on the far side of the living room.

"He's going to hate this."

Cam chuckled from in front of the master bedroom door. "I know."

He scooted sideways. Miska tucked herself beside him, Tracy on her other side. In front of the windows, Matt and Jordan crouched behind the overstuffed chair.

Garrett walked into the living room from the main hallway.

Someone groaned.

"Sorry." He wiggled his eyebrows. "I blame the chili dog."

More hushed sounds of disgust spread through those closest to the hall.

Garrett sprawled across the couch and turned on the TV. "He'll be here any second. Grin and bear it."

Miska whispered in Tracy's ear. "I don't have anything for him."

"It's okay. We're just hanging out."

Did Tracy not know? Had Dillan kept what he'd seen to himself? "He won't want me here."

"So what? I do."

People near the hallway shushed, and she heard the faint sound of a lock turning. The door squeaked open, and Garrett turned in his seat. "Hey, man."

"Hey." The door closed. "Aw, Garrett. What's wrong with your bathroom?"

Dillan appeared, and people jumped up at him. "Surprise!"

He froze beside the island, his gaze flying around the room. People blew noisemakers and clapped, reached out to pound him on the back and tell him happy birthday. His look of shock faded to bemused acceptance. Miska hung back. She'd let him enjoy his friends before she wished him a happy birthday and left.

Garrett made his way behind the island and waved Dillan over. Two chocolate cakes, large circles of yumminess, sat on the counter.

Dillan gave a happy moan. "Is that what I think it is?"

"Portillo's chocolate cake? Yeah."

"Can it be my birthday every Friday?"

Miska smiled while the crowd laughed.

"Thank you all for coming. Have a safe trip home so I can be alone with my cake."

"Hey now," someone said.

He grinned. "Fine. I'll share."

Garrett raised a hand. "Since this is Dillan's last year in his twenties, we decided we should have a party for him before he gets his wheelchair and can't get around. Right, Cam?"

Cam gave him a thumbs-up. "Thank goodness for elevators."

People laughed again, easily amused at the prospect of cake.

Miska looked back to see Dillan's eyes shift from her to the cake, his easy grin gone.

Her own smile vanished. She shouldn't be here.

Garrett continued. "We thought about putting twenty-nine candles on the cake, but we didn't want to char the thing so…" He held up two fat number candles, one a two and the other a nine. He stuck them in the cake, the nine in front of the two. "Happy birthday, Dillan."

Around her people clapped and cheered. Miska clapped too as Dillan rearranged the candles. Someone started the birthday song, and she mouthed the words while Garrett lit the candles.

"Make a wish," Matt hollered, and Dillan pursed his lips, head tilted, and studied the cake.

Garrett crossed his arms. "Dude, wax is not a frosting."

Dillan blew out the candles. There was more clapping, more cheering. Loud chatter took over as people broke into groups, spreading throughout the tight space. Miska moved forward, intent on getting out of Dillan's sight, but Cam and two women blocked her way.

Someone grabbed her arm, and she turned. Jordan grinned at her. "Good to see you, Miska."

She doubted it, but Jordan's smile said it was the truth. "You too. Where's your man?"

She chuckled. "Don't you start."

"What?" Miska smiled. "Aren't you two a couple? He seems like a nice guy."

"He is, but… We were dating when he left for the Marines. That ended quickly. Then he calls me two months ago." She shrugged. "I don't want to go through that again."

"You seem like a smart girl. You'll be okay."

"Well, thanks, Miska. I knew I liked you."

Matt stopped beside Jordan, three cake-filled plates in his hands. "Ladies. For you."

"Thank you." She took her plate.

"Have you had Portillo's cake?" Jordan asked.

"Don't think so."

"Best stuff ever," she said around a mouthful.

As Miska ate and listened to Jordan and Matt, she studied the crowd. Tracy and Garrett stood by the refrigerator, talking with two other couples. A handful of unfamiliar faces mingled with people she remembered from Monday night. But how things had changed. Tonight no one sent curious looks at her and Dillan, because Dillan stood on the other side of the room, talking with Cam and three women.

Here, in this group, she felt invisible.

She shifted, aware that she was in Dillan's line of sight if he looked past the redhead flirting with him.

Instead he nodded and said something to her. She cocked her head, and he laughed.

"Miska?"

She turned her back to Dillan, shifting her gaze to Jordan. "Sorry. What?"

"I asked what you thought about coming to that Bible study Wednesday night."

Oh, gag. While the side effects of living the Bible way seemed okay, there was no chance she'd buy that stuff—and no way they'd want her, once they knew her like Dillan did. "Thanks, Jordan, but I don't think so."

She shrugged. "If you change your mind…"

The redhead Dillan had been talking to patted Jordan's shoulder as she walked by. Jordan lifted her fork in a wave.

Who was Dillan talking to now? "So was he surprised, you think?"

"Dillan? Definitely, and he's tough to surprise. We only pulled this off because we planned it last minute. He had a youth group activity tonight so we knew when he'd get back."

"Youth group activity?" She pictured a bunch of teenage girls with long hair, no makeup, and ankle-length skirts sitting in a circle, praying about something.

"Laser tag, I think."

Oh.

Jordan laughed. "What were you expecting?"

So Dillan wasn't kidding about her poker face. "I never went to youth group. Or church."

"Oh, yeah? You should come sometime."

No matter how nice these people were, she couldn't see herself talking about the Bible. Mom had had no time for it, and Wade and Zane had made jokes anytime someone mentioned it. Of course those two weren't any great representations of mankind either. "I'll think about it."

Jordan shrugged her acceptance.

Behind his sister, Dillan squeezed through the crowd, his back to Miska. Matt followed her gaze and smacked Dillan's shoulder. "Hey, bro."

Dillan turned, eyes on Matt. "Thanks for coming, man."

"Wouldn't miss it." He pointed at Jordan. "She wouldn't let me."

Dillan shot Jordan a smile. "I'm guessing you had a hand in this?"

"I plead the fifth."

"In other words, guilty."

Jordan stuck a bite of cake into her mouth and gestured helplessly.

"Right. Can't talk." Dillan shook his head. "Whatever." He moved on.

Miska stilled. He hadn't looked at her, hadn't even acknowledged her. She drew in a slow breath, hoping Matt and Jordan wouldn't notice the snub.

But they locked eyes onto each other. Jordan cleared her throat. Matt pressed his lips together and looked around the room. "Now where did—"

"Guys, it's okay." She should have expected this, but she'd hoped—though she hadn't known it—she'd hoped Dillan would forgive her. "He's got a lot of people to talk to. I'll see him later."

Jordan rested a hand on Miska's arm. "I don't know what to say. That seemed so rude, but that's not like him."

"I know." But he'd been rude. He'd treated her as if she didn't exist. As if she wasn't worth his time.

Was that how it was? That someone like her wasn't even worth looking at? Wasn't worth talking to? Was she really worthless to these people? If so, how long before Jordan caught on? Before Tracy?

The room swam. "I think I'll head out."

"Oh, Miska." Jordan's mouth turned into a heartbroken frown. "I'm so sorry. I'll beat him up for you."

"No." She forced another laugh, her throat tight. "Don't say anything. He'll feel bad."

"He could stand to feel bad."

"Really. It'll just make it awkward. I'm sure he didn't mean it."

"If you're sure."

"I am." The condo seemed too small. "You guys have a good night."

"You too, Miska."

She wove her way through the crowd. The handful of people blocking the door let her pass, calling goodnight. She smiled, waved, and slipped outside where the only sound was the muffled chatter coming from Dillan's place.

Dillan, the man who refused to look at her.

She raised her chin as she unlocked her door. If that's the way it was, then fine. Life was simpler without him, anyway. If he wanted to be left alone, that was okay.

Because she wanted to be left alone too.

Just her and her condo. Just her and the view out her window. She walked to it and stared at a sleeping Buckingham Fountain and the blackness that was Lake Michigan.

Only tonight the blackness didn't comfort.

CHAPTER TWENTY-FOUR

A nother night as a third wheel.

Dillan opened his bedroom door, letting it bump the wall to warn Tracy and Garrett that he was coming out. Not that they were the making-out type—well, Tracy didn't seem to be—but one never knew. In three months they'd be married. At this point waiting was probably difficult.

Garrett and Tracy sat on the couch, his arms spread across the top. He was saying something quietly as Dillan neared, and Tracy laughed, smacking his knee. "Stop it."

Garrett glanced over his shoulder, his carefree grin in place. "Dillanetics. What's happenin', man?"

"I'm hungry." He opened the refrigerator and scanned the contents. Milk, mayonnaise, ketchup, a mostly empty container of sour cream, half a sub, and a package of red grapes.

Nothing.

SportsCenter's bump music came on, a hockey clip playing. The second game of the Stanley Cup Finals had been tonight, but Sullivan didn't seem to be around.

Dillan tapped the counter. Forget Miska. He was here for food.

"Popcorn's above the microwave," Garrett said.

"Thanks. You guys want some?"

"We're good."

He set a bag in the microwave and started it, then leaned against the counter and watched the seconds tick by.

"Did you finish your cake?" Tracy asked.

"Ate the last piece for lunch. Sorry."

"I was just curious. Jordan said Miska had never had it before."

He narrowed his eyes. Amazing that there were things she hadn't done.

Why she'd been at his party made no sense. It had to be Tracy. Or Jordan. Or both. Those two didn't get why a guy wouldn't want her around. Fortunately, the packed condo had made it easy to ignore her, and he'd been relieved when he'd realized she'd left. The less he saw her, the better.

Some silhouetted woman was being interviewed on SportsCenter.

He should ask someone out, even though no one interested him. There was that new woman—Amanda, the redhead. She seemed nice. He'd better ask her quick before Cam got to her.

The popcorn had just begun popping when Tracy gasped. "Garrett, go back."

Garrett sent her a confused look. "Go back to what?"

She grabbed the remote and rewound the interview. When it played again, the voiceover was midsentence. "And she's not the only one making a living off professional athletes and talking about it. The writer of the blog *My Kept Life* makes her living off two professional athletes, both of whom think they're the only one."

The picture changed to a blog title's fancy red script.

"We asked her for an interview, but she didn't respond. Her blog only goes back seven months, but in it she details how she keeps these two lives separate and why she does what she does, the first relationship a romantic one while the second is purely business."

Tracy sagged against the couch. "That's Miska."

It did sound like her. Scary to think that there were others like her.

Garrett took the remote. "What do you mean it's Miska?"

"I mean it's her." Tracy shot Dillan a look of concern. "That's *her* blog. Miska's blog."

She blogged about it? He walked around the island. "Are you kidding?"

"Come on, Trace. How do you know?"

"It was on her laptop. She had the dashboard open, and I read the title."

Unreal. "So she tells the world about it? What a—"

"Don't you say it." Tracy aimed a finger at him, jaw tight. "You don't know what she writes. It's not what you think."

He snorted. "Right. It's all about her horrible guilt from living like she does."

Garrett cleared his throat.

Fine. Dillan opened the microwave and grabbed the corner of the bag. He'd shut up. He didn't want to talk about her anyway.

"So you've read it?" Garrett asked.

"Yeah. It's sad."

Sure it was.

Tracy spun in her seat. "But, hey, don't read it, okay? It's not—it's not good, all right?"

Finally. They agreed on something. He opened his popcorn bag. "Fine by me." He tossed a kernel into the air and caught it in his mouth. Ow. Hot. "You guys have a good night."

Adrienne moved the cursor over the play button on her laptop's screen. "Ready?"

"I guess." Miska eased onto a stool. Adrienne had called to ask if she could stop by after work. The request wasn't unusual—Adrienne usually called first—but this time she'd been serious. Somber. This wasn't girl talk.

The clip was from SportsCenter. The male host talked about women making a living off professional athletes by being paid safe-sex partners in a city the athlete routinely visited, being available only to them.

Miska shifted on her stool. Why was Adrienne showing her this?

The picture changed to a woman's silhouette, a woman who tweeted about her life with a pro athlete.

Oh no.

The interview ended, and her blog appeared on the screen. The host told how she blogged about her relationship with two athletes. How she hadn't responded to their requests for an interview.

When had they asked for an interview?

The clip ended, and only then did she realize she'd raised a hand to her mouth. Seeing her words splashed across a TV seemed bigger than anything she'd ever imagined. However many people had read her thoughts before, it had to be so many more now.

Adrienne minimized the clip. "A friend showed this to me. Did you know?"

"No."

"Have you checked your blog lately?"

"Not since Kendall—" She lunged for her laptop on the desk. Two days had passed since her blog had been featured. What could have happened in that time?

She set it beside Adrienne's computer and woke it. In a few moments she was at her latest blog post.

Comments were on.

She sucked in her shock. "Someone hacked it."

"What?" Adrienne leaned in to see.

Miska's fingers flew over the keypad. Her password had been changed, but she requested a new one. "I turned the comments off in January. People were one extreme or the other."

She logged into the blog's dashboard and scanned the information. Eighty-three comments beginning at eleven Sunday night. Three hundred and two comments today.

"What are they saying?"

She could read the first line of the comments as she deleted them. Offers to keep her company when her men weren't in town. Suggestions. Lewd, despicable, perverted things. She fought off a shiver as she deleted more comments. "Perverts. All of them."

"Men are gross."

These men were. She thought back to Eric. Allen. Kendall. Her fingers shook, and she balled them into fists and pounded the island.

"You okay?"

"I feel—I feel like someone broke in."

"You feel violated. I know. You need a good password, girl. A crazy difficult one."

She continued deleting comments. "I can't believe this. These disgusting people. Like they know me."

"They're not worth your anger, Misky. Delete them, change your password, and move on. Don't let them keep you from blogging." Adrienne grinned. "Think how many are listening to you now. Your following has exploded."

That didn't comfort.

"You need to track this. Get Google Analytics on there."

"They can't figure out where I live, can they?"

Adrienne shrugged. "I don't think so. What's your bio say? Just that you're in the Midwest, right? You'll be fine."

This, right now, didn't feel fine.

In a few minutes the comments were gone. Miska grabbed paper and pen. Time for a password they'd never expect from her—a Bible verse.

She Googled Genesis 1:1 and read it silently. *In the beginning, God created the heavens and the earth.*

Okay. How was she going to make this into a password?

Adrienne leaned over her shoulder, staring at the screen. "What are you doing?"

"I'm making a password they'd never suspect."

"I love it." Her sister laughed. "You should find a verse about adultery."

No, she didn't want to go there. "This'll work."

"Well, you look like you've got it under control." Adrienne closed her laptop and slipped it into her bag. "Let me know if you get hacked again. I know someone who can help you."

"You're leaving? You just got here."

Adrienne checked her watch. "Ten minutes ago."

"I thought we'd hang out. Get dinner or something."

"Sorry. I have plans. I'm already late." Adrienne hefted the bag onto her shoulder. "I just wanted to make sure you'd seen the clip. Good thing, huh?"

"I guess. Thanks."

"No problem." Adrienne started for the hallway, then paused. "I heard Relentless Hearts is closing. Don't you do a lot of work for them?"

Miska dropped the pen onto the counter. "Melissa told me last week. So it's been announced?"

"No, just rumored. What are you going to do?"

"Honestly I don't know. With Mark and Kendall coming, I'd forgotten about it."

"And I had to bring it up."

Miska shot her a smile. She'd have remembered soon enough. "Melissa's got three months of work for me."

"Three months? Could be worse. Could be none."

"Yes, well…" She whacked the pen against the pad. "Something will turn up."

"Good girl. You keep your chin up."

Like she had a choice.

Adrienne adjusted her bag. "I gotta go. Call if anything changes with the blog."

"Will do." Miska followed her. "Don't have too much fun without me."

"No promises." Adrienne opened the door. "I'm—"

Tracy stood in the hallway, her fist raised to knock.

"Well, hey there." Adrienne sent Tracy a patronizing smile. "Tracy, right?"

"Yes. How are you, Adrienne? Miska?"

"Oh, we're just fine." The fakeness dripped. "What are you doing here?"

What Adrienne had against Tracy, Miska would never know. "We're watching *Downton Abbey,* season two. You want to join us?"

"How quickly you forget that I have plans."

Let her think that. "Next time."

"Absolutely." Adrienne sent Tracy another sickening smile. "You two have fun. I'll see you later, Miska." Adrienne waved her manicured nails and slipped into the hallway.

Tracy stepped inside. "She does not like me, does she?"

Miska motioned toward the living room. "Adrienne doesn't like a lot of people. Don't take it personally."

"I don't." Tracy pulled the DVD case out of her purse. "So are we ready? To find out what happens with Matthew and Mary?"

Miska followed Tracy around the couch and sank onto one end of it, feet tucked beneath her. "What do we watch after this? Season three?"

Tracy's smile faded. "I have an idea of something to do, but—well, I think it's an awesome idea. I'm not sure you will."

"Tracy, I refuse to go skinny dipping in Buckingham Fountain."

Tracy's eyebrows rose. Her mouth fell open, and laughter erupted.

Miska joined in.

"Oh. My. Goodness." Tracy ran her fingers through her hair. "That would draw a crowd."

"Like I said. Ain't happening."

"Good, because climbing in to give you a towel would be awkward. Plus we'd both get arrested." She shuddered. "Moving on. Here's my idea." She took a breath and squared her shoulders. "We should read a book together."

"Fiction? I'm not big on non-fiction."

"Well, I was thinking..." From her purse she pulled a thin paperback. "We should do a Bible study together."

Miska eased back. The title read *John*, and a man's name sat low on the cover.

"I used to be right where you are. I thought the Bible was boring, outdated. Then I came to a point where I needed something beyond myself." Tracy set a hand on Miska's knee. "Miska, I think you're there."

Whatever she thought of this book, the concern and love in Tracy's eyes made her pause. She wanted to say no, to get the book out of sight. But Tracy had become a true friend, a friend who hadn't thrown her away when she'd deserved it. A friend who seemed as steady as her dad was unsteady. Everything she'd seen in Jordan and Tracy and Garrett and Dillan—at least, before he'd seen her with Kendall—all of that made her hesitate.

Maybe this book made them the way they were?

Tracy held her gaze, almost as if she knew her thoughts.

No, she couldn't toss the idea out. Not without thinking about it. Tracy deserved that much. She took the book and stared at the cover, if only to have somewhere else to look. "Why, Tracy?"

"Because this is where it began for me. This book completely changed my world, Miska, and I wouldn't be any kind of friend if I didn't share it with you."

Her throat tightened. She turned to the back and pretended to read. "I'll think about it."

The truth, though, was that Tracy had already convinced her. Because what kind of a friend would she be if she said no?

CHAPTER TWENTY-FIVE

Iced tea in hand, Mark eased onto the overstuffed chair.

Darcie's image filled the great room's TV. Her wavy bob bounced around her jaw as she updated viewers on last night's fire. He hated to admit it since he preferred long hair, but the short haircut looked great on her. She'd said something about it bringing out her cheekbones. He'd agreed. What was he going to do, tell her to glue it back on?

He set his glass aside and grabbed the laptop off the matching ottoman. The screen showed the blog one of his teammates had laughed about, the woman who lived off two pro athletes. Evan had said he needed to find himself a woman like that to make road trips easier.

Initially Mark had ignored talk about the women on the SportsCenter clip, but when Evan wondered why a woman would take on a second man if she was in love with the first, he knew.

Revenge.

This Midwestern woman—could it be Miska taking revenge on him?

He ran through the evidence he'd accumulated so far. She was in love with the first athlete, who was married. The second athlete helped make ends meet, particularly the mortgage she was trying to pay off.

Miska had told him she'd bought more house than she could afford, but she hadn't moved—because he'd helped her, right?

The woman lived in a major Midwestern city on a lake. That could be Milwaukee, Chicago, Cleveland, Detroit. Maybe the Twin Cities?

Plus Miska loved words. He could see her blogging.

He scrolled back to the first entry. She'd just met a pro athlete who'd suggested a proposition that would benefit her financially. She debated because the money was amazing. A couple years with him, and she could be set. But she felt guilty because she loved another athlete, a guy who'd forgotten her.

That wasn't a match. He'd driven down to see her a good five times last off-season.

He read on. She'd accepted this second athlete's offer because the men's sports were in opposite seasons. She'd checked their teams' schedules and their paths wouldn't cross.

So the second athlete seemed to be a winter athlete. Basketball? Hockey?

Which meant the first athlete had to be a baseball or soccer player.

How had he missed that?

He grabbed paper and pen from Darcie's desk. He read on, writing down everything that fit. Her love for her city; Miska thrived off Chicago. The foot and a half of snow that had fallen January eighth; Milwaukee and Chicago had each received close to eighteen inches of snow; Detroit, twelve; Cleveland, nine; Minneapolis, three.

Okay, it was Milwaukee or Chicago.

Her guilt over the second athlete seemed to fade as he continued reading. Either she didn't care anymore or she was falling for him.

Darcie's voice interrupted.

Mark scrutinized her banter with the weather guy. Did she seem overly friendly? Or was he reliving the past?

The most recent blog entry was May 22. The woman wrote about her first close call, one athlete coming on the heels of another. He tried to think of anything that stood out from his last visit to Miska. What day had he arrived?

His calendar stilled him. That same night.

He read her words again. *You won't hear from me for a while. They're coming in one after another, something I was sure would never happen.*

Okay, this was something concrete.

He checked Chicago's NBA schedule. They were playing Cleveland in the playoffs, but the games had been in Chicago while Mark was there. Once he left, the series went back to Cleveland. A quick check of Chicago's soccer team showed they'd been playing on the East Coast.

So it wasn't Chicago.

Relief rushed through him. He fell back against the chair and chuckled at the ceiling. See? He'd worried over nothing. It wasn't Miska.

So what city was this woman in?

Milwaukee's NBA team was out of the playoffs. And they didn't have an NHL team—

Chicago did. And they were playing Boston for the Stanley Cup.

In a few keystrokes he pulled up the schedule. Game one of the Finals was May 28. A day and a half after he'd left Chicago.

He stared at the screen.

Was this woman seeing a hockey player?

He studied the schedule again. His shoulder throbbed, and he tried to work his fingers deep into the muscle the way the team's trainer did. Stanley Cup games three and four, yesterday's and tomorrow's games, were in Boston. Games five and seven were in Chicago.

It could still be Chicago. It could still be Miska.

He re-read her texts. The word choices seemed similar, the style like the blog. But he was no expert. He could be seeing a match because he was paranoid.

Was he paranoid?

After Darcie flirted on local TV? After she took advantage of his schedule? He remembered pitiful glances from the clubbies. Oh, yeah. He was paranoid.

He scrolled through the blog again, scanning a line here, another line there. There had to be something—

The fountain outside my home turned on today. Every spring I live for this day. It's like a fresh start, a promise that the cold and bleakness of winter are gone. A promise that from now on it's all sunlight and lake breezes.

The date was the end of his first road trip to Chicago, the Thursday he'd left. The time posted, 1:15 p.m.

He'd been at Wrigley Field by then. Miska had been on her own.

What're you looking at?

Buckingham Fountain. Isn't it beautiful?

He'd surveyed her instead.

He propped his elbows on his knees. Blew out an anguished breath. It had to be Miska.

And it sure sounded like this second guy was taking better care of her than he was.

He rubbed the sides of his throat.

On TV Darcie talked about a near-drowning on Lake Michigan. She'd almost left him for her old weather guy, some twerp five inches shorter than him who looked decent in a suit and tie. Not good. Decent. Some loser who'd only wanted her because of who she was married to.

And Miska?

She'd sold herself for money—something, frankly, that he could understand. Wasn't he with Darcie for the same reason? His money?

He scrolled through the blog posts, rereading the ones that talked about her guilt over athlete two. He tapped a finger against the laptop. Before he did anything, he had to be certain. He had to make sure it really was Miska.

He stretched his shoulder, pantomimed his pitching motion. The sharp jolt of pain was still there. He'd had worse. He could play through this, still be seventy percent.

But perhaps it was time to tell the trainer about the injury he'd been hiding. Miss a start, take a few days off, and figure out exactly what Miska was doing—and with whom.

CHAPTER TWENTY-SIX

"Dude, you read it yet?"

His brother's words made no sense. Eyelids drooping, Dillan glanced up from where he filled the dishwasher before calling it a night. "What?"

Garrett leaned against his bedroom doorway. "Miska's blog. You read it?"

"No. Tracy said it wasn't worth reading. I already knew that."

"It's not that. She wrote about you."

He closed the dishwasher and dried his hands on a towel. "About *me*?"

"Oh, yeah. You made an interesting impression on her at one point."

"What'd she say?"

"That she *wuvved* you. Wanted to marry you."

Dillan tossed the towel at him.

Garrett snagged it, laughing. "Read it yourself. Tell me what you think."

"Give me something."

Garrett waggled his eyebrows. "Nope. Read it and see."

His sermon wasn't coming. Again.

Dillan stared at the computer screen, seeing the type but not registering it. Why was he having such a tough time? What was wrong here?

He shoved back from the desk and strode down the hallway to the windows in the living room. Far below, Buckingham Fountain calmly sprayed while tiny people meandered around it.

Pastor Frazier had asked him to fill in Sunday morning, to preach where he'd left off in 1 Corinthians. Dillan mentally ran through the passage, the first half of chapter six where Paul dealt with Corinthian church members suing other church members. That part was no problem.

It was the three seemingly out-of-place verses that ended the section, the verses that listed those who wouldn't inherit the kingdom of God—idolaters, adulterers, homosexuals, thieves, drunkards, and others. And then the final verse reminded readers of the letter that they had once been such people.

That verse always fascinated him. *Such were some of you*—until God got a hold of them. How cool would it have been to be in that church? To see idol worshipers, adulterers, and thieves changed into God-honoring people? How amazing would that have been?

Were any of them like Miska?

That sobered him.

He couldn't believe he'd fallen for her, a little. Then again, women didn't come much more beautiful or feminine than her. The farther he stayed away, the better, because he was weaker than he'd realized.

Now every glimpse of her reminded him who she really was, of the deep soul danger she represented. Every glimpse filled him more and more with disgust.

If he read her blog, he'd probably be even stronger.

"Garrett, you moron," he muttered.

He wandered back to his office, leaned against the doorjamb, and stared at the computer. All he had to read was the last month. If she'd written details about Scheider or Sullivan, well, he didn't need to read those.

He plopped onto his chair and searched for her blog title which had branded itself into his mind. Her blog was the first listing.

Her profile described her as a Midwest girl loving life in the big city, doing her best to make ends meet.

He snorted. *Buy a house in the suburbs and you won't have to prostitute yourself.*

The most recent entry detailed her two worlds almost colliding, something she'd never expected.

Whatever.

The next entry talked about the beautiful spring weather she wished she felt deep inside.

Oh-kay.

The third entry, "Wait For It," made him pause.

> *I confess I love a good historical romance, especially one set in the Regency or Victorian era when people were such prudes. So much potential for scandal makes for a fun romance. But I'm glad that's not how we live today.*
>
> *Can you imagine trying to get a good workout in a corset or petticoats? Or posting a picture on Instagram where you and a friend of the opposite sex are—gasp—touching and being shunned for it?*
>
> *Or actually waiting until marriage for sex?*
>
> *I've met someone who thinks we're still back in olden times. Who believes in waiting until after he says, "I do."*
>
> *That's right. Some man said that to me.*
>
> *We've all been told to save it. You know, wait until it's someone you really love, someone you can see yourself with long term. But wait until marriage?*
>
> *He tried to talk me into that view today. We had a nice, heated discussion about it and his views on how we came to be—that Adam and Eve story. The one that says God made everything out of nothing.*
>
> *He's the epitome of the religious nut. A pastor.*

Dillan clenched his teeth.

> *He says he's waiting for the right woman. In all his twenty-eight years, he's never had sex with a woman.*
>
> *I find that hard to believe.*
>
> *Would a decent-looking guy wait that long? He's all male, rather good-looking in an un-GQ way. Can carry on a*

conversation if you start it. Is into sports and running. A guy like that waits?

On the other hand, he's a pastor. A Bible thumper. A man who buys into all that nonsense. Not very manly if you ask me.

Let's be honest—have you ever seen a truly masculine man of the cloth? Look at what the Catholic Church has dealt with in recent decades, all those priests with gay tendencies, even as they denounce homosexuality and preach abstinence or marriage.

This guy wouldn't be the first to lie about having sex, would he?

Dillan growled.

So maybe he hasn't had sex with a woman. At least, not in a very long time. Maybe he's a gay man hiding it under the guise of waiting for—

Dillan stormed to his feet, stomped to his door, stomped back to the computer. What an idiot he'd been, what a fool to share the truth with her. Trying to give her answers. Trying to point her another way.

And here she was, telling the world he was gay.

Well, he'd had it with her stabbing him in the back, with her fake friendliness and questions. He'd call her on it.

He sent the post to the printer.

The hum of the machine pounded in his head. She deserved a piece of his mind. How smug would she be when she found out he knew what she'd written?

He pounded on her door, chest thumping with the speed of his breathing. "Come on," he muttered. He raised his fist to pound it again.

The knob turned.

Miska opened the door, her forehead marred by questions. "Dillan? What is it?"

"This." He held the paper in front of her, aware that he was shaking with anger. "This garbage you wrote on your blog."

She took the page from his hand and stared at it, backing up a bit as she read.

He barged into her hallway, letting her door bang behind him. "The things I could write about you. The way you pretended interest in what I thought. The way you asked me what you should do about Mark. And here he was, only one of your men."

"We had just argued, Dillan. If you bothered looking at the date, you'd remember this was right after you told me you were waiting."

"Well, you sure took it and ran with it. Wrote some great fiction there. Attached my name to it."

"I never gave your name."

"Tracy knew it was me."

"I'm sorry, but I never imagined you'd see this—"

"No. Really?"

"Dillan, you were an anomaly. I'm serious. I'd never met someone who believed this way."

"So let's mock them, huh?"

"Look, I'm sorry." She crumpled the paper. "I told Adrienne about you, and she said people like you existed."

"Yep. Put us in the zoo."

"Dillan, stop it. What do you want me to do? Right a retraction on my blog? Take it all back? It's a stupid blog. What does it matter?"

"What does it matter?" He took a step closer, relishing the way he towered over her. "You called me gay!"

"I was trying to make sense of it, and that was the only thing that fit."

"Are you *kidding* me?"

"Real men don't wait. Real men, in my world, don't make it to twenty-nine—"

"Like you would know a real man."

She rolled her eyes. "Here we go."

"You think Mark's a real man, that Kendall's a real man? Why? Because they use you?"

"It's how they make me feel, Dillan. They know how to take care of a woman—"

If he hadn't been mad before. "They're *using* you, Miska. Wake up!"

"Fine." She clenched her fists, stepped up to him. "Call it how you see it, I don't care. But a real man knows how to make a woman remember she's a woman—"

If that's what it took— He grabbed her shoulder, pushed her back against the wall. His mouth covered hers.

She caught her breath, her soft lips open in shock.

Good. He kissed her again, pressing against her to make his point.

Her hands settled low on his chest. Her lips moved against his.

Oh.

Oh, man.

His hand slipped to the wall behind her, flattening her curls.

Her hands slid up his chest.

He pulled back just enough to give himself a better angle, and she came with him, like metal filings to an industrial-sized magnet. He wrapped his good arm around her back as her hands glided up over his collarbone and neck. Her fingertips slipped into the hair around his ears, the length of her fingers blazing against his skin.

He groaned against her mouth. She was so soft, so much woman. And the way she responded— He didn't want to stop. He couldn't stop.

She stretched up against him, back arching beneath his palm. "Dillan," she breathed against his mouth. Her kiss turned aggressive. "Oh, Dillan."

His breath came even faster. He had to stop. He'd made his point. But he didn't want to let her go. Her body against his felt so amazing.

"Dillan," she groaned. He stumbled back a step, and she followed his movement again. "Let me show you. Please."

He pulled his mouth from hers. Show him?

"Let me show you how wonderful it can be."

What had he done? What was he doing? He raised a shaky hand to his hair, rested it on top of his head. *God, no. Please. No.*

"We can take our time. Go as fast or slow as you like."

No. No, he couldn't. "Oh, God," he begged, everything in him shaking with longing and shock. What was he doing? What was he thinking? To treat her like this? To touch her? Kiss her? He closed his eyes and backed away, his fingers clenching his hair. "Oh, God. Help."

"Dillan, it's okay. We'll just—" She grabbed his elbow, tried to pull it down. "We'll go slow."

"No!" He jerked away. "Get your hands off me."

"Dillan—" She reached for him again.

He frantically grabbed for her doorknob and yanked on it. The door flew open, and he raced the few steps to his door and banged it open. He slammed it behind him. Flipped the deadbolt.

Safe.

He sagged against the wall and stared at the thick white baseboards. His chest heaved as if he'd finished a set of sprints. He leaned over, hand pressed to his thigh. What was wrong with him? What kind of a man was he?

He swallowed. *God, what have I done?*

A knock sounded on the door.

He startled and stared at it.

"Dillan?" Miska called. "Will you open the door? Please?"

She'd come after him?

"Dillan, let me in."

He backed away.

The knob twisted. "Dillan!"

The woman had no shame. No remorse. No soul.

She knocked again.

He crossed to the far corner of the living room. Still he could hear her knocking. He opened the door to Garrett's room and slipped inside.

Shadows hung in each corner.

He closed the door and sat on Garrett's perfectly made, king-sized bed. He stared through the partly open curtains and catalogued the view—blue water, white boats, clear sky.

But all he could remember was Miska in his arms, her lips responding to his, her voice in his ear.

Let me show you.

CHAPTER TWENTY-SEVEN

Sitting uncomfortably on her hallway floor, Miska pressed an ear to her front door.

Voices, but they were going the other way.

She stretched her legs. Three hours had passed since Dillan had kissed her, kissed her thoroughly. She'd never imagined he'd look at her, much less kiss her, but he had.

Now he wouldn't open his door.

So here she sat. If she could catch Garrett before he talked to Dillan, maybe she could get inside the condo and make Dillan listen. He needed to know that she hadn't viewed him as gay for a long time.

Her laptop clock said seven.

Yawning, she set it aside and struggled to her feet. Of all the days for Garrett to get home late. Where was he?

Keys jangled.

Miska looked through her peephole.

Garrett stood outside his door.

She stepped into the common hallway. "Hi, Garrett."

He didn't look up, searching his keys instead. "Hey, Miska."

He seemed tired. Worn out. Sick maybe? "You okay?"

He glanced up. "Yeah. Fine. What can I do for you?"

"I just—" She had to pretend this was an ordinary coincidence. She shrugged one shoulder. "I had a question for Dillan. Is he home?"

"Far as I know. Come on in." He unlocked the door and pushed it open.

She followed him in.

Dillan sat in front of the TV, in navy blue sports shorts and matching Fighting Illini T-shirt. His hairy legs were spread, his forearms covering each arm of the chair. He stared at the TV as if he wasn't seeing a thing in front of him.

Good. He was still thinking about it.

Garrett stepped into the kitchen and hefted his briefcase onto the island. "Dill. Company."

Dillan's head turned, his eyes meeting hers. He jumped to his feet. "What are you doing here? Garrett, what are you thinking, letting her in?"

Garrett turned from beside the refrigerator, eyes wide.

Miska rounded the couch. "Can we talk? Garrett can stay—"

"No way. I want you out of here." He kept the chair between them, fingers gripping the seatback, eyes dark.

He couldn't be mad. "I know you didn't mean it, Dillan—"

"Get out."

"Don't you owe me a minute? After what you did?"

Rolling his eyes, he let go of the chair and marched around the far side of the couch.

She ran back the way she'd come, trying to cut him off before he escaped down the hallway. "Dillan!"

They made it there at the same time, almost colliding. She reached for him. "Please. Let's—"

He yanked himself back, hands up by his shoulders as if she were vile. Infected. "Don't touch me." He slipped past her. Another second and he was at the door, wrenching it open and rushing outside.

The door banged shut behind him.

Trash. Worthless. Her shoulders sagged. Her vision blurred. She pressed her fingertips against her eyelids. Was that how he viewed her? Scum? Tramp? Whore?

Garrett still stood by the refrigerator, mouth open. He blinked. Shook his head. "What was that?"

He'd hear it from Dillan eventually. Hear Dillan's side anyway. She motioned to the couch. Maybe Garrett would know what to do. "You got a minute?"

Night approached by the time Dillan returned.

Silence greeted him as he stepped off the elevator and turned down his hallway. He'd spent the last hour and a half in the gym. He needed a shower, but that could wait. First he had to pack, because in the morning he was leaving.

As he neared his door, he eyed Miska's.

It stayed shut.

Good. He slowly turned his doorknob and let himself in, then sneaked to his bedroom.

The condo was quiet. No TV. No NBA Finals. No ESPN. Where was Garrett?

He dug a suitcase from his closet and plopped it onto his bed. A stack of shorts went in one corner. He grabbed jeans and arranged them in another.

"What're you doing?"

He stilled at Garrett's voice behind him. Man, he didn't want to talk about this. But Garrett had seen him and Miska. Garrett wouldn't stop until he knew all the details. Like how good of a kisser she was, how far—

He dropped the last pair of jeans into the suitcase and stared at it.

Garrett sniffed. "You all right?"

"Yeah." He grabbed a handful of books from his nightstand.

"Miska told me what happened."

Garrett probably had her tell it twice, just to have details to lord over him. He shoved the books between his jeans and shorts. "Did she?"

"Yeah."

"Hmm." He crossed to his closet and grabbed sweatshirts from the top shelf. He tossed them at the suitcase, not caring that they fell half in, half out.

"What's with the suitcase?"

"I'm leaving. I'll stay at Mom and Dad's until I figure something out." Returning to his childhood bedroom made him sick. He wasn't running home, but he had to get out of here, away from her, and right now home was his only option. "Maybe Cam has a spare room."

"Don't go, man."

"I can't stay." He faced Garrett. "Not with her next door. Not with Tracy bringing her over and including her every time I turn around."

"That won't happen."

"Where have you been for the last month?"

Garrett stared at his feet. "Tracy won't be bringing her here anymore."

"So you already told her what happened. Awesome. Thanks."

"No." He straightened and shoved his hands into his pockets. "Tracy called off the wedding."

What? He stared at his brother. Just the night before, he'd seen them leaving the singles' group, laughing over something. "What happened?"

"She found out I was…" He shuffled his feet, rubbed his jaw line. "I was seeing Adrienne."

Dillan's eyes closed. *Aw, Garrett.* Suddenly he felt so tired and sick of it all. He sat on his bed, beside the suitcase, and propped his elbows on his knees, rested his head on his good hand. What a mess. And not just Garrett.

He was a mess too.

Garrett coughed. "Stay, man. I don't—" He cleared his throat. "I don't want to live alone right now."

Dillan doubled over, rubbed the back of his neck. He wanted to leave. Run. He had to leave, didn't he? He was weak. He couldn't stay.

But Garrett… Dillan wouldn't want to be alone either. Together the two of them could be tough. For a while. Then Garrett would be better and he'd have figured out another place to live.

Aching, he raised his head, stared at his open closet. "I'll stay."

"Thanks." Garrett pushed off from the doorjamb.

"Gare."

His brother looked back, eyebrows raised.

"I'm sorry."

Garrett quirked a shaky smile. "My fault."

Dillan watched him go. There'd been more to his "I'm sorry" than he'd been able to say, but Garrett hadn't caught it.

Later.

He set the books back on his nightstand. His Bible lay on top, and he flipped through it, the words merging in a smeared, unreadable line.

How had this happened?

He sniffed, blinked a few times. His Bible lay open to 1 Corinthians. He scanned the pages, reading here and there until a familiar phrase stopped him.

Such were some of you.

He backed up to the beginning of the chapter and began to read. Every single word.

Chapter Twenty-Eight

Her father's story was heartbreaking, though he tried to shrug away his abusive childhood as if it weren't that big a deal.

Curled up on her couch, Miska hurt for him. "I'm so sorry, Dad."

He held out his hands. "What are you going to do? Can't change it. Can't stop it. I guess we learn and go on." He rested an ankle on his knee and fiddled with his loafers. "Can I tell you something? Something you probably won't like?"

"Why would you do that?"

"Something you said the other day… I think it might give you hope."

"Even though I won't like it."

"You don't have to hear it if you don't want to."

Man, he was good at the guilt trip. "By all means, go ahead."

He scooted to the edge of his seat. "I helped one woman raise a child."

"You raised one of your kids?"

"No. Jake wasn't mine."

"Jake, huh?" Some kid who didn't share a drop of DNA had gotten his time while those who could donate an organ had not? "How long were you with his mom?"

"Until she died. Jake was fourteen when I met her. His dad was like my dad, cruel and evil when drunk—which he was a lot. We were together two years when she found out she had cancer. She died six months before Jake turned eighteen. She named me as his guardian and made me promise to raise him until he was of age."

"You were a single father."

He chuckled. "I hadn't thought of that."

"How is Jake now?"

"He's good. Just graduated from college. I went to his graduation."

Of course he did. "You're right. I don't like that some guy had four years with you, years he remembers. How is this supposed to help?"

"Remember what you said about your nephew, that you wished some good man would step in and be his dad?"

"Yes?"

"Well." He spread his hands. "I checked on him."

"You've seen Liam? How is he?" Almost five years had passed since she'd held his tiny body, four and a half years since she'd seen him rocking back and forth on hands and knees. After Zane and Lacey split, Lacey had cut the whole family off. They'd been—no, *she'd* been too wrapped up in her mom's final days to protest.

"Liam's fine. Tall. Looks like your mom. Better than that, he has a good dad."

"Lacey's re-married?"

"A year ago. Good guy. Loves Lacey, loves Liam like he's his own."

"Hates Zane."

He grinned. "We didn't go there."

She laughed. "How astute you are."

"Yeah. So it seems your prayer has been answered. Liam will be okay."

"I'm glad to hear that, but I didn't pray for him."

"Then your prayer was answered before you even prayed it."

What did he mean? "Do you believe in prayer?"

"Sometimes. I've prayed for things to happen, and they've happened. Other times I've prayed for things and—nothing."

"Which proves it isn't real."

"I don't think so. I mean, what is God? A genie? That's a slave, not a god."

Her heart beat faster. "Dad." She slid to the edge of her seat. "Do you believe in God?"

He looked out the window. "I think so. I look at people, and I'm pretty sure there has to be someone."

The possibility of a god out there, a god beyond her world, made her shiver. But if he *were* real, wouldn't it be best to find out? To know what he wanted?

How did she do that?

Her phone rang. The screen showed Tracy's picture. "You mind if I take this?"

"Go ahead. I need to leave anyway."

"Okay." She answered the call. "Tracy, can you hang on a sec?"

"Sure."

She pressed the phone to her shoulder.

Dad picked up the messenger bag he carried everywhere. "Thanks for lunch."

"Thanks for coming over."

He kissed her temple and left.

After the door shut, she raised the phone to her ear. "Tracy? Sorry. My dad was just leaving."

"I didn't mean to chase him away."

"You didn't. What's up?"

"I should have called earlier. Now you're working and—"

"Don't worry about my schedule. I can edit later."

"Really? I was praying you'd say that. Can I come over?"

Tracy had prayed she'd be free? If God were real, then he'd just listened to Tracy, had just said yes to what she'd prayed.

What had she been thinking before Tracy called? Wondering how she could know if there was a God, if he were real.

"Miska? I don't have to come over now—"

"No, you do." She relaxed her grip on the phone. "Now is perfect."

"I'll be there in ten."

Tracy settled onto Miska's couch. "It doesn't look like you've heard."

Miska set her glass on a coaster. "Heard what?"

"That Garrett and I broke up."

Miska's mouth fell open. She grabbed Tracy's hand. "Oh, Tracy. No! I'm sorry."

"It's all right. I did the breaking up."

Why? "Are you okay?"

The question filled Tracy's eyes, and Miska ran to the kitchen for a Kleenex box. When she returned, Tracy was wiping beneath her eyes, blinking rapidly. She grabbed a tissue and dabbed at them. "I can't believe there are still tears."

"We're women. There are *always* tears."

Tracy laughed, a sniffle interrupting it. "Sadly, that's true." She folded the Kleenex, sniffed, and squared her shoulders. "Okay. Garrett's been seeing Adrienne."

"What?" Miska rose up on her knees. "Adrienne? My sister?"

"Yep."

If Adrienne was involved, then— "By seeing, you mean…"

"Oh, yes." Tracy looked out the window. "You got it."

How could Adrienne have done this? "Tracy, I am so, so sorry."

"It's not your fault. I knew you'd have said something if you knew."

She was definitely going to say something. "How did this happen? When?"

"All those evenings he had to work? Came home for dinner, then got called in?"

All those nights she and Tracy had spent together, becoming friends, her sister and best friend had been destroying the couple. Miska pictured Adrienne hunched over her phone, texting someone, then telling Miska she had a date. All that time…

"Remember the night my car had a flat?"

"He stayed with Adrienne."

"He did."

Miska sagged against the cushions. "I don't understand it. Adrienne hates men. She's not the kind of girl a guy brings home. Why would he do this with her?"

Tracy looked down.

Was it because they were waiting? Was that what she was going to say? That if she could do it over, she wouldn't make Garrett wait?

Don't say it. Tracy was right; Dillan was right. They *had* to wait.

The really good men did.

"You asked me once what Garrett's past was. If you knew, it would make sense."

"What *is* his past?"

Tracy rubbed her forehead. "I'm so mad at him, I don't even care. He was in a sex club in law school. A couple underage girls got in and cried rape. It was big news out there. Garrett was just fortunate that he'd never... been with them. But a couple friends were arrested. It shook him up. Made him think. Or so he said."

If that's how he was, Garrett and Adrienne were a better match than she'd thought.

But what about the night Miska'd propositioned him, the night he'd been a perfect gentleman? "I don't—I don't get it."

Tracy grabbed another Kleenex and blew her nose. "Don't get what?"

"You were three months from getting married. How could he throw that away?"

"If not Adrienne, it would've been someone else."

"How do you know?"

"There've been warning signs. He's been—he's not the man I met." Tracy grabbed another tissue.

It popped out of the box, leaving an empty hole.

She leaned over the box and peered inside. "Really, Miska? Three Kleenex? Three?"

Miska stifled a giggle. Tracy met her gaze. Her lips tightened, and she burst into laughter. Miska's own laughter erupted, and they doubled over, laughing until they hurt.

By the time they calmed, tears streamed down their faces. Miska found another Kleenex box, and Tracy made a show of pulling out the first three tissues, finding a fourth, and nodding in satisfaction. The laughter began again.

"My stomach." Tracy wrapped an arm across her middle. "Between crying and laughing, there'd be room to spare in my wedding dress."

The comment killed Miska's giggles. "How did you find out?"

"I had yesterday off. " Tracy set the Kleenex aside. "I decided to surprise Garrett for lunch since we never get to do that. So I went to his building and waited in the lobby. I heard his laugh and looked up, and there he and Adrienne were, coming out of the elevator." She sniffed. "He had his arm around her, and they were rushing, like they were in a hurry."

They probably were.

"By the time I got outside, they were getting in a cab."

"Where'd they go?"

"A hotel. Honestly, I'm surprised the driver didn't get in an accident."

Miska closed her eyes. *Adrienne...*

"I spent the afternoon cancelling everything but the church because that would get back to Dillan before I could get to Garrett."

"Good thinking."

"I went to his building and waited until he left work. And you know what got me?" She sat up, her finger pointing. "He walked right up to me, that stupid smile on his face, and tried to give me a hug."

"I wish I could have seen you light into him."

"Oh, I did. I'm not necessarily proud of it now, but I let him have it, right there in the lobby." She flopped backward. "It was horrible."

Miska shook her head. Adrienne had messed with relationships before, but she'd never done it to one of her friends. "Wait until I get a hold of her."

Tracy shrugged. "He was ready for some woman, any woman. I see it now. I don't completely blame Adrienne. It's not like she forced him."

Still.

"When I met Garrett, he was only months removed from the club, from seeing his friends arrested. He was quiet, serious." Her smile gave away the ache she felt. "He was where I'd been, way back in high school. I hurt for him."

"You wanted to fix him."

"Maybe. I knew how different my life was. I wanted it for him, but now I wonder if he's just like he used to be, you know? Over the last few months—since we got engaged really—he's been changing."

"How?"

"Comments he makes, innuendos, jokes. Trying to go farther than we'd agreed to."

Wasn't that how guys were?

Not Dillan.

She thought back to his kiss, to the way he'd seemed to pray for help right before he left, seconds after she'd been so sure she'd be his first.

Oh, God. Help.

Dillan never said God's name like that. Never. His words were a prayer—and his prayer had worked.

Did that mean Garrett hadn't prayed? Or that if he had, he and Tracy would still be together? That didn't seem fair.

But then there was Tracy's prayer that Miska would be free—right when Miska wondered about God. "Tracy, do you believe in prayer?"

"Yes. Why?"

"How does it work? Or does it work?"

"No, it works." Tracy tore the corner of her tissue. "Miska, God is my heavenly father—a perfect father—and prayer is how I communicate with him. So every time I pray to him, talk to him really, I know that the answer he gives will be what's best for me."

"Okay, but how do you get what you want?"

"Prayer isn't about what I want."

"But you prayed that I'd be free today. And the other day Dillan prayed—" She squeezed her hands together. Couldn't go there.

"Dillan prayed what?"

"He prayed for something, and it happened. Right away."

Tracy raised her eyebrows.

"I know. I didn't catch it until today—I didn't realize he was praying. He just… said something."

"Here's how it works." Tracy's eyes, dry and clear, focused on her. "When we pray about something, God says one of three things—yes, no, or wait."

Dillan had prayed for help, and a second later he'd been out of her arms, racing for his place. "What determines the answer?"

"What's best for us. What God's will is."

"God's will."

"Like when Garrett's grandfather passed. We prayed that God would heal him."

"What was wrong?"

"Just old age. He'd had a third heart attack. We prayed for healing because they didn't want to see him go. But at the same time, they knew he'd be in heaven. He'd be better off there. So we prayed, 'God, heal him if that's your plan,' knowing that it might be God's will to take him to heaven."

"So your prayer didn't work."

"No, it did. We made our request known, but at the same time it was with the idea that God's will be done. Our prayer for his healing was for us, so he would be here longer. Eventually we all die. In his case, he'd lived a long, full life. His body was weak. What was best was that he went home to be with God."

Miska held her lip between her teeth. She thought of Liam, of Tracy's prayer that she'd be free to talk, of Dillan's prayer for help.

Help to get away from her.

It had been answered. Which meant what was best for Dillan, God's will for Dillan, was to keep away from her.

Her nose tingled. Her eyes filled.

"Miska?" Tracy grabbed her hand. "What's wrong?"

She shrugged. How could she say it? Tracy would probably agree. She wasn't good for Dillan. Wasn't right for him. God, if he were real, had made that clear.

"Honey. Tell me."

How calm Tracy was, how concerned for her when twenty-four hours ago she'd caught her fiancé cheating. Miska shook her head again. "I can't."

Tracy studied her.

Now her nose was running. She held out a hand for the Kleenex box. Tracy passed it, and Miska pulled out three tissues, nodding when another popped up.

Tracy smiled.

Miska blew her nose and dried her eyes. "I shouldn't be crying."

"Miska, can I tell you something?"

She balled the tissues. "What?"

"Do you know I prayed about you? Before we even met. And God said yes."

She swallowed, that annoying tingle returning. "What did you pray?"

"That you and I would be friends. That I'd be able to tell you about God."

Here they were, true friends, and she'd listened to Tracy talk about God more than once. "Why would you pray that?"

"Because I knew you were lost."

She closed her eyes. How true that was. "I'm tired of feeling lost, Tracy."

"I know."

"How does God fix that?"

"He fixes it by making us his child. We humans who rejected him, who sinned and cut *ourselves* off from him—for us God sent Jesus to pay our punishment. On our own, we're heading for hell. But when we accept Jesus's sacrifice and give him our lives, then we become God's child—and we realize how free and safe we are, that everything we've been searching for was in him, *was* him."

"And that's why he's home?"

Tracy smiled, tears in her eyes. "Exactly."

God, are you real? Miska closed her eyes. This was crazy, talking to someone who wasn't there. But it had worked for Tracy, for Dillan, the people she respected most in the world. She swallowed her uncertainty. *Tracy's starting to make sense. Is that because... you're there?*

CHAPTER TWENTY-NINE

Feet propped on top of her headboard, back flat on the mattress, Miska prayed to whoever was out there that this phone call with Mark would go well, that they'd both sense they were right for each other. "How's your shoulder?"

"Bad, and I'm just resting."

News about his injury had hit the media Friday afternoon. The article she'd read said he'd had two MRIs, one with contrast and one without—whatever that meant—revealing mild strain in some muscle.

"When did you throw last?"

"Wednesday."

"That's three days ago."

"Yep." He sighed. "Not good."

"You're worried?" He'd sounded so calm before. Maybe it was more serious than he'd let on.

"It's not the usual pain, you know?"

"Can't say that I do."

He chuckled. "You know what the good side of this is?"

"What's that?"

"I can come see you."

Her feet slipped off the headboard, and she pushed herself upright. "Oh. Umm—"

"You okay?"

"Sure. I just— Hang on." She opened the drawer of her nightstand. "Sorry. I'm getting my calendar out."

"Why? You busy?"

"Actually, yes." Where was her Mark-and-Kendall calendar? "Lots of editing."

"That's great. Last we talked you were losing a client."

She mashed her lips together and made a fist. Right. "Still losing them, but I'm overbooked right now. Trying to make money while I can."

"You've got to have a few free hours."

She found the calendar and flipped it open. "I'm swamped, Mark."

"Miska." He groaned. "I want to see you. What about Tuesday?"

Kendall was arriving that noon for Wednesday's game. "Tuesday doesn't work."

"Wednesday?"

"No. Not Thursday either. I have a big deadline that day."

"What book?"

Seriously? "You know I can't talk about them."

He sighed. "What about Monday?"

"This coming Monday?"

"Yeah. If I head out when Darcie leaves, I can be there by ten. We can order in. I can leave by one."

She squeezed her eyes shut. She had to make it work. "Monday should be okay—"

"Oh, wait. Got a meeting."

Relief spilled through her. Having them here so close together was risky. She needed to end things with Kendall.

But the money…

"Miska?"

She startled. "I'm here."

"Did you hear what I said?"

"Yes. Monday doesn't work. Sorry I'm so busy."

"I'll have to settle for thinking about you."

She smoothed the hair on the back of her head. He sounded okay with her no. "If I get my work done early, I'll call you, okay?"

"Please do. Hey, Darcie's back. Gotta run."

They hung up. She lowered the phone and let gravity pull her across her bed. That had been close.

But she'd prayed. *How'd that go, God?* What answer fit best? Yes, no, or wait? And how long until she found out?

CHAPTER THIRTY

When Dillan came in from his run Wednesday morning, Garrett stood in the living room, knotting his tie and watching SportsCenter. "What's it like out there?" Garrett asked.

"Kinda cold, actually." Dillan wiped his forehead on his sleeve. "For June, anyway."

"I hear it's summer in the 'burbs. We should visit Mom and Dad."

"Maybe they'd feed us."

"That'd be spectacular."

Behind the TV, something thumped against the wall.

Garrett stilled. "What was that?"

"Got me."

He muted the TV. "Sh."

A faint voice broke the silence. A man's voice—angry, raging. Another thud. Another sound. A cry?

Dillan stiffened. "Miska?"

They dashed for the door.

Garrett reached the hall first, only to freeze.

Dillan slammed into his back. "Garrett—"

Mark Scheider slumped against the wall but jerked upright at the sight of them.

Sounds of a fight filtered into the hallway.

Dillan tried Miska's door. Locked. "Who's in there?"

"Kendall Sullivan. I walked in on them—"

Something shattered. Miska screamed.

Dillan shook the knob, threw his shoulder against the door.

Garrett kicked it. "You call the cops?"

"No. No cops."

"Are you kidding?" Dillan pounded the door. "Call them now!"

Garrett held out a hand to Mark. "Hey, your keys."

Dillan flung himself against the door.

"Your keys!"

He spun.

Mark stared at Garrett.

What was the matter with this guy? "You coward! You got in there, didn't you?"

"She can't have us both. She has to learn—"

Garrett rammed Mark against the wall. "Gimme your keys. Before I take them."

Mark dug them out of a pocket.

In seconds Garrett unlocked the door. "Call the police," he hollered.

Dillan pushed him forward, and they raced inside.

The living room looked trashed—Miska's desk toppled, a lamp shattered beside it. An end table destroyed, her coffee table flipped—

Beside the master bedroom, Kendall jerked Miska up.

"Hey!" Dillan hurdled a toppled chair, relishing the startled expression on Sullivan's face. Garrett went around the couch, and Sullivan dropped Miska to face them.

Blood streaked her face.

Dillan got to him first. He grabbed Sullivan's shirt and shoved him into the wall.

Sullivan swore, fists flying.

Dillan blocked his right hand, but the man's left got past his casted arm and connected with his cheek. Pain flashed through his vision, and he stumbled back. He blinked away the sting in time to see Sullivan double Garrett over.

That was *it*.

Sullivan turned to him, throwing another right hook.

Dillan let it fly by, then drove his fist into the unprotected side of Sullivan's face. The blow rocked through his hand, but it sent Sullivan toppling to the floor.

Gritting his teeth, his hand throbbing, Dillan hauled Sullivan up.

The man's head wobbled. He wasn't a threat anymore.

Behind him Garrett coughed. "You okay?"

"Yeah."

"Nice job. What'd you do there? Trip him into submission?"

"This clown didn't know he was fighting a lefty. Isn't that the first rule, Sullivan? Know your enemy?"

"And here he thought he was fighting a woman."

Sullivan shook himself.

Dillan let go. "You're a real catch, beating her up like that."

The loser wiped his nose with the back of his hand. "What do you know, huh? Or maybe you've slept with her too." He glared at Miska, curled in a ball in the doorway. He called her a name and kicked her leg.

Dillan grabbed him again, plastered him against the wall.

Sullivan's head banged the doorway's trim, and the man grimaced.

Pleasure soared through Dillan. "Do it again, Sully. Let's see how you leave then."

Sullivan raised his hands in silent agreement, Dillan let him go, and the man eased away.

In her bedroom doorway, Miska pulled herself to a sitting position, bent over, shoulders shaking. A red slice glared across her exposed back. Only then did what she was wearing register, a silver, lacy spaghetti-strap nightgown with a low back.

And probably a low front.

The bed's silky red comforter caught his eye. He stepped past her, tugged it free of the sheets, and draped it around her shoulders.

She clutched it tightly.

In the living room, Garrett spoke to Sullivan.

Dillan searched her bedroom for anything that belonged to the creep. A closed suitcase sat tucked into a corner. Men's shoes lay beneath one corner of the bed. Dillan lugged the suitcase to the living room and tossed the shoes after it.

"His wallet's on the dresser."

Dillan studied her, huddled beneath the comforter. "You okay?" he asked.

She nodded.

"Anything else I'm missing?"

She raised her head to look.

Dillan sucked in a breath at the bruise forming on one cheek, the blood that had spilled from her nose and split lip, the space where tears had washed her face clean.

"No," she whispered.

He shouldn't feel sorry for her. She'd caused her own mess. What did she expect from sleeping with two athletes? For money? He grabbed the wallet and walked into the living room.

Sullivan stood by the island, zipping a tablet cover.

"He about done?" Dillan asked.

Garret nodded. "He's cutting it close, don't you think? Cops have got to be just outside."

Sullivan sulked as he jammed his feet into the shoes. One eye was swelling shut. Huh. Right where he'd nailed the guy. He'd done good there.

"Dill, whatcha got?"

"His wallet."

Sullivan jerked his head up and reached for the wallet. Garrett snagged it first. "What do you pay her, Sully?"

He growled his answer. "None of your business."

"Hmm." Garrett pulled out a stack of plastic. "Let's see. We got a Visa. Two Visas. Oh, look, Dill. His library card—"

Sully snatched the wallet. Still holding the cards, Garrett propped his hands on his waist and cocked his head like he was appalled.

Dillan snickered.

"Give me my stuff."

"You pay her?"

"I told you it's none—"

"Miska." Dillan glanced over his shoulder. "What's this guy owe you?"

She shook her head.

"What about damages?"

"I'm done with him. I want him gone."

Good. "You heard her. Get your stuff and get out before the—"

"Cops get here." Sully snatched the plastic. "Yeah, right. What cops?"

True. They should have been there by now.

He took a few steps toward Miska, and Dillan stepped between them, ready for him to try it.

Sully grabbed the suitcase. "I'm leaving. You can have your whore."

Garrett tsked. "And what you did here doesn't make you a whore?"

Sullivan shot him a deadly look.

"Dude." Dillan waved a hand toward the hallway. "Go already."

Sullivan straightened and started to leave, swaying a little. Garrett followed, Dillan behind him. At the door, Sully flashed them an obscene gesture, then left.

Classy guy.

Dillan caught the door before it closed and poked his head into the hallway. Sullivan vanished into the lobby. The rest of the floor was silent. Empty. "That idiot Scheider left without calling the cops."

"Figures. Hey." Garrett nudged him. "'Dude'? Really?"

"Works for you."

"It does. Thanks for having my back."

"You too. Let's not do it again." He stepped over the remains of Miska's desk, something crunching beneath his shoes.

Miska glanced up at the sound, then ducked her head.

She was ashamed. Or embarrassed. Or... something.

He crouched before her, where she could see him if she wanted to.

She kept her head lowered and sniffed, wiping the corner of her eye.

What could he say to make a difference? "How's your nose?"

"Fine."

"You think it's broken?"

"No." She sucked in a deep, shuddering breath.

"Miska. Let me see you."

Slowly she raised her head. Tears pooled in her big, dark eyes. Her lip had started to scab over. The bruise on her cheek was already darker, discoloration sneaking up to edge her eye. She'd wiped the blood off her face—or tried to.

He pushed to his feet. She needed a washcloth.

In her bathroom Sullivan's toiletries were all over the counter.

He stared at the towel on the floor, the toothpaste-covered toothbrush that had fallen—or been thrown—to the tile. So this was what had been happening when Mark walked in.

He grabbed a thick cream washcloth from the linen closet and ran it under cold water. In her bedroom, he crouched before her again and offered the cloth.

She took it, her fingers shaky, and dabbed her face.

"He hurt you anywhere else?"

She ran the cloth over her lip, wincing. "I'll be fine."

"Miska."

She wiped the skin between her lip and nose.

Garrett stopped behind her. "How you feeling?"

"I'll be fine," she repeated, sounding robotic.

Garrett looked at Dillan.

He shrugged. "She's not saying."

"You tell her about Mark?"

She looked up.

So here was his power. "Haven't told her."

She tried to look at Garrett. "What about Mark?"

Dillan ignored her. "Where else do you hurt? Ribs? Back?"

"Dillan—"

"Tell me where you hurt."

She sagged. "My ribs."

"How bad?"

"Just bruised, I think. My leg aches. He kicked me."

He would have done so much more if they hadn't walked in when they did. "You know your back's got a bad scratch?"

"That's why it burns." She dabbed her mouth. "What about Mark?"

Garrett spoke. "We found him in the hallway, listening to you scream. Did he call the police? No. Did he unlock the door to let us in? No. He decided you needed a lesson. Nice guy, Miska. *Great* guy."

If the news upset her, she didn't show it. "What about Adrienne, Garrett?"

His tight mouth sagged. His crossed arms loosened until he tucked his hands into his pockets.

"You know she's bisexual, right?"

Dillan caught his breath.

"She hates men. Just likes to mess with them." She looked at his knees. "Why, Garrett?"

He glanced away, then vanished into the living room.

Miska went back to dabbing her mouth.

What a complete mess.

She opened up the washcloth, straightened it, folded it into a square. Studied it for several seconds. "Thank you," she croaked.

In the living room something thudded into a plastic trashcan.

"You're welcome."

She shook her head, gaze still on the washcloth. "My mom would be so ashamed of me. Of what I've done." Her face crumpled. Her shoulders shook and she doubled over.

Dillan scooted closer, putting an arm around her as if she were Jordan at six, crying over skinned palms. She shook against him, her forehead buried in his neck. He patted the comforter on her back.

She cried a minute longer, finally pulling back to wipe her face and eyes. She kept her head down, her hair a tangled shield.

"You need anything?" he asked.

"No."

"Something to drink? Eat?"

"You don't need to stay."

"Let me make sure you're okay. Can you get up?"

"I think so."

He offered her his hand.

She hesitated, then put her hand in his and held on. She clutched the comforter close as he helped her up.

Once she sagged against the doorframe, he set his hands where he thought her waist might be, steadying her. "You all right? You dizzy?"

She flashed a shaky smile. "I'm okay, Dillan. Really."

"Just being careful. Can't have you tipping over and landing on your face."

"That would be embarrassing."

He chuckled at her attempt at humor. Her good cheek flushed a little, and Dillan cocked his head. What was going on inside her?

"I need to sit."

He led her to the bed and helped her ease onto the edge.

"Would you get the robe on the back of my closet door?"

"Sure." He found a silky black robe and carried it to her. "This it?"

She nodded and started to rise.

"Hang on." She might have forgotten what she was wearing, but he hadn't. "Give me your washcloth. I'll rinse it."

In the bathroom he took his time running the cloth beneath the water, rinsing away the blood, squeezing the water out. Squeezing it out again.

When he returned, her room was empty. He found her in the living room, leaning against the wall, staring down at Grant Park.

In the kitchen Garrett tied a trash bag. He jerked his head at Miska as if to ask about her.

Dillan shrugged. *Time to go?* he mouthed.

Garrett nodded.

When Dillan looked back, Miska faced him. The morning light caressed her face, the bruise on her cheek morphing into clear, velvety skin. Her eyes seemed bright, large, fine, and the sun backlit her curls, glimmers of purest light sparkling through wild wisps of hair.

She looked so innocent. So perfect.

She took the washcloth. "Dillan?"

"Umm—" Oh, right. "We're gonna go."

"Okay."

"We'll be next door if you need us." Somehow he'd gotten a step closer. Her neck lengthened as she looked up at him. "Do you need anything?"

Her voice was as delicate as her skin. "No. Thank you."

"If you do, just knock." He swallowed, realizing he was staring. "Have—have a good day."

What?

He swept past her couch. Behind him Garrett told her he'd left their cell numbers on the island. Not to open the door unless she knew who it was. Useful stuff. Careful stuff.

Dillan stepped into the hallway. No Sullivan. No Scheider. No losers. Scratch that. Just him.

Why did she affect him so much? Why? Just because he was still single? Hadn't he seen what she was? Known the things she'd done? How could a woman like her get to him? *How?*

Garrett closed her door. "You all right, dude?"

"Sure. Think she's okay?"

"Yeah." Garrett led the way inside their condo. "But it couldn't hurt to let Tracy know. She'd kill us if she heard about this later." Garrett hopped onto the granite island. "You mind texting her?"

"I'll do it."

Hands deep in his pockets, he wandered into his bedroom. He'd text Tracy, let her take over. Then he had to get his mind off Miska—for good.

He had work to do.

CHAPTER THIRTY-ONE

Four hours had passed. Mark still hadn't called.

Which was ridiculous. *He* should be calling *her*, if only to make sure she was alive. Was it true what Garrett had said, that Mark had stood in the hall and listened? Had he locked her door behind himself and then refused to let Dillan and Garrett in? Would Mark do something so low?

She slid her finger over his number. His phone rang four times, then went to voicemail. She ended the call and tried again. It rang four more times and went to voicemail.

Idiot.

She called again. The phone rang once. Twice—

Someone knocked on her door.

Miska stared down her hallway. Who was out there? Mark? Kendall?

The knock came again.

At her door, she peered through the peephole. It was Adrienne, texting someone. Miska's shoulders sagged. Not the person she wanted to see right now.

She unlocked the door and opened it, backing up to allow her sister inside.

"Hey, girl," Adrienne said, fingers flying across her screen.

"Hey." Miska slow-walked back to the couch. "What are you doing here?"

"I was free for lunch. Thought I'd stop by and—" Adrienne halted by the empty space where the desk normally sat, the barren wall scraped by the lamp Kendall had thrown. "What happened here?"

Miska eased onto the couch.

Adrienne turned to her, and her mouth fell open. "What happened to you?"

"Kendall."

"Kendall did this?" Adrienne flew to the couch. She rested a warm hand on Miska's leg. "He hit you? What happened?"

Her hand rose to the bruise she'd done her best to hide. "Mark showed up."

Adrienne groaned. "What dumb luck. Good thing he was around to stop Kendall."

"Mark left me with him." Understanding had dawned in Mark's eyes when Kendall had walked out of her bathroom. Mark had held up his hands and said he hadn't known, hadn't realized. He'd backed out of her bedroom—and she'd made the mistake of scrambling after him.

"You're lucky that's all Kendall did."

"What's lucky is that my neighbors stopped him before he killed me."

"Your neighbors…"

"Yes, *those* neighbors."

"Oh." A smile slipped across Adrienne's lips. "Good for them."

Good for them? "How could you do it?"

"Do what?"

"Don't play dumb. I know what you did to Tracy and Garrett."

Adrienne laughed. "That had nothing to do with Tracy—"

"She's my friend. How could you do that to my friend?"

"She wasn't your friend when it started. I didn't think—"

"Exactly. You don't think. You're just like Wade and Zane."

"Don't you compare me to them." Adrienne's neck tightened. "It's Garrett's fault Tracy got hurt. We were just having fun."

"Please. Since when do you have fun with men?"

Adrienne jumped to her feet. "Shut up, Miska!"

Her anger and hatred froze Miska. She stared at her sister, at the pinched features that conveyed her revulsion.

Adrienne stomped around the couch, her stilettos punctuating each step.

"So you're just gonna' leave? Can't handle being called out? You know it's true—"

Adrienne whirled. "Go look in the mirror, Miska. What you're doing to that poor girl in Wisconsin isn't any different than what I did with Garrett."

"You know it's not the—"

"Yes, it is." Adrienne stomped one threatening step closer. "The only difference is that you don't know her. She doesn't come over at night and watch stupid dramas with you. But you know what? I did a little research. She loves *Downton Abbey*, loves going to Milwaukee Bucks games in the offseason with her *husband*, and hopes to start a family with him. So if anyone here is doing something wrong, messing around with a *married* man—"

Miska clenched her teeth. "Stop it."

"If anyone reminds me of the loser men in our family, it'd be you. Just like your brothers. Just like our father. Aren't you?"

The insult stole her breath. "I am not."

Her phone rang, the ringtone Mark's. She glanced at the screen, then up at Adrienne.

"It's him, isn't it?" Adrienne stormed away. "Enjoy your bruises, Miska. You've earned them."

She ignored the words, waiting for the door to close.

Adrienne banged it shut, one last bit of drama, and Miska answered the phone. "Mark."

"Hey."

Holding her breath, she waited for him to apologize for leaving her to Kendall, for standing outside and listening.

But he didn't.

"Did you really stand in the hall and let him hit me?"

His hesitation proved it. "Of course not. I heard you half a second before those two came out."

"Then what took so long?"

"I don't know. I guess we all panicked. You know how it is. You're in a hurry and your fingers don't work."

Liar. She sighed and rested her head against the back of the couch.

"Are you okay?"

"You mean how badly did he hurt me?" She traced the mark on her thigh, the one starting to resemble a heel. "I look like a battered woman. How's that?"

"Sorry."

That was his apology? "Why were you here? I told you I was busy."

"Whoa! What about the man in your bathroom wearing your towel?"

"He doesn't mean anything to me. We're done. I told him to get out."

"Then *why*, Miska, was he there?"

The agony in his *why* warmed her. Mark cared. He wanted her. "It was... money, Mark. That's all."

"Money."

"I thought we were over. I met him, and he made me this—" She swallowed. "This offer."

Mark said nothing.

"It was just so I could handle my mortgage. You know how I struggled—"

"Which is why I took care of you!"

"I know. You have, but back then I hadn't heard from you in a month. I thought you'd chosen Darcie. When you came back, he was just a safety net."

His laugh was harsh. "So it's my fault you were with Kendall."

"I messed up, Mark. I'm sorry. Please. I don't want to lose you."

"You telling him the same thing?"

"No!" She bolted upright. Pain shot across her ribs, and she winced, covering them with her palm. "Mark, I want you. Only you. Please believe me."

"I don't know."

A tear rolled down her cheek. Too bad he couldn't witness the reality of her pain. She sniffed the tear away. "I've felt guilty every second with him. Give me another chance."

He let out a deep sigh. "I don't—I don't know."

No. She wanted to beg him again, plead with him to forgive her this wrong. Another tear rolled down her cheek, and she swiped it away. *Oh God, please don't let him go.* How would she make it without him?

"I think we should just…" He sighed again. Dread pooled in her chest. "We need a break."

"Mark—"

"Don't argue with me."

"Please don't—"

"Miska," he snapped.

She folded in on herself, silencing her tears with her hand.

"I need to think things through, see if we really love each other—"

"Mark, I do love you."

"I need time, okay?"

She fought the panic. "How much time?"

"I don't know."

"Then I'll call you—"

"I don't want you calling me. At all. You got it?"

At all? "But, Mark—"

"We need a break. *I* want a break. If and when I'm ready, I'll call you. So no matter what happens—got that? No matter. What. Happens. Don't call me."

So this was the end. Here she sat, bruised and hurting, while Mark walked away.

"Don't call me," he repeated.

She ended the call. Silence was better than that.

Her ribs ached from holding back her grief, and she trudged to the kitchen for more ibuprofen. The mirror above the sink reflected an image she'd never seen. A scabbed lip, a soon-to-be black eye—no surprise there. But the rest of her, the part whole and unmarked, still seemed weary. Worn out. Almost—old?

He doesn't care about her. He wants one thing.

Just like that, they were done with her. They'd used her up, and now they'd find someone younger, fresher. Someone willing to do what they wanted—until they tired of them and threw them away too.

She set the cup down and stared deep into her sink. Dillan's words were prophetic, it seemed. He'd known what he was talking about, and she hadn't listened, not really. His words had seemed so foolish, but they'd been true, and she'd ignored them.

What was she ignoring now? What words of wisdom had she'd laughed off? How would life be different if she'd listened?

Mark watched his screen fade. She'd hung up on him. Now it was too late to call her back, to make himself plain. Had she caught what he'd said? Had she understood at all?

His teammate Nick grabbed a glove from his locker. "You all right, man?"

"Yeah." He had to convince Nick that it was really over. He forced himself out of his chair and set the phone in his locker. "Thanks for the advice."

"Any time."

A picture of him and Darcie sat beside the phone, the two of them smiling on a boat just off Maui's shores. He couldn't look at it and reached for an undershirt. Somehow he had to put all this behind him. For a while, anyway.

"Scheider." Nick fiddled with the glove. "You did the right thing."

He grunted. Didn't feel right.

"You can go home to Darcie and know you're not living a lie. It'll get better. Trust me."

Enough already. He yanked his shirt off, wincing at the pain in his shoulder, and flashed what he hoped was a sad smile. "You're right. Thanks for being here while I called her. I appreciate it."

More than he'd ever know.

Chapter Thirty-Two

The woman he'd kissed one week ago stood motionless at the edge of the fountain's pavilion.

Dillan pulled up behind her, a dozen white seagulls cawing nearby, and wiped his forehead on his sleeve. Coming to Miska's rescue yesterday had been one thing, but what about now? What was he supposed to do when they crossed paths?

Why was she even out here? She couldn't be running. He tried to follow her gaze. Across Lake Shore Drive there was nothing but lake. What was she doing, looking at all that water?

She wasn't thinking... was she?

He strolled her way, clearing his throat to announce his presence.

She glanced over her shoulder and smiled. Her bruised cheek looked worse.

He stopped beside her and shoved his hands into his pockets. "Morning."

"Morning. How are you?"

He should have asked first. "All right. You?"

"I'm okay. Just enjoying the view, you know?"

"Yeah." She wasn't just saying that, was she?

Silence settled between them. Dillan gnawed on his lip. He couldn't leave, as much as he wanted to. He needed to make sure she really was okay.

You need to deal with what you did to her.

He inhaled slowly, exhaled loudly. "Hey, I need to apologize."

She faced him, her expression startled. "For what?"

"For the other day." He swallowed. "When I kissed you. I—"

Chuckling, she turned away. "You're apologizing for a kiss? I don't think anyone's ever done that." She flashed him a smile. "Thank you."

"Sure."

"You remember that talk we had by the lake?"

"No."

"When you said men like Mark were after one thing."

Now he remembered.

"After yesterday I realized..." She searched his face. "You were right. You gave me good advice, the right advice really, and I ignored it."

He studied his shoes. What was there to say? *I told you so?*

"How's your cheek?"

"Hmm?" He looked up at her.

"Your cheek. You've got a bruise."

Her finger breezed over the spot where Kendall had landed one decent punch. "I barely feel it. How about your ribs?"

"Okay. Don't make me laugh, though."

"Then what do we talk about? When our childhood pets died?"

She wrapped her arms across her rib cage. "I told you not to make me laugh."

He raised his hands, a smile sneaking free. "Sorry."

"No, you're not. You've probably got jokes racing through your head."

"Want to hear them?"

"Only if they're groaners."

"Oh. Well. I got nothin' then."

She chuckled and hissed in a breath. "Dillan," she growled.

"You're easily amused."

She doubled over a little.

Oh. She wasn't kidding. "You want to sit down? There's benches by the fountain."

"Too far. Let's sit here." She eased onto the top step that led to street level.

Dillan sat beside her, a good two feet between them. *Now what?*

Her mouth twisted as if she wrestled with something. "I talked to Mark."

Of course she had.

"I called him. I know it made me seem desperate, but I had to know if he'd done what Garrett said."

"And?"

"He lied. He said he hadn't had time to go back in, that he couldn't make his hands work."

Yep. He'd lied.

"You know what really makes me mad? That I *knew* he'd locked my door on his way out. It won't lock on its own. So he purposely locked me in there with Kendall, made it so no one could help me." She ground her fists against her thighs. "And I still begged him not to end it with me."

So they were over. He stared at the water. She didn't see it yet, but Mark ending the relationship was a good thing. An extremely good thing.

"He told me not to call him. No matter what. He wants time to think. If he wants to see me again—*if* he wants me—he'll call, and I'm supposed to jump into his arms and pretend none of this ever happened."

She was surprised by this?

Her lips trembled. "Things were supposed to be different here. Better. All the bad that happened in the suburbs, none of that was supposed to follow me—"

Her wail erupted without warning. She doubled over, hands over her face, her ponytail flopping over one shaking shoulder.

People walking by stared. Good grief, *he* was staring.

He slid a little closer, unsure what to do. She buried her face in his chest, and reluctantly he put an arm around her.

Her sobs rang out, her agony on display for everyone to see.

A middle-aged woman left the sidewalk and walked toward them, her gaze moving from Miska to Dillan and back.

Like she could help. He tried to stare her off, but she kept coming until she stood on the step beneath them.

"Is she okay?" the woman asked.

Clearly. "She's fine."

The woman held her ground.

All right then. He pretended appreciation for her concern. "She just found out that her, uh, pet... pig has... rabies."

Against him Miska's sobs shook into something else. She raised her tear-streaked face. "My what?"

"Your potbelly pig. You know." He shrugged.

"Are you okay, honey?" the woman asked.

"No, but it's not his fault. He's helping."

He was?

The woman pointed to her cheek. "He do that to you?"

Oh, great—

"No." Miska straightened. "He's the good guy, but he makes me laugh when my ribs hurt. Make him stop."

The woman grinned at him. "Stop, honey."

"Yes, *honey*." Miska flicked his arm. "Stop it."

His skin warmed. "I'm just sitting here."

"Looks like you're in good hands, sweetheart. You lose the other guy and keep this one."

"Will do."

His face burned. The woman walked back to some man who'd been smart enough to stay by the street, and Dillan rubbed his stubble-covered chin. "Well, that was... awkward."

Miska laughed, sniffed, wiped her cheeks. "Ah, Dillan." Another sniffle and hiccup escaped together. "How I wish I'd met you first."

And now it was way, way past awkward. He looked away. "How I wish I could tell you a joke."

Miska forced her laughter into a smile while Dillan gazed down the street, his cheeks pink. She longed to curl into him again and feel the weight of his arm around her. It was almost enough to make a girl fake-cry.

He leaned forward, elbows on his knees, and stared at the lake.

She memorized his profile—the dark hair that stood thick and nicely messy across his head, his angled jaw covered in stubble, his broad shoulders and long arms, the curve of his bicep, and the muscles that pulled beneath the skin of his forearm while his fingers fiddled with his cast.

His head swiveled, and his eyes connected with hers.

Heat flashed across her face. She jerked her gaze away.

Now why had she done that? Why not hold his gaze and let him know she was interested?

Because he'll reject you.

Already had, actually.

His feet scuffed the ground, and she looked back to see him standing, one hand running over the top of his head in the gesture that meant he was embarrassed. He spoke to the fountain. "Think I'll head in."

Not yet. "What do you think about Tracy?"

He glanced down at her, his forehead lined. "Tracy?"

"I've always thought she was perfect for you." Not really, but she couldn't say she wanted him for herself. He'd avoid her completely.

"Not again, Miska."

He helped her up, and they headed toward the fountain. "You don't see the two of you together?"

"After she dated my brother? No."

"You can't hold their relationship against her. She's the sweetest person ever."

"Doesn't mean she's right for me."

"Then who is, Dillan? Or are you waiting for perfection? Because she ain't out there."

He stopped and looked down at her. Cocked his head. "Don't think I've ever heard you say 'ain't.'" He held the back of his fingers against her forehead. "You okay?"

She smacked his hand away. "Stop it. What's the matter with you that you can't find a woman?"

The sound he made was a cross between a huff and a laugh. "What's it matter to you?"

Just say it. She swallowed and looked past his shoulder. "I don't know."

"You starting a matchmaking business or something?"

Yes. You and me. She looked into his eyes, those brown eyes that made her feel like she actually mattered. "You and Tracy believe the same."

"There's more to it than that."

"Like?"

"I don't know." He turned toward their building, his pace slow.

"So what are you waiting for?"

"For God to bring the right woman."

"Define *right*. A woman who believes like you do? A woman who's waited?"

"Sure."

"Then where does that leave me?"

"What?" He stared at her, eyes wide.

"What about women who didn't grow up believing like you, who've done things they regret? They're not good enough now?"

"If you're talking about Tracy, I wouldn't hold something in high school against her."

High school mistakes—sure, those were the years where everyone was stupid. So that was forgivable. But now that they were adults and should know better... She fought the urge to tell him off. "Good to know."

He stopped again, fingers splayed on his hips. "I'm sorry," he said, his voice conveying how clearly *not* sorry he was. "Am I missing something here?"

"No." He would laugh if he knew how much she thought of him— laugh, or grimace in disgust. She couldn't handle either. "I'm going in."

"What a coincidence. Me too."

His sarcasm wasn't funny. As they walked, she kept her head down, but from her peripheral vision she caught the glance he sent her.

All she'd wanted this morning was to hide, to fade into the park where he wouldn't notice her, wouldn't make her long for him. She tugged her hair out of the ponytail and shook it, letting it cover her. Hadn't she been just fine enjoying the waves before he came over? Before he—wait, why *did* he interrupt her? She grabbed his arm, hauling him to a stop. "Why did you come talk to me?"

He sent her another confused look. "What?"

"I was fine all by myself this morning. You're the one who came to me."

"Umm, you were the one who smiled at me. Can't walk away from that. That's rude."

"Who suggested we sit and talk?"

He laughed and held his hands out. "What is this?"

His incredulous smile ticked her off. "Why were you watching me, Dillan? For real?"

"For real? You want real? Okay." He looked at the fountain, then back at her. "Because I wondered if you were thinking about killing yourself in the lake."

She sucked in her breath.

"Are we good now?"

"I was admiring the view. You ever do that? Watch nature because it's beautiful?"

He looked over her head. Shook his own. "My bad for being concerned. Next time I think you might be contemplating suicide, I'll keep walking."

"You think my life's so bad that I'd kill myself? Over Kendall? Over Mark?"

"I didn't know, Miska. Sheesh. Clearly I don't know you very well."

"No, you don't." She shook her finger at him, furious at all the signals he'd missed, furious that he'd only spent time with her because he feared for her life. "You are so stinkin' clueless."

"Agreed. 'Cause I have no idea what this is about."

"You idiot." She half-stomped, half-limped away. No, she wasn't done with him. She stomped-limped back, her finger in his face again. "Ever since I've known you, Dillan, you've intrigued me. More than any man I've ever met."

"Uh—"

"Don't interrupt. I'm not done."

He raised his eyebrows, lips pressed together.

"Did you even have a clue of the crush I've had on you? You made me wish I believed like you did, just so I'd have a chance with you."

His eyebrows lowered. His shoulders pulled back.

"And you wonder why you're still single." She smacked his arm, catching his flinch. "Well, pay attention!"

He stared at her.

Oh, honestly. "Just so you know, this is where any sane man grabs the girl who's confessed her feelings and lays one on her. But no, not you, because she has to be perfect—from the day she was born. Newsflash, Dillan. That isn't realistic. Not for me, not for you, not for anyone. So get over yourself."

His mouth fell open.

There it was. He knew how she felt. Still he stared at her, and her shoulders sagged. Now he'd avoid her for sure.

Like Kendall. Like Mark. Now Dillan. "And they say the third time's the charm." She turned for home. "See you." Not likely, but as he'd said, walking away would be rude. She trudged past the fountain, listening for his footsteps, waiting for him to say something.

Did he ever think about their kiss? The way she did? Did he ever wish things could be different?

She stopped and turned.

Dillan still stood where she'd left him, but he faced the lake now, both hands on his head.

What did that mean? That he was doubly embarrassed?

With a sigh, she turned back. Never before had she been ignored when she'd told a man how she felt. But it figured. The one man she wanted more than any other—he'd be the first to let her walk away.

CHAPTER THIRTY-THREE

News about Relentless Hearts came out Friday. Adrienne texted about an editorial opening at her house, but the pay wasn't nearly enough.

It was time to be honest. Man-money had kept her living on Michigan Avenue. There wasn't an editing job out there that could keep her here, not without Mark and Kendall.

The plan for the evening had been for Miska to meet Tracy at her place to go over that John book, but when her morning walk resulted in pain and stiffness, Miska texted Tracy.

She agreed to come over but would be praying feverishly that she didn't see Garrett.

Please, God. Don't let Garrett see Tracy.

"Are you feeling better?" Tracy asked after successfully avoiding him.

"Some, if I'm not moving."

Tracy pointed to her own cheek. "That bruise must be a doozy."

"It is. Honestly, though, the visible stuff hurts the least."

Tracy nodded, face sober. "I understand."

She did, didn't she?

They reached for each other at the same moment. Dillan's arms hadn't felt nearly this good. Being with someone who understood soothed like nothing else.

Tracy pulled back, wiping one eye. "I'm so sick of crying, you know?"

Oh, did she.

"I get so nervous before church. I'm afraid I'll fall apart in front of him and everyone else. How embarrassing would that be?"

Probably quite like Miska's confessing her feelings to Dillan.

"So far I've been okay, but seriously it's been by the grace of God."

The grace of God? After Garrett betrayed her for meaningless sex?

"I lost you, didn't I?" Tracy laughed. "My brothers say I talk too much, but talking things through helps me."

"So talk. How are you? Other than before your church meetings?"

"Work is fine since I'm busy. It's after work that's hard, when I come home and don't have plans for the night. No texts from Garrett. No wedding details. Nothing." She waved her words away. "But enough about me. What's going on with Mark?"

"Nothing. He ended it."

Tracy nodded.

"You think it's good he dumped me."

She sighed. "I hate that you're hurting. And I'm sorry for how things ended, but he wasn't good for you."

"Just because he's married—"

"Miska, he stood in the hall and *listened* while Kendall beat you. Dillan told me they could hear you, clearly, all the way out there. That he refused to let them in. He didn't even call the police. Kendall got off because Mark didn't call. How can you miss a man like that?"

"Can you blame him? He walked in, thinking he'd surprise me, and here was this other man. What would you have done if—" *Oh.*

Tracy toyed with her fingers.

Miska's face and neck heated.

"What I would do, Miska, is go to the person who betrayed me and call them on it, then end it. Don't justify how he acted. A good man doesn't do that."

"But you thought Garrett was a good man."

"To be honest, I had considered pushing the wedding back and evaluating things, but I told myself he was just tired of waiting, you know?"

"How do you think Dillan does it?"

"Does what?"

Why had she gone there? "How he waits? Do you think there's any chance he's messing around?"

"Dillan? No way. He wouldn't be able to look anyone in the eye."

"What if he just kissed a woman?"

"What, like some random woman?"

Did he consider her some random woman?

"Enough about Garrett. Did you read the first chapter of John?"

"I did." She picked up the paperback from the end table. "Trace, I'm just going to say it. This made me feel dumb. I don't get it."

"I remember. That's normal."

"Why?"

"Because you're looking at God's wisdom for the first time in your life. You've spent thirty years listening to the world's wisdom, and God and this world are enemies. What God says is right and honorable, the world says is wrong and disgusting. It makes perfect sense that when you first come to the Bible, it's going to confuse you. Even the Bible says it will seem like foolishness to those who don't believe."

The open book drew her eyes. "I don't know that I saw it as foolishness. Just confusing. Some of it made me stop and think, but I didn't think it was dumb."

"Show me what you connected with."

"Okay." She drew in a deep breath. *God, if you're real...* "There's this idea throughout of the world not knowing this light. Verses four and five—that the light shone in the darkness but that the darkness didn't get it."

Tracy opened her mouth.

Miska held up a hand. She had to get this all out if she was going to make sense of it. "But then verses ten and eleven really hit me. 'He was in the world, and the world was made through Him, and the world did not know Him. He came to His own, and His own did not receive Him.'" Miska lowered the book. She'd read those words over and over, wondering, then needing to understand them. "What does it mean?"

"It's talking about the world—all people—rejecting God, the one who created them. Then Jesus came, specifically in those verses you read, and his own people, the Jews, rejected him."

Miska read the words again. All these years, she, Mom, Wade, and Zane had scoffed at the idea of God. Was this talking about her? Had she rejected him? She certainly didn't know him.

But one comment from Dad, a month of friendship with Tracy, with Dillan, and she was beginning to wonder if her family had been wrong. "Can someone who hasn't known God, who hasn't received him, change that? Is it too late?"

"You're talking about yourself."

She nodded.

Tracy sucked in a breath. "Miska—"

"I'm just thinking."

"As long as you have life, you can have reconciliation with God."

Reconciliation? Had she wronged God?

"What else struck you?"

Miska scanned the verses. "Okay, this one—the language was beautiful. I don't understand it, but as a writer it spoke to me."

"Which one?"

She began to read, aware of the awe in her voice. "And the Word became flesh and dwelt among us, and we beheld His glory, the glory as of the only begotten of the Father, full of grace and truth."

"Do you know who the Word is?"

"That's one of the things that threw me. But when I read it here—" She closed her mouth and shook her head. How did she put into words this feeling she didn't understand, that these words were of utmost importance? "So the Word is a person?"

"It's Jesus, God coming to earth and taking on human form. Living on earth with us. Going through all the things we go through."

"Christmas."

"That's 'the Word became flesh.' But then it goes on. The Word dwelt among us. John's sharing his story. He was one of Jesus's closest followers. He spent three years with him, day after day. Eating with God in the flesh, talking to him, listening to him, learning from him. And what did he think of that experience? 'We beheld His glory,... full of grace and truth.'"

"So John and Jesus, the Word, were friends."

Tracy's voice rang with wonder. "Can you imagine?"

"What does it mean? Why is it so special?"

"It means that God loved us so much that, even though we'd ruined the world he created, he lowered himself to become like us. Think of it. A perfect God taking on the form of a lowly human, someone people didn't pay attention to. It's like—I don't know—Prince William taking a job cleaning toilets without the paparazzi following, without it being broadcast on the news. It was a great sacrifice, something God didn't have to do, something he was so far above."

"And he lived with them."

"He did. He ate, slept, was hungry. The Bible even says he cried over the death of a friend and the family's sorrow. He went through all the things we go through, quite possibly even the death of his earthly father."

Miska wet her lips.

"And then there were his own brothers who rejected him while he lived on earth. He was just their brother, they thought. He couldn't be God. So they didn't believe him until after he'd died, risen, and returned to heaven. Which means he understands rejection too."

Miska curled her toes. *The Word became flesh and dwelt among us.*

"What matters right now, Miska, is that you understand who God is. That he's this perfect, holy, wonderful, unchanging God who humbled himself to live with us so we could have a future with him. He's not a god who hates us, who relishes being a dictator. He's a just God who loves us more than anyone on earth ever could. And it wasn't just talk, Miska. He *showed* it."

He'd shown it? *Show me,* she begged. Her fingers trailed down the page. "Can we read it again? Now that I understand more?"

"Absolutely." Tracy began with that first verse, that the Word was there in the beginning, that the Word was with God and was God. That all was made through him and that he was life. And light.

And this time, it made sense.

CHAPTER THIRTY-FOUR

The parking lot at Tracy's church wasn't as full as it had been on Mother's Day. Miska parked near the entrance. Evidently Father's Day didn't carry the same church status.

Tracy hurried down the main stairs as Miska stepped from her car. "You made it. Any problems getting here?"

"Nope. Boringest drive ever."

"Yay, I think?"

Miska followed her into the auditorium which was starting to fill.

Tracy chose a row close to where Dillan sat on Mother's Day.

What would he say when he saw Miska? Anything? She looked around for him.

Instead, a guy in his mid- to late twenties walked into the row ahead of them, his eyes—and his smile—on her. He was a new face, someone she hadn't seen at the Fosters' home or at Dillan's party. His dark hair set off bright blue eyes. He stopped and shot Tracy a charming smile. "Hey, Tracy. How are ya'?"

"Fine, Ethan."

Miska shot her a look. She sounded annoyed.

"Thought I'd say hi to your friend." He held out his hand. "Ethan Doebler."

She shook it. "I'm Miska."

His smile widened, leer-like as if her name meant something. "Garrett and Dillan's neighbor?"

Who'd told him that? "I am." More importantly, *what* did he know?

"Cool." He nodded rhythmically. "I've heard about you. Plus Tracy mentioned you the other day."

"So you remember." Tracy glared at him. "I thought you forgot."

"Nah, but we have to make our guests feel welcome."

His smile reminded her of Eric. Of Kendall. She couldn't look at him. "What am I missing, Trace?"

Ethan shrugged. "She asked us men to leave you alone when you came."

What?

"Ethan!" Tracy's mouth hung open, her eyebrows fighting to connect.

"You didn't want her to know?" He winked at Miska, like they shared some secret. "Tracy's a bit extreme, isn't she?"

He was definitely in the category of Tracy's first Ethan. "I'm good with her extremeness."

"Yeah, well." He dropped his palms against the top of the pew. "We all love Tracy. She knows that."

Tracy snorted. "Did you need something?"

He flashed Miska that foul smile. "Wanted to invite you two to join us for lunch, if you don't have plans."

"Like I want to eat with Garrett." Tracy rolled her eyes. "Go away, Ethan."

He sent Miska another practiced smile. "I'll be in the back later."

"Mmm. Okay." No thanks.

When he was gone, Miska turned to Tracy. "He's appropriately named, isn't he?"

Tracy slapped a hand to her mouth. "Oh, wow. That never dawned on me." Giggles took over, and she slouched in her seat.

"He's awful."

"I know. I'm sorry."

"Is he why you told the guys to leave me alone?"

"Miska, dear, you are drop-dead gorgeous. You are—" She held up a hand. "Let me wax poetic. You are the ultimate fly zapper, and men are flies who cannot ignore you."

"Fly zapper? Really?"

"You don't like it?"

"Not much."

Across the auditorium, Dillan entered from a side door. Someone stopped him to talk.

"I wondered what was going on. I assumed they all had virgin radar."

Tracy choked. "Had what?"

"They all said hi and backed off."

But Dillan hadn't left her alone. He'd sat beside her, talked to her, run down the field with her on his back. "Every time Dillan talked to me at his parents' house, the other guys were watching, like something was going on. I get it now. He wasn't leaving me alone."

"Miska, I just wanted you to be able to focus on God. I didn't want some guy with romance in his eyes to distract you."

They wouldn't have, not with Dillan nearby. She glanced back at him.

He was gone.

She searched the auditorium.

There he was, walking across the front, and his eyes were on her—until her gaze met his. He looked down at his tie, up at the wall, across the room.

Yep, embarrassed. Wondering how to avoid her. What to say if he absolutely had to speak to her.

He set a book down a couple rows ahead of them. His ice-blue tie swung away from him, and he caught it with his palm as he straightened, smoothing it against his stomach. "Hey, Tracy."

"Morning, Dillan. How are you?"

"Good." He swallowed. "Thanks." His gaze flitted to hers. "Miska." Skittered away.

Her voice was weak. "Hey, Dillan."

He sped down the aisle, for someplace away from her.

Tracy fidgeted. "What is up with everyone this morning?"

"Nothing, Trace. He just got the message."

"Message?"

"About leaving me alone."

"I never told him to."

Tracy didn't have to, not when Miska took care of it herself.

The last savory bite of salmon melted against her tongue.

Across the table, Dad scooped up buttery sauce with salmon crumbs and a stray green bean.

It *was* a good meal.

He leaned back in his chair and plopped a hand against his stomach, his cheeks puffed out. "I am full. Very good, Miska. Thank you."

She smiled her thanks as she stood. "There's more."

"More? I can't. That was the best Father's Day dinner ever."

"I bet you always say that." She slid his card from the drawer in her new desk. "Here's the grand finale. For what it's worth." She held the blue envelope over his empty plate. "Happy Father's Day."

He stared for a moment before taking it, holding it with both hands. His thumbs slid across the envelope, just touching. Just... feeling.

"Dad?"

He slid the card out.

"I hope you like it. Took me forever to pick out."

"I can imagine." He sniffed, nose twitching. "I'm guessing they don't make too many thanks-for-waltzing-back-into-my-life cards. 'Hey, Dad,'" he quipped, "'you're the best absentee father ever. Happy Father's Day.'"

"That's terrible."

"You don't think Hallmark should jump on it?"

"No."

He read the inside of the card where she'd thanked him for risking contacting her. When he spoke, his voice was gruff. "Thank you, Miska." He closed the card and studied the front again. "You know what this is?"

"What?"

"My first Father's Day card."

Her breath caught. How could that be? "What about that kid you took care of?"

"Got a couple you're-like-a-dad-to-me cards. Of course the women bought cards—when I was with them—and signed the kids' names. But this is the first card I've received from one of my children."

No one else had remembered him today?

"I will treasure this forever, Miska. This means more than you know. More than I thought it could."

"Thank you." Her sinuses warned that they were going to overflow soon if someone didn't do something. She pushed her chair back and stood, grabbing empty serving platters. Oh, to not be a woman for a moment.

Dad spoke behind her. "Let me help."

"No, no. It's Father's Day. It's illegal, I'm sure."

He followed her to the sink, plate and silverware in hand.

"Have a seat, Dad. I'll take care of it."

"Let me help you. It's the least I can do after…"

After all the cooking she'd done. She turned the faucet on. Water splattered and landed on her cheeks. With the back of her hand, she wiped it away.

He craned forward to see her face. "Are you crying?"

She laughed. "The water got me."

"Oh." He set the dishes in the sink and wiped his hands on a towel, then nudged her with his hip. "I'll help. Then we can both sit and relax."

She let him take her spot.

He tossed her the dishcloth. "Wipe off the table, daughter."

With a smile, she did, finishing with a gaze out the window. Late afternoon sunlight shone golden across the lake and treetops. Peace blanketed her after a full day—a pleasant morning with Tracy, a glimpse of Dillan, words from the Bible that piqued her curiosity, and dinner with Dad.

A year ago, she would never have believed it.

Two months ago she would never have believed it.

She returned the dishcloth to the sink.

Dad did a double take. "What are you smiling at?"

She'd been smiling? "Just thinking. Life is good."

"Really?"

"Yes."

"Despite your client issues? Despite whatever caused that bruise on your cheek?"

Her smile fell away.

"You did a good job with makeup, Miska, but it's still there. What happened?"

She gripped the edge of the island. "I don't want to talk about it."

"Did Mark do that?"

"No."

His forehead lines deepened. "Who?"

She shook her head.

"Are you involved with another man?"

She couldn't help glancing away. Her gaze landed on the new desk, dark and sleek like her floors, the new lamp a faded red. "Not anymore." She kept her gaze averted.

A glass clinked against the sink. Silverware clattered.

"What about your neighbor, Dillan? Where does he fit?"

"He doesn't."

"No?"

"I see him some. He's nice to me when it's just the two of us." She blinked at the truth of her words. When they were around other people, he shunned her.

How had she not seen that? She rubbed her arms. His birthday party, then this morning at church. She remembered Ethan and his immediate awareness of her identity. Did she already have a reputation at Dillan's church? Was that why he avoided her? Because they knew—

"Miska."

She jolted at his touch.

But it was just Dad, eyes tight with concern. "You okay?"

Of course she was fine.

He pulled her to him, his arms enveloping her. A hug—the first she'd ever received from him. At least, the first that she remembered.

No way was she going to ruin it by crying.

She shoved her emotions down. Closing her eyes, she inhaled his scent—Polo and a warm, male body, the smell of a man who'd been outside, taking in the sun.

Then there were his arms around her—holding her close, holding her the way a father should hold his little girl. Holding her like she'd never been held before.

She wrapped her arms around his waist. "I'm glad you're here, Dad."

"Me too." One big hand rubbed her back. "Because nobody cooks like you do."

Laughing, she pulled away and smacked his shoulder. "Sweet talker."

CHAPTER THIRTY-FIVE

The beginning of the week flew in a haze of work, morning jogs, and that crazy John book, the one that wouldn't leave her alone. Between Melissa Leach's call on the last Relentless books and the steamy romance she was editing, verses kept popping up.

I am the voice of one crying in the wilderness: Make straight the way of the Lord.

Behold! The Lamb of God who takes away the sin of the world!

Jesus answered and said to him, "Before Philip called you, when you were under the fig tree, I saw you."

Because I said to you, "I saw you under the fig tree," do you believe? You will see greater things than these.

Greater things… What had Dillan seen? What had Tracy seen?

Miska texted Tracy verses that captured her, and Tracy explained the story John was sharing about this Savior who hadn't come to free them from Roman oppression but from the oppression of sin and its judgment.

She thought of Mark. Kendall. Had Jesus freed her from them? Was that what had happened?

A full week had passed since Mark told her not to call him. It was like he was gone, like he'd never been. Would he ever darken her door again?

Did she want him to?

If it meant keeping her home, yes. Mark was no Dillan—that was a given. He'd made a stupid move by letting Kendall beat her. A smart woman wouldn't take him back.

A desperate woman would.

His team would be in town late Thursday night, maybe early Friday morning, for a series with the White Sox. The real question was, would he stop by?

When you were under the fig tree, I saw you.

Did this God see her? If he did, then he knew all that she'd done.

The possibility made her dive back into her work.

Storms rolled in late Tuesday and lasted throughout the night, thunder rumbling comfortingly in the distance. For the first time since Kendall's attack, Miska slept well and woke completely rested.

Outside, rain poured. She dressed, grabbed her keys, and took the stairs to the seventh floor gym. The place was packed, every elliptical, bike, and treadmill filled. On two treadmills in the corner, Garrett and Dillan ran side by side. Garrett caught her eye and flashed five fingers. She nodded her thanks and picked her way through the machines until she was behind them.

"Hey," Garrett panted.

"Morning, Garrett. Dillan."

He jerked his chin at her.

They were flying on their machines, running as if they were racing each other. She listened to the treadmills' hums, to Garrett's and Dillan's pounding feet, watched their arms pumping—

Dillan's cast was gone.

He moved too much for her to get a good look, but his forearm was clearly pale and a bit scrawny. Her gaze trailed past his elbow to the tanned biceps and triceps that showed from his gray sleeveless T-shirt.

Something beeped, and they slowed their machines, Garrett slowing to cooling-off speed. He pulled his T-shirt up and wiped his face. "How you been, Miska?"

"Good. You?"

He shrugged. "Okay. Heard Ethan hit on you Sunday."

"Was that what that was?"

Garrett chuckled.

Dillan glanced her way.

"When'd you get your cast off?" she asked him.

"Yesterday."

"How's it feel?"

"Fine."

"Fine?" Garrett snorted. "You should see the broken dishes. He keeps dropping things. Says his arm's 'weak.'"

"Dillan? Rebuttal?"

"Dropped one glass."

"Then all that skin came off." Garrett shuddered. "You should have seen it, coming off in sheets—"

Dillan reached across the gap and shoved him.

Garrett kept his balance. "Seriously, sheets. I think that's the reason his arm is smaller. All that dead skin—"

"All right, all right. You're grossing me out." She remembered how disgusting Wade's leg had looked after his cast came off, how he'd chased her around the house, threatening to put skin crumbs in her hair until Mom yelled at him to stop.

"She look grossed out to you, Dill?"

Both watched her over their shoulders.

She wiped the smile from her face. "High school memory. I'm back."

Garrett's treadmill stopped, and he stepped off. "And I'm done. All yours."

"Huh-uh. Wipe that thing down."

"What?" He grinned. "Like you're not gonna get sweaty."

"It'll be my sweat. Not yours."

Miska stretched while he cleaned the machine.

When he finished, he held his hand out with a flourish. "All yours to dirty up."

She stepped onto the machine and programmed it.

Garrett left, stopping near the door to talk to someone. A woman on an elliptical eyed him.

Girl, he is not worth it.

While she warmed up, Dillan ran silently beside her, his labored breathing hard to ignore. She sped up to her favorite speed, then realized her feet and Dillan's were pounding the treadmill together. Just to be different, she slowed, but her forced attempt made her falter, and she caught herself on the rails.

"You okay?"

"Yeah. Just stumbled." She stood outside the tread and watched it whir beneath her. For once, she couldn't think of anything to say to him. What was the point? He didn't want to talk—

"Ethan hit on you, huh?"

She looked at him.

He was slowing his machine.

"He did. Seemed to recognize my name. Any idea why?"

"Nope. I avoid the guy."

Silence fell again, as awkward as the silence between Garrett and Dillan had felt right. She stepped back on the treadmill. "Tracy and I are reading John."

His treadmill stopped. "No kidding."

"You sound surprised."

"No, I mean—" He shrugged. "That's cool. What do you think of it?"

Verses that had come to be her favorite ran through her mind. "I like it. Frankly, it's raising more questions than answers, but—"

"If I can help, let me know."

Really? Where had this come from? Or was this what pastors did? Her burst of happiness dimmed. "Thanks."

"Any time."

He took the spray bottle off the wall, grabbed a wad of paper towels, and returned to the machine.

She lowered her speed. "Can I ask a question now?"

"Go ahead."

"We just finished the second chapter."

"Where Jesus turns water to wine and drives money changers from the temple."

She raised her eyebrows. He knew that? Just by her saying what chapter they were in?

He chuckled. "What's your question?"

"What was the point of all that? Especially the part in the temple? He seemed angry over nothing."

"Well, it wasn't nothing. The temple was where the Jews worshipped, and the money changers were in cahoots with the priests, forcing people to buy sacrificial animals at inflated prices. They needed to go."

"Why weren't they allowed to make money?"

"They weren't just making money. They were ripping people off, like a combination of collusion and kickbacks."

Interesting. "What was the point of the water to wine?"

"To prove he was God come down to earth. He came as an ordinary man, you know? Nobody special, they thought. But then there were his miracles—healing the blind and crippled, bringing the dead back to life—"

She raised her eyebrows.

"Keep reading. You'll get there."

"What chapter?" she teased.

He blew out a breath, searching the space between them. "Somewhere in the middle. Try eleven or twelve."

"You're messing with me."

"Am not." His smile created one of her own. "It's what I do all day. Study the Bible, learn what it says. Stuff like that."

"Huh." She'd seen Tracy's Bible. Big book. He knew where everything was? "So the water to wine was a sign that he was God."

"It was." He pursed his lips. "Anything else?"

"No. Thanks."

"Sure." He slung his towel around his neck and grabbed his empty water bottle. "Have a good day."

"You too."

He stepped around occupied bikes and ellipticals.

The same woman surveyed him, eyes darting up and down.

Miska turned up the speed and prayed for dry skies in the morning.

Miska was reading John?

Dillan leaned on the pedestal sink in his bathroom, staring at the mirror. First church, now a Bible study with Tracy. He would have bet money that would never happen.

Garrett's footsteps approached.

Dillan pushed off from the sink. Time to shower and scrape off the dead skin that kept flaking off his arm.

Garrett stopped in the doorway. "You got plans for dinner?"

"Probably not until after church. You want to get Chipotle?"

"Sounds good. I'll order it."

"Great."

Garrett didn't move.

"What?"

"Don't you think it's interesting? Miska being at church again?"

"I guess. Why? You gonna' ask her out? She is single."

"Dude, I'm pretty sure she's got a thing for you."

Dillan rolled his eyes and grabbed his razor.

"You wouldn't be interested if she became a Christian?"

"Would you marry a woman like her?"

Garrett blinked at him.

Oh. He scratched his arm. "Sorry, man. I didn't mean..." Sheesh. Foot in mouth.

"Guess my dating options are thin, huh?"

Dillan shrugged.

"No, it's true. I felt it when I moved back home, and, man, do I feel it now. Got to date the new women before they hear too much. I was going to ask Amanda out, but Cam—"

"Beat you to it?" Dillan grinned. "Me too."

"You like her?"

"No. I mean, she's fine. I guess I was thinking that if you ask them, they'll be the one."

"Got it."

Which sounded stupid, now that he thought about it. "You and Tracy are really over?"

Garrett rubbed the edge of the doorjamb. "I made a mess of it. She's done."

"No second chance?"

He shook his head, eyes thin, mouth twisted.

Despite the stupidity of what he'd done, Garrett had really seemed to love Tracy. Now he seemed… less without her.

"Did Pastor tell you we're meeting each week?"

Dillan raised his eyebrows. "No."

"Thursday nights." Garrett cleared his throat. His gaze stayed glued to the chipped doorjamb.

"Pastor's idea?"

"Mine. We've already met once."

"Good for you, man."

Garrett's shiny eyes met his, then slipped away. "I'm sick of struggling. Will you pray for me? That I kick this thing once and for all?"

Garrett had never asked him to pray. "I'll pray, man." Hard.

CHAPTER THIRTY-SIX

S o this was Jordan's and Tracy's Bible study.

A crowd of twenty- to thirty-somethings filled a roomful of metal folding chairs. Jordan and Matt sat in the back row, lost in conversation, and at the opposite end Cam sat next to the redhead from Dillan's party, his arm across the back of her chair. He lifted a hand in greeting, and Miska waved back.

Seated in front of Cam, Miska glanced around the packed room. Lots of familiar faces, but where was—

There. Near the front. Dillan sat hunched over, elbows on his knees and fingers linked while he talked with someone.

One of the men on the front row walked to the podium. "Guys, we're going to get started," he said, adjusting the podium's height.

The chatter dwindled.

"We're on chapter three tonight in our study guide, which also covers the third chapter of John."

Miska sent Tracy a puzzled look.

Tracy leaned closer. "We're studying John for the summer."

No wonder Tracy knew so much about the book. "Who's the guy?"

"His name's Austin. He's doing an internship. Why?" Tracy grinned. "You interested?"

Miska rolled her eyes.

Behind her Cam began reading about a man named Nicodemus who asked Jesus how he could be born again. Then Matt took over as Jesus asked this man who was a teacher of Israel how he didn't know these things.

Miska's finger stayed next to one of the verses Cam had read, and when the group finished the chapter, she went back to verse two and reread what this man had said—that they knew Jesus was from God because no one could do the signs he'd done unless he was from God.

Just what Dillan had said that morning—which meant this conversation was probably important.

The discussion began, people sharing answers to the book's questions and asking questions of their own. Concepts swirled around her, the idea of the world being condemned, of God sending his son so that anyone who believed could be free of condemnation.

God and Jesus had always been a swear word, an outdated lifestyle, but now she wasn't sure. Living like Dillan, like Tracy—where was the bondage in that? Tracy hadn't slept with Garrett which turned out to be a good thing, and Dillan waited for a woman who would be loved more than any woman she'd ever known. His waiting now seemed like the most wonderful thing ever.

When the discussion finished, they divided into groups to pray. Amanda—the redhead dating Cam—joined Tracy and Miska. People huddled together, heads bent close, voices rising throughout the room as they prayed to this God who was far wiser than anyone she'd ever met.

While Tracy prayed for Amanda's new job, for Matt's friends who'd just deployed, and for some other guy's sister who was away from God, Miska sent up her own frantic prayer—that somehow God wouldn't ignore her, that she'd be good enough for him, that he'd look past everything she'd done.

That somehow he'd give her a chance.

What *did* God think of women who slept with married men?

She'd always comforted herself with Mark's words, that the marriage was about to end. She hadn't been the one to break it up; Darcie had done that.

The truths she knew now didn't match Mark's story. They were trying to have a baby. They were known to go to NBA games. None of that sounded like a marriage about to end.

Had Mark been stringing her along? All this time?

More importantly, would he show up at her place tonight?

After giving her condo a thorough cleaning, Miska met Adrienne at a salon for a mani-pedi. Adrienne went on about a new author they'd signed, how good the book was, how great the sex scenes were, but the details didn't thrill Miska like they used to. All she could think of was what the poor woman would deal with when she was all used up and discarded. Because that's how it would end in real life. That's how it always ended.

Even with Tracy and Garrett.

So what's the point?

The thought hounded her. She picked up a Lou Malnatti's pizza on the way home, sans garlic, and bought an extra one for her freezer, just in case Mark wanted some.

While the pizza cooked, she watched SportsCenter for details on Mark's game in Colorado. It had gone into extra innings. She checked the clock. Another hour until his plane left, an hour and a half for the flight. She calculated time for the plane to be emptied onto buses, for the buses to reach the hotel, for him to get his room like he always did, and pack a smaller bag for her place. Four hours from now she'd know where she stood with Mark.

But where did he stand with her?

She still needed him. She hadn't felt the financial pinch yet, but give it another month, and she'd have to make some decisions. If Mark showed up, well…

She blew a deep breath against her fists.

Tracy had asked about her plans for the weekend. She'd answered as truthfully as she could, that it depended on Mark.

"Will you be safe?" Tracy had asked.

Mark wouldn't hurt her. "I'll be fine," she'd answered. No matter what happened.

At one in the morning, Miska slipped out of her body-hugging skirt and beaded tunic and went to bed.

On Friday, she stayed up until midnight. The game against the White Sox had been over for two and a half hours.

On Saturday afternoon, she watched him pitch seven innings and give up three runs. The clock slowly ticked from six to seven to eight to nine to ten.

He wasn't coming.

One last game tomorrow at one, but as soon as the game ended, the team would drive home to Milwaukee. She checked his schedule. He didn't come back to Chicago until late July, his last Chicago trip of the season.

What was she going to do?

There was no point in borrowing trouble. Maybe by his next trip he'd have forgiven her. She could make it until then.

She put her glass in the dishwasher and turned off the lights. Warm, rectangular lamplight from her bedroom fell on the living room hardwoods, guiding her to her bed, to sleep, to a new day that was empty because she'd cleared it for Mark.

So she'd fill it. With Tracy. With Dillan.

With church.

Chapter Thirty-Seven

Tracy eased back in her chair, hand over her stomach. "Best pizza ever."
Miska had invited Tracy over after Sunday morning church to eat the pizza she'd bought for Mark. "I know. The garlic makes it."

"Totally, although I don't know how anyone's going to stand talking to me. Those poor kids tomorrow."

"Maybe they'll pass out before you stick them."

Tracy laughed. "You might be on to something." She scooped up her plate and silverware and carried them to the kitchen. "So whatever happened with Mark?"

Miska grabbed her own dishes. "He never showed."

"Did he call?"

"Nope." She set her dishes beside the sink.

Tracy rinsed them.

"I hoped he'd at least stop in, you know? See how things felt."

"I'm sorry, Miska."

So was she. Sort of. "I'm okay. I've got other things in my life."

"Like?"

"You. My dad. Work. Church." Dillan, sort of. He'd sat three rows ahead of them this morning. She'd had the hardest time keeping her gaze off him.

"You feel like you fit in there?"

"Between you and Jordan, yes."

"Good. You do belong, you know."

She shrugged a shoulder. She'd caught looks from a couple single guys. Whether it was because they knew her history or not—either way it made her uncomfortable. "When I'm at your church, I'm intrigued, but I don't really belong."

"Sure you do."

"No, I don't. I'm so different than everyone else."

"Come on—"

"I *am*." She shook her head, surprised at the emotions clogging her throat. "I look at someone like Dillan and—" Had she really just said that? "And that Austin who leads the John study, all those other guys—Cam and Matt—they'd never look twice at me, not once they knew."

Look at Ethan. He knew something. He might not have been at church that morning, but he'd be back. If he hadn't shared his knowledge with others, he would when someone mentioned her.

Could she go back once it all came out? Because the only person who would stand beside her was Tracy.

"I can guarantee Austin won't look at you. I hear he's engaged. Frankly, I think you and Dillan are cute. You should have heard the teasing he got after Memorial Day. Everyone gave him a hard time about flirting with you."

"He wasn't flirting."

"Umm, yeah, he was. Dillan plays it safe. He doesn't do anything that might make a woman think he's interested, but the way he acted with you..." Tracy grinned. "The guys gave him a hard time."

"Wish I could have seen that." She bit her grin into a nonchalant smile. "Does he blush?"

"He was blushing all over the place. Poor guy."

"Why is he still single?" The words were out before she could think them. She sucked in a breath, praying Tracy wouldn't see the obvious.

But Tracy studied her. "I've wondered that. I tried setting him up, but he wasn't interested. Said he'd wait for God to bring her at the right time. I think he worries about causing problems with women at church if it doesn't work."

"He told me that."

"You've had this conversation?"

Her skin warmed, remembering how he'd talked about waiting for his wife, waiting to give all of himself to her. No baggage. No past. "Awhile back."

"Hmm."

She couldn't meet Tracy's gaze and fingered the counter's edge.

"Miska, he's a great guy."

"Yeah."

"Miska."

Tracy's tone pulled her back. "What?"

"It's okay. I won't say anything."

How was she going to get over Dillan? "I feel like such a dork, like I'm back in middle school and hitting puberty."

Tracy laughed.

"It's not funny." She smiled anyway. "I don't know how to act around him. I can't read him. And he knows so much stuff about me—which never bothered me before—but I know how he lives. I know he's waited. Tracy, what do I do?"

"Honey, you're not right for him. Not now. You can't be a couple unless you believe in God the same way he does, and you can't fake that. I'm serious. He'll know in a second whether it's real or not."

"So…"

"You learn about God. You study his Word and decide for yourself what you believe. From there…" Tracy shrugged.

It sounded so good, like maybe she had a chance, but Tracy didn't know everything. "Even then he'd never look at me. He wants a virgin. Someone clean and perfect. Someone the opposite of me."

"You don't know that."

"I do know that. He's said so."

Something shifted in Tracy's eyes. "He said that?"

"He did." She could still hear him asking how she'd feel if someone waited for her, if it wouldn't be a gift. She swallowed her regret. "I wish I'd known that there were men like Dillan, but I didn't, Tracy. All the men I know take. They take and take, and I was dumb enough to give it to them. To think that what they offered was good."

"Now you know."

"And it's too late."

"Miska, it's not. Now you know, and it can change your future."

She shook her head. Not when the man she wanted had such high, high standards.

Such wisdom had come far too late.

Tracy stayed another hour before collecting her purse and keys. Miska followed her to the door. "So John four for Wednesday?"

"John chapter four." Tracy paused. "Have you read it yet?"

"No."

"You should read it."

She thought of Dillan's words in the gym, about Jesus raising someone from the dead. "Why?"

"Because it shows how much God loves us, no matter what we've done. Read it. Give me a call. Okay?"

"I will." How could Dillan's God love like that?

Tracy stepped into the hallway. "Thanks for the pizza—"

Dillan's door swung open. He walked out, laughing over his shoulder at a smirking Garrett right on his heels.

Miska took in Dillan's black shorts, gray T-shirt, and tennis shoes before she realized his laughter had faded.

Garrett eased his door shut. "Tracy."

Her name floated in hushed, reverent tones.

Miska glanced from Garrett to Tracy, who pressed her teeth into her lower lip. They should have been more aware.

"Do you—" Garrett swallowed whatever he'd been about to say. "You got a minute?"

"Not really."

"Please. Right here. Miska and Dillan won't leave."

Dillan looked up from his shoes as if to make sure she was staying.

Oh, his eyes, so warm and brown. His hair, a little long for him, so thick, so touchable.

She wet her lip as he neared her, trading places with Tracy who took a handful of reluctant steps with Garrett. Miska studied Dillan's profile as he watched them. He wasn't a man of many smiles. But when he did—

He ducked his head, then looked at her.

She flashed him a wan smile and glanced at Tracy.

Her friend listened to whatever Garrett was saying, but pain lay beneath her indifferent mask.

Poor Tracy. Poor Garrett.

She blew out a breath and looked back at Dillan. Still he watched her. Her stomach tightened. What did he think when he looked at her like that, all silent and indecipherable? "Going to the gym?" she asked.

"Running outside. I talked Garrett into living dangerously." He leaned against the wall and crossed his arms. Uncrossed them and shoved his hands into his pockets. "How are you?"

"Fine."

"Good."

"You?"

He nodded, looking down the hallway. "Can't complain."

She waited for him to say more, to lead this conversation wherever he wanted it to go.

He blew out a deep breath, then turned back. "You were at church again today."

"Yes. Is that okay?"

"Of course. I just—" He dragged his fingers down his neck. "I remember you laughing that off."

Had she?

"One of those days you fed me."

The day he'd admitted to being a virgin. She remembered the way she'd rolled her eyes and mocked him. She'd given him every reason to be rude.

He'd been nothing but a gentleman.

"Dillan, I'm so sorry for how I treated you."

Straightening, he blinked. "It's not a big deal."

"Why are you always nice to me?"

"I'm not always nice to you. There've been times I've blown it." He shifted again. "Why have you been coming to church?"

"Because it's starting to make sense."

His eyes roamed her face.

"You don't believe me."

"It's such a change."

"A lot *has* changed."

"Like?"

Down the hall, Garrett listened to Tracy's muffled words. "It'd be easier to list what hasn't changed. Here I am, reading part of the Bible. And not just once. The thing has me hooked."

"What part?"

"All of John so far. In the first chapter it was the stuff about the Word becoming flesh and dwelling with us. Then that verse that said God didn't come to the world to condemn us because we were already condemned. I can't stop thinking about that."

"We don't have to stay condemned, you know." He cleared his throat. "What about chapter four? You read it yet?"

"No. Why?"

He shrugged. "No reason."

"Tracy asked me that too, and I'm sure you know what's in it."

His soft laugh warmed her. "Busted."

"Yes, you are."

"Ever hear about the woman at the well?"

"No."

"Oh. Well, that's chapter four."

"Woman at the well—that's pretty vague, Dillan."

He pressed his lips together in a not-telling smile.

"You're trying to up my curiosity so I read it right away."

"If it works…"

"It won't." She crossed her arms and challenged him with a smile of her own. "I might get busy this week. My work, you know."

"It would be your loss."

"Really?"

He nodded, eyebrows arched.

"So convince me. Whet my appetite."

He ran his hand down his jaw. "Okay. The woman at the well is a Samaritan. Jesus is a Jew. The Jews hated the Samaritans, and the Samaritans returned the favor. Their hatred for each other was so great that they wouldn't travel through each other's land."

"Then how does Jesus meet this woman?"

"Read and find out." He looked to the side, and Miska followed his gaze.

Tracy walked toward them, head down, while Garrett watched, shoulders slumped.

"Well, looks like that went..." He pressed his lips together and glanced her way. "See you." He nodded to Tracy as he passed her, then gripped Garrett's arm and turned him toward the elevators.

Once they disappeared into the lobby, she wrapped her arms around Tracy. "You okay?"

Tracy nodded and pulled away enough to wipe an eye. "He wants another chance. Can you believe it?"

Yes. Yes, she could.

CHAPTER THIRTY-EIGHT

Wednesday was half over before Miska worked up the nerve to face John four.

Why she'd held off so long—why she'd been afraid—she wasn't sure. It probably had to do with Tracy and Dillan asking if she'd read it. What did it say that made them think of her?

While she ate lunch, she read about Jesus sitting alone at the well, tried to solve the riddle of him having living water, and reread where he told the woman all about her past—that she had no husband, that she'd had five husbands, that the one she had now was not her husband.

He knew.

If he was really God, then he knew. Just like Dillan knew—

No, Dillan could only guess that there had been others. If Jesus knew this woman's past, he would know about Jared, Gordon, and Rob. He would know all the details about Craig, about Brandon, Evan, the second Craig, and Jon—

Sir, I perceive that You are a prophet.

He was no prophet. The only one who could know that information was someone who'd been there through it all. Someone who'd… who'd authored her.

More names ran through her head—high school boys, college men, men in New York, men in Chicago. Men who'd taken advantage of her. Men she'd taken every advantage of.

Tracy could read this and think of one name. This woman at the well could name six. Miska could double that—and still have forgotten some.

Like Alex, Todd, Kellen—

God, make it stop.

She wiped her nose on a napkin while she read that this woman worshiped what she did not know but that the hour was coming when true worshipers would worship the Father in spirit and in truth. "For the Father is seeking such to worship Him."

God was seeking this woman who slept around in a day when sleeping around wasn't accepted? He welcomed her?

It shows how much God loves us, no matter what we've done.

How could God love her like this? She closed the book and eyed it. How could he?

None of this made sense. Dillan talked about how God said to wait, to stay pure, yet here was this same God inviting *this* woman to be a follower. How could the two go together?

Look at Garrett. He lived more like the woman at the well, and it sure didn't seem to be okay—

Understanding settled around her. This woman wouldn't be allowed to follow Jesus and stay the same.

If she were to buy into this stuff, she'd have to change. Jordan, Tracy—they'd expect her to be like them, to live like them. What was the point? Dillan still wouldn't value her.

Forget Dillan. How could God value her? No man ever had, not even her dad. This woman at the well was one thing. But Miska—she was another.

This Bible was messed up from start to finish. To be held in bondage to one man, to hold no power over him to keep the relationship fresh... People had a right to be happy, to move on when things got bad. And things *did* get bad.

Look at her and Mark, her and Kendall. Those relationships were over, and she was fine. She'd knocked a hundred thousand off her mortgage. Good move, financially. But if she bought into this John book, there'd be no more money, which meant she'd have to move back to the suburbs, get an office job, and answer to someone else's schedule.

No. She wouldn't change when she'd always be *this* woman to Dillan. To Tracy.

Maybe she could find someone else. She'd handled Mark and Kendall okay. If she met another man who'd take care of her…

She pushed away from the island. Tracy and Dillan's beliefs were certainly intriguing—she'd give them that—but she didn't belong. Ethan had made that clear. She could try to fit in, but she never would.

Besides, there'd undoubtedly been other women at other wells who'd said thanks, but no thanks—and she couldn't blame them.

Because saying no to this God was the only real option she had.

All through small group, the seat beside Tracy—the seat she'd reserved for Miska—remained empty.

Dillan fought to keep his attention on Austin. He was supposed to give the intern feedback, after all, supposed to coach him through two months of leading the singles' study. But his mind kept wandering to where Miska might be, to what had kept her away tonight.

When the discussion ended and people milled around, Dillan caught Tracy's eye.

Her lips turned up, but her gaze reflected his concern.

Something had gotten in Miska's way.

"Will you shut that thing up?"

The gravelly male voice opened her eyes. Miska blinked at her closed closet.

Behind her, the bed shifted, and she held still. Her shirt and bra lay scattered nearby. Last night's skirt lay closer to the door.

What had she done?

Somewhere her phone rang.

She eased up and held the covers against herself.

A dark-haired figure rolled over in her bed, his arm covering his head.

The phone rang again, close to her door.

She slipped out of bed, hoping he wouldn't look her way. Beneath her skirt lay her bag, half-buried. She rifled through it, a headache knifing between her eyes. The call ended as she found the phone, a number she didn't recognize displayed across the screen.

The man cleared his throat. "What time is it?"

Faint memories of Friday evening came to her—memories of the man she'd danced and flirted with. But that man had been blond.

"Hey." He sat up, palming his eyes. "You hear me?'

She glanced at her phone. "Eleven-forty."

He moaned. "A whole morning wasted. Remind me not to get so drunk next time."

Next time? After he'd declared her a waste? "Don't puke in my bed."

He lay back down and rolled over.

Who was this guy?

Her phone chimed. A text—the same number. *Need to talk to you asap. Call me. Dillan*

How had Dillan gotten her number?

Her phone chimed again, and she jumped.

The text was from Tracy. *You ok? Dillan's looking for you.*

What was going on?

She tried to text back, but her fingers wouldn't cooperate. She tossed the phone at her purse. It'd be easier to go next door and see what had gotten into Dillan.

The man snored softly.

She grabbed her underwear and bra and slipped into them, hoping she hadn't done anything too awful.

Woman at the well. Her mouth twisted. What did God think of this? He had to be done with her—if he'd ever been concerned with her to begin with.

In her closet she slipped into yoga pants and a workout shirt, but her reflection in the mirror stopped her. Her hair was a Medusan mess, more evidence of a night of things she couldn't remember. She grabbed a hair tie and fought it into some resemblance of decency. But then there was the smeared eye makeup. She rubbed away what she could. She looked puffy and—

So what? She grabbed a breath mint from her dresser top. It was just Dillan needing something.

She crept away, easing her bedroom door shut. She'd take care of it, then get the drunk out of her home.

Someone pounded on her front door.

Could the man not wait another minute? She ran for it, head pounding with every step. She needed Advil right away—Advil, food, and water.

The pounding came again, loud enough to wake the man in her room.

She yanked the door open.

Dillan lowered his fist.

Garrett stood behind him, hands on his hips.

Dillan's breath escaped in a rush. "You're okay."

"Of course I'm okay." She stepped into the hall and let the door bump her backside. "Some people sleep in on their day off."

Garrett raised an eyebrow.

Whatever. She crossed her arms and glared at Dillan. "What's got you all hot and bothered?"

"We need to talk."

"So I gathered. Talk."

"Not here." Dillan eyed the empty hallway. "Can we come in?"

With some stranger in her bed? "Just tell me."

"You don't want me to tell you here. Not where people can hear."

"There's no one out here, Dillan. Spill it already."

Garrett leaned forward. "Miska, really. Can we—"

Her headache grew. "I don't have time for this." She turned to go. "Tell me now or—"

"Darcie Scheider is dead."

CHAPTER THIRTY-NINE

Dillan's words hit like fists. Her legs failed, and she fell against the door.

He caught her wrist and arm while Garrett's hand shot above them, holding the door steady.

"Darcie's…" She couldn't say it.

"We just heard. They found her this morning."

Her legs wouldn't work. She clung to the doorknob. Darcie was dead? Suspicions and *what-ifs* began to form, but she shook her head, a fist against her mouth.

"Let's sit down." Dillan pulled her hand from the knob.

She concentrated on the feel of his fingers.

He turned her like he had Garrett on Sunday and steered her toward the living room. Her couch had never looked so welcoming.

Dillan held on until she found a seat on the edge. She fingered the cushion's tight seam. This was where Mark had sat, his arms around her, his lips in her hair, promising that they'd be together once the marriage was over.

Now it was.

Dillan sat beside her, Garrett beside him. They both studied her, Dillan with concern, Garrett like she knew something.

She knew nothing, which was terrifying. "Darcie's really dead?"

Dillan nodded.

"Are they saying—" She couldn't go there. "How? What happened?"

He shrugged. "She was inside, by her front door."

"So…" She pressed her fingers into her eyebrows.

"They haven't said whether it's foul play or not."

Hearing Dillan go where she'd been afraid to freed her thoughts. "Who would kill her?"

"Miska." Garrett slid to the edge of his seat. "You've been seeing Mark."

She darted to the window, to her view of the lake and fountain and treetops.

Already they were turning that dingy green, the dirt and smog of a few million people tarnishing their spring freshness.

Her head throbbed. Her stomach burned. "Mark and I are done—for over two weeks now. I haven't heard from him since he and Kendall—"

What had she been thinking? Mark, Kendall, the stranger sleeping off a hangover in her bed. Why had she ever thought a night with men could offer real happiness? She knew better.

Miska eased onto the overstuffed chair. "I'm sorry she's dead, but it doesn't affect me. Not anymore."

Dillan shifted. "You don't think it'll get out about you and Mark? Won't that make people look at it differently?"

"We're over. If someone killed her, it wasn't Mark. He's in Arizona. The team would have arrived Wednesday night." Unless he hadn't gone. She covered her mouth. "Don't tell me he stayed behind."

"He went. They say he found out at the ballpark this morning. I guess he's already on a flight back."

She buried her face in her hands.

Dillan's voice soothed. "What're you thinking?"

She shook her head.

"Miska." Leather squeaked beneath Garrett. "Do you think Mark might have done this?"

She lowered her hands. "Why would he?"

Garrett and Dillan held her gaze.

"Why would he?" She raised her voice. "We're over. I told you. I haven't heard from him in two weeks. He told me not to call no matt—"

No matter what happened.

Behind her, the bedroom door clicked. "What's going on—whoa. Who are these guys?"

She couldn't turn, but Garrett's and Dillan's faces said it all. Dillan's mouth fell open, and Garrett scowled. "Dude. Get some clothes on."

Dillan jerked his gaze to the floor between his feet.

The bedroom door banged shut.

Garrett shot Dillan a look, but Dillan didn't catch it.

She pressed her fingers to her cheeks, feeling them burn. Another man for Dillan to see her with. Some naked guy standing in her doorway, demanding to know who Garrett and Dillan were when she couldn't even remember his name.

The door opened again. "Miska, where'd my jeans go?"

Her face flamed beneath her hands. "I don't know. Go look—" She waved her hand over her shoulder. "They're in there somewhere."

"Well, I can't find them." His voice faded as if he'd turned to survey her bedroom.

Garrett rolled his eyes. "For crying out loud." He shoved himself off the couch. "Come on, Dopey. Let's find something to put over your birthday suit."

She wrapped her arms around herself, something tight and unforgiving encasing her. She knew it well—the shame that followed a night like she'd had. Funny how she always forgot about it until the morning after.

Dillan didn't look at her, his fingers fiddling with each other. He sat back in his seat and placed his hands on his knees, then ran a hand through his hair and leaned forward again, rubbing his chin as if he needed to scrub something off it. He heaved a sigh and cleared his throat.

He was about to speak, and she couldn't let him go first. "I'm sorry," she whispered.

"Don't apologize to me." He finally looked at her. Studied her. "Who is he?"

Something with a T. Tony. Trevor? That sounded right. "It's Trevor."

"Well. Good for you and Trevor."

The silence returned, releasing a muffled voice from the bedroom. Trevor's, it sounded like. She couldn't wait for him to go, for Garrett and Dillan to leave her with her own repulsion.

A muffled phone dinged.

Dillan dug his out of his pocket and read the screen.

"What is it?"

He shrugged. He probably couldn't stand to look at her. "There's a report that she might have died from an allergic reaction."

"To what?"

"Guess she had a peanut allergy."

She'd read that somewhere, way back when she'd first discovered Darcie's existence and had scoured the internet for ammunition against Mark. Now she was dead from that allergy. "How awful."

The phone dangled from his hand.

"So it wasn't foul play."

"Guess not." He returned the phone to his pocket, then clasped his hands and studied them. If only he would look at her, give her the tiniest bit of hope that it would be okay. That the rest of her life wouldn't be like this, waking up to some stranger with a hangover.

"Dillan, I'm sorry."

He shook his head.

"Really, I'm sorry. I didn't mean—"

"You know what, Miska? It's your life. You want to screw it up? Feel free. But don't drag me into it. I'm not involved."

Behind her, the door opened. This time she looked. Trevor stepped out, fully dressed down to a scowl on his green-tinged features.

Garrett followed. He clapped a hand to the guy's shoulder. "Well, Barry here is ready to face the world."

Barry?

"I thought it was Trevor," Dillan said.

The guy snorted. "Trevor's my cousin."

Oh, right. Memories returned to shame her further.

"So where are we?" Barry asked.

She clenched her teeth.

"Someone going to tell me?"

Dillan made a sound of disgust. "The Loop. Michigan Avenue."

"Seriously?" Barry stepped into view.

"Look out the window," Garrett said. "Buckingham Fountain's right there."

"Sweet." Barry walked past her, assaulting her with a whiff of last night's cologne and BO. He stood before her window, hands on his hips. "Nice view, Miska. Really nice view."

Her name on his tongue felt dirty. What had she done with him? With Trevor? She ached to curl into a ball and give in to a good cry.

Garrett popped his palm against his fist. "All right, Barry. You know where you are. Time to go."

"Yeah, sure." He turned enough to peer down at her. "Can I get your number? See you again sometime?"

Dillan and Garrett remained where they were, Dillan's arms crossed over his broad chest.

How she wished they grasped her deep regret, understood that the *no* she'd give Barry was the same answer she'd give if they weren't there.

But they wouldn't.

She wiped the moisture building in her eyes. "No."

"Excuse me?"

She looked up.

He leaned toward her, his button-down emphasizing his stocky build. He'd looked so good in the dark lights of the club. In daylight and the aftermath of a hangover, not so much. "Hey, sugar. You in there?"

His words snapped her teeth together.

Even Dillan straightened.

"I said no. Now get out."

"I get it." He smirked at Garrett, then Dillan. "Got these two to keep you company." He pulled his wallet from his back pocket. "When you get bored, gimme a call." He tossed a business card onto the coffee table.

She lunged for it, grabbed it, and threw it back. "Get out."

He swore at her, and Dillan jumped to his feet.

Barry froze and stared at Dillan as if it had just dawned on him how tall Dillan was.

But it was time she took care of things herself. She shoved Barry, satisfied when he stumbled and caught himself on the windowsill. "Leave. Now."

He snorted. "Be all uptight. You'll call." His smile scalded her. He kicked the business card her way and walked toward her front door, hands stuffed in his pockets. "You all have fun now." He opened the door and saluted her before disappearing.

Her shoulders sagged.

Beside her Dillan shifted. "We should go."

What a mess her life was. She rubbed her hands against her arms. If she told them she didn't want to be alone, would they stay?

"Yeah, I think the game's about to start."

They were leaving her for a game?

"Game of the week's on early. That's where we heard about Darcie. You should watch. Maybe they'll have an update."

She nodded at Garrett. A tear spilled down her cheek. She hid her face again, fought the shake in her shoulders. Not now. Not while they were still here.

Someone tugged her to his chest.

She opened her eyes—Garrett's Bulls T-shirt. She let her forehead rest against his warmth.

"It's okay," he said as if it were a commonly known fact.

But it wasn't. Tears dripped off her nose. "I don't want to be like this. I don't want it, Garrett. Why do I do it? Why does it always end like this?"

"It doesn't have to."

Look who was talking. She pushed back, and he released her. She wiped her eyes, too aware of Dillan watching.

"He's right, Miska."

Easy for virgin boy to say. "It's not that simple."

Garrett shifted. "It's not simple. Real change isn't simple. I know."

She looked at him.

"Where were you Wednesday?" he asked.

Out partying. Barry wasn't the first kiss of the week.

"Did you read chapter four?"

"Pry much, Garrett?"

He chuckled. "Yeah. Is that a problem?"

She smiled. "Yes."

"Too bad. I'm changing—for real this time. If I can change, you can too."

Dillan chewed his lip. Did he believe Garrett? His mouth slanted to the side, one eyebrow cocked just enough to say that no, he didn't believe his brother.

Neither should she.

"You coming to church tomorrow?"

"Garrett—"

"You want to change, Miska? Spend some time there instead of at a club with losers like Barry and, well, the old me. And start listening, really listening."

She had been listening. That was the problem.

Dillan scratched his neck. He probably wanted out of there.

She'd leave too, if she could. How had she become such a skank? Garrett was right. She wasn't going to meet decent men living the way she'd been. She forced a look at Garrett. "Thanks for telling me about Darcie."

"We didn't know if you were okay or if something had happened to you too. But it looks like you're fine."

"Oh yeah, I'm great."

Dillan smiled at the floor.

Garrett picked up the business card. "You want this?"

"No."

He flipped the card over. "Lindros Construction. Huh. Lindros is his last name."

The huge company that advertised all over Chicago sportscasts? It cost a fortune to advertise there. The company was massive. Loaded.

Which meant Barry was loaded.

Oh. *Oh.* She wrapped her hands around the back of her neck. Desire flickered. She held her breath. No, she couldn't go there again.

But desire burst into a bonfire, an addiction she couldn't shake. Her home, her mortgage. Security. Stability.

No. No! She wouldn't sell herself for money, not anymore. She couldn't live that way again.

But the money…

"You sure, Miska? You don't look sure."

She stared at the card between Garrett's fingers. What could it hurt to call him— "Get it out of here." Anguish blew up inside her. *Let me have it.*

"Will do." He palmed the card. "You ready, Dill?"

"Yeah." Dillan glanced at her. "Take care." He strode around the couch and down her hallway, Garrett on his heels.

When Dillan disappeared, Garrett paused and looked back. "See you tomorrow?"

"'Bye, Garrett."

With a shrug, he left.

Alone at last.

She lowered herself to the coffee table's edge. Lindros Construction— what would the woman at the well do?

She could Google the company and find a phone number, but Barry wasn't a man she could live with. How tired she was of men like him. She wanted more than a life of flings, a few months with one guy before being abandoned again. "God, I'm sick of this."

But Lindros Construction…

In the bedroom her phone chirped.

What now? If it was Adrienne, she didn't want to talk. Adrienne had let her take some stranger home.

The phone chirped again.

With a sigh, she walked to the bedroom. Her phone lay on top of her skirt, and Tracy's name filled the screen.

What would Tracy think of what she'd done?

She surveyed the rumpled sheets and thrown-back comforter. Two slept-on pillows. A dark sock peeking from beneath the bed.

He'd left a sock?

She grabbed it and stormed into her bathroom, threw the thing into the trash. She smacked the counter. "I'm not going to live this way. No more!"

Where was the other sock?

She jerked the bedding to the floor, yanked free the fitted sheet, and wadded everything into a trash bag. Five hundred dollars—wasted. But she'd sleep on a bare mattress before she'd slip between those sheets again.

Now where was that sock?

It wasn't beneath the bed. She searched the bathroom. Her closet. Traced her usual path from her front door to the bedroom. Nothing. He'd left with one sock?

She woke her phone and opened Tracy's message. *You ok?*

Spectacular.

Want me to come over?

Her fingers flew across the phone. *Why do you care?*

Half a minute passed. Her phone chirped. *Because.* :)

She wilted. How could Tracy love her like this?

Because she didn't know the real Miska.

If she did… Miska had to know. *Come over.*

On my way.

She set the phone aside and returned to the trash bag, ready to toss her garbage and start over.

Again.

CHAPTER FORTY

The news online was simple—a friend called the police when she couldn't reach Darcie. They'd had morning plans, but Darcie hadn't shown and wasn't answering her door, even though her Infiniti sat in the driveway.

Police called Mark in Arizona to see if he'd heard from her.

He hadn't. He gave them permission to enter his home and waited to hear what they found.

She was dead just inside her front door. A teammate offered to fly home with Mark, but he said no and grabbed the first flight out.

Darcie Henderson Scheider was thirty-five, the oldest of four sisters. She left behind a grieving husband and shocked coworkers who'd said a casual good-bye Friday afternoon. She and Mark had been together seven years, married for four. There was no official cause of death, but an autopsy would be performed. Mark was on bereavement leave with no date when the club expected him back.

Miska stared at her laptop. It sounded like Mark had nothing to do with it. He'd been eighteen hundred miles away. But Dillan and Garrett wondered, and Mark's last words echoed in her head.

Don't call me. No matter what happens. Got that? No matter. What. Happens.

Those words carried a different meaning now.

She swatted the thought away. He'd never hurt his wife.

He listened while Kendall beat you.

Death by allergy wasn't something Mark could control. People with peanut allergies were extremely careful about what came into their homes. It had to be a fluke.

SportsCenter coverage showed Mark's team standing outside their dugout, hats off, heads bowed as the stadium paused for a moment of silence. In the next clip, the team's manager, surrounded by microphones, said Mark had spoken with his family and Darcie's before flying back to Milwaukee. That he was obviously in shock. That he'd waited in the clubhouse with teammates for that second police call, every passing moment making it clear that the news wasn't good.

No kidding.

She pulled up Mark's information on her phone. Garrett and Dillan were right; if news about her leaked, people would look suspiciously at Darcie's death.

But she and Mark were over. He'd bought her affection for a while, used her, paid her nicely. But he'd had his fill. He'd moved on, either with another woman or with Darcie.

If it were with Darcie, then she felt truly sorry for both of them. "I never meant to mess things up."

Would Darcie be alive if Miska and Mark had never met?

The thought tortured her.

She set her phone down, turned off the lamp, and stumbled across the dark living room. In her bedroom, she wrapped a winter blanket around herself and curled up on the bare mattress.

Darcie lay on a cold metal slab.

Something told Miska she didn't deserve any better.

Friday night at the club; now Sunday morning at church. How quickly things changed.

Miska followed Tracy down the side aisle toward Tracy's usual spot.

Ethan Doebler stood in the way, talking with another guy. He nodded at them and stepped aside, but his gaze lingered.

Tracy turned into a row, and Miska glanced over her shoulder.

Ethan wore a knowing, gut-churning smirk.

Garrett stopped beside him and backhanded him in the stomach. "Knock it off."

Ah, Garrett. Her hero.

She sat beside Tracy.

Footsteps sounded, and Tracy looked up, then clamped her mouth shut.

"Ladies." Garrett perched on the seat beside Miska. His gaze flickered to Tracy, then back to Miska. "How you doing?"

"Good. Thank you." Despite Ethan, it felt right to be here. "Thanks for pushing me yesterday."

"Anytime. I'm a great pest."

"You're a pro."

He chuckled, glancing past her to Tracy. "Morning, Tracy."

She studied her fingernails. "Morning."

"Well." Garrett slapped his hands against his thighs. "About Ethan—feel free to smack him if needed. He's a moron."

"Good to know." She sent him a grateful smile. Having her honor defended by a man who knew how little honor she had... that was new.

He left.

Miska glanced at Tracy who didn't look up. "He's gone, Trace."

She rubbed her bare finger. "I know."

What if Garrett did change? What would Tracy think? What would Dillan think?

At the front of the aisle Dillan walked toward his usual spot a few rows ahead of them. He set down a stack of books. His hair, shorter than yesterday, looked thick and dark—good hair on a strong masculine face that had grown on her more than she'd thought possible. He eased onto the seat, his arm across the back, his body turned toward her—his eyes on her.

Miska stiffened. She'd been staring?

"Morning." He nodded at her. "Good to see you."

It was? "You're talking to me."

His eyebrows lowered. "What?"

Embarrassment flashed through her. "We don't talk when I'm here. I thought—" She twisted her hands together. "Never mind."

Dillan glanced at Tracy.

Tracy shrugged back.

He *did* ignore her. Sent all kinds of signals that he didn't want her around him here. She laughed it off. "Sorry. I'm still kind of fuzzy after—"

Yesterday. She swallowed. Did she really have to remind him?

Like he'd forgotten.

Dillan stood, books in hand. "Mind if I join you?"

Her stomach flipped. "Feel free."

They slid down, and he filled the space beside her, warmth and masculine cologne scenting the air. His lips pressed into a tight smile.

She smiled back. The urge to rest her head against his arm was tempting. So tempting. No other man made her feel this safe. She pushed down emotions that were far too close to the surface. "Thank you. For yesterday. You and Garrett—I don't know why you guys care, but I'm grateful."

"Don't mention it."

She wouldn't, if it would make him forget. *God, Dillan's so special. Is there a way, somehow...*

Jordan and Matt sat on the other side of Tracy. A friend of Dillan's joined him, and they all slid down, making room for one more.

As she settled into her new seat, Miska savored being in the middle, as if she were truly part of them. She wasn't, but for one morning she could pretend that she belonged, that she bought into everything Dillan, his family, and Tracy believed. Everything that the woman at the well believed.

Dillan left to open the service, but his spot beside her remained empty, a promise that he'd be back.

Miska savored the feeling of waiting for the return of a man who wouldn't use her or take advantage of her.

When the pastor began speaking, Dillan spread his Bible over his knee and pointed out where they were.

She read the words as the pastor read them, breathing in the comfort they gave.

When the service ended, the contrast of yesterday and today remained. Dillan introduced her to his friend. Jordan hugged her and asked how she'd been. Amanda stopped to chat.

There was no going back. Miska knew it. There was something here, something in the words in Dillan's Bible, something more precious than anything she'd encountered before.

All she knew was that she needed it.

But as she followed Tracy to the main aisle, as Tracy made lunch plans for them with Jordan and Amanda, Ethan Doebler stood near the back, eyes on her, hand covering his mouth as he spoke to the man beside him, a man whose eyebrows rose while his mouth curved in cynical amusement.

And her sense of belonging faded.

CHAPTER FORTY-ONE

Monday, the last day of June, wilted beneath storm clouds building in the southwest. Not that Miska could tell from her east-facing windows, but the storm was a big story on the news. The lightning, wind, and heavy rain weren't supposed to arrive until later.

Dad called to see if they should cancel their dinner plans. No way. They'd leave the restaurant long before the storm hit. Besides, she hadn't seen him since Father's Day.

A knock sounded as she ended the call. Miska opened her door.

Adrienne smiled and strutted inside like she lived there. "Hey, girl. Just had a lovely run-in with your neighbor."

Her stomach tightened. "Which one?"

"Garrett." Adrienne grinned. "His brother was there too. So fun."

Had her sister always been like this? The onslaught of memories told her she had. How had she ever found it amusing?

"They were coming inside from a run. All hot and sweaty." Adrienne waggled her eyebrows. "I walked in behind them. They had no idea until we got to the elevators."

How twisted Adrienne was. Miska dumped the contents of her purse on the island and sorted through them.

"You should have seen Garrett. His face turned sheet white. Then that bump-on-a-log brother of his saw me—"

"Hey." Miska pressed her palms against the granite. "Leave Dillan alone."

Adrienne cocked her head. "What's this? Are you into him?"

Yes. Oh, yes. Her mouth cemented open, and, in the awkward silence she couldn't fill, complete understanding registered on her sister's face.

"He's not your type, you know." Adrienne ran her fingers down her neck. "He'd never pay attention to you, although it'd be fun to try."

"Leave him alone, Aid."

"Why?"

"Because it's not right."

"Please."

"It's not."

Adrienne tapped her toe. "Does this have something to do with Mark?"

Miska fingered her lip gloss. Sure. Why not? "Maybe."

"Maybe? Girl, he's single all of a sudden. I know how you feel about him."

Felt about him.

"Have you talked to him since... it happened?"

"It?"

"Yes. *It.*"

"Can't you say it?"

"You don't say it, Miska. It's bad luck."

"Oh. Well. Lucky for you then that your mom didn't die because you'd have all kinds of bad luck. People ask, you know, and you'd have to tell them. You'd have to say that she'd *died* and—"

Adrienne stepped back, eyebrows raised. "I think I'll head out."

That sounded wonderful.

"You got plans for the night?"

"I do." With Dad. What would happen if she said that?

"Anything like Friday night?"

"No."

"Anything you're going to share?"

"No."

"Then that would be my cue to leave."

Good.

But Adrienne pulled Miska into a hug. Despite everything, Miska rested in her sister's embrace. *This* felt right. So right.

When Adrienne released her, Miska stepped back, eyes on their feet, and wiped her nose. "Thank you."

"Sure."

"Sorry for being a brat."

"No, I should have realized how everything would affect you. Sometimes I'm not very sensitive, you know?"

"Adrienne Insensitive Tomlinson."

Her sister laughed. "We should hang out, work together like we used to. Next week maybe?"

"Sounds wonderful."

"We'll do it." Adrienne's phone buzzed inside her bag. "Gotta run. You be good tonight," she called, already at the front door.

"I will."

Adrienne vanished down the hall.

Partway through their ceviche platter, Dad brought *it*, as Adrienne said, up. "I've been following the story about Mark's wife."

She half-expected the restaurant chatter to vanish, but no one paid attention. "It's sad, isn't it?"

"Sad, yes. Odd. Strange. She knew she had an allergy, so how did she die from it?"

"People die from allergic reactions, don't they?"

"Yes, although…" He sighed. "Jake has a peanut allergy."

Miska set down her fork.

He smiled at the tablecloth. "I caused an attack once. I didn't know about his allergy and brought home a Snickers, accidentally spread some crumbs. Jake touched the counter and started reacting."

The image in her mind changed from some faceless kid to Darcie.

"Janet knew right away. Grabbed his EpiPen. Stuck him in the thigh. Yelled at me the whole time." He chuckled. "We went to the ER, but he was fine. Thankfully."

"So he was okay."

"Yes, but my point is the EpiPen. Where was Darcie's? She would know where her pen was at all times. At least Janet and Jake did. So why didn't she use an EpiPen?"

"Maybe she did, and it didn't work."

He shrugged. "Maybe, but then she would have gotten medical help. Except she didn't call 911. She stayed inside and died. She should have had time to get help. Why didn't she?"

She speared a piece of fish. "Mark was in Arizona, you know."

"So how did he do it?"

Her fork slipped to the floor. "Dad."

"What?"

"Mark wouldn't kill his wife."

"You sure about that?"

Their waiter stood two tables over. Miska snagged his attention, and he came immediately, flashing a wide grin. "What can I get for you?"

"New fork, please."

"Absolutely. I'll refill your water too."

The man hurried off.

Dad lifted his empty Coke glass and clinked ice around. "Think he'll bring me a refill?"

"Of course."

Dad snorted. "Just like you're determined to think it's a coincidence that his wife dies the same summer he's having an affair."

"I don't want to talk about it."

"I think you better, because if he killed his wife, he did it for you."

She glared at him. "Stop it."

"I'm serious."

"So am I. I never asked him to do that. Besides, we're over."

The waiter returned, fork and water pitcher in hand. "Here you are, miss."

She took the fork, careful not to smile at him. "Thank you."

"And your water. Anything for you, sir?"

"Another Coke."

"Be right back with that."

He left, and Dad sighed. "If he did it, he'll call. Try to get things going again."

She filled her fork. "Mark's smarter than that."

"Not if he killed his wife."

She ignored him and took a bite.

"What will you do if he calls?"

"He's not going to call."

"Humor me, Miska. What will you do?"

He wasn't going to let it go, was he? "I'll hang up on him."

"Wrong. He'd think you suspect and are about to go to the police. You'd be in trouble."

"You've thought this through. Why don't you use it for a novel? Make some money off it."

He flushed. "Don't hang up on him. Tell him you heard about his wife, that you're sorry for his loss, and slip it in there about your new boyfriend."

"Who doesn't exist."

"He doesn't need to know that."

"Come on, Dad. If he killed Darcie—for me—don't you think a new boyfriend will tick him off?"

The waiter set the Coke above Dad's plate, sent her a look, and left.

"Good point. So what do we do?"

"Nothing, because he didn't kill her—and he's not going to call. There's no way I'll hear from him."

"At least change your locks."

That wasn't a bad idea. "Can we talk about something else?"

"I guess. How's work?"

"Good. What I have of it, anyway."

"What are you going to do?"

"I don't know."

"You could… If you had to sell your place, you could live with me until you found something cheaper."

"I'm not selling my place."

"Mark would have a hard time finding you."

"Dad!"

He held up his hands. "Something to think about."

She tossed her napkin on top of her plate.

"My apologies, Miska. But I worry. I don't want anything to happen to you."

"Nothing will."

"So I pray."

So would she.

The wind picked up during dinner. Dad hailed Miska a cab and sent her home. By the time she reached her building, the wind had transformed into a downpour.

Inside her condo, she changed into a dry shirt. Goose bumps faded and warmth returned. She searched the quickly darkening sky for lightning. Thunder rumbled, but she couldn't see its source.

The fountain's center jet shot high, wind arcing it toward the lake.

From her purse on the island, her phone rang.

It was a flat ringtone, one that meant the phone didn't recognize the number. No name on the screen, just a phone number she didn't recognize, an area code she couldn't place.

Why was she so nervous?

It was Dad's fault, of course. His comment that Mark would call.

It could be a publisher she'd contacted. Potential work that would keep her in her home.

She answered. "Hello?"

"Miska."

Mark's voice buckled her knees.

CHAPTER FORTY-TWO

M iska grabbed the countertop. "Mark?"

"Yeah. Hi."

"Hi." She swallowed. What did this mean? Was Dad right? "Mark, I'm so sorry about Darcie."

"Thank you. It's been—" He blew out a sigh. "It's been a rough few days."

She couldn't imagine. "How are you holding up?"

"I'm all right. Our families are here. The team's supportive. I'll make it."

"Good." Faint noises sounded—Darcie's family? A TV? "Where are you?"

"Home. Alone. First time since Saturday."

"How's her family?"

"They're pretty shook up. Doing okay, though. I told them they could stay at our place, and they took me up on it."

"When's the funeral?"

"Friday. July fourth. Going to be a long week."

Then a long month, year, two years to follow. He had no idea.

"They did the autopsy."

"What'd they find?"

"Haven't heard. They're expediting the toxicology report. Should have results in a couple days."

"I've heard it might have been her peanut allergy."

"Yeah. Guess she'd been eating when she died."

She flinched. Could he really just say that?

"You're probably wondering why I called. I needed to talk to someone who knew things weren't perfect between us."

Had she ever really known how things were between them? "Are you sorry she's gone?"

"Of course! I tried, Miska. I tried everything to make it work. I never wished her gone. But there was just too much junk. The affair—some things you can't get over."

The affair would be Darcie's, of course. His wouldn't count. "I'm sorry."

"Me, too." He sighed again, then groaned. "Miska, I miss you."

"Don't say that. Your wife isn't even buried."

"I know. It doesn't make sense, but it's true. I didn't want to end things between us. But I talked to a teammate, and—"

She jerked upright. Someone else knew?

"—he said I had to give Darcie a chance."

Her heart pounded. What if word about their relationship got out?

"You have to know how sorry I am about that day. I was confused. I was… torn."

What was he saying?

"You there?" he asked.

"Yes."

"I want to see you."

"No." She squeezed the phone. "We can't do that."

"Miska—"

"If people knew you had an affair, they'd look at things differently."

"How can you say that? I wasn't even in the same time zone."

"You shouldn't be calling me."

"I'm on a prepaid phone. Just call this number."

He thought she'd call him?

"If you need more time, fine. We can wait until the season's over."

Three months? What was wrong with him?

"Miska, please. I need you, even if we just talk. Don't push me away."

Like he'd done to her. She rubbed her forehead.

His voice shook. "Miska?"

"I'm here."

He sniffed. Coughed. "Sorry. I don't mean to fall apart on you. I've just never dealt with anything like this."

Nothing could prepare someone for the loss of a loved one, no matter how imperfect that person had been. "I know."

"I guess you do."

Lightning flashed over the lake.

"What are you doing tonight?"

"Watching it storm."

"Wish I could join you. That'd be perfect."

No, it wouldn't.

She toyed with a curl. Did she really not want him? She'd be financially secure.

But if she welcomed him back, she'd have to say good-bye to Dillan's church, to words that made more and more sense, words she was beginning to cling to.

"You're quiet."

"Just thinking."

"About?"

"I don't know." She dragged a hand across her forehead. How had things become so complicated? "I just don't know."

"About us?"

"Five minutes ago there wasn't an *us*."

"Things have changed."

Yes, and she prayed he'd had nothing to do with it.

"Look what's happened, Miska. Fate's made it so we can be together. I know you want that."

He had no idea how much she'd changed. He had no idea who she was or what she wanted anymore.

"Have you changed your mind? After everything—" He swore softly. "Don't do this."

Whatever she decided, now wasn't the time to bail. "Mark, I'm glad you called. I'm glad we could talk."

He snorted. "But."

"We should wait until the season's over. That'll give you time to grieve. We'll both have time to decide what we want."

He growled in her ear. "I know what I want."

She closed her eyes, glad he couldn't see how her hand shook. "For your family—and Darcie's—we need time. Okay? It won't look good if we start dating right away."

Lightning flashed near Navy Pier. Thunder clapped right behind it, her windows rattling.

"I don't like this, Miska."

"I know."

"I love you. I want you." He swore again, and something banged. "They're back. I've got to go. Talk to you later."

"'Bye—"

He'd already hung up.

Miska set the phone down.

Mark didn't sound like a husband in mourning. He sounded like a man eager to get on with life. That couldn't be normal.

On the other hand, his marriage hadn't been well for a long time. *According to him.* Darcie'd had an affair, and he'd never gotten past it. He'd never forgiven her.

That didn't mean he'd killed her.

Rain pelted the window.

She hugged herself and leaned against the glass, staring at the darkening sky. Hopefully she'd bought herself some time, but eventually he'd demand an answer, and she prayed he'd accept her *no*.

Because she didn't see any way that Mark would be part of her life again.

Monday's storm lasted through Tuesday. Wednesday brought clear skies and heat with a vengeance. The morning air was already thick, the temperature over eighty. Miska ran past Buckingham Fountain anyway, guzzling water.

"Miska!"

She turned.

Dillan jogged her way. He looked great in navy-blue shorts and a gray T-shirt promoting some camp in Wisconsin.

She watched him near, unable to hide a smile.

He returned it. "You look happy."

"It's a beautiful day."

He surveyed their surroundings. "It's disgustingly hot and humid."

They fell into step, crossing Lake Shore Drive and jogging down the stairs to the lakefront. This time they turned north, toward the skyline and Navy Pier jutting into the lake.

Dillan panted as they ran. "You hear the latest about Darcie?"

The air suddenly felt suffocating. "There's news?"

"Yeah. She was a few weeks pregnant."

Miska stopped, chest heaving.

"I guess she died from an allergic reaction, and the police are still investigating."

"Still investigating? Why?"

"I don't know. Maybe they don't think it was an accident."

Mark couldn't have... Her breath came faster. She eased onto the grass. "Oh, Dillan."

He sat beside her. "You okay?"

She shook her head. Far from it. "He called me last night."

"Scheider *called* you?"

"I know. He's an idiot."

"What'd he say?"

"That he misses me."

His eyebrows rose. "What'd he say about the baby?"

"Nothing. Do you think she hadn't told him? Or didn't know herself?"

He shrugged. His gaze traveled over boats bobbing in the harbor. "What are you going to do?"

"I don't know."

"Would you go back to him?"

She shook her head.

"Well, good." He blew out a sigh. "Good. You tell him that?"

"No."

"Why not?"

"Dillan, he wanted to see me, and I told him no. He wasn't happy."

"He threaten you?"

She bit her lip.

"What'd he say?"

"Think of what he's going through. It was just stress—"

"You reacted, Miska. He said something that felt like a threat."

"If I believed he killed his wife, then yes, it could be a threat. But just because he had an affair doesn't mean he killed her."

"But add in him calling you and wanting to see you—a man doesn't do that when his wife dies."

She rested her forehead against her knees. "I can't think about it."

"If he killed his wife, you have to think about it."

If he killed his wife, Darcie's death was her fault. That baby's death was her fault. She raised her head. "Dillan, why do you care?"

"Don't get off topic."

"Why do you?"

"This is serious. You have to wonder if he killed her."

"Yes, but I can't go to the police. What if it was just horrible timing? Then I've ruined his name. I have to *know*."

"What about when he wants to see you again? If he killed her, what will he do to you when you tell him no?"

That had been tiptoeing through her mind. "I can't think about it."

"Miska, you have to. He's already said something—"

"No, I don't!" She swallowed. "I told him we had to wait at least until the season's over. I've got three months."

Dillan stared down the running path, his jaw tight.

"What?"

He shrugged, his mouth turning into a frown.

"*What?*"

"He'll call again."

He probably would.

"What will you say?"

"I don't know."

"Well, figure it out."

"What's that supposed to mean?"

"It means if you don't have a plan, you'll end up with him again."

So that's what this was about. "Let me ask a second time, Dillan. Why do you care?"

"Miska—"

"I want an answer. Why does this matter so much?"

He scowled. "Because it's wrong, you with him. It isn't right."

"You mean…"

"It began as an affair. Nothing good can come from that."

She jumped to her feet. "Why does it always have to be about right and wrong with you? Why can't it ever be about people? About *me*?"

He rose, staring at her.

"All you care about, Dillan, is black and white. Whether what I'm doing is right or not. But once, just once, I'd love to hear that you care about what happens to me for me." She jabbed her chest with her finger. "For *me*."

He said nothing, just looked at her.

"Well?"

He wet his lower lip.

"What? No thoughts in there? Are you going to crawl inside your shell and hide—again—while you demand I share everything in my head?"

His shoulders drooped. "I can't."

"Can't what?"

"I can't care about you. It wouldn't be right, you and me—"

Her fist flashed out and smacked his chest.

"Hey!"

"There you go again. Right and wrong. I'm so sick of it—"

He grabbed her arms. "You don't believe in God. I do. It *would* be wrong."

Inside her, hope crumbled. She jerked free.

"It wouldn't work, not like you think it would. Before long we wouldn't agree on anything, wouldn't care about each other, wouldn't love each other—"

Her gaze snapped to his. "Love?"

His eyes bore into hers. "You don't know how often I've wanted to tell you what I really think, how much you tempt me, but we can't get caught—"

"That's what I am? A temptation? Some evil to be avoided?"

"This is avoiding you?"

"You're right. You want to change me so you can do whatever you want to me."

He straightened. "I never—"

"You're just like the rest, trying to use women."

"Stop it. When have I tried to—"

She stepped close, almost touching him.

His eyes widened, and he pulled back.

"Oh, that's right," she breathed. She looked at his mouth, then up at his eyes. "You're not like ordinary men." She shoved him away and raced for home.

CHAPTER FORTY-THREE

Dillan clenched his teeth as Miska ran, her ponytail swishing behind her.

Why do you care, Dillan?

She vanished up the stairs. The top of her head bobbed out of view.

A horn blared.

He jerked and strained to see the road.

What if something happened to her? What if Mark was a killer and came after her? Forget that. If Mark was a killer and she went back to him, she'd always be in danger.

He rubbed his chest where she'd punched him. While it had made him angry, it hadn't hurt. As strong as she was, she'd be no match for a ticked-off Scheider.

And the truth was that he did care. Too much.

Maybe he should tell her.

If she knew people cared, if she knew she had options—

Dillan took the stairs two at a time. At the crosswalk he waited for a gap in traffic, searching for Miska. The spring green of her tank top flashed into view. She was already near the fountain—and moving fast.

He crossed the road and darted around tourists and a biker, barely keeping her in view. He reached the western edge of the fountain and another street. Waited again for traffic to clear. Ran across the bridge above the train tracks.

The street curved to the right, leading to their block. She crossed Michigan Avenue, the walk sign flashing. He pushed himself to catch it, but the sign changed. Traffic pinned him where he was. He leaned over, hands pressed to his thighs, and sucked in air, watching her slow to a walk.

Good.

What was he going to say? What was the right thing to say? A frustrated chuckle escaped. How did he make her see that caring about the right thing *was* caring about people?

The light changed, and he jogged across the street, a cramp in his side.

She reached their building and vanished inside.

Dillan pushed himself to a run.

At the entrance, he caught a glimpse of her entering the elevator bank. He sprinted down the hallway, flashed a smile at the day doorman, and yanked open the glass door to the elevators.

An elevator was closing.

He prayed it belonged to Miska and stuck his hand between the doors.

They slid back, revealing her slouched against a wall.

Her eyes widened. "What are you doing?"

"Trying to convince you that I'm not out to use you."

She rolled her eyes.

The doors tried to close. He pushed them back. "I *do* care about you, Miska. I don't want to see you hurt."

"Wow. Such a gentleman. Like when you completely snubbed me at your party."

His neck warmed. "I'd just seen you with Kendall. You—it disgusted me."

"*It* disgusted you? You were going to say I did, weren't you?"

"It was right after I gave you a ride home. We had fun, Miska. I shared myself with you, and then to find out how you really lived and that you had to be laughing at me—"

"So it's not about me. It's about you. About how dumb you feel."

Man, she knew how to get under his skin.

"Isn't it?" she asked.

"Can I finish?"

"Go ahead. You're doing great."

"I don't talk to women about things we've talked about—"

"What things?"

Like she didn't know. "About waiting. About how guys think."

"So?"

"So I did with you."

She raised one eyebrow, her head tilted.

"Come on, Miska. How can you say I don't care when we've talked? Really talked?"

She laughed. "That's talking? Yikes. I'd hate to see you clam up."

Fine. He was done. He stepped out of the elevator. "Have a nice day." He turned his back, waited until the doors whooshed shut and the elevator hummed. He pressed the call button and turned.

Miska leaned against the wall, her arms crossed.

"What are you doing?" he snapped.

She pushed off the wall with her shoulder. "Sorry. I was intentionally baiting you."

"No kidding. Really?"

Her eyes narrowed. "I just apologized."

He groaned and ran a hand down his face. "Yeah. Sorry."

She nodded. "Well?"

"Well what?"

"You were defending yourself. You said you wanted to finish."

Oh, he had. "I'm done, Miska."

"Dillan." She grabbed his forearm, and he looked down at her soft brown hand. "Tell me why you bother with me. Please."

He stepped back, freeing his arm. How honest should he be with her? How much should he say?

Hadn't he chased her down to be honest? Finally?

He had. So here it went. "I think you're the most beautiful woman I've ever met."

She blinked at him.

"I used to think that was why I couldn't get you out of my mind. From the day I knocked you and Scheider over, I tried to avoid you. We had nothing in common, you know?"

Her eyes lowered to his chest.

"But I kept running into you. I blamed Tracy, but then she and Garrett broke up, and we still crossed paths."

She toyed with her fingernails.

"Somehow, Miska, we've become friends—of a sort. I'd hate to see anything happen to you. I care—" He gulped down the words. Man, this was hard. "I care what happens to you. I care about *you*. Every time you're at church, every time you ask about God, I get excited. I can't help it. He means everything to me, and I know how much your life would change if you'd follow him." There. He'd said what he could. He planted his hands on his hips and waited while she worked her fingers.

She started to speak, but an elevator dinged. The doors slid open, and a man dressed for the office stepped out. He sent them a curious glance as he left.

She kept her gaze on her hands. "You said we were friends of a sort. If I became a Christian, how would that change?"

Now there was a place he couldn't afford to go. He forced a grin. "I don't know. Why don't you do it and we find out?"

"Dillan, I'm serious." She raised her eyes to his. "I'm being completely open with you. How would things change?"

There was honest pain in her eyes. He searched their dark depths. Was she saying she was interested in him? Still? That crush she'd mentioned a few weeks ago? She didn't feel that way anymore, did she?

He rubbed a hand across his shirt. He couldn't go there. He really couldn't go there. What on earth did he say to this?

"Dillan?"

He hung his head. Even if she did become a Christian, would he ever trust her? She had such a wild past. Two athletes at once, some naked guy whose name she didn't even know—and there was no way they were the first.

Not even close.

Could he ever be serious about a woman like her? As much as he was drawn to her, there was no way they could build a life together. Even someone like Tracy would be preferable to her.

He could never say that.

She pressed the call button.

Dillan watched her profile.

She stared at the wall, her mouth a straight line, then turned away, but not before he caught a tear skimming down her cheek.

"Miska," he groaned, stepping toward her.

An elevator dinged behind them, and she stepped away, toward the opening doors.

He followed her in.

She yanked her hair out of her ponytail, and the dark strands fell around her face, hiding her.

Dillan pressed the eighteen. The doors closed, and the elevator rose.

She rested her head against the wall.

"Miska."

"Hmm."

"I didn't mean to hurt you."

She shrugged. "Don't worry about it."

The words ratcheted up the guilt. "I mean it. I'm sorry."

She flicked her hair aside and looked at him. Her cheeks were damp, the only evidence that there had been tears. "I'm not being passive-aggressive. Let's move on."

But now he couldn't. "I can't say how things would change between us because I don't know. We'd have God in common, which is a big deal. So at some level we'd be better friends."

Sadness coated her smile. "That's good to hear."

He nodded. Clearly it wasn't the answer she'd been looking for. She *had* wondered how far their relationship could go. If they could have a romantic relationship.

And he'd made it plain they could not.

The elevator dinged. The doors opened.

Dillan held out a hand for her to go first. At least here he could be a real gentleman.

Inside her condo, Miska set her phone on the island. Well, she knew. She'd wanted to know, and she knew. Even if she chose to believe like Dillan, there could never be anything between them.

The lake sparkled through a window, but she ignored it and plopped onto the couch. She'd put him in an awkward spot. She should have known better, really.

Hadn't she sat with Tracy through the other side of the situation? Listened to her say that she'd never be able to believe that Garrett had really changed? Hadn't Dillan watched his own brother go back? Was it any wonder he refused to get involved with her?

She tucked her arms between her knees, hands clasped, and stared at the coffee table. For the first time in a long time, she was alone. No men in her life, if she didn't count Mark. It was strange to know that she was completely on her own. Finally she could focus on what was best for her.

But she still had bills. If she stayed single, she'd have to get roommates again. Or sell. If she didn't, she risked losing the condo and the entirety of Mom's legacy.

She wouldn't do that.

Her laptop lay open and waiting on her desk. She forced herself off the couch. She needed to get some work in.

But the John book, peeking beneath a bill, caught her attention. Had it only been a week since she'd read about the woman at the well? She flipped through the pages, stopping at chapter five, the chapter the church group would discuss Wednesday. Tonight.

The chapter was full of miracles—a man healed, five thousand men fed with five loaves and two fish, Jesus walking on water—and in between them were words that seemed to be written to her.

He who hears My word and believes in Him who sent Me has everlasting life, and shall not come into judgment... I am the bread of life. He who comes to Me shall never hunger...

Her life was constant hunger.

Lord, to whom shall we go? You have the words of eternal life.

Simon Peter's words were hopeless and hopeful at the same time. There was no one else but Jesus because He alone had the words of life.

Was that true?

She flipped back to the beginning of the passage and read it again. Was Jesus the only one who had the truth? Did he alone offer answers?

Dillan's life—and Tracy's—gave compelling evidence that it was true.

This is the will of Him who sent Me, that everyone who sees the Son and believes in Him may have everlasting life...

Did she believe? And if she did, why?

Because it couldn't be for Dillan anymore. He'd made that clear. If she was going to choose this Jesus, this God, then it had to be completely because she believed it, not because it might get her a good man.

Do not labor for the food which perishes, but for the food which endures to everlasting life...

Certainly she'd been working for things that perished. For food which had to be bought again and again. For clothes that snagged. For furniture that broke. For clients who shut down—

Was there something more?

Tracy thought so. Dillan thought so.

He who comes to Me shall never hunger.

How she was tired of hungering. Of always chasing another man, another night that failed come morning.

Lord, to whom shall we go?

If God alone had the words of life, then she owed it to herself to find out.

Tonight.

CHAPTER FORTY-FOUR

The singles' room was filling up.

Already seated, Dillan looked up from his notes for Sunday as Garrett sat beside him. "Hey, Gare."

"Hey." Garrett sent a nod to Ethan across the room before resting his gaze on Tracy.

Who sat beside Miska.

Dillan cleared his throat. "Haven't seen you with Ethan lately."

"That's on purpose." Garrett stretched his legs beneath the chair in front of him. "Miska's here again."

That had been a surprise. He'd looked up just as she'd entered, and she'd sent him a painful smile he did his best to return.

"You talk to her lately?"

"This morning."

"How'd that go?"

Dillan rubbed his nose. "Great."

"Had she heard about the baby?"

"No. Mark called her, though."

Garrett swiveled in his seat. "For real? Wow. That is messed up."

Austin stepped to the podium, and the room quieted.

Dillan locked his fingers together. He shouldn't have said anything. Garrett had never been good at keeping things to himself. "Don't repeat it."

Garrett flashed him a look that said Dillan could trust him.

It wasn't any comfort.

The study began. After reading the passage, people asked questions and pointed out things that caught their attention.

Austin called on Miska.

When she spoke, her gaze remained on her open book. "There've been a lot of verses that stood out, but the main one for me is where Jesus calls himself the bread of life. He says that whoever comes to him will never hunger. Last week he called himself living water." She looked up. "It's clear what he's saying. So how do we know if it's true? Because either he's right or he's wrong."

Dillan held his breath.

Austin nodded. "It's a good question and one we've all faced. How do we know that the Bible is true?" Austin flipped through his book. "One of the study questions asked us to share how we became a Christian and how God satisfies us. Who wants to start?"

Amanda volunteered. She'd come from a Christian family, saved at age eight.

Great. Not at all like Miska. Didn't answer her question one bit.

Jordan was next. Saved at five. Currently going to a Christian college where she saw God answer prayer requests from herself or her friends every day.

Good. Nice. Not much help.

Someone else spoke up. Surprise, surprise. Another person saved as a kid, their parents taking them to church. He looked around the room. Most here had been saved as kids. Wasn't there someone Miska could identify with?

What about you?

He was just like them. Saved at seven. Grew up with a desire to serve God. From age sixteen, there'd never been a doubt that he'd serve God fulltime.

But there'd been other doubts, different doubts. There'd been days when his faith felt puny, days when it had been tested.

God, do I say that?

"Pastor Dillan."

He jerked his head up to meet Austin's gaze.

"You look like you have some thoughts."

So the answer was yes. He leaned back in his seat. "I was thinking how my life is like almost everyone else's. Saved young, grew up in church, in a Christian family. The big sin I had to repent from was being rude to an obnoxious little brother."

Snickers spread.

Garrett stilled, then straightened. "That would be Fred, our brother who died." He gestured at Jordan. "You weren't born yet."

Laughter grew, and Dillan chuckled with them. "Yeah, poor Fred."

Garrett shook his head tragically.

"Anyway, during college I faced whether my faith was mine or my parents'. I believed in God. I knew he was the bread of life, the living water. I'd seen him work in my parents' lives, but I hadn't experienced much in my own life. Being on my own made me examine what I really believed."

Memories returned, sweet and satisfying. "For the first time I had to face whether God was God enough to do everything he'd promised. I had to decide if he was big enough to trust."

Miska turned toward him.

He saw only her. "And God was. Over and over I went to him, prayed about situations and struggles, and each time he stepped in and did what was right for me. He met me, and he was completely enough. He was everything he said he was.

"I think, Miska, there comes a point where it's faith. We all came to Christ based on faith that what he said in the Bible was true. We hadn't seen it yet; we hadn't experienced it yet; but we chose to believe and, well, put everything in his hands.

"Those of us who did, whether we were saved at eight or twenty-eight, would tell you that he doesn't fail us. No matter what happens, he's there and working on our behalf to make us stronger. It doesn't mean life is easy—because it isn't—but we go through all the trials with him. We aren't alone. And he never drops the ball."

The words were full of clichés, he knew, but around the room heads nodded. Dillan studied his hands. They all got it. If only Miska would too.

From the back, Cam spoke up. "I get Miska's question. I was saved at twenty-eight. I remember wondering if I was losing it since this stuff was

making sense. All I'd say, Miska, is read the Bible. Don't be afraid to ask
the hard questions. Yes, it takes faith to believe, but it takes faith to reject it
too. When you really want the truth, God opens your eyes and you get it.
At least, that's what happened to me. You couldn't pay me to go back to
my old life."

Couldn't pay me. Dillan rubbed a knuckle against his lip.

The discussion continued. Miska listened intently.

And Dillan couldn't help remembering that elevator ride with Tracy,
two months ago, when she'd wondered if they lived next door to Miska for
a reason.

Sure looked like Tracy had been right. Tracy, with the strongest faith.

We aren't alone. And he never drops the ball.

The words played in her head all Thursday. During a wedding scene in
the romance she edited. During a pre-lunch workout. While she cleaned
before Tracy arrived with dinner.

Like her dad had said, God wasn't a genie. He was powerful, in charge.
So the real question, the one she'd ignored all day, was what she was going
to do about it. Would she try to turn him into a genie like the people who
followed him for the miracles? Or would she be like Simon Peter who said
there was no one else to go to?

Tracy arrived with a Chinese feast.

Miska paid her back, despite Tracy's protests, and joined her on the
couch, eating while the sky hinted at dusk.

"Some days I think I could live off Chinese food," Tracy said around a
mouthful of General Tsao's chicken.

"Some days I think you and I are twins." Miska ate another bite of
broccoli, then pointed her fork at Tracy. "Move in here."

Tracy, mouth full, raised an eyebrow.

"You're still looking for a place to live come September, right? Be my
roommate. I've got two spare bedrooms. You can pick the one you want
and have your own bathroom."

Tracy's shoulders fell. "Honey, I'd love to be your roommate. If you lived anywhere but next door to Garrett, I'd do it."

Garrett. Right. "I forgot about him."

"I wish I could forget about him. In fact, let's talk about something else. What did you think about last night?"

"Honestly? I've gone over it all day."

"What exactly?"

"About how it seems like I know all I need to know. I'm not sure where I go from here, though."

Tracy set her plate on the coffee table. "You know what I did?"

"What?"

"I confessed my sin to God, asked his forgiveness, and accepted Jesus's sacrifice. I asked him to take me as his child, Miska. I gave him everything."

Everything was a massive commitment. "What's with the father/child analogies? That's not reassuring."

"Except that God is the perfect father. He doesn't hurt us, humiliate us, or leave us. Instead he does what's best for us. He won't mess you up."

It was all too good. "If he's so perfect, how can he care about me?"

"Because he made you, honey. No one will ever love you like God does."

She rolled the words through her head. "I don't know."

"What don't you know?"

She shrugged. "I just—I can't measure up."

"To what?"

"To God. To the way he says to live. I still won't be a virgin."

"Is this about Dillan?"

Was it? "I don't think so." She rested her head against the back of the couch and stared at the ceiling. "Listening to everyone—you're all good. No one has a past like me."

"I do."

Miska sent her a gentle smile. "No, you don't. You've been with one guy. I'm not sure I could give you an accurate number."

"It doesn't matter."

"Of course it matters. How could it not?"

"Miska, when we repent before God, he forgives our sins. The Bible says they're as far from him as the east is from the west. Think about that."

"People don't forget."

"People don't matter."

Sure, they did. Some. Moaning, she covered her face with her hands. "Tracy, I've done so much. I've done things people in that group would never even think about."

"How do you know?"

"I've listened to them. They're so... innocent."

"But they're not." Tracy grabbed her hands. "It doesn't matter how much you've done, whether it's one sin or a million sins. They both have the same punishment—hell, eternal separation from God. When Jesus died on the cross, he didn't die for the twenty-sins-or-less crowd. He died for everyone who would believe, whether they were a six nine pastor who picked on his brother or a woman who couldn't say how many men she's slept with. He died for you both, Miska. God loves you just as much as he loves Dillan."

Her vision blurred. "But what does he expect from me, Tracy? What on earth do I have to give him?"

"Just your love and obedience. Just a lifetime in perfect friendship with him."

The knock on the door came at ten o'clock.

Dillan knelt on the living room floor, picking up the popcorn kernels he'd spilled. Garrett turned off the kitchen faucet. "I'll get it."

The door squeaked open. Tracy's voice sounded. "Is Dillan here?"

He set the bowl on the couch and stood.

Garrett held the door open, and Tracy hurried past him toward Dillan, tears rolling down her cheeks. "She did it, Dillan. She asked God to save her."

He opened his arms a moment before she threw herself against him. She shook once, twice, while he held her, dazed. Miska had become a Christian?

Tracy stepped back and wiped her cheeks.

Garrett stayed by the door, watching.

"What happened?"

"We've been talking all evening. She's so ashamed of her past, Dillan. She almost couldn't get over it. But then she just made up her mind."

Her words settled in his brain. "She really believes?"

"She does. She was so ready for someone to tell her about God. So ready." Tracy laughed. "You should see her."

He couldn't imagine.

"She asked me what she should start reading. I told her to keep going in John. We ran out, bought her a Bible, and read through two more chapters." Tracy laughed, ending it with a hiccup. "Dillan, I'm so excited. Already she's different. You can see it in her face, hear it in her words."

Miska—saved.

"Don't tell her I told you, okay? I think she wants to tell you guys herself, but I couldn't keep quiet. I had to tell someone." She sent Garrett a soft smile, and Garrett sent it back. "I'm still giddy. Part of me can't believe it. I don't think I'll sleep much tonight."

He might not either. "Thanks for telling us."

"Thanks for everything you did, Dillan."

He hadn't done much. Tracy was the one with the burden.

"I need to get home." She gave him another hug. He patted her back. She gave Garrett a quick hug too. "See you guys Sunday."

Dillan stayed rooted by the couch, his gaze locked onto the door as Garrett shut it behind her.

His brother looked his way. "What do you think?"

What did he think? He'd hoped she'd get saved, and then he'd doubted, and then he'd hoped— "I think it's awesome."

Garrett searched his face, as if he expected more.

Dillan ran a hand over his hair. He could guess what that look meant— and he wasn't going there. "I'm tired. See you in the morning."

Garrett stepped aside and let him pass.

In bed, the lights out, he could still picture the emotion on Tracy's face, the certainty that Miska had made that life-altering decision.

And suddenly he couldn't wait to see for himself if this quasi-friend who'd once laughed at God had really become brand new.

CHAPTER FORTY-FIVE

Dillan was coming up the lakefront stairs when Miska reached Lake Shore Drive the next morning. His sweaty shirt clung to his chest, and he plodded across the road, breathing heavily.

What would he think of her news?

Miska waited where she was.

He didn't notice her until he was within arm's reach. Then he pulled up and chin-nodded, panting for breath. "Hey."

"Morning."

He wiped his forehead on his sleeve. "You're out here late."

"Yes, I—" She tented her hands over her mouth, trying not to give it away. "I read some of the Bible before running."

He raised his eyebrows. "You read the Bible."

She nodded, lowering her hands. There was no point in hiding the grin. She could hear it. "I bought my own yesterday. I had no idea how expensive they could be."

"No eight dollar gift-and-award Bible?"

"I saw those. No, I decided if I was going to buy one, it was going to be nice. Real leather, nice chocolate color."

"Hmm."

"And get this. It has the words of Jesus in red so they stand out."

He smiled as if she amused him. "Really."

"That's what I read this morning, where the red words started."

"So you started in Matthew."

How did he know that? "Chapters five, six, and seven. And don't tell me what it was about. Because I know."

He chuckled, the sound warming her. "Tell me."

"There were a bunch of verses with blessings."

He nodded, his eyes looking happy. Was he?

"One struck me right away, that those who long for righteousness—who hunger and thirst, I think—would be satisfied. I realized that's me. Last night—" Her voice shook. "Last night I asked God for his forgiveness. I believe him, Dillan, and I realized this morning that it's true, that I have been satisfied."

His smile broadened. He wrapped an arm around her, then another, pulling her close. "I'm happy for you, Miska."

"Thank you." She rested against his damp shirt and closed her eyes. "I'm happy for me too. Are you surprised?"

He chuckled.

"You're not." She pushed out of his arms. "How did you know?"

His grin touched every part of his face—cheeks, jaw, eyes. "Tracy told us last night. And you reading the Bible—that would have given it away."

"Ever since that woman-at-the-well story, I've been thinking about it—fighting it. Then last night, talking to Tracy, it just clicked. I couldn't believe I'd doubted."

"You're looking through God's eyes. Everything will be different."

Everything? She hoped so. "Do you remember when you did this?"

"Honestly, not all of it anymore. I was seven—long time ago. I remember going to my dad, though, and telling him I needed to be saved, that I didn't think I'd go to heaven if I died. I remember being scared." He stared toward the lake. "I remember he cried afterward."

Just like Tracy. Happy tears, she'd said.

Dillan smiled at her.

She smiled back.

He said nothing, and after a few seconds, awkwardness set in. She looked down at his feet.

"You off today?" he asked.

"Just the afternoon. Then I'm going to Tracy's for dinner and fireworks. You?"

"Same—I've got some work to finish up. Then fireworks."

She nodded. Maybe they'd end up at the same place.

"Well."

The word announced he was about to leave. She forced her smile to stay.

"I'm really happy for you, Miska."

"Thank you."

He checked his watch. "I need to head in. Stay, though."

"I will. Enjoy the fireworks."

He moved into a jog and tossed a final smile over his shoulder, then loped across the pavilion.

Well.

He did seem happy about her news. For that she was grateful. But there'd been nothing more.

She closed her eyes and relived his smelly, sweaty hug. What would God think if she prayed about him? Would that start her off on the wrong foot? Because she wanted so much—

Oh, God, please.

She jogged across the street, her feet slower than they'd been.

Miska never expected such excitement over a decision that affected only her, but there it was—Jordan, Amanda, and Tracy hugging her, their laughter contagious, their excitement recharging her own.

"So, Miska," Amanda said as they sat around Tracy's table, "you know what this means. Cam's going to ask you out."

Jordan and Tracy laughed.

Miska frowned at Amanda. "I thought you were a couple."

"It was never serious."

"It's what Cam does," Tracy said. "He asks the new girl out. It doesn't last long."

Jordan agreed. "I remember Garrett being relieved that he asked Tracy out before Cam could."

Tracy's mouth curved into a cynical smile, her eyes on her glass.

"How long has this been going on?" Miska asked.

"I've been here three years," Tracy said. "So at least that long."

"Why doesn't it last?"

Jordan and Tracy shrugged, but Amanda pursed her lips.

Jordan smacked the tabletop. "Amanda knows something."

"Maybe. I think it has to do with what he said Wednesday—about his life before he was saved."

Tracy shrugged. "I don't know anything about that."

"Because he won't talk about it. All I got out of him is that he's the only Christian in his family. You ask about them, and he's got this wall."

"So he just clams up?"

"He changes the topic. I don't think he lets anyone get beyond the surface."

Of course not. Miska nodded. "He doesn't feel worthy."

"Why not?" Jordan asked. "We don't care about his past. Whatever it was, I wouldn't hold it against him. Would you?"

Amanda shook her head.

"It's easy to say, but what if you found out..." The only thing she could think of was her own story. "What if you're falling for a guy, and you find out he'd..." Why was it so hard to say? "That he'd slept with a lot of women? That some hadn't meant anything—" Her throat tightened, the ache swelling until she feared she couldn't hold it down.

"Miska." Amanda squeezed her hand. "If a guy holds that against you, he's not worth it."

"Would you want that in your relationship? Especially if you'd waited?"

"What are you talking about? STDs? So you get tested. You go from there."

The STDs she'd had had been curable, but her guilt... "It isn't that simple."

Jordan arched an eyebrow. "It should be."

"You don't get it. You all grew up in church and were Christians before you hit puberty."

Amanda snickered.

Seriously, she and Jordan had no idea how life changing the order of those events was. "Dillan said his big sin was picking on Garrett. Really? That's what haunts him at night? I can't let anyone know my story because I *have* slept around. I've been with more men than I can count on my fingers and toes. Which makes me feel incredibly inferior."

Jordan frowned at her. "Do we make you feel that way?"

"Of course not."

"Then you shouldn't feel that way."

Tracy leaned forward. "Regardless of how we should or shouldn't feel, the fact is that sometimes we do feel worthless." She sighed. "I felt that way. When Garrett told me where he'd come from, I felt better. We both had pasts, you know? He couldn't condemn me."

"Tracy." Jordan whispered her name. "You're one of the best people I know."

Tracy flashed her a tremulous smile.

Amanda ran a finger through the condensation on her glass. "Tracy, I thought you grew up in church."

"No, I…"

She held up a hand. "I don't need to hear it. All I know is who you are now—a Christian who's kind and sweet and doesn't deserve what her fiancé did to her. No offense, Jordan."

Jordan widened her eyes. "I'm with you."

"If people are holding your past over you, they're in the wrong. But if you're holding your past over yourself—" She shook her head. "How crazy is that? It's gone. Move on."

The words were beautiful, but Miska wasn't ready to stand on them. "What do you do when someone's talking about you?"

Amanda glanced at Jordan. "You mean Ethan."

So he *was* talking about her. She closed her eyes and locked her fingers behind her neck. "What's he been saying?"

Jordan grimaced. "Do we have to go there?"

"What's he said, Jordan?"

She rolled her eyes. "Ethan's a perv. The guy's hardly ever at church—"

"But sometimes he is," Tracy interrupted. "So what does he know?"

Jordan sighed. "He knows about a certain night you were drunk."

Of course he did. And everyone else soon would if they didn't already.

"If it helps, Garrett feels bad."

It didn't. "What do I do?"

Amanda lifted a hand. "Beat him up."

Jordan laughed.

Tracy smiled. "I'll help."

"While that might be cathartic, I don't think it'll help my cause."

Amanda shrugged. "Then beat him to it. If you tell people your past, what's left for him to talk about?"

"But you said to move on."

"Well, of course. You don't need to go into detail. But share how God saved you, what he saved you from. Put it out there as neat or messy as you want. Then who cares what he says? You said it first."

Dillan knew enough without her going into detail. Or was his imagination worse than the truth?

In her purse by her feet, Miska's phone rang, that dull ringtone.

Mark was calling? She glanced at the clock. The funeral was only eight hours ago. What did he want? She picked up her bag, pulled out her phone, and caught Tracy's eye. "It's Mark."

The phone rang again.

"Who's Mark?" Amanda asked.

Tracy gripped the table's edge. "Don't answer."

"Who's Mark?" Amanda whispered to Jordan.

Jordan grimaced and shook her head.

It rang again. He'd just keep calling. How clear could it be? He wouldn't take no.

She pushed her chair back.

"Miska, turn it off."

"I have to face him. Can I use your bedroom?"

Tracy groaned but pointed to a closed door off the living room.

Miska shut herself inside and answered. "Mark?"

"Miska." He heaved a sigh. "I was beginning to think you wouldn't answer."

"Sorry. I'm with some friends." She cringed. What a stupid thing to say to a man who'd just buried his wife.

"How are you?" he asked.

"Okay. You?"

"Needing to see you. That'd make today bearable."

She bit her lip. "I'm sorry."

"Me too."

What was there to say? *Sorry for your loss, for the baby you never knew. Please don't call me.*

"Darcie's family leaves tomorrow. Tell you what—that can't happen soon enough."

"Mark."

"You spend a week with people who think your wife was an angel and glare at you every second you're not mourning her."

Darcie's family was upset with him? "Why? What do they know?"

"Know? About what?"

"I don't—I mean—I don't know. I'm sorry."

"What?"

She squeezed her hair. "I don't know what to say. I feel caught in the middle, and I don't want to be. I'm sorry Darcie's gone. I'm sorry for your loss and for the baby—" Her mouth shook. "I never meant to ruin your marriage, Mark. I'm so sorry—"

"Miska, stop it. You made it bearable."

"How can you say that? You were trying to have a baby with her. You had to love her."

"Of course I did. But it's time to move on. With you."

Tears trailed down her cheeks. "How can we have a relationship after this?"

"Miska—"

"I took away Darcie's chance at a good marriage. She never had a chance while I was around."

"What are you talking about? She's gone, Miska. This is our chance to *have* an honest relationship."

No relationship with him could be honest. "A lot's changed with me."

"Please. What could be that drastic?"

"I mean it. I've been rethinking things."

"Like?"

Everything. "What I believe about life. How I want to live."

"Winters in Fiji. Remember?"

She pulled up the memory of Dillan's sweaty hug. "Mark, I don't think it'll work."

"What aren't you getting?" he hissed. "Darcie's gone. You wanted her gone, and she's gone."

No. He didn't mean... "What have you done?"

"I didn't do anything!" He swore. Swore again. The phone banged on his end, and something thumped. His voice rang loudly in her ear. "Listen to me. I didn't do anything. Got it? I was in Arizona. In a hotel. Then at the ballpark. Talk to anyone there. How could I have done a thing if I was in Arizona? Hmm?"

"Mark, you're not—" She sorted her thoughts. "You're grieving. You're not yourself right now."

"Sure. Whatever."

How could he be so flippant? "You're not ready for us."

He growled.

"Listen. I've been where you are, okay? When someone passes, everything's messed up. Nothing's right. I know. I understand. Okay? Okay?"

There was another thud on his end. "Yeah."

"You need time. You need to work things through."

"I don't want time."

"But you need it. You're angry at her. Don't you see? You have to deal with that, Mark. For our sake." She bit her lip at the lie, hoping he'd buy it. "Take some time to let things inside you die down. Take some time to... to enjoy being single again."

He said nothing.

"Mark?"

"Yeah."

"I'm sorry about everything."

"None of it's your fault. So don't be."

It wasn't true. She'd gotten between a husband and wife.

"Miska, I need to see you."

"No."

"Stop saying no."

"It's not safe! Your wife just died."

"Don't yell at me! You think I don't know that?"

She plopped down on Tracy's bed. "Mark, I told you we couldn't—"

"Let's meet somewhere in the middle, near the state line."

She sucked in a breath. "I can't."

He breathed a curse. "When will it be okay? Give me a time frame here."

Her own ultimatum rose before her. Had that factored into Darcie's death? *Please, God. Don't let him have killed her.*

"Miska."

"Let me think about it."

"No. I want—"

"My friends are calling. I need to go."

"Wait—"

Cringing, she ended the call. She'd never heard him like this. Never.

What kind of a man was he? Truly? If she kept saying no, what would he do?

The door opened. Tracy poked her head inside. "Everything okay?"

Nothing was okay. Mark wouldn't let her go. And no matter how much she'd changed, her past wouldn't let her go either.

CHAPTER FORTY-SIX

A full week passed. Then another. Miska continued her habit of reading her Bible, then going for a run and savoring what she'd read. The words were coming alive, full of hope and promises, conviction and encouragement. She pored over the John book and the passages the head pastor taught each Sunday. She arrived early to small group and stayed late, relishing her new friendships… and catching every glimpse of Dillan that she could.

Cam remained his usual friendly self. Ethan stayed just outside her vision, but his gaze was always leaving her whenever she noticed him. Mark returned to baseball, starting two games before reinjuring his shoulder. He hadn't called since the funeral, but now that he was on the disabled list again, she expected another call.

Not that she wanted it.

Adrienne stopped by on Monday, laptop in hand, and they spent the evening devouring homemade guacamole while they worked. Adrienne asked about the blog, and Miska confessed that she hadn't looked at it in, well, almost two months. She made a mental note to close it down. No way could that part of her life get out.

Adrienne spent the night, and it felt like their best days together, like the year Adrienne had moved in while she swore off relationships and figured out life. There was no arguing, no disagreeing. Just quiet, enjoyable companionship.

Sometime during Miska's run the next morning, Adrienne left. Miska threw sheets from the guest bed into the wash, then showered and started her last Relentless Hearts edit, a steamy time-travel set in modern-day and

Roaring-Twenties New York. As she read one graphic scene after another, the characters' behavior—once so similar to hers—rubbed her wrong. By early afternoon she stopped editing, head in her hands.

How many sex scenes had she edited over the years? She knew the effect they had on her. What about the people who read the work she'd helped perfect? What did God think of what she'd done, was doing still?

If she was really going to follow God—and she wanted to—it couldn't be okay to continue this. But what was she supposed to do?

Dillan's words resurfaced, how he'd gone to God and how God had met him, had been enough.

Was God big enough for this?

She pursed her lips. The real question was, did he care?

The blue summer sky called from the window. She wandered over. Buckingham Fountain was in the middle of a water show, the central jet flirting with cotton-ball clouds that glided over the lake, darkening water and dimming boats.

How far did God want to go in her life? Did he care where she worked? What she did? Books were just words—

No. She shook her head. This work she'd done for so long flew against everything she'd learned about God. The last thing she wanted was to go against him, and she was doing just that. She knew it.

"Okay, God. But I need to eat. Pay my bills. I can't do this anymore. So..."

She wet her lips. *Just say it, Miska.*

But they were so much more than words. They were a completely new way of living. Once she put it out there...

What if he didn't answer? What if nothing happened? What if...

There just comes a point where it's faith. We hadn't seen it yet; we hadn't experienced it yet; but we chose to believe and put everything in his hands.

Dillan never said how terrifying it was to trust God with everything. It had been so much easier to accept Kendall's offer, so much simpler to invite Mark in for the night. So much easier to live on her terms.

Closing her eyes, she leaned against the window. "I need a new job. I can't edit these books anymore. And that hurts because my entire life has been stories and—" She wiped fear from her eyes. "This is *me*, God. *Me.*" She clenched her fists. "I can map out my life in books. How can it be wrong to edit? What else am I supposed to do?"

Nothing happened.

Where was the answer? How long was she supposed to wait? When would she know that he'd heard? Or hadn't?

She opened her eyes. Treetops called for her to enjoy their shade.

But she couldn't. She had work to do. She'd already contracted with Melissa and another publisher to edit three books. She'd finish those jobs, and then she'd...

She'd what?

"I'll quit editing for them."

It was the right thing. But what about after that? How was she supposed to live?

She lifted her chin. She'd figure it out later. That's what. For now, she needed to escape, and a run through Grant Park sounded perfect.

Late July in Chicago didn't get nicer than this. Temps in the low eighties, a breeze off the lake, and just enough clouds for occasional shade. Why work in a white, windowless bedroom when all of this was outside?

Dillan checked his watch. He'd been sitting by the fountain for an hour, but he'd made good progress on his Sunday School class. He cross-referenced a verse and found himself reading words that had caught his attention after he'd kissed Miska—the list of people who wouldn't inherit the kingdom of heaven.

The last verse in the section had become his favorite. *Such were some of you; but you were washed, but you were sanctified, but you were justified...*

The verse had initially hit him because of Garrett—then because of himself. He couldn't believe how he'd treated Miska, but enough time had passed for it to make sense. He'd looked at her as trash. He had. He'd viewed her as without value.

All he'd cared about was making sure he looked good.

Today, though, the verse made him think of Miska. A month ago she wouldn't have inherited the kingdom of heaven. Now her sin was gone. Like the verse said, she was washed, she was sanctified, she was justified.

Garrett had bugged him about asking her out before Cam—or someone else—did. The thought was tempting. There had always been something about her that drew him, even when he knew the worst. But she was still a baby Christian. If he barged in now, he'd never know how real of a change God had made in her.

Not that she had to prove herself to him. Not if she truly was saved. And the early evidence pointed to that. He smiled, remembering her expression when she'd told him she'd become a Christian. How she'd gone running later than usual because she'd wanted to read her Bible.

In the weeks since, she'd routinely come out later. Either she was sleeping in or...

How tempting to move his run back half an hour.

But he couldn't. He wouldn't. He'd vowed he'd never force a relationship. If God wanted him with someone, then God would have to bring them together at the right time.

He just wished it were soon.

He looked up from the page he'd been staring at.

A tour group on segues rolled past the fountain, and Miska headed his way, dressed in gray shorts and a pink tank top.

He straightened. What was she doing, running in the afternoon?

Her ponytail bounced from side to side as she ran, seemingly unaware of the people she passed, like the two college guys who stared after her. Her gaze swung in his direction. Her eyes connected with his, and Dillan felt it through his chest.

She veered his way. He closed his Bible and commentary and set them on the yellow notepad beside him. She slowed to a walk and blew away strands of hair around her forehead.

"You always run in the afternoon?" he asked.

"No." She glanced at the empty space beside him. "Am I interrupting?"

"Nope. Have a seat."

She sat down and blew out another deep breath, staring at the fountain. "Well." She wiped her fingers across her forehead and swiped them on her shorts.

Her legs caught his attention, and he made himself look away. He set an ankle on his knee and tugged free a loose piece of his sandal's sole.

"What are you up to?" she asked.

"Just work. Got tired of staring at four white walls. You?"

"I needed to think. It looked so gorgeous out here that I was sure I'd figure things out if I went for a run."

"And?"

She sent him a rueful look. "Nothing yet."

He nodded, fighting the urge to ask.

"Dillan, how do you know if God hears you?"

Verses filtered through his mind. "Well, we know if there's sin in our life, sin we're entertaining, he won't hear us. But other than that, if we pray, he hears."

"What if you were sinning and didn't know it?"

What was she thinking of? Mark? Someone else? He hoped not. "If you realize you're involved in something wrong, then you stop it, ask God for forgiveness, and move on. Replace it with something right."

She held his gaze as if she was rolling the words around in her mind.

"You want to share?"

"Yes. I guess." She fiddled with her nails. "I just realized, like you said, that I'm involved in something wrong. I want to stop, but it leaves this huge hole."

He waited for her to elaborate.

She didn't.

"Are you talking about Mark? Or—"

"Oh, no. No way. That's over."

Good. Great.

"Anyway, I prayed about it just now. I asked God to show me what to do, and—nothing."

"Ah. You didn't hear from him, no writing on the wall. Got it."

She cocked her head. "Sometimes he writes on the wall?"

He couldn't help laughing. "No. That's—no." He shook his head. "Sorry. I'll explain that one later."

She shrugged, her smile saying she didn't mind his laugh. "Okay. So?"

"We know God hears us if we're right with him, but answers don't always come immediately. Sometimes we wait. Sometimes we wait awhile."

She slouched against the bench. "I don't have awhile."

"Why? You going somewhere?"

"Maybe an overpass. Maybe Lower Wacker Drive."

He frowned at her mention of the two-level street. "What's going on?"

"You know I do freelance editing, right? Well, the book I'm working on is pretty—" She blew upward, and hair fluttered around her forehead. "One of the lines I edit for is erotica. You know what that is?"

He tried to hide his surprise. "I'm familiar with it. With what it is, I mean."

The corner of her mouth turned up. "I realized today that I can't keep doing that. I can't work on fiction that's got sex scenes all over the place and people..." She waved a hand. "You know. So much fiction has that, even if it's not erotica. So how am I supposed to make a living? I prayed about it. I asked God what to do, and—" She held up her hands. "Nothing."

"Have you told them you're done working for them?"

"No, but I'm going to. I thought about what you said, about God being big enough for our problems. I figure there's no better time to find out than now, right?"

Wow. She'd changed.

"I've considered moving to the non-fiction side, but that means connecting with editors who don't know me or my skills. It's doable, but it'll take time to rebuild my client list. Time I don't have."

He picked up the commentary he'd been reading and looked at the publisher's name. "Have you checked with Christian publishers?"

She stared at him. "With what?"

He turned the spine toward her. "Christian publishers. This one's in Chicago."

She grabbed the book. "Are you kidding me?"

A smile spread over his face. Here was her answer. How cool was this?

She flipped the book open a few pages. "I've never heard of these guys."

"They've been here forever."

"Seriously?"

"And there's another Christian publisher in the suburbs."

"And people work for them? Like fulltime? With benefits and everything?"

He shrugged. "I would imagine."

"Do they do fiction?"

"Some do. I don't know about this one."

"Oh, wow." She hugged the book to her chest. "I can't believe this! Why didn't I think of that? When I moved to New York, I heard there were Christian lines, but when you work in erotica, you roll your eyes. I'd completely forgotten." She ran her hand over the burgundy cover. "Are there many publishers like this?"

"I've got an office full of books. You're welcome to look."

She gave the book back. "Now?"

He laughed. "You mean this second?"

"Come on, Dillan. I'm about to be homeless. Help a girl out."

He set the book on the notepad. "I don't know," he drawled.

"Dillan—"

"It's really nice out. Tomorrow's supposed to hit ninety."

She smacked his arm. "You're messing with me." She dramatically pooched her lip. "Please? I need to see those books."

Grinning, he stood. "All right, all right."

She jumped up, hands clasped beneath her chin. "Thank you, Dillan. So much."

"You're welcome." Afternoon light warmed her cheeks. "You realize what this means?"

"What?"

He chuckled. She was so new to this. "God answered your prayer. Right?"

She covered her mouth with her hands. "Oh, Dillan, he did." Her eyes filled. "Oh, Dillan." Tears raced down each cheek. She ducked her head, but her shoulders shook.

Her emotion hit him, and he pulled her close, there beside the fountain, and held her while her tears soaked his shirt. God had answered her prayer, and, even better, he'd let him be a part of it.

And why not? They were both washed. They were both sanctified. They were both justified.

And he'd never forget it.

CHAPTER FORTY-SEVEN

Miska was a new woman.

Jogging beside her, Dillan couldn't get over it. She looked the same, but everything else—what she said, the giddiness in her speech—was completely different.

They'd spent an hour in his office the previous afternoon, Miska looking through books and writing names of publishers. That had led to her flipping through titles that caught her eye, and when she left, she'd taken five books and a list of twelve publishers.

She'd grinned like never before.

This morning, when they found themselves heading outside at the same time, Miska confessed that she'd gotten up earlier than usual to read one of his books.

He'd shaken his head and smiled.

Different woman indeed.

They jogged toward the fountain. "Got any leads?" he asked.

"You have no idea. The two Chicago publishers?"

"Yeah?"

"Editorial openings at both."

"Really."

"I found a dozen houses that publish fiction. Sent resumes to four. Looked at their books online. Ordered eight—"

"Not bad for an almost homeless woman."

She flashed him a smile. "I know, right?"

"Now what?"

"I finish the books I'm contracted for and pray one of these places hires me fast."

"When will you resign?"

"Did it last night."

Holy cow. He slowed to a walk, then doubled over and held his thighs, chest heaving. Miska barely looked winded. "What will you do until then?"

Her smile vanished. "I'm gonna sell."

He straightened. She'd move?

She eyed him. "You don't look happy."

He forced a dry laugh from his throat. "Just surprised. Where would you move to?"

"Somewhere in the 'burbs where I can buy a house and live off the remains of the sale. It'll need to be close to church and hopefully one of the publishers here. Oh—and close to Tracy's job."

"Tracy?"

"We're going to be roommates—if I stay in the area."

She'd even leave Chicago? "Sounds like you've got it all worked out. I'm happy for you."

"Are you?" Her eyes narrowed. "You don't look it."

"It'll be weird not having you next door." He forced another fake chuckle. Man, he was getting good at those. "Who will I run with in the morning?"

"You mean you'll miss me?"

"Of course." He ignored her faint smile and wide eyes. "It's been fun, seeing how you've changed."

"I have changed, haven't I?" She looked around the park. "A month ago I couldn't bear leaving, and now I'm fine with it. It's like—" She froze. "Dillan." She stared into the trees north of the fountain.

Dillan followed her gaze. "What?"

"It's Mark."

"Where?" Beneath trees beyond the Fountain Café stood three people, two tugging a leashed dog, the other looking their way. Dillan craned his neck, trying to make out the figure's face. "You sure?"

"Yes." Her voice hushed with fear. "What's he doing here? Why is he just standing there, watching?"

The man slid further back into the shadows, mostly disappearing behind the building.

Whatever his reasons, they weren't normal, weren't safe. Dillan clenched his jaw. "What do you want to do?"

Her fingers traced her collarbone. "I should talk to him. Act normal, you know?"

"Not by yourself. I'll go with you. You're not going anywhere alone with him, okay?"

She swallowed. "Agreed."

She led the way toward the cluster of trees. The shadowy figure straightened as if debating what to do, then took a step closer.

Dillan caught his breath. It *was* Scheider.

He wore a weathered hat with the curved brim pulled low, but the thick, blond beard did the most to hide his identity. Khaki cargo shorts hung to his knees, as if he'd lost weight, the faded retro Mountain Dew T-shirt too big.

Hands buried in his pockets, Scheider took a step closer, his gaze locked on Miska.

Dillan kept his features hard. The guy needed to know he'd step in if needed.

Miska stopped well out of reach. "Why are you here?"

"I came to see you."

"I told you no."

"Now I know why." Scheider focused on Dillan, anger heating his eyes. "Sure explains why you were so quick to save her from Sullivan."

Dillan took a step forward. "That's 'cause I'm actually human."

Miska held up a hand. "Mark, really. We're just friends."

"Right. Which is why you two were out here yesterday too."

Dillan stilled.

Mark snorted. "Got no reply, do you? Because you know I caught you being all friendly. What happened when you went inside? After that hug? Tell me that."

Miska smiled. "We looked at books."

He laughed. "Come *on*, Miska. Be a little creative here. You looked at books? How dumb do you think—"

"Hey." He'd gladly get into a fight with this guy, if just to shut his mouth. "She's telling the truth. We're not a couple."

"I see. Friends with benefits. So I was the sucker who had to pay for it—"

Dillan got in his face. "Leave, Scheider."

The guy stepped forward, his chest bumping Dillan's. "That a threat? Assault's a crime, bro."

Miska tugged Dillan back. "What do you want, Mark?"

"You." He shrugged. "That's all. I haven't seen you in weeks. I'm going crazy. Send this loser packing and give me ten minutes."

"You just called me a prostitute. Why would I—"

"Technically you were." He held up his hands. "I'm not saying that's how I viewed you, but if the details were to get out, that's how the law would see it."

This scum. "Blackmail's a crime too."

Scheider grinned. "Then we've all got stuff to hide, don't we? Listen, Miska, you and me—we struggled because Darcie was between us. Don't let Sir Trips-A-Lot get between us too."

How he'd love to lay this guy out. He bit his tongue and waited for Miska's response.

Instead she kept quiet, eyeing Mark. She wasn't... considering him, was she?

Scheider reached for her hand.

Miska jerked away.

He jammed his hands into his pockets. "I'm sorry. I shouldn't have said that about you. But this guy—" He jerked his head at Dillan. "I can't stand seeing you with him. It's wrong."

"No." Her voice was concrete. "You and I were wrong. We never should have—" Her face twisted, and she covered her mouth, eyes shut, forehead crumpling.

Dillan released his breath as she struggled.

The old Miska would never have turned Mark down, even if he had called her a prostitute. How clearly he remembered her crying over him, even after Mark had left her for Kendall to abuse.

She wasn't that woman anymore. Not even close.

And suddenly he couldn't quite breathe for the beauty of the moment. It was like she was being... remade right in front of him. And it was far more magnificent a thing than he'd ever realized. Far, far more amazing.

He touched her elbow. "You want to go?"

She pulled herself up and shook her head. "In a minute."

Mark smirked.

"How did she die, Mark?"

The words destroyed his smile. He blinked at her. "How? Just—an accident. Something she ate that had peanut stuff in it."

Peanut stuff?

"What about her EpiPen?"

"It was damaged. Had gotten hot, I guess."

She nodded. "So she called 911?"

His jaw clenched. "What are you getting at?"

"Some people think it's odd she wasn't able to get help."

"Yeah, well, she had asthma."

"Which means?"

"It makes the reaction much more severe, much faster." Mark ducked his head. "She didn't have time to get help."

Miska crossed her arms again, shoulders hunched. What was she thinking? And what was Mark thinking, now that she'd asked him if he'd killed his wife? What would he say if he knew they all suspected?

Mark glanced his way. "You find this funny, Foster?"

His name on Scheider's tongue—the guy remembered his name?

Scheider took a step closer. "You think you've won? Think you've got her wrapped up? Let me tell you something." He jabbed his finger into Dillan's chest.

Dillan smacked it away. Stood his ground.

"This isn't over. You think you can sweet-talk Miska into your bed, but you can't. Got it?"

Another finger jab.

Dillan knocked it away again. "Shut up, Scheider."

"She and me—there's too much history—"

The finger came again. Dillan stepped into it, grabbed Scheider's wrist, and yanked it down.

Scheider's other fist flew at him.

"No!" Miska jumped between them.

Mark's fist grazed her scalp.

"Miska!"

She staggered into Dillan.

He cradled her against him, sending Mark a look of hate. "You idiot."

Mark hovered over her. "Baby, I'm so sorry. I didn't mean that for you."

She pushed herself up.

Dillan held her arm, watched her closely.

But she looked strong and steady. "I want you to leave."

Scheider took a step closer. "I know that was stupid—"

"Mark, we're over. I'm sorry for everything that's happened, but you need to leave."

His features twisted. "We're not over. We can't—"

She grabbed his hand, silencing him. "I'm sorry."

He swallowed, staring at her hand over his. "I love you. I know you loved me."

Her mouth curved, but there was no pleasure there. "It wasn't love, Mark. Love doesn't do what we did. I get that now." She stepped back. "Good-bye. I wish you the best."

Scheider blinked at her.

Miska turned to Dillan, her eyes clear, her voice quiet but strong. "Let's go."

Gladly.

They turned away.

"What if you had something to do with it?"

Miska stopped and looked back. "With what?"

"Darcie's death. The police are looking for someone to pin it on. Maybe you wanted her gone. What about that?"

What was this moron doing? Dillan stepped toward him. "You're saying she was murdered?"

Mark glared.

Miska grabbed Dillan's arm. "I'm sorry your wife is gone, Mark."

Dillan let her turn him around and fell into step beside her. But he needed to know and looked over his shoulder.

The space beneath the trees was empty. Scheider was gone, as if he'd never been there.

Dillan glanced at Miska. If only he never *had* been there.

CHAPTER FORTY-EIGHT

*W*hat if you had something to do with it?

"Miska? Miska." Dillan pulled her to a stop.

They were on the southern end of their block. How had they gotten there?

"Is your head okay?"

Her head?

"Where Mark hit you." His eyes betrayed his concern. "You haven't said a word since we left him."

"My head's fine." Cars and buses flew by. "I'm sorry for what he said."

"What'd he say?"

"You know. About us."

"Oh. Well. I'm not broken up about it, so don't you be either." He nudged her. "Okay?"

Nice of him to make light of it, but his words didn't touch the guilt burning inside. All those months she'd spent hassling Mark to make a decision—she'd never meant for him to kill Darcie. Or his child.

She would never have thought it of him. Never.

"Come on, Miska. We know the truth."

The truth?

"We haven't done what he said."

"Oh. Right." Their building's entrance called her. "We did kiss. Once."

Dillan didn't respond.

They reached the revolving doors, Dillan gesturing, as usual, for her to go first, his eyes avoiding hers.

The doorman nodded hello as they entered the elevator bank.

Miska stepped inside a waiting elevator and pressed the eighteen.

Dillan followed. He still didn't look at her, even though he had to know she was watching him.

The elevator rose.

She moved before him, and he finally met her gaze. "Well?" she asked.

He kneaded the back of his neck. "I apologized for that."

"I didn't want an apology, Dillan. I didn't want you to think it was a mistake."

"Even though it was?"

"It was not." She laughed out her hurt. "Don't you ever think about it?"

He shook his head. "No. Never."

Never?

He looked away.

Liar. The way he'd kissed her again and again, the way he'd held her close—how could he not think about it? She was getting warm, just remembering. "Are you telling the truth?"

He heaved a sigh and shot his gaze to the ceiling. "Can we forget about it?"

The elevator stopped. "If it meant that little to you." Behind her came the sound of the doors opening. "But I'd love to see how you kiss a woman when you mean it."

Dillan's gaze flew past her, his skin flushing.

Miska turned. Adrienne stood in front of the open doors, eyebrows arched.

"Adrienne." Miska forced a smile. "What are you doing here?"

Dillan brushed by.

"I came to see you." Adrienne pointed after him. "But if I'm interrupting…"

Dillan halted. "You're not," he snapped, his eyes dark. "She's all yours." He vanished down the hallway.

"What was that about?"

"Nothing." Miska closed her eyes. "Why are you here?"

"Nothing? You were talking about kissing. You got something going on with him?"

Miska ground her teeth together, fighting the urge to stomp her foot. "For the last time, no. I have absolutely nothing going on with him."

"Yikes, girl. Sor-ree."

"Adrienne, what do you need?"

"To talk to you. Privately."

Miska sighed. "Come on then."

They turned down the hallway. Dillan wasn't there.

"How's the editing going?"

"It's going."

"Have you replaced Relentless?"

"No." She unlocked the door and opened it. "Why?"

"Because I have an offer for you."

Miska set her keys on the island and eased onto a stool. "I'm listening."

Adrienne pulled a manila envelope from her bag. She opened it and slid out a sheaf of paper with rows of black text. It looked an awful lot like...

The pages met her hands, the words springing to life—Adrienne's publishing house named as the publisher, Miska Tomlinson named as the author. "A contract?"

"For two books." Adrienne's heels clinked against the rungs of the barstool as she seated herself. "We want the entire blog with additional content. As a book. Details about you and the men filled in. We think it will sell well."

Miska flipped to the third page of the contract and scanned the dates and financial figures. The advance showed their high expectations. For both books. "I don't understand. Why my blog?"

"Because of the attention it's received since SportsCenter featured it."

She flipped through the rest of the pages.

"Paul, our acquisitions editor, saw it on SportsCenter and read it. He's the one who showed me the clip. He raved about it—thought it had great potential—but the others didn't. So he's spent time accumulating data on how many people are reading the thing."

People still read it?

"You don't know? It was trending on Twitter for a week. I told you to put some analytics on it. We could have had this to you sooner."

She flipped back to the first page, rereading the words that weren't quite connecting. "So you want the blog turned into a book?"

"Paul wants every blog entry included and expanded on, plus life in between."

But she'd written about Dillan. Had made fun of him. "I don't know, Aid—"

Adrienne held up her hands. "You're in shock. It's a lot to take in. But don't say no. It's a good deal."

Miska flipped back to the terms. Why so good? Were that many people still talking about what she'd written?

"We'd like you to come in and meet with Paul and Kelly, our publisher. We'll go over what we're looking for."

She set the contract down. "What have you told them?"

"Not much. Just expanded on what you wrote in the blog. You know." Adrienne flicked Miska's knee. "That blog entry on Dillan—Paul loved it. He has it up on his corkboard, right there in the center. It was one of the first things he showed everyone. He wants more of that."

She closed her eyes. "Adrienne."

"You know it's funny. Dillan won't care."

She pressed her fingers against her lips. He did care. "What's this about a second book?"

"We want the full story on you and… and Mark."

Her hand fell to her lap. "You told them about Mark?"

"The deal wouldn't have been this good otherwise—"

"You told them about *Mark?* And Kendall?" She slid off the stool and stormed away, fingers clenching her hair. "Did you tell them Dillan's name too?"

"Of course not. Dillan doesn't matter—"

"Yes, he does!"

"I mean to them, Misky. He's not famous. Mark is. It's his name that matters."

How could Adrienne? "You had no right to tell them. They're strangers. They have no right to know my business—"

"Miska." Adrienne stepped toward her, palms out. "Miska. Listen. Please. I did this for you."

She snorted. "Really."

"It's coming out. It is. This story with Mark—it's about to explode. Whether you like it or not, your name's going to be out there."

"Why? What's happened?"

Adrienne blew out a breath. "We have a contact in Milwaukee's police department. They believe he killed his wife."

No.

"Right now they're getting their ducks lined up, but it's a matter of time. And too many people know about you and Mark—"

"How did he kill her? He wasn't even there."

Adrienne sighed. "Misky."

"*Tell* me."

Adrienne ran her thumb over her nails. "There was peanut oil in her salad dressing."

"I thought peanut oil didn't cause the same reaction as peanuts."

"This was cold-pressed oil. Which would cause an allergic reaction."

"So the oil got in there during packaging—"

"The bottle was half empty."

Miska's eyes squeezed closed. "So someone added it after..." Her throat tightened.

Mark had killed his wife. For her—because of her. She'd caused a woman and child to die—

She sank to the floor, her head in her hands. No. No no no.

Adrienne grabbed her shoulders. "Miska."

The tears wouldn't stop. She shook her head. "It's my fault."

"No, it's not. Not unless you told him to kill her."

"I told him he had to choose! Me or her, Adrienne. That's what I told him. Me or her. And he killed her."

"It's not your fault—"

She laughed at her sister's blindness. "It *is* my fault."

Adrienne shook her. "Miska, wake up!"

The movement startled her into silence.

"The only way it's your fault is if you told him to kill her. Or if you knew he planned on doing it and did nothing. Did that happen?"

"No," she whispered.

"So he did it alone? Without you knowing?"

She nodded, wiped her nose. "But it doesn't matter."

"You wanted him to divorce his wife. That's all. He's the one who chose to kill her."

She stared at the floor between her and her sister, this sister who refused to acknowledge the truth. "Nothing will change the fact that I told him, repeatedly, to leave his wife. To choose me over her. And finally he did. It wasn't the way I expected, but he did what I asked."

"You had an affair. Yes. People will judge you for that. But you're as guilty of her death as Amber Frey was of Laci Peterson's murder."

Miska huffed out a laugh. "I knew he was married. I knew." But what did Adrienne care? She'd known Garrett was engaged. Had even met Tracy. "I never should have listened to him."

"But you did. Now you have to think about yourself. Very soon your name is going to leak out, and people are going to be hounding you. For interviews, for your story. Look at the contract, Miska—"

"Stop it."

"Look at it! You want to know why that advance is so big? Because these are the kinds of offers you're going to get. You don't think Melissa Leach will be conference calling you with her publisher? You think that other house you freelance for isn't going to call?"

She gritted her teeth. "I don't want their money."

"Oh, come off it—"

"I don't want their money!" Her voice echoed in the sudden silence, her shout repeating in her head.

Adrienne stared at her.

Miska unclenched her fists. "I'm sorry, Aid. I didn't—none of this is your fault."

Adrienne looked away.

Miska rested her forehead against her palms, her elbows digging into her thighs. How would she go on after this? How could she ever look people at church in the eye again? And Dillan—what would he think when he found out?

Adrienne sighed. "If it makes you feel better, no one knows your name. I filled that in myself. So your secret's safe. For now."

It wouldn't be a secret long. Not if Mark was arrested.

"Miska, I'm so sorry." Adrienne's arm settled across her shoulders. "I wish you weren't dealing with this. If I could, I'd make it go away."

Miska nodded, her gaze on the floor.

"But I can't. Neither can you. No one can."

Not even Dillan. "Why couldn't I have met him first?" She met her sister's gaze. "You got to live next to people like him—and you didn't want it. Why couldn't I? Why couldn't I have met him in high school? Do you know how different things would be?"

Adrienne's forehead wrinkled. "You lost me."

She shook her head. "It doesn't matter." Adrienne was right. No one could make this nightmare go away. Just like she couldn't rid her past of all the men she'd been with.

No matter how badly she wanted to.

"Are you okay?"

No. She forced a smile for Adrienne. "I'll be fine."

"What will you do when the story breaks?"

She shrugged. What Christian publisher would hire her with her name and face plastered all over the evening news? "I don't know." What *would* she do? Her shoulders slumped as reality set in. She'd already turned in her notice. What on earth would she do?

"Miska, right now the thought of profiting from this disgusts you. But in another week or two, you'll think differently."

"I will not—"

Adrienne laid a finger over her mouth. "You don't have to make a decision today. Or this week. Give yourself some time to let things clear out and settle down, okay?"

The contract landed in her lap.

"You need income, and the numbers here provide it. The advance alone could pay for, what? Half of what's left on your mortgage?"

She nodded. Almost.

"You'd still be editing, plus you'd have time to search out new clients. Since we're fast-tracking the blog book, you'd potentially have royalties in eighteen months. All of which means you could stay here."

Live next to Dillan and watch him avoid her? Because he would, once the story broke. He was a pastor; he'd have to.

"Look. I shouldn't—" Adrienne swore. "You can't repeat this, okay? You know some agents. Get yourself a good one. Have them talk to Paul. They could get you more, probably a lot more. Paul just wanted to sign you before everyone else found out."

Publishers would pay more? For details on how she'd destroyed lives?

"You think about it, okay?"

Never.

Adrienne caught her eye. "Okay?"

"Sure." Whatever got her out of there. "I will."

"Okay then." Adrienne climbed to her feet.

Miska pushed herself up, still fingering the contract.

Adrienne stayed around a minute longer, forcing exuberance into her words, but Miska refused to be affected. Finally her sister left, and in the silence that rumbled through her condo, Miska spread the contract across the island.

So much money—and Adrienne said she could get more.

No way could she make money off Darcie's murder. But somehow she had to make a living. How?

She climbed onto a stool. "God, I came to you because I want to live right." A knot of emotion clogged her throat. "I've already quit my job. I'd planned on doing editing that honored you."

Not anymore. That dream had died. She dropped the contract and clenched her fists on top of it. "There's only so much I know to do. I can edit, and I can—I can—" The pain overwhelmed her. "Where *are* you in this? Why don't I have options?" She scrubbed her hands across her face. Was God done with her already? He'd finally realized who she was, and he'd dropped her? Because that's what it felt like.

She read the contract. The blog book, the tell-all book about her relationship with Mark—both for six figures. Her sin sensationalized for entertainment in exchange for a roof and utilities, for groceries when Mark's gift cards ran out—

She groaned. "I can't use those."

She left the island for views of Grant Park. Buckingham Fountain still held court in the center, the outside jets spraying water over the center basins.

Whatever happened, this part of her life, this dream of downtown Chicago, was over.

It was all over.

She pressed her hand against the sun-baked glass. "I don't have any options, God, except to keep following you. Just—please." She mashed her lips together. "Please don't let me go."

Like her father had. Like her brothers had. Like all the men in her life had. Like Dillan would, once he found out what was coming.

Because he needed to know. Everyone did, really. Tracy, Amanda, Jordan, Matt, Cam—they all deserved to hear it from her.

And when it was over, it'd be just her and God. And maybe Tracy.

Probably Tracy.

That would be enough. It had to be.

She pushed off from the glass. Just her and God. And whatever bits of life he left her.

CHAPTER FORTY-NINE

Dillan entered the singles' room that night with a growling stomach and a headache. He picked a row halfway back and sat as the room filled. Garrett and Cam took the chairs beside him while Tracy, Miska, and Amanda chose the other end of the row in front of him.

Just as he'd hoped.

It seemed like everyone had shown up tonight. Even Ethan walked in and plopped onto the chair beside Garrett, going right into his usual shtick.

Dillan ignored him and leaned forward, elbows on his knees, fingers linked.

Miska smoothed her cream pants over her knee, then smoothed them again. And again.

He tilted his head to get a better view.

She was quiet, somber. Tracy and Amanda talked beside her, seemingly unaware that something was off.

Ethan leaned into his vision. He grinned and tipped his head toward Miska. "You like?"

"Knock it off." Dillan sat back, tucking his legs beneath the chair in front of him.

"No one would blame you, man. Who wouldn't want some of that?"

Garrett stiffened between them.

Dillan reached across Garrett and grabbed the jerk's arm. "Shut your mouth, Ethan. Don't say another word about her."

Ethan wrenched his arm away, eyebrows jumping toward his hairline, and nudged Garrett. "He doesn't know?"

If the man said a word—

Garrett pushed Dillan back. "Dillan's right, dude. No more. Let her start fresh."

Ethan studied Garrett, then shrugged and slouched in his seat, arms crossed.

"Dude." Garrett hissed in Dillan's ear. "Chill."

He sucked in a deep breath. "I can't stand him."

"Really?" Garrett's mouth twitched. "I say you ask her out already."

Honestly... He looked Miska's way again. It was tempting.

"No excuse this time? Whoa. I need a moment."

Cam leaned in from Dillan's other side. "What are you girls whispering about?"

Garrett leaned across Dillan. "I'm expounding on the wisdom of him asking Miska out."

Cam grinned at Dillan. "He's a little stupid."

He was stupid? "Says the guy who dates the new girl for two weeks, then ends it."

"Except this new girl. Why do you think that is?"

Cam was waiting for *him* to ask Miska out?

"Do it, Foster."

"Right. Like she'd—"

Cam deepened his voice. "Do it."

Garrett snickered.

Throughout the night, Dillan continued to watch her. While she listened to the discussion, she didn't contribute, and the sadness on her face never faded.

She looked heartbroken. Why?

She glanced over her shoulder, her dark eyes meeting his.

He wrinkled his eyebrows in question. If only he could pull her close and ask what was wrong. Ask if there was anything he could do. Anyone else he could tell to back off.

Her mouth shifted into a smile. She shook her head a little, then looked back at Austin behind the podium.

Dillan didn't look away. Who cared who noticed? Her past didn't matter to him. It shouldn't matter to anyone else either.

Garrett and Cam were right. He should ask her out.

The discussion wrapped up, and Dillan closed his study guide after Garrett did, aware that he hadn't caught much of the night. Austin could have been teaching Islam for all he knew. He glanced Miska's way again.

"Prayer requests?" Austin asked.

Miska shifted in her seat.

Four people shared requests for job concerns and sick family members.

Then Miska raised her hand.

Austin nodded at her.

She stood, fingers twisting together. She sent a nervous smile over the room. "I, umm, have something I need to share."

Dillan's gut tightened.

She took a deep breath. Exhaled. Met his gaze, then looked at her feet. "You all know I became a Christian a few weeks ago. Tracy helped me get there. I'll always love her for that."

Tracy flashed Dillan a smile.

He forced one back.

"Some of you know where I've come from, but most of you don't. I want to clear that up."

No. He gritted his teeth. What was she doing?

"If you'd known me three months ago, you would have said I'd be the last person to become a Christian. I was—"

Silence hummed.

Dillan clenched his fingers together, his knuckles turning white. She didn't have to do this. Didn't she know that? Who had planted this crazy idea in her head?

She sucked in a deep breath. "I guess you could say the woman at the well had nothing on me."

Garrett's arms were crossed over his chest, one hand fiddling with his collar while he stared at the seatback in front of him. Beyond him, Ethan mirrored his position, but his eyes were locked on Miska.

"I was involved with someone for a while. This man who—" Her words vanished. She rubbed her fingertips across her throat. "His wife recently died, and…"

Dillan leaned forward, ran his hand through his hair. A whisper from the back floated across the room. He should say something. Shouldn't he? Because it didn't matter. Not anymore.

"I'm telling you this because... because..."

Dillan bit back a groan. "Miska—"

She lifted a hand to silence him. "I want you all to hear it from me. I've learned that the police believe he killed his wife and that they'll be arresting him. And I know my name—" She shoved hair away from her face. "My name will be linked to his."

Miska. Dillan rested his forehead in his palm, studied the smudge of dirt on his Nikes.

"I'd asked him to leave his wife for me, and realizing now what he did, because of what I said—" Her voice trembled. "I have so much regret. I never meant for him to—to—"

Tracy's quiet voice reached his ears. "Miska, we know."

Dillan lowered his hand over his eyes, used his ring finger to clear one eye, then another.

"I don't even know what to ask you guys to pray for. I want to find out the truth of what happened to his wife. I need to know how much I'm to blame for it, and where—" her voice shuddered "—where to go from here. I've been working for some publishers, editing stuff a Christian has no business editing, and as soon as I realized that, I quit. I've applied for jobs with Christian publishers. I want to live for God, you know? But now I find out what Mark's done and..."

He forced himself to look at her. Her hair had fallen around her lowered face, but he could still see her mouth quiver. Hear her draw a shaky breath.

"I have no job, and no one is going to hire someone involved in a scandal like this."

Behind the podium, Austin shifted. "Maybe they won't hear about it."

"They'll hear. It's Mark Scheider."

Ethan's hand dropped from his mouth. He stared at Garrett, then glanced over his shoulder at the back of the room, shaking his head at someone.

Miska was right. The story would be all over ESPN, all over the internet, all over national news.

"I've been offered money for my story, but I can't do that. I just—I don't know what to do. I need a job. I need direction on where to go from here and how to… how to handle this, how to get up in the morning knowing another woman is dead because of me." She laughed a harsh, biting laugh. "A woman and her child." She twisted her hands together and dropped onto her seat. "Thank you."

The room stayed silent, but people glanced at each other.

Dillan looked at Austin who looked back with wide eyes. *Go on,* Dillan mouthed.

Austin blinked, clearly at a loss.

Yeah, this wasn't the type of thing you discussed in Bible college. *Pray,* he mouthed.

Austin asked for volunteers to pray for Miska and the other requests. Cam volunteered. Then Garrett. Jordan. Two others. Austin never looked Dillan's way, never let him volunteer.

Maybe that was for the best. Miska needed to know how much this group loved her, regardless of her history; and as the prayers rose, one after the other, it was clear that they did.

The prayers destroyed what little control she had.

Cam prayed that she'd know God's forgiveness and that He'd give her direction for the future. Garrett prayed for safety and wisdom when the story became public. Jordan prayed for comfort through whatever was coming. On and on the care went. It was enough. It was too much.

And yet it wasn't enough; Dillan had stayed out of it.

Sure, he'd said her name once, tried to stop her before she spilled it all. But once she had, he hadn't been able to look at her, had kept his gaze on the ground.

The prayers ended, and she tried to erase her tears, but people surrounded her, loved on her, gave her hugs and encouragement. Garrett and Cam even gave her decent guy hugs and told her to hang in there, that it would be okay.

Would it?

People she didn't know very well told her they'd be praying for her. She thanked them but couldn't help looking past the people around her at the one person who mattered most. The one who'd stayed out of the circle of support and talked to Austin beside the podium.

What did he think now?

He gave Austin a pat on the back, glanced at the crowd around her, then left.

No, it would never be okay.

CHAPTER FIFTY

On the other side of the kitchen island, Dad sat up on his stool, eyebrows raised. "When you make up your mind, you don't waste time, do you?"

Miska closed the oven door on the tilapia, smiling at the truth in his words. Dad's thoughts about her quitting New York were just like Mom's words when she'd moved there before she'd even found a job.

Mom, Dad, a family she didn't even know— "You ever think about getting us all together?"

"Yes. At least the seven of you who speak to me."

"I'd love that. We could be a family for the first time."

"Family's important."

Words she'd never expected from him. "It is."

He opened his mouth to say more, but a familiar knock sounded on her door.

Miska grabbed the counter's edge.

"What is it?"

She held a finger over her mouth. "It's Adrienne." Of all the days for her sister to drop in.

"Get the door. I'll keep quiet."

"No, hide in my bedroom. Shut the door, and don't make a sound."

He hurried away.

The knock came again.

Miska sucked in a breath and blew it out. "Coming," she called, hoping her voice sounded normal. She took her time down the hallway and opened the door, pretending surprise. "Hey, girl. What're you doing here?"

"I came to ask you about the contract." Adrienne brushed past her. "Have you made up your mind?"

"Oh. No. Not yet." She followed Adrienne to the couch. "I thought you said I could take a week."

"Paul doesn't like that you hid the blog. Keep it up. We can post that the book is coming and increase your readership in the meantime."

No way was she putting the blog back up. "Adrienne, I'm not taking any book offer."

"Of course you are. It's the only thing that makes sense.

"I won't profit from it."

Adrienne rolled her eyes.

"Mark may go to jail because of me. Darcie and a baby are dead because of—"

"Because of you. I know. When will you realize that you're not responsible for what he did? You're not taking advantage of him or anyone else. You're just making the best of a sad, sad situation."

"No. I could never live with myself."

Miska held Adrienne's gaze. Her sister broke eye contact first. Sighing, she glanced at the kitchen. "Smells like you've got fish cooking—" She straightened. Her gaze landed on the table set for two. "What's this? Got a date?"

She swallowed the sudden rush in her throat. "He'll be here soon."

"Who is it? Dillan? If you're already cooking fish, he must be nearby."

Closer than Adrienne realized. "It's not Dillan."

"Garrett?"

"Seriously? You think I'd date Tracy's ex?"

"Why not? They broke up."

"Thanks to you."

Adrienne waved the words away. "I'll go. Have fun with your mystery man."

"I will." Miska followed her around the couch.

"You're not dressed for a date, though."

"Maybe I'm not dating the way I used to."

"Whatever makes you happy, Miska." She paused beside the island. "But just because—" Her gaze locked onto something by the barstools. She stepped closer and tilted her head.

Miska did the same.

Dad's leather messenger bag leaned against the barstool's legs.

Adrienne nudged it. "Whose is this?"

Miska's hand covered her mouth before she could stop it.

Adrienne looked up.

Miska lowered her hand to her neck, hoping for nonchalance.

"Is that Jack's?"

"No, it's—"

"Don't lie to me." Adrienne twisted, looking for him. "Where is he?"

"He's not here, Adrienne."

Adrienne swore at her, her eyes narrowed and dark. "You told me you weren't seeing him. You said—"

"You forced me!"

"How could you lie to me?"

"How could I want to have a relationship with one of my parents? How could I want to know the one family member I actually look like?"

"He doesn't deserve to know us. It's wrong."

"It is *not* wrong. You can make your own choices, Adrienne, but you can't force them on me. My mom is gone. My brothers—" She laughed out her frustration. "Like we ever see each other. Dad is all I have left."

"*Dad?*" Adrienne stepped back. "You call him Dad?"

The ultimate betrayal. Miska knew it. "It's my decision to make. Not yours."

The bedroom door clicked open, and Adrienne turned toward the sound.

Dad—Jack—stepped out, his smile wan. "Hello, Adrienne."

She raised her jaw, stared down her nose at him.

He walked closer. "Now you know. We've been getting together almost weekly for... how long, Miska? Two months? Three?"

What was he doing? "Awhile."

Adrienne's gaze bore into her peripheral vision.

"I meet with all of my kids. All except you and Alec." He stopped at the other end of the island.

Adrienne clung to her corner.

"I don't get together with the rest as much, but Miska and I—" He sent her a warm smile. "She and I are the closest."

"That's enough." Adrienne pushed her bag's strap higher on her shoulder. "I can't pretend this is okay, because it's not. It's me or him, Miska."

"Adrienne, calm down. Just—wait a minute. Think."

"Oh, I have. Either he stays a part of your family, or I do. There isn't room for both."

"You don't mean that." Miska reached for her, but Adrienne stepped back. "Just like that? You could throw away all the years we've had together? Because I want to know my father?"

"He was *never*. Our. Father." Her teeth clenched together, lips revealing the polished hatred within. "You're the one throwing me away. And for what? A man who'll abandon you again? Just wait. It's coming."

"No." He took a step closer, and Adrienne retreated further. "I'm a different man. I would never—"

Her sister turned her shoulder on him. "What is it, Miska? Who goes?"

"Adrienne." The name released her anguish. "Please."

"*Who*, Miska?"

How could she pick? Adrienne was the only sister she'd ever known. She'd never been perfect, but they were sisters. They'd been roommates. They'd picked each other up when things went wrong. They'd shared the same kitchen, the same condo, had loved the other despite their differences. Could she give that up? "I won't choose."

Adrienne's shoulders slumped. Her bag's strap slipped down her arm and yanked on her elbow. "Then that's your decision."

"Never. That's *your* decision." Her voice cracked. A tear escaped, then another, and suddenly more vaulted from her eyes. She reached for her sister.

Adrienne jerked back.

"Listen to me. You know I love you—"

"Not if you're choosing him." Her sister turned her back and started down the hallway.

"Adrienne, stop!"

Adrienne turned the knob.

"You can come back." Miska wiped her cheeks. "Any time. You know I love—"

The door closed. Adrienne was gone.

Miska sagged against the island.

"Miska. Oh, Miska." Dad's arms circled her. "My poor girl. My poor baby girl."

She let him hold her while her grief seeped across his shoulder.

When she finally raised her head, nothing was better. Dad was still there, and Adrienne was still gone.

"You chose me," he whispered to her. "You chose *me.*"

Had she? Or had Adrienne made the choice for her?

"You need to write that book, Miska."

His words didn't make sense. "What book?"

"The contract she offered you. A book about you and Mark, right?"

"I can't. It's wrong."

"No. You're making lemonade out of lemons. That's all. Take the contract."

She stared at him.

"Take it."

"That's what you'd do?"

He nodded. "Write it. It's the only way forward."

Forward. Was that even an option anymore?

CHAPTER FIFTY-ONE

"So you're finally gonna ask her."

From his seat on the couch, Dillan glanced at Garrett in the kitchen, then back at his phone where he searched for the perfect first-date restaurant. "It's been two days since we ran together—since I've seen her. All I think about is how she's doing, what she's thinking."

Garrett planted his palms on the countertop. "You miss her."

He did. "You should see how she's changed. It's like—" He set the phone aside. "I don't even see her as the Miska before. She's completely different. I just want to... be near her."

"Well, bro, it's been real. Invite me to the wedding."

"The wedding. Right. I haven't asked her out."

"So what are you waiting for? Go. Ask."

"Now?"

"You got a better time?"

"I don't know. I could wait for the stars to align."

"Oh, of course. Absolutely. Suddenly I understand how you've been single so long."

Smiling, Dillan stood and ran his hands over his hair. He stretched up on his toes, tensed his arms and neck as he arched his back.

Garrett snickered.

"What?"

"It's funny seeing you like this. Nervous, stalling. Giddy."

"I'm not giddy."

"Dude. You're giddy. You were grinning at the windows for five minutes before you said you were gonna ask her out. I stood here and watched. Gid. Ee."

"What do you think she'll say?"

Garrett pursed his lips and studied the ceiling. He nodded to himself. "Prolly no."

"Dude."

Garrett cracked up.

Dillan laughed with him. "Thanks a lot, man."

"I love it when you go all *dude* on me."

"Yeah, well, you're not helping any, *dude*. I think I'll head next door and ask her before you completely maim my confidence."

"You go, girl."

Dillan waved him off. "Shut up."

Garrett's laughter followed him out of the condo.

But in the hallway, he sank against the wall opposite Miska's door. What would he say? Seriously. How was he not better prepared for this?

With his foot, he pushed off the wall and stepped in front of her door. He knocked three times, the sound strong and confident, everything he wished he was.

His fingers drummed against his shorts. Dinner tomorrow night would be a good start. They could go north, maybe walk through Millennium Park—

Inside, Miska spoke to someone. The lock jingled, and she swung open her door, smiling unsteadily. "Dillan. How are you?"

"I'm fine. Good." He should ask about her. "You?"

"Not bad. What's up?"

"Oh. I just—" He wet his lip. "I hadn't seen you in awhile. Wondered how you've been."

"You mean after Wednesday night."

He'd forgotten all about that. "You know you didn't have to tell everyone."

"No, I did." She glanced into her condo, then stepped closer, keeping the door cracked open with her heel. "I'm glad I did it. Everyone reacted so much differently than I'd expected. Now I don't have to worry about..."

"About Ethan."

She looked down at her feet.

Why was she so withdrawn? This wasn't like her. "Miska, what's happened?"

"Nothing's happened."

"Mark hasn't called you? Threatened you?"

"No."

"Then what's wrong? You're not you."

She bit her lip. "I have to be careful."

"Of?"

"Dillan, I'm going to be all over the news. Fox, CNN—they'll all be talking about me. There'll probably be reporters outside the building." Her dark eyes shone. "I'm going to be known for months—years—as the woman who destroyed a family."

Yes, and none of that was a newsflash. "That's who you were. You're different now—"

"But it's too late. I can't change what I was. What I did."

She'd lost him. "God doesn't expect us to change the past. He saves us, and we move on."

She sagged against the doorjamb.

"Not to sound calloused here, but I'm not getting the problem. Mark's going to pay for what he did. You'll—" Oh, boy. "Yes, you'll be dragged along with the story, but you've got people who'll be there for you." He swallowed. "I'll be here for you."

She looked at him.

"I mean it, Miska. I—" How did he go from this to asking her on a date? What did he say? "I've missed you. Missed our runs. Missed seeing you in the morning, hearing about the verse you read that just blew your mind."

She closed her eyes. "I can't drag you into this."

"You're not dragging me into anything."

"I can't have your name tied to it. You're a pastor. You can't afford to be associated with me."

"Whoa." He stepped closer. "Don't tell me I can't—"

"You *can't*, Dillan. I won't destroy your name too."

"You won't." He held back a frustrated growl. "I choose to be there for you. Regardless of the cameras in your face."

Silently she watched him, arms crossed. She was trying to make him think that she was holding herself together, that she was fine. But she wasn't. Here she was, a baby Christian, facing a trial that a mature Christian would struggle through. He wouldn't let her face it alone. "Don't shut me out because of what I do. You need a friend. I—" He needed her. Or maybe he was going crazy from loneliness.

No. He needed her.

She covered her eyes with her hand.

He took a step closer. She smelled like spring, like flowers. He studied her bare hand, his fingers curling with longing. "Miska."

She sniffed.

"I want to spend time with you. I want to know you better. Pray together, study the Bible together." Okay, he hadn't meant for all that to come out. Might as well just propose while his mouth was running.

But she raised her gaze to his. Her eyes, so dark, searched his face. *Yes.* She was softening.

He smiled out his hope. "I'd like to take you out for dinner. Are you free tomorrow—"

"Hey, Miska?"

Dillan froze at the man's voice inside the condo.

"I finished in your bedroom."

What? He straightened, staring through the door as if he could make out the man inside her home.

Miska pushed her door open.

A thirty-something guy wearing khakis and a light-blue button-down, the sleeves rolled up, smiled at her, camera in hand. He saw Dillan and stopped. "Oh. You're busy. I'll wait in your living room."

"It's okay. Mitch, this is Dillan, my neighbor."

The man stepped forward and smiled broadly as he held out his hand. "Mitch Johnson. Photographer for Miska's realtor."

A photographer. For her realtor. Dillan took his hand, pumped it once. "Hey." He smiled his relief. "Nice to meet you."

Mitch held up the camera. "I'll be in the living room."

"Okay." She watched him go, then turned back to Dillan.

And he'd thought—he laughed the idea from his head. "Getting the place listed, huh?"

She nodded, her somberness back. "Yes. Just a photographer. Not another man."

He'd pretend he hadn't heard that. "So what do you think? Are you free tomorrow—"

Her fingertips landed on his arm. "We're not ready for this."

"Of course we are."

"No. You're not. I have enough of a time, living with myself. It's too fresh for you."

"Miska, I'm sorry—"

"I know, Dillan." Her hand slid down to his palm. He tried to capture it, but she slipped away. "I need to go."

"Please don't." Whatever she'd seen before, she had to see how sorry he was, how much he longed for her.

But her smile was weak. "We'd just hurt each other. You'd never trust me, and I'd always feel guilty."

"That's my fault, not yours."

"It'd be my fault if I ruined your name." She pushed her door open farther. "Bye, Dillan."

The door closed. Her lock clicked.

He'd just blown it. The wall between their doors held him up. Oh, man, had he blown it. He tipped his head back, closed his eyes against the ceiling.

How stupid. *Stupid.* She'd been about to say yes. He'd talked her into it, and then that camera dude had to call out. He planted his hands over his face, dragged them down his cheeks.

Maybe—terrible thought—maybe she was right. Maybe he'd never be able to forget the Miska he'd first met. Or Mark. Or Kendall. Or Barry.

He blew out a deep, deep breath. How he wished he could forget. But it was too late.

She'd caught him, and the damage was done.

Just like her and him. Done. Over before anything could start.

"You're an idiot, Foster," he muttered. A real idiot.

He shoved his door open before remembering Garrett was inside. Too late. At least he'd get it over with.

Garrett popped out from the kitchen and grinned at him, an open Lucky Charms box in hand. "What'd she say, bud?" he asked around a mouthful.

Dillan jammed his hands into his pockets. "She said no."

Garrett quit chewing and stared.

Dillan clenched his jaw as the finality of it struck him. "She said no," he repeated and slipped inside his room.

CHAPTER FIFTY-TWO

A phone was ringing.

Miska opened one eye. Morning sunlight peeped around the edges of her silvery damask curtains. The phone, charging in the kitchen, rang again, and she lifted her head enough to see her alarm clock.

Seven thirty.

"It's Saturday," she whined. The only day she could sleep in, now that she was a good, church-going girl.

Well, a church-going girl at least.

She forced her legs to the floor and padded into the kitchen. The sunlight was bright, and she squinted as she picked up the phone and read the caller's name.

Dad.

She croaked a *hello*.

"Morning, Miska. You just wake up?"

Her laugh sounded froggish. "I did. You woke me."

"Oh. Whoops. Forgot to look at the time."

"That's okay. I needed to get up and run anyway." She'd skipped yesterday. Running without Dillan was no fun.

"You could use food, young lady."

"Yes, well. You buying?"

He chuckled. "Hey, I got a phone call this morning." He was grinning—she could hear it. "I've been working on this book. It's not done yet, but I pitched it to an editor at a conference last week. She loves what I sent her, and she wants to see more."

"Dad, that's fantastic. Congratulations."

"Thank you. She wants to take it to her editorial board next week, and I wondered if you could help."

"Of course. What do you need?"

"Just a fresh set of eyes. I'm going to be polishing chapters as much as possible, and I need to brainstorm the ending, get your take on how it should wrap up."

"What's it about?"

"It's kind of a memoir about our family."

"Our family?"

"Yeah. See, I've been taking notes on my meetings with you kids, writing down what happened and everything. It's a memoir about a truly dysfunctional family, about a dad who abandoned his kids and how I've rebuilt a relationship with most of you. Kind of the modern, messed-up family makes good. What do you think?"

He was writing about them? About her? His messenger bag flashed before her, the time she'd stormed out of the restaurant and caught him still in his chair, writing furiously.

"Miska?"

Her voice wouldn't work.

"You there?"

It couldn't be as bad as it sounded. "Sounds... interesting. Different."

"That's what the editor said. Can you help?"

She had to see what he'd written. "Sure."

"Great. When can we get together?"

"Umm." She swallowed. "I'm looking at houses today, but I can cancel—"

"Don't do that. I want to finish more before you read it. What about later tonight? I can bring dinner by your place."

Could she really eat before reading the thing? "That works."

"Thanks, Miska. I owe you."

It certainly sounded like he did.

Her realtor, Ian, had five houses to show her. Tracy met her at the first one, and they toured them together. One was too close to O'Hare, another too far north. One had potential foundation issues, but the other two were possibilities.

Neither appealed, though. Nothing would appeal, not until she'd read what her dad had written.

On the way home, Ian's office called to say an agent wanted to show her home that night, around eight thirty. Would that work?

She'd make it work.

Dad showed up at five with two Lou Malnati's pizzas, one spinach and one sausage with garlic. Just what she needed, a garlic stench in the place. She wrapped the pizzas up as soon as they finished eating and set a timer to go off around seven. She'd bake a batch of brownies and hope the smell of chocolate covered any lingering odors.

"So." Dad made himself comfortable on her couch and from his bag pulled out a manuscript somewhere over one hundred pages. "Here's what I've got so far. Tell me what you think."

He set it in her lap, and Miska stared at the first page, a prologue dated almost two years before she was born. The pages were like a boulder against her legs, but she picked them up and began to read.

It was his version of leaving Jody, the same story Adrienne had told her in May. She read as he made the decision to abandon his wife and kids, how he packed his suitcase while his wife pleaded for him to stay, how she clung to him as he headed for the front door, and how he pushed her away, ignoring the crash and scream that followed.

It was just like Adrienne had said.

Except that Adrienne wasn't in his version—just him and Jody. There were no kids crying out their fear and confusion. No children left with a mom who would stay physically but abandon them emotionally.

A tear splashed onto the page.

The couch creaked. "Miska?"

"I can't do this, Dad. Not with you here. I can't read this now."

"But it's not about you. It's about Jody."

"And Adrienne. And Alec. Adrienne already told me this story, and it's just like you said, except she and Alec were there too."

"Were they?" He squinted at her. "I don't remember."

"That explains a lot, doesn't it?"

His eyes cleared. He straightened and eased back in his seat, pinching his lips together as he stared at her window.

What had he said about her and her brothers? About Mom? He'd been dead on with Jody. What would she learn about her own family? Was she ready to hear the truth?

He cleared his throat. "I should leave."

He reached for the manuscript, but she clutched it to herself. "I want to read it."

"Miska—"

"Don't I have a right to know what you wrote? Don't all of us kids have a right to know what you're saying?"

He stared out the window again.

She pushed herself off the couch and walked to the kitchen, the manuscript still in her arms. "Why did you write this?"

He said nothing.

She set the manuscript on the far end of the counter and grabbed a brownie mix from the cabinet.

Still nothing.

She set out a bowl and mixer, found the oil and eggs needed. Ripped open the box and tugged the bag out of the box.

"I thought it would be good."

She stilled and studied the back of his head.

He rubbed his hands together. "I thought it would sell."

He wants money.

Adrienne's words couldn't be true. "So after you started meeting with us, you got the idea to write it all down."

He said nothing.

"Right? Dad?"

His shoulders rose then fell, and finally he twisted enough so he could see her. "Miska..."

But he couldn't finish. Because she wasn't right. All along, this getting to know her and the rest of her half-siblings—it had all been for money. Never for love. Never for reconciliation or relationship.

She and I are the closest.

She smacked the brownie box, sent it flying off the counter. "You used me. You lied to me!"

"No, Miska—"

She rounded the island, her teeth clenched as tightly as her fingers. "No more lies, Jack!"

He paled. "Miska, listen to me. The ideas came together—"

She grabbed his bag from the coffee table and threw it at him. His wallet, pens, a pack of gum, and half-used writing pad fell out. She kicked the pad toward him. "There's your paper, *Dad*. Your pen. Quick, write it down while it's fresh. Write down how much of a failure you are, how your kids will all find out what a liar—"

He reached for her. "Miska."

"—and despicable man you are."

"Stop it—"

"No! You stop it!" She buried her face in her hands. "I gave up my sister for you. My friend. Do you even care?"

"She didn't care about you."

"Neither do you." She collapsed onto the couch. How could she have bought his act? The Father's Day card, the pizza she'd fallen in love with—a complete betrayal of Mom—how she wished she could take it all back.

"I'm just a man, Miska. I'm not perfect."

She gave him her back. "So I'm learning, Dad."

Dad.

Her throat swelled. Her eyes burned, and she squeezed them shut.

Behind her came the sounds of him packing his bag, then his footsteps moving toward the door. Somewhere near the island he stopped.

Miska blew her pain away. She would not cry. Not over a lousy narcissist who couldn't even fake a good father.

"Miska, I'm sorry."

Of course he was.

"I didn't mean to…"

To hurt her. He couldn't even say it, because it wasn't true.

Her door opened and closed.

When she finally stood, the shadows of Chicago's high rises stretched into the lake. She moved around the kitchen like a frozen person, purposely numb. She'd bake the brownies, then read the manuscript and see how much of her pain he had shared for profit.

CHAPTER FIFTY-THREE

Night cloaked the distant reaches of Grant Park. Around the fountain people waited for the nine o'clock light show to start, taking pictures and video in front of the splashing water.

Somewhere nearby sirens screamed to life, and people turned to look. Dillan kept going, past the fountain. Tonight he didn't care.

He should have planned something. Garrett had been out most of the day, but Dillan could have called Cam or Matt, seen if they wanted to shoot buckets. He focused on the blackness of the lake. He'd never been by the waterfront at night. The running path probably wasn't busy. Seemed like the perfect place to forget.

Traffic on Lake Shore Drive was sparse. The traffic sign flashed permission for him to cross, and he did, headlights from a cab and a Mustang shining on his legs. He reached the stairs to the lakefront and started down.

He veered north, toward the glittering skyline and Navy Pier and the huge, lit-up Ferris wheel. The path was empty with sporadic lampposts lighting his way.

Up ahead someone sat near the bottom of another staircase leading to street level. The person was hunched over, back curved as if he—she?—was hugging her knees to her chest. The woman lowered her head.

Dillan paused. Whoever it was wanted privacy too.

Except the person on the stairs looked kind of familiar. Kind of like...

He glanced over his shoulder as he turned. The figure looked his way. It was Miska, rocking back and forth, her arms clenched around her stomach as if she were in pain.

"Hey." He stopped. "You okay?"

She said nothing, her silky straightened hair falling between her face and his.

He hesitated. If she wanted him around, she'd say so. And yesterday she'd told him no.

But she was clearly hurting in a way he hadn't seen before, in a way worse than after Kendall had beaten her.

"Miska?" He neared her. She sniffed, and he paused, foot on the step beneath her. "What's wrong?"

She raised her head and swiped her nose, moist cheeks reflecting the dim lamplight. Her fist ground against her thigh. "My dad. He—" She crumpled before him, her hands covering her face as her whole body shook in silence.

Dillan eased onto the stair beside her and waited, not touching her lest she not want it.

Why was he always crossing paths with this woman? She'd already turned him down for tonight, and now he had to stumble across her on his attempt to forget her. Why?

Beside him she sucked in a shuddering breath. "Why do you always have to see me at my worst?"

He couldn't help the chuckle.

"What are you laughing at?"

"Nothing. Not you. Sorry."

She peeked at him.

He smiled back. "You gonna be okay?"

She stared at the lake, like she wondered that herself. "My *dad* is writing a book about his reunion with all of his kids. He decided to meet us so he could make money off us."

Dillan furrowed his eyebrows. She had to be kidding.

"Adrienne told me he was after money. I didn't believe her. And now she won't speak to me because of him."

No loss there.

"Better yet, I learn from reading the manuscript that my father never cared about my mom. She was just—" Her jaw tensed. "His first marriage wasn't going well, so he found this cute, blonde thing at work and used her to forget. Just—" She threw her hand up and let it flop onto her lap. "And then, *then*, she ends up pregnant with twins, Jody finds out and lets him have it, and he leaves her because she's going nuts. Decides to stay with my mom awhile. They end up in Vegas and get married, and he realizes he's made a mistake. He never loved my mom. Never loved my brothers. Never loved—" Her voice cracked.

Dillan tugged her hand from her lap.

"He says he loved Jody. And the two women after my mom. But not her. And not us." She faced him, her eyes glossy. "He told Adrienne that he and I were the closest, and now I see it was a lie."

What did he say? What could anyone say to make it better?

"You know what's worse? I think he told this editor about me and Mark."

Dillan stilled.

"I found a piece of paper that looks like notes from a conversation, you know? One of them says, 'Include chapter on Miska and Mark.' He told her, Dillan. Or him. Whoever. He told this editor about Mark, and now that publisher is interested in his book."

He squeezed her hand.

"When does it stop?"

It was a good question.

"Why does all this keep happening? Why doesn't God step in and do something? Doesn't he care?"

He laced his fingers through hers. "He cares, Miska."

"I don't feel it."

"I know. Sometimes we don't. But he cares."

She studied the lake. "Maybe for you."

But not her? "Why wouldn't he care about you?"

"Do I have to spell it out for you? Do you want names? Is that it?"

"That's gone, Miska. He doesn't see it anymore. He sees you as pure and perfect as Jesus."

"Well, I still see it."

"Then the problem's with you, isn't it?"

A breeze lifted her hair from her shoulders, blew it gently across her face. She swiped it away. "I can't stop the news about me and Mark from leaking. I can't stop you from picturing the men I've been with. All of that will always be there."

She tried to tug her fingers away, but he held on. "I'm sorry I hurt you. I didn't mean to."

She ducked her head, protecting herself again with her hair.

He brushed it aside and slid a finger along her chin, turning her toward him until she had to meet his eyes. "Miska." Just saying her name was enough to leave him weak. "I really like you. I do. From the day I tripped and wiped out in front of you, you've fascinated me."

Her mouth tipped at one corner.

"I tried to stay away from you, but it didn't happen."

A tear slid down her cheek. "I'm sorry."

"No." He wiped her hurt away. "I wonder now if God wanted us to meet, to talk. That's why I couldn't avoid you. I watch you grow as a Christian, and I…" *Just say it, Foster.* "I wonder sometimes if he doesn't want us together for good."

Her fingers stilled in his hand.

"I just freaked you out, didn't I?"

She laughed, and he chuckled with her. "No. Shocked me maybe, but scared me?" She peeked at him, shook her head.

He wet his lip to continue, and her eyes darted there. He swallowed. Breathed deeply. In and out. In. Out.

She squeezed his fingers, her skin soft and smooth. "I can't imagine why God would want you with someone like me."

"Why wouldn't he?"

"You're so… so…" The sorrow in her eyes made him ache. "You've waited, Dillan, for one woman. And I haven't."

"Well, I would hope not," he joked.

"Be serious."

"I am. I'm nowhere near as perfect as you make me out to be."

Somehow they'd moved right next to each other, her arm snug against his. She rested her head against him. "You're pretty close," she said, "even if you do like to speed."

He chuckled and nudged her up with his shoulder. "See? We are right for each other."

Her dark eyes glowed in the deepening night.

"Miska, I hurt you yesterday, and I hate to say it but I'm sure I'll hurt you again, somewhere down the road. I'm just a guy. And a pretty average one at that."

"You're way beyond average."

She leaned against him again, her other hand covering their joined hands. He spread his feet wider to support her and watched the lake breezes tease her hair. All he wanted was to wrap his arms around her and turn her face up to his, kiss her for a completely different reason than the reason he'd had before.

"I want to date you, Miska."

She stayed against his side. "You are *so* messed up."

"I'm serious. I want to see what the future holds."

She straightened and looked at him. "Honestly, Dillan. Why?"

"Because of who you are. Who you've become. Because when we talk, I hear the fire in you to know God, to love him with everything you have." He bit his lip and forced his gaze to stay on her eyes. "You've gone through a lot in a short time, and you haven't given up."

"It's been tempting."

"Sure, but you haven't."

She watched him back.

"I look at you and see—" Should he say it? He swallowed. "I see the most beautiful woman I've ever met. There's just... something about you, Miska. I want to know you better. Spend time with you. Spend my money on you—"

She ducked her head.

Dillan reached for her chin again and tipped her face up. Her eyes glimmered, and he lowered his head, kissed her gently once. Twice. Waited to see what she'd do.

She stayed where she was, a breath away from him, giving him permission for one more kiss.

Just one more.

He made it last, relishing the way she kissed him back.

When he opened his eyes, she was already watching him.

He lowered his hand and smiled. It'd be great if she said something. Told him how she felt maybe.

But she didn't.

He cleared his throat. "You want to stay out or go in?"

"I can't go in. I have a showing."

Already? "How long should that take?"

"Another half hour maybe?"

Lake water splashed onto the concrete. Footsteps sounded on the sidewalk behind Miska, but Dillan ignored them. "I think the light show's started. You want to watch?"

"Sure." She smiled at him but didn't move.

So she didn't want to leave either. How tempting to stay here and go on kissing her, go on loving her. He couldn't look away and leaned in for one more kiss.

The footsteps began to run.

CHAPTER FIFTY-FOUR

Miska met the gentleness of his lips. The way he kissed her, like she was his treasure—had anyone kissed her this way before?

Dillan pulled away and looked past her.

She heard it, turned and saw it—a dark-hooded figure racing at them, a step away.

The figure's fist caught Dillan square in the jaw.

Miska screamed.

Dillan fell against the concrete stairs, and the man kicked him in the side. Kicked him lower. Dillan cried out and curled into a ball.

"Stop it!" She grabbed the man's arm and pulled, but he shoved her down and kicked Dillan again while she climbed to her feet.

Dillan didn't move.

She wrenched the man's sleeve, and he turned on her, the street light revealing his features.

Mark.

He snapped his arm free and grabbed her forearms. "You whore," he hissed. "How could you?"

She pushed against his chest, but his fingers tightened, pinching her skin. "Mark, stop it. Let me go."

"I'll let you go. When I'm good and done with you."

He marched down the concrete, dragging her from view of anyone who might walk by the stairs. She tripped and fell to one knee. He yanked her up, leaving skin to mark where she'd been.

Blood trickled down her shin. "Mark, please."

The burn in her knee set in, and she tried to dig her sandaled feet into the concrete. Her wrist flamed beneath his grip.

"After everything I did for you." He yanked her arm, and she bounced up against him, pain shooting through her shoulder. He held her tightly, his chest heaving against hers. "After *everything*, this is how you repay me."

"I didn't ask you to kill your wife!"

His jaw clenched. "You begged me. Don't think you're innocent."

"No." She shook her head. "I'm not innocent. I'll never forget that, but you made the decision to murder her."

He swore, spit landing just below her eye. His fingers dug deeper into her arm, and she forced herself still.

She'd never seen him like this. Never imagined he could be angry enough to—to kill. She took a deep breath, tried to think, tried to slow her racing heart. "Why are you here?"

One hand loosened its grip. "Because I needed to know where we stood." He drew in a shuddering breath. "And I know, don't I? You're with him." He groaned, and his hand relaxed a little more. "*Why*, Miska?"

She'd destroyed his life. Destroyed Darcie's life. Destroyed their child's life. Tears flooded her cheeks. "I'm so sorry, Mark."

His eyes shone as if tears threatened him too. "You begged me, Miska. You begged me not to end it. I didn't want to, but I had to so it would look like—" He let go of one arm and turned toward the darkness of the lake, fighting for composure. "I just want to know what happened."

She longed to look back to see if Dillan had moved, if anyone had seen him crumpled at the bottom of the stairs. But she didn't dare. "You said it was over. I believed you."

"I didn't mean it. I never meant it."

"You could have divorced her." Her voice trembled. "It didn't have to be this way."

He gripped her again. "Come with me, Miska. Love me. Let me love you. We were so good together."

No, they weren't.

"Remember?" He shook her. "Don't you remember?" He shook her harder, her head bouncing. "Please, Miska. Don't make me do this!"

"I can't. It would be wrong—"

His laugh was bitter and painful. "I shouldn't have wasted time on you. The guys said you weren't worth it. My life's a nightmare now—because of a piece of trash like you."

He pulled her close, pressed his mouth against hers. She tried to escape, but he snaked an arm around her waist and held her flush against him, his other hand gripping her head, forcing her face to his.

She couldn't move. Couldn't hardly breathe.

He kept kissing her, moving around the concrete as if he were forcing her to dance. She braced both hands against his chest and, with everything she had, pushed.

Mark let go.

Lake Michigan enveloped her, the cool water closing over her and erasing the view of his hardened jaw. Her feet kicked the corrugated harbor wall, and she twisted, pushing for the surface.

When she broke through, Mark crouched on the edge of the sidewalk.

She sputtered and reached for the wall, but he grabbed her hair and jerked her face forward, down into the water.

He was trying to kill her.

She fought the realization, feet toeing the wall. She grabbed his wrist and tried to pry his fingers from her hair.

His palm flattened over her head, his fingertips digging into her scalp and pushing her deeper, deeper toward her death.

Panic burst through her chest. She clawed for the top of the wall. She grabbed its edge and clung to it, the metal biting into her skin. But his strength won, and she plunged further into the water.

His hand slipped off her head.

She fought back to the surface and gasped for air.

Lying on his stomach, Mark grabbed her head with both hands and plunged her into the water again, one hand gripping her neck. She clawed at it, scratching and digging. She kicked her legs and twisted. Air. She needed air.

Mark's fingers tightened on her neck, then banged her head against the metal wall. His fingers released, fumbled across her skin, scratched. Vanished.

She was free!

But the darkness of the night had entered the lake. Her lungs betrayed her, and she sucked in water. Her fingers screamed up the wall, searching, clawing, grasping—

A hand bumped her face, grasped her hair, another hand gripping her shoulder. She latched onto the wrist as it tugged her to the surface.

She sucked in air, coughing out water.

Dillan's face greeted her above the sidewalk. "Breathe, Miska! Come on. Breathe!" He grabbed her armpit and braced his other hand against the seawall. "You're okay. You'll be okay."

Beyond him Mark sat up, blood cascading down his forehead.

Dillan's other hand plunged into the water. He grabbed her side and heaved her up.

Mark wobbled to his knees.

"Dill—" Water in her lungs cut her off. She coughed, choked.

"I've got you."

No. She tried to shake her head, but the cough overwhelmed her. She smacked his shoulder, shoved his face.

"Stop it. Calm down—"

Her throat cleared. "Mark!"

Dillan let her go and spun.

Miska clung to the metal edge as Mark stumbled toward them.

Dillan leaped to his feet, took one step, and tripped.

Mark dove toward where Dillan should have been, but Dillan was already falling to the ground. His head clipped Mark's knee, and Mark fell sideways onto the concrete. A smack sounded, then silence.

Dillan pushed up to his knees and stared at him.

Was Mark out?

Dillan crawled back to her. "Miska." His voice wobbled. He grabbed the back of her arms and pulled her onto the concrete.

She collapsed beside him, coughing.

The faint wail of sirens rose above the slapping water.

"Are you okay?"

She nodded and cleared her lungs again. She sucked in a deep breath, felt her lungs expand. "I'll be fine."

Piece of trash.

Dillan reached for her, and she filled his hand with hers, keeping out of the hug she knew he'd meant. "Are you hurt?" she asked.

He ran a hand along his jaw. "I'll survive. But only if you do too."

You weren't worth it.

Dillan pulled her close.

She gave in and let him hold her, water leeching from her clothes to his. Back where Mark had punched Dillan, two silhouettes huddled at the bottom of the stairs, watching.

Dillan followed her gaze as sirens parked behind the trees.

Mark groaned.

"Miska, baby, stay here. I'll make sure he can't get up."

He left her, and her body chilled in the late July night. Mark was right. She was a piece of trash, and Dillan deserved better than her.

Three officers rushed toward them, hands at their belts. Another officer stopped by the two gawkers and spoke to them. They nodded and pointed and gestured toward her.

"Miss? Are you hurt? You need an ambulance?"

She stared at the officer who knelt before her. "I'm all right." She looked at Dillan who stood, talking to the cops. "Make sure he's okay."

"We will. Tell me what happened."

She closed her eyes, buried her face in her hands. The story had really broken now. "That's Mark Scheider."

"The baseball player?"

She nodded.

"And the other guy?"

"He's not involved. Please. Leave him out of this."

"Tell me what happened. People said a man was holding you under water. Which guy was it?"

"It was Mark."

"Mark Scheider tried to drown you?" He pulled out a notepad and a pen. "You know why?"

"Because—" She sniffed, shuddered, coughed again. "Because I was his mistress." *Piece of trash.* "And I think he killed his wife for me."

When she wasn't even worth it.

CHAPTER FIFTY-FIVE

The clock on Garrett's Lexus said it was going on two a.m.

Dillan's heavy eyelids agreed. He forced his eyes open and watched the lamp-lit sidewalks of Chicago slide by.

"Dude." Garrett jerked his chin toward the backseat.

Dillan turned, the seatbelt pressing against his sore ribs. Curled up in the back, Miska looked asleep, her lashes dark against her cheek, her hair—a wide, tangled mess—spread across the seatback and draped along her neck where a bruise flashed to life beneath a streetlamp.

"She's been out awhile," Garrett said. "You look beat too."

"Ha ha."

"Sorry. No pun intended."

Dillan glanced at Garrett to see if he were serious. He seemed to be. "Thanks for coming to the station."

"No problem. Just don't make me do it again."

"Yeah, well, Mark can't post bail any earlier than Monday. So we're good through then."

"Can't believe he tried to drown her."

Again Dillan saw Mark bent over the walkway's edge, his arm buried in Lake Michigan. He clenched his fingers, opened them, pressed his hands against each other. "I can't talk about it." His head and groin and ribs had still hurt when he'd managed to sit up and see Mark send Miska into the lake. He'd struggled to his feet, adrenaline pushing him past the pain and down the lakefront where he'd knocked Mark's forehead into the seawall's metal edge.

But the water had been so dark—and Miska hadn't popped back to the surface. For one heartsick moment he knew he'd lost her.

He glanced her way again.

She shifted as if she was trying to get comfortable, but her eyes didn't open

He settled back in his seat and moaned. "I've gotta be up in five hours."

"Dude, sleep in. You need it."

"It's Sunday. I can't miss."

"Yes, you can. I called Pastor and told him what happened. He said to take the day off and rest."

Sleep—and Advil—sounded fabulous right now. "I wonder how long before this hits the news."

Garrett glanced at the clock. "Three, four hours ago."

"Come on. For real?"

"For real. I've talked to Mom and Dad, Jordan, Matt, Cam, Ethan twice—he called after seeing it on ESPN's ticker. Just concerned, you know."

Dillan scoffed. "Creeper."

"Yeah, well. Hey, Tracy even called."

Garrett lapsed into silence. Familiar buildings flew by.

"So what were you two doing by the lake? I thought she'd told you no."

"We ran into each other. She had a showing, and I was bored."

"Guess that changed, huh?"

That it had.

"Oh, dude." Garrett slowed as he passed their building. "There's guys with cameras outside."

Dillan looked through the car's back window. Four dark figures walked along the sidewalk, television cameras on two of their shoulders.

"Maybe you'll end up on TMZ."

Garrett was kidding. He hoped.

Dillan slumped in the seat and traced the edges of his raw forehead.

His brother turned into the building's garage and parked beside Dillan's SUV. Other than the security guard at the exit, no one was in sight.

Dillan eased the seatbelt across his sore ribs and slipped out of the car.

Miska still rested in the back.

"Dill, you should probably wake her."

Yeah, although watching her sleep wasn't all bad. After what she'd been through, she needed it. A near drowning, a long night making an official statement to the police...

"Umm, today, bro?"

He shook free of the sleep settling over him and opened the back door.

She barely stirred.

He leaned inside and ran his knuckle down the silkiness of her cheek. "Miska."

She pressed her cheek into the seatback.

A chuckle rose in his throat. "Miska, baby, we're back." He touched her shoulder. So delicate. So fragile. "Miska. Honey, come on. We're home. Let's get you inside."

Her eyes opened. She blinked at him, then looked around the car.

He held out his hand. "I'll help you out."

She grasped his fingers and slid across the seat until her feet touched the floor. She rose shakily.

Dillan used it as an excuse to rest a hand on her waist. "You okay?"

She nodded, eyes avoiding his.

Miska said nothing until they were inside their building's elevator. Even then she kept her gaze locked onto the paneled wall. "Thanks for getting us, Garrett."

"No problem." Garrett frowned over her head at Dillan.

He shrugged back.

At their doors, Garrett said goodnight and made a quick exit.

Miska fumbled with her key.

"Need some help?"

She shook her head as she inserted the key into the lock.

"Miska."

She stilled, her gaze on her door.

"Everything's gonna be fine."

"Maybe."

"Maybe?" He leaned against her doorjamb. "You won't be alone. You've got me."

Her head lowered.

She was just tired. He reached for her hair. She'd tried to finger comb it at the station, but it had dried a matted, tangled mess. A curl sprang beneath his touch and flipped out of his grasp.

"Dillan." The way she said his name knotted his stomach. "About last night—"

"Take Mark out of the picture, and it was the best night of my life."

"I can't let you throw yourself away for me."

He should have known she'd go there again. How many times did he have to tell her that her past was the past? "I meant everything I said. I care about you. A lot. And after what he did to you—"

"I deserved it."

"What?" He ducked his head to hers. "No, you didn't."

"Mark's right—I'm not innocent. I had an affair with a married man. I asked him to leave his wife. You deserve better than that."

"Quit telling me what you think I deserve. All I want is you."

She shook her head violently. "I won't ruin you, Dillan. It's bad enough that you were there tonight."

If he hadn't been, she'd be dead right now. "You're exhausted. Let's get some sleep and talk tomorrow." No, it was already tomorrow. "Today. After lunch. I'll order a pizza—"

She grabbed his arm. "Listen to me. Let me go. I'm not worth it."

"Miska, stop it—"

"No! Somewhere there's a woman who's waited for you. A woman who's kept herself pure for you."

"I don't care about that."

"Yes, you do. You want a woman who loves God and who comes to you a virgin. Just like you are."

"You love God, Miska. The rest doesn't matter."

"It does to me." Her eyes searched his. "I won't have people whispering about you."

"They won't—"

"I heard what Garrett said about Ethan calling. About the men with cameras. I won't ruin you."

He grabbed her shoulders. "Listen to *me,* Miska. I don't care what anyone says or thinks. I've seen the old Miska and the new one. I know who you are."

"Do you? Do you know how many men I've been with?"

"I don't care."

"There was Gordon. Jared. Rob. Alex. Todd. That was high school."

"Miska—"

"In college I let it all go. It wasn't the number of men I was with. It was what I did—"

"It doesn't matter."

"Evan. Jonathan. Craig. Travis—"

"Stop it."

"—Brandon. Troy."

He grabbed his doorknob. Locked. "I don't need to hear this."

"You do, because you don't even begin to know the way I lived. I was so broken. So messed up. So *used.*"

"And now God's got you—you and me. I wouldn't trust us with anyone but him."

She smiled faintly. "You are the most beautiful man."

He grabbed her hand. "Let's talk over lunch. You can share whatever you want then."

"You mean the rest of the names. Like Geoff. Craig—"

"You already said him."

"Different Craig."

He gritted his teeth. "This isn't doing us any good. Let's get some sleep. We'll talk later."

She kept quiet.

Good.

She unlocked her door and pushed it open.

"Good night, Miska. Sleep well."

"'Bye, Dillan."

She didn't mean that.

Her door closed.

She couldn't mean that.

CHAPTER FIFTY-SIX

Miska slept until knocking woke her.

Dillan stood outside her door, Dillan and a pizza. She told him she wasn't up to it and went back to bed, trying to forget the anguish in his eyes, the sag in those broad shoulders.

Local news stations led with the story and a live broadcast beside the lake or in front of her building. Every friend, work associate, and then some called. Even Wade and Zane phoned. Miska told them all, including Tracy, that she needed a few days—time to heal and figure things out—before she saw anyone.

For the next three days Dillan knocked on her door. She never answered, instead curling up on her bed while the tears ran.

She had to let him go.

Ian, her realtor, showed the house every day. Each time, Miska escaped to the roof deck where she could hear Chicago honking and bustling far below. How she would miss this.

How she wanted to leave.

She skipped Wednesday's small group. Just before nine o'clock, Tracy's distinctive—and perhaps irritated—knock sounded.

Miska pushed herself off the couch. She shouldn't have been surprised. If it was just Tracy, she'd let her in. She couldn't escape the real world forever.

But four days of wallowing sure had been nice.

When she opened the door, Tracy raised her eyebrows. "So she's not dead. Holy cow."

"Don't start on me." She motioned Tracy inside. "I'm still sore. Did you notice the reporters outside?"

"That's why you're ignoring everyone. Because you're sore and don't want your picture taken."

So this was how it was going to be. Miska flopped onto the overstuffed chair. "Let's get this over with. Say what you came to say."

Tracy's eyes widened. "One of the most amazing men in the world is in agony next door because you won't speak to him, and this is what you say? 'Let's get this over with'?"

Why wouldn't Dillan let her go?

"Miska, the guy is sporting some crazy concrete burn on one side of his face and a lovely brown and yellow number on the other. He deserves for you to listen to him."

"I have listened to him, Tracy. But he's not listening to me. Don't you get it? He's too good for me."

Tracy shook her head. "How?"

"My life isn't going to be sane or normal or private until this whole nightmare goes away. Which could take years. He doesn't need to be dragged through that."

"He doesn't care, Miska! All he wants is to be with you, to help you through it. And in case you missed it, Dillan was the guy who saved you from Mark. He's part of this now, whether you want it or not."

"I can't involve him further. It wouldn't be fair."

Tracy flopped against the couch's back. "I don't get it. I really don't. If he's too good for you, then how come I'm not too good for you?"

"That's different. You're my friend."

"Maybe you don't know this, Miska, but love—marriage—is supposed to be a friendship. It's like dark chocolate, a favorite sweatshirt, a day at the beach, and a good workout all mashed together."

Miska couldn't hide a smile. "Look, I appreciate you coming over. I'm sorry I've kept you away. I won't anymore."

"And Dillan?"

Miska sighed. "Tracy—"

"Right. You're not good enough. Got it." She slapped her palms against the leather cushions. "Hey, what part of the Bible have you been reading?"

The sudden change threw her. "Uh, Matthew. And John."

Tracy nodded.

"Why?"

"Just wondering how much of the Old Testament you know."

"Old Testament?"

"That answers that. It's the part of the Bible written before Jesus's birth."

"Haven't gotten there yet."

"Hmm." Tracy pondered her coffee table.

"Okay. What?"

"You ever hear of Rahab? Tamar?"

Who hadn't heard of Rahab? "Who's Tamar?"

"She was a woman who pretended to be a prostitute in order to have children. You know what's interesting about them? They're ancestors of Jesus."

Okay. That mattered how?

"You know who Bathsheba is?"

"No."

"One of King David's wives. He had several. But this one he had sex with while she was married to another man. And when he found out she was pregnant, he had her husband killed so he could hide what they'd done. They're both ancestors of Jesus."

King David—she'd heard about him. What was it someone had said a couple weeks ago at small group? Something about God being close to David? How was that possible when he'd had an affair with a married woman and killed her husband?

"If God chose them to be in the line of Jesus, then you can't say you're less than what Dillan, a mere mortal, deserves. Can you?"

Prostitutes, adulterers, and murderers in Jesus's line? God allowed that?

"But that's not the issue, is it?"

Miska stared at this friend who was far too perceptive. "What do you mean?"

"You're afraid Dillan will leave you too. Like your dad. Your brothers. Mark. Kendall. Every other man you've known. Now that you've met an amazing guy, you're afraid you won't be enough for him."

The words sliced through her.

"You're not protecting him. You're protecting you."

"What if I am, Tracy? Can you blame me?"

Tracy's smile bled sympathy. "No. But you're comparing apples and... well, rotten apples. You've never dated a man like Dillan. He doesn't play around. I've known him three years, and in all that time he dated one girl twice. Honey, he doesn't toy with people."

"But he's never dated someone like me, someone with a past."

"The awesome thing about the word *past* is that it means it's behind you. It's not around any longer. Ever thought about that?"

"My past isn't staying behind me. Dillan doesn't know what he's getting into."

"I think he does. He's a pastor, girl. He deals with people. Chicago people, not angels."

She couldn't think of anything to say.

"Jordan says Dillan's crazy about you. She thinks you're the one."

"Stop it."

"Yep, she brought it up, in fact. She's wondered ever since Memorial Day. You weren't a Christian then, so she kept quiet. But she told me last Wednesday—after you shared that past we should all be so terrified of—that she thought Dillan had found the woman for him. You."

That couldn't be. "Why would she say that?"

"Because he's never looked at another woman the way he looks at you. He's never talked about a woman the way he talks about you. I can see it. Jordan can see it. I hear even Garrett sees it." Tracy snagged her hand. "Quit trying to shove him onto another woman who'll never love him like you do. Take a risk, Miska—and if something happens and he hurts you, well, I'll buy you dinner."

"Wow. Step out on a limb."

Tracy grinned. "Fine. You can double my rent."

"No thanks."

"Come on. He's the third best thing that's ever happened to you. Don't push him away just because you're scared."

She wasn't scared; she was petrified. "Wait, third best?"

"God. Me. Then Dillan."

"At least you come after God."

"Good to see you smiling again." Tracy pulled Miska to her feet and hugged her. "Now that my work here is done, I need to go. Some of us have jobs tomorrow morning. Are we looking at houses this weekend?"

Miska followed her. "Probably. I'll send you any links Ian sends me."

"Good. Please talk to Dillan."

She wasn't sure she'd ever be ready for that. "We'll see."

"I love you, Miska. You know that, right? I just want the best for you."

Like she wanted the best for Dillan. And security for herself.

Tracy opened the door. "You know what? You need to read the book of Ruth in the Old Testament. It's a short one. You'd like it."

"I've never heard of Ruth."

"Didn't think so." Tracy stepped into the hall. "She was from a country that practiced human sacrifice, a country that clearly didn't know God. But God loved her anyway. A lot. Read it. Tell me what you think."

Somehow the story would take her back to Dillan.

She knew it.

CHAPTER FIFTY-SEVEN

For the rest of the week, she thought about reading Ruth.

Thought about it when Dillan knocked on her door Thursday and Friday and then when he didn't Saturday.

Thought about it when she came late to Sunday's service and Dillan stood up front, leading the music. He almost froze, his arm up in the air.

Miska sat in the back row and buried herself in the song's words, but every time she glanced up, his eyes were locked onto her.

She wasn't ready for him. She couldn't do this.

She left before the song ended.

Dillan knocked on her door around one.

Miska didn't answer.

Ian called on Monday to say that two offers were coming in. They'd priced the home aggressively to drive people to it, and the plan had worked.

On Tuesday, the Chicago-based publisher asked for an interview. Hope rose in her throat, but Miska shoved it down. She scheduled it for that afternoon, and, in their offices ten minutes north, the woman looked at her funny as they shook hands, probably wondering why she recognized her. The interview went well, but when it was over, Miska told her about Mark, that she was a new Christian committed to living the way God wanted, not the way she had been.

The woman's face shuttered.

Miska left, knowing she'd never hear from them.

Ian called with the two offers. They countered both, and the next days were spent negotiating. Miska and Tracy filled Saturday with house hunting and found a home fifteen minutes from church, ten minutes from

Tracy's work, and smack dab in the middle of Miska's uncertain future. She signed the contract, and Ian called later with the news that the all-cash offer on her condo would close by the end of August.

She released a deep breath. Things were starting to even out. Finally.

On Sunday she went back to church. On time. Friends greeted her as if she'd been gone forever. People she didn't know told her they'd be praying for her.

Dillan stayed on the other side of the auditorium, nodding once when they locked eyes.

How she missed him.

Ian called that afternoon. She had the house she wanted with closing scheduled the same day as the condo's closing.

Now if she could only find a job.

The phone call came Wednesday morning while she emptied her walls. The publisher she'd interviewed with asked for a second interview.

Hope surged through her wounds.

During the interview, they talked about their fiction, asked if she'd read any of their titles.

She'd read six of their latest releases.

Of course they wanted her thoughts.

She took a deep breath, told them what she loved about her favorite, talked about the others that she'd enjoyed, and shared as kindly as possible why she wasn't fond of one of them.

They nodded with her.

They liked her skills, they said. Her New York references were good. But they wanted to know more about this change in her life. Could they talk about that?

She was in the news. Of course they had to be careful.

Miska set caution and security aside and kept nothing back.

Home again, she found herself wandering, fingering her Viking stove and lingering by the living room windows. Her words from the interview haunted her—her relationship with Mark, Tracy's determination to show her the truth, her realization that she'd lived her first thirty years completely wrong.

How could this publisher look past her oh-so-public sins? How could anyone? How could God?

Really, how could he?

Buckingham Fountain's jet climbed into the sky.

The more she read the Bible, the more it seemed like she'd broken every rule there was. How could God see past that?

"God, please."

Her words startled her. Silence had reigned in her home for so long; she couldn't voice her truest thoughts. Not anymore.

Please, she tried again. *Don't let me go. You're all I have. Everything else— everyone else is gone.*

She mashed her lips together, then forced herself to speak. "I need this job. I don't deserve it—I know I don't deserve anything from you. Not forgiveness. Not a second chance." Hurt chased dampness down her cheeks. "Not love—yours or… anyone else's."

Dillan's face swam before her.

If this was as good as life got, she'd be content with it. God had saved her, that much she knew. She might not ever be good enough for him or any man to love, but that was okay. Because more than anything, she couldn't go back to the life she'd once lived. Never. All the security and money in the world couldn't keep her anymore.

The week passed, then another. She packed until boxes stacked the walls of the smallest bedroom. She was down to paper plates, Solo cups, and a deep skillet.

Tracy called her each night, giddy with excitement. This move couldn't happen soon enough.

On Wednesday—the second-to-last day in August—her phone rang.

Miska set down the skillet she'd been scrubbing and dried her hands as she checked the caller.

The publishing house.

Adrenaline shot through her, burning her stomach. She dried her hands and picked up the phone. Stared at it, then answered.

"Miska, this is Connie Gilbert in HR. How are you?"

She moistened her lips. "I'm well. You?"

Connie chuckled. "Wishing I could take my office outside today. Can you believe it's August?"

Really? She was making small talk? "Hard to believe."

"We're all going to fry tomorrow, they say. I already told my husband we're having a picnic tonight."

Miska closed her eyes. *God, make her just say it.*

"Anyway, listen. Nancy Thompson let me know an hour ago that they'd made their choice for the editing position."

So it wasn't her.

"She wanted me to apologize for taking so long to get back to you, but—"

The true depth of unacknowledged hope squashed her. Had she really thought they'd look past everything and hire her? She'd known better than that.

"—and then after surgery it got infected and… anyway, she's missed a lot of work. So that's why it's taken so long."

Surgery? "I'm sorry—what happened?"

"Nancy broke her leg. Had surgery to put a screw in it. You should hear the jokes around here. Like I said, the job is yours if you'd like it."

"Mine?"

"Absolutely. You can take some time if you need to, but we'd like to know by the end of the week."

The job was hers? She caught her breath. "I accept."

Connie laughed. "Nancy will be thrilled. She wanted to call you herself, but she knew you'd understand how buried an editor gets when she misses six days of work. I'll let her know you accepted, and she'll be in touch when she gets a moment. Is that okay?"

She pressed a trembling hand to her mouth. "That's fine."

"Great. Does Tuesday work as a start date?"

"Tuesday's good."

"Wonderful." Connie spent another minute detailing information Miska needed, then ended the call.

Miska grabbed her desk chair and sank onto it.

Was this real? She stared at the phone shaking in her hand. Did she truly have a job editing Christian books? She broke into tears, deep, loud sobs that echoed off her bare walls. How could this be?

"Oh, God—" She couldn't finish the prayer, but the *thank you* rang deep within her. She buried her face in her hands and let the tears flow.

God loved her after all. He hadn't just saved her. He loved her. She mattered—and now he'd taken care of her. All that worry, all that fear—for nothing.

She caught herself smiling through the tears. Only God could take the mess she'd created and turn it into something perfect. As long as she lived, she'd never forget this... this miracle. This gift. This love.

She dried her face and blew her nose. From the corner of her desk, her Bible called to her. She flipped through the Psalms she'd discovered after Tracy had mentioned David and Bathsheba. Since that frank conversation, she'd spent every day reading Psalms and stories Tracy had mentioned, but she'd ignored that book Ruth, unsure what Tracy was up to. She searched the table of contents and found it.

Short, like Tracy had said.

She read about Ruth leaving everything she knew for Naomi and a foreign land. How Miska identified with that. She searched online to fill in the gaps Dillan probably knew backwards and forwards—who Ruth's Moabites were, their history with Israel, the gods they worshiped.

When Boaz told Ruth to stay in his field and take what she needed, Miska's tears returned. How silly she'd been to think that God hadn't been there before. How many people over the centuries had he provided for?

When Boaz told Ruth that he'd heard she'd left her father and mother and the land of her birth and had come to a people she didn't know, the tears flowed again. Ruth understood. Boaz understood.

God understood.

And then *she* understood why Tracy had told her to read the book. Ruth went to Boaz and asked him to take care of her. To provide for her. To be her husband.

That Tracy.

She read on, realizing at the end that this Boaz, this Ruth, had been part of the line that belonged to King David. This foreigner who had come from a godless, wicked society had left all for the faith of Israel.

And she'd been welcomed.

And loved.

Loved!

Her Bible cross-referenced Matthew, and Miska looked up the verse. Ruth's role as a many-times grandmother of Jesus wasn't hidden. Anyone who wanted to see it, could. Ruth, Rahab, Tamar, David, Bathsheba— they'd all been placed out in the open as ancestors of Christ. Anyone who wanted to know—it was there.

If God had chosen them for his own son, might he really have chosen her for someone like Dillan?

The thought was staggering.

The closings were both tomorrow. She had to have her place empty and the keys to Ian before nine. She packed and cleaned late into the night, this time skipping small group because she had to in order to be out on time.

But she prayed while she cleaned. About Dillan. For Dillan. About what she should do. She'd thoroughly turned him down, and clearly he believed she meant it. He'd never resumed knocking on her door and stayed on the other side of the auditorium.

So if anything was going to change, it was going to be up to her. She had to take action.

Just like Ruth.

CHAPTER FIFTY-EIGHT

On the last day of August, Miska woke before the sun.

She showered and dressed, fixed her hair and put makeup on, even though she expected to go for a run. Smiling, she tossed her pajamas into the laundry bag on her empty closet floor. The only clothes left were the white shorts and gray, cotton T-shirt she'd wear after her run.

Moving day clothes. She couldn't wait.

She filled her water bottle and left her condo. She'd wasted so much time, hiding out instead of enjoying her last days in Grant Park, but no longer would she look back.

Today was all about the future.

She leaned against the wall opposite Dillan's door and waited.

Five minutes.

Ten.

Fifteen.

He should have come out already.

The door opened, and Garrett flew out, his pace taking her back to when Dillan had barged into her life, knocking Mark flat.

How right that had been. And she hadn't even known it.

"Miska." Garrett sent her a curious smile as he locked his door. "What are you doing out here?"

"Waiting for Dillan. Is he coming?"

He took in her running clothes and makeup. "Is this what I think it is? You have a ring on you?"

"Stop it." He laughed, and she backhanded his arm. "Keep it down. He'll hear you."

"He went running early. Has been all week."

"He's out there already?"

Garrett checked his watch. "A good forty minutes. Hurry; you might catch him."

She raced for the elevator.

Dillan wasn't by the fountain or in the trees or paths nearby. Praying he hadn't taken the route back by the Art Institute, she jogged across Lake Shore Drive and down the stairs to the running path.

August wind blew her ponytail off her neck. Water slurped at the concrete's edge, and she stopped, unwilling to face the northern path where Mark had almost destroyed her. She looked south, toward Adler Planetarium and Shedd Aquarium.

No perfectly tall man stood out in the joggers.

That left only one place. She took a long, slow breath. It was daylight, she reminded herself. Mark was still in jail. She swallowed, turned, and looked north.

Far down the running path, Dillan faced the water, hands in his pockets, watching her.

She stayed there while her lungs filled, then swallowed the terror that crashed through her. Why didn't he move?

Maybe he'd had enough. She wouldn't blame him if he had.

But maybe he hadn't either.

She kept to a walk as she approached him, kept her eyes trained on his, on those guarded brown eyes that watched her near. He held her gaze until she was close, then looked down, one Nike kicking the ground like he'd done so long ago when they'd first talked beside the fountain.

"Hey." She forced a calm smile. "I'm glad I caught you."

His eyes returned to hers, his smile tentative, maybe even hopeful. "Yeah?"

"Yes." She dropped her gaze. "Dillan, I want to thank you for everything you've done."

He shrugged. "It's not a big deal."

Not a big deal? "You saved my life. More than once. You and Tracy—you two mean everything to me."

Caution filled his eyes.

How she'd hurt him. "I've treated you terribly, Dillan, and I have to tell you how sorry I am."

His lips twitched. He looked across the lake.

Clearly he didn't want to hear what she had to say, but she needed to try one final time. "Tracy told me I should read the book of Ruth. You know that one?"

"Sure."

She laughed. "Rhetorical question."

A wary smile broke. "I don't know it all."

"Me either." She reached for his hand, took his long, masculine fingers in hers. "What I do know is that I've twice told the most amazing man that he deserves better than me—when all I want is to see him every day."

His Adam's apple bobbed.

"Dillan." She swallowed, wrapped both hands around his, and glued her gaze there. "I'm about the worst woman a pastor could date. I don't know the Bible well, I've got a past that I wish would disappear, and I'm so scared that I'll hurt you or that…"

His fingertips slid along her hairline. "Or that I'll hurt you."

She couldn't look at him. Her voice wobbled. "That's crazy, I know. I've done so much that I have no right to think you might—"

"Miska." He stepped closer, his warmth enveloping her. "Can I see you tonight?"

She caught her breath. Oh, his eyes. "Tracy and I are moving."

"I'll bring movers. And pizza."

She smiled tremulously. "Lou Malnati's?"

He chuckled. "If that's what you want."

"I just want you, Dillan."

The words hung between them. She shouldn't have said them. But there was her deepest desire, laid before him, waiting his response.

He didn't look away. "Do you have plans for Friday night?"

"No."

"What about Saturday lunch? And Sunday afternoon? Because I'd like to spend them with you."

She could hardly breathe. "Please, Dillan."

A deep, relieved smile broke over his face. He reached for her again, fingertips gliding along her cheek, tracing the curve of her jaw.

She closed her eyes and cupped his palm to her face.

"Miska," he breathed. He pulled her to him, and her head rested against his broad chest, his arms circling her.

She wrapped her arms around his waist and held him close while people jogged past them. While his heart thudded beneath her cheek.

She'd done nothing to deserve this love, this grace.

"Dude, you kiss her yet?"

A grinning Garrett stood behind them, phone up as he recorded everything. "Am I too late?" he asked.

She looked up at Dillan who narrowed his eyes, even though his mouth fought a smile. "Yes, you're too late," he said. "Go away."

"Liar. Kiss her already."

Dillan smiled down at her. "What's the rush? We've got time."

Perhaps a lifetime?

But he lowered his head anyway, brushed his gentle lips across hers, pressed his mouth to hers again.

Yes, a lifetime of this…

They broke apart, and a deep smile creased his face. "Miska," he whispered.

He hugged her close, and she tightened her hold. Why God would give her so much when she offered nothing—she'd never understand it.

But she didn't have to. Dillan's God—*her* God—loved her, despite her sins.

Despite her ignorance.

Despite her mocking.

If she'd known a year ago that love could be so pure, so chaste, so perfect, she wouldn't have wanted it. But God had wanted her for himself, had wanted her for Dillan, this incredible man who linked fingers with her and refused to look away.

This God would keep her, would keep Dillan, would keep them both. And she'd keep trusting him. No matter what came.

Jude 1:1b-2—To those who are the called, beloved in God the Father, and kept for Jesus Christ: May mercy and peace and love be multiplied to you.

Dear Reader,

I can't tell you what a thrill it is to meet you here at the end! I hope you enjoyed Miska and Dillan's story as much as I did. They're very special to me, and if you'd like more time with them, please visit http://sallybradley.com/sallys-books/extras-for-kept/ which will take you to a page just for *Kept* readers. There you'll find deleted scenes, the ending written from Dillan's point of view, and a fun interview with them about where their relationship has gone.

My goal is for this book to be the first of many. With that in mind, a review on the site where you purchased the book would be extremely helpful. If you'd like to be notified when my next book is ready, please subscribe to my newsletter. You can visit me at my website, sallybradley.com, or my Facebook page, Sally Bradley, Writer. I'd love to connect with you.

Until we meet again, I'm praying that you find plenty of stories that build you up and point you back to God.

Sincerely,
Sally Bradley

ACKNOWLEDGMENTS

I used to think that a book was the effort of one person. And while that's partly true—writers write, after all—there are so many people who influenced me and helped in some way.

My first thank you goes to my local writers' chapter—the fabulous ACFW Kansas City West—who brainstormed and critiqued with me. Many thanks to the crew that helped me plot that crucial opening chapter. Your comments and viewpoints were right on. The rest of the group critiqued it until they had to be sick of it—and worked a ton with me to choreograph that first scene in the hallway. I'd be bald without you guys. And my readers would be lost. Thank you!

I have to give a big shout-out to my beta readers—you all are the best! Ginger Aster, Ane Mulligan, Lora Young, Terri Poss, Jennifer Fromke, Joy Melville, Elizabeth Kramer (if the costuming gig doesn't work out, you should be a macro editor!), Rebecca Barlow Jordan, Elizabeth Runyan, Michelle Massaro, and Heidi Blankenship. Thank you, thank you, thank you for your time, encouragement, and insights.

To my Christian Indie Authors group—what a wealth of information everyone's been! It isn't easy going from writer to writer *and* publisher. Thanks to so many farther down the trail who shared their business knowledge and experience.

Christina Tarabochia, thank you for your insightful edits! I'm so glad I took a "risk" on a new author a few years back and read your book. I've so appreciated getting to know you and hearing your thoughts about *Kept*.

Elizabeth Kramer, thank you for being my go-to medical and mayhem person. We have too much fun thinking through all the injuries my characters face. Let's hope the NSA never listens in to our calls. Miss you, friend.

Kristin, thank you so much for sharing your story with me. I've only known the "after" version and not the "before," but I can't picture you as the woman you say you once were. You're an amazing trophy of God's grace. Thank you for being open with me.

Of course I have to say a huge thank you to my family. Mom and Dad, you paid my way through college and let me major in something I was unlikely to make a living on. Better yet, you lived for God and taught me the importance of following Him. I've been incredibly blessed by your faithful testimony and love. I can't imagine that there are better parents anywhere in the world. My sister, Andria, thank you for always being a fan and letting me talk about my dreams. I'm sure that got tiresome at times, me being the older know-it-all sister.

To my husband, Steve, who's always believed in me. Seventeen years ago, when I talked about writing a whole lot more than I wrote, you told me that the world wouldn't be sorry if I never wrote. Those words have stuck with me and reminded me that I had to stop dreaming and start doing. You've always believed in me, and I can't even say how badly I needed that. Thank you for supporting my indie journey. You're the best. We should grow old together.

And to the world's best kids—Ty, Alison, Luke—you guys have enriched my life so much. It seems cliché to say, but it's true that because of you, I'm a better woman. You've filled our lives with lots of laughter and companionship. Ty and Alison, what a help you've been as I've worked on *Kept*. This book wouldn't be available yet without you two stepping up and helping out where needed. Thank you for understanding that Mom had her own dreams and goals and for being excited with me at each step. I love you all so much. You guys make me proud.

Thank you, God, for giving me this writing dream. And thank you for making me wait. The wait has made it that much sweeter. I pray that everything I write will bring glory and honor to you always.

ABOUT THE AUTHOR

 Sally Bradley has been a fiction lover for as long as she can remember—and has been fascinated by all things Chicago (except for the crime, politics, and traffic) for almost as long. A Chicagoan since age five, she now lives in the Kansas City area with her pastor/cop husband and their three children, but she and her family get back to Chicago when they can for good pizza and a White Sox game. A freelance editor and former president of her local writing chapter, Sally has won a handful of awards for *Kept* and another work-in-progress. Visit her online at sallybradley.com.

23359483R00258

Made in the USA
San Bernardino, CA
19 August 2015